THE UNDEAD CHRONICLES VOLUME 3

Dead of Winter

PATRICK J. O'BRIAN

FIDELI PUBLISHING, INC.

ISBN: 978-1-955622-73-8

Special thanks to Ron Meikle, Brad Wiemer, Korby Sommers, Jobina Wiemer, Kevin Sommers, Jeff Groves, Dave Blackford, Kendrick Shadoan, and John Herrick.

Other novels by Patrick J. O'Brian include:

The Fallen

Reaper
(Book 1 of the West Baden Murders Series)

The Brotherhood

Retribution
(Book 2 of the West Baden Murders Series)

Stolen Time

Sins of the Father
(Book 3 of the West Baden Murders Series)

Six Days

Dysfunction
(Book 1 of the Terry Levine Detective Series)

The Sleeping Phoenix

Snowbound
(Book 4 of the West Baden Murders Series)

Sawmill Road
(Book 2 of the Terry Levine Detective Series)

Ghosts of West Baden
(Book 5 of the West Baden Murders Series)

Red Rain
(Book 3 of the Terry Levine Detective Series)

Sin Killer
(Book 4 of the Terry Levine Detective Series)

The Doomsday Clock
(Book 6 of the West Baden Murders Series)

Hallowed Grounds

The Undead Chronicles Volume 1: Home and Back Again
Uncertain Terms
The Undead Chronicles Volume 2: Darker Days

Non-fiction works by Patrick J. O'Brian include:

Risen from the Ashes: The History of the West Baden Springs Hotel
Pluto in the Valley: The History of the French Lick Springs Hotel

Learn more about Patrick and his projects at:
www.pjobooks.com

One

Nearly Two Weeks Ago

Never in his life had Bryce Metzger felt more abandoned than the moment the military cargo plane began to taxi down the runway, leaving him behind.

Instead of traveling back to the safety of a Virginia military installation with his brother, he stood near the end of the runway surrounded by the undead, a civilian he barely knew, and a wound that surely meant his life was measured in hours or days. Fortunately, most of the undead were lying on the ground, shot or stabbed through their skulls, meaning they couldn't return to life again.

Bryce winced as he clutched his right trapezius muscle, the fresh bite still burning despite him quickly shooting the zombie that inflicted the wound. Knowing such a bite proved fatal to any living person, he understood his time on Earth was limited, but he still had a few objectives to accomplish. Dangerously low on ammunition, with more undead staggering in his direction, Bryce looked to his sole ally as the cargo plane left the ground farther down the runway.

"I'm not sure this can get much worse," he commented to Molly, his brother's friend who stepped from the plane to assist him, only to get stranded with him at the small New York airport.

"It's about to if we don't find a way out of here," she replied. "Do we go after him?"

She looked to her left where a man ran away from them as fast as humanly possible. Their last remaining tie to the man who created the apocalypse they now lived in, Xavier Fournier, escaped the cargo plane at the last second. Bryce wanted to pursue the man after spending so much time tracking him down and capturing him, but he possessed a contingency plan for locating the lackey.

"We need to move," Molly said, ushering Bryce along as he ignored the pain, watching Fournier from the corner of his eye while spying the zombies drawing closer.

"See any vehicles?" he asked.

"A few cars near the hangars," Molly answered, beginning to move in that direction. "We're going to lose Fournier if we don't catch up to him soon."

"No, we won't," Bryce assured her, keeping up with her pace.

"You got some sort of satellite or drone you didn't tell me about?"

"Not exactly," Bryce answered as they neared a gray Prius.

He tried the driver's side front door, finding it locked.

"Who locks a Prius?" he lamented. "This would've been perfect."

Molly unzipped her pack, handing him a bottle of water.

"What's this for?" he questioned, since danger continued to surround them.

"Clean your wound," she said. "Maybe you can buy yourself some time, or maybe it isn't as bad as it looks."

Bryce couldn't see the wound very well because the bite occurred close to his neck. He saw blood, and felt the pain from teeth sinking into his flesh. He poured some of the water on his shoulder, rubbing it against the wound and feeling the bumps where teeth had pierced his flesh. Whatever virus the undead carried could be transferred from their bites, and presumably any mucus or blood that spewed from them, mingling with open wounds. Already accepting his fate, Bryce simply needed to escape the immediate danger and educate his companion about how to track Fournier.

"Over here," Molly said, finding the door of a tan Chevy pickup truck unlocked.

She tried the glove compartment, a middle storage console, and finally the sun visors before finding a set of keys hidden beneath the driver's side floor mat.

"Let's hope she has gas," Molly said as she inserted the key and started the truck.

Bryce heard a groan behind him and whirled, finding a zombie dressed in blue coveralls with a stubble beard stumbling towards him. In no mood to receive a second bite, he raised his firearm and fired one shot into its skull, downing it permanently. He climbed into the passenger's seat, his mind already contemplating the best course of action.

"If we don't go after him now, we may lose him," Molly said as she glanced in the direction Fournier darted, still not clear of the small airport.

Bryce reached into his back pocket, pulling out a device slightly larger than a smartphone, pressed a button and watched the screen power up, illuminating a simple, green GPS map.

"Are you listening?" Molly pressed.

"I am," Bryce answered, waiting for a red dot to appear somewhere on the map, and when it finally did, moving slowly across the screen, he breathed a sigh of relief.

He turned to Molly, holding up the device.

"When I rendered Fournier unconscious in the city, I slipped a small tracking device into one of his pockets, because my orders were to let him slip away if possible so we could track him."

"That's all well and good until he changes clothes, or it slips out."

"It's not perfect, but if we question him, it's doubtful he'll give up Nadeau's whereabouts. Strangely enough, my superiors thought this was the best plan of action if Fournier tried to escape."

Several zombies smacked against the truck's windows, attempting to get to the pair, succeeding only in distracting them momentarily.

"He may not even *know* Nadeau's location," Bryce added. "If there are more hoops to jump through before they rendezvous, we'd be blowing our one and only chance."

"Your people left with the paperwork and any information from that safe house," Molly stated. "There's an excellent chance they can decipher the next location from that."

"You're saying you'd prefer to leave this to chance?"

More zombies made their way over, joining their kind at the truck, pawing at the windows, looking for movement inside.

"I'm asking if this is really what you want to do with what little time-"

Molly let the sentiment linger.

"You can say it."

"I don't need to."

"This is who I am, and what I do," Bryce assured her. "The problem is I won't be able to finish the job. Someone would have to carry the baton."

"I see," Molly said ambiguously, openly concerned about completing the task at hand.

"If you aren't willing to track Fournier, we might as well use this device to film a farewell speech to my family. I'm not sure finding Nadeau will help solve anything, but I wouldn't mind personally putting a bullet in his forehead after torturing him a few hours for some answers. Surely you've lost loved ones as well."

Molly flushed a bit with anger.

"I've lost everyone in my life, some of whom were in my care, but that doesn't give you the right to use the guilt trip card."

"Our other option is to clip him with this truck and torture him, or flat out run him over," Bryce countered. "I know this man killed a lot of people you knew, including my own parents, but I'm willing to see this through the right way. If we deal with him right now, we'll both feel better, but that doesn't bode well for the fate of mankind."

"You're as stubborn as your brother," Molly said, shaking her head. "If we do this, promise me this son-of-a-bitch will see justice."

"I'm guessing that'll be up to you," Bryce said, forcing a smirk.

Awkward silence filled the truck momentarily.

"How do you propose we handle this?" Molly finally asked.

"Let him escape the airport before we move," Bryce suggested. "He'll think this truck is disabled and escape cleanly. We want him to feel comfortable so he leads us to the next step."

Both turned to look, seeing Fournier nearly clear of the busted fence at the opposite end of the property. A few zombies attempted to pursue him, but proved far too slow to catch their quarry. Bryce held his sidearm sideways, ejected the magazine, and saw three rounds left inside. Molly followed suit, finding only four rounds left in her pistol

"Not much if we make a last stand somewhere," she muttered.

"Once I'm certain this thing works, we need to find shelter and more firepower."

"What kind of range does that have?"

"It's guided by satellites, so in theory it should cover the globe," Bryce answered. "As long as I keep it charged, we should be able to track him."

Bryce hadn't taken much time to consider his own mortality, and his impending doom caused by a simple bite of all things. Over the years, he considered the horrific ways of dying at sea, like going down with his ship, being devoured by sharks, or his body being torn to shreds by any number of enemy projectiles.

He contemplated how to leave a message for his family, assuming Molly or some other stranger somehow delivered it later on. Even that scenario sounded farfetched to him, but he couldn't imagine Isabella raising their son alone, though she'd practiced doing so for years while he was away on tours. Life aboard a ship wasn't easy, though it remained regimented. The apocalypse ensured he wouldn't get to retire, driving around with a military license plate on his truck, or attending VFW events in his later years.

Now he wouldn't even see his family one last time, which weighed on him. Knowing the remains of his government might bring Nadeau to justice fueled his passion to continue until he couldn't function any longer. He hadn't seen the stages of illness and decay that followed a bite from the undead personally, but he understood his time was extremely limited.

"Where are we going?" Molly asked once Fournier distanced himself from the airport.

"We need to stick to a suburb," Bryce answered. "Going into Buffalo would be suicide if we got surrounded by a horde."

"There are plenty of buildings in Lancaster," Molly suggested. "They're just down the road."

"That'll work. Let's try for something residential to see if we can find food and guns."

Weaving around stalled vehicles, the undead, and other random debris throughout the business district, Molly made her way to several streets containing houses. Bryce noticed several neighborhoods he considered favorable because the undead population appeared diminished, and some of the houses looked undisturbed. Molly continued to drive until they reached a street that appeared to have limited access routes, and the houses looked upscale, like the kinds of residences producers might have their characters living in within a television sitcom.

"How do you even know about this place?" he questioned.

"Between family in the area, and jobs that required me to travel, I know some of the suburbs rather well."

Molly chose a brick house with two stories, an unopened front door, and black shutters on each of the numerous windows. A car remained in the driveway, the front door was closed, and no evident signs of life, or undead, were visible in the area.

"Familiar place?" Bryce asked.

"My great-aunt lived here when I was a kid," Molly answered. "Always wanted to see how it looked after she passed away."

"Let's hope your aunt's successors had a penchant for firearms."

"If they didn't, someone in this neighborhood surely has a gun collection."

Bryce hoped any abundance of firearms weren't used against them when they set out to explore the neighborhood. Once Molly parked in the driveway, he stepped out of the truck, listening for nearby danger. A few undead staggered in circles down the street, not yet aware that the living dared invade their feeding grounds. Holding his firearm in a ready position, Bryce walked to the front door while Molly walked to the back side of the house.

After opening the storm door, Bryce turned the doorknob, finding it secured.

"Shit," he muttered, ready to head to the rear entrance when he heard Molly call his name in a subdued yell.

He went around the house in a hurried walk, finding Molly at the rear door, ready to enter. She used her left hand to turn the knob back and forth without pushing the door, indicating they had means to enter without forcing a door or window. Bryce nodded, and she opened the door, quickly looking from floor to ceiling for traps or signs of the undead.

Suddenly thankful the house was built with numerous windows that flooded the house with natural light, Bryce stayed by Molly's side as they navigated the mudroom into a narrow hallway before entering the kitchen. Hearing no indications of anything else inside the house, Bryce stepped into the family room while Molly opened a door leading into the attached garage. His eyes scanned the room, finding two chairs and a large couch as though the family left after the start of the apocalypse and never made it home.

Built-in bookshelves remained along one wall, fully stocked with novels, encyclopedias, and coffee table books. Bryce saw the living room beyond this family space, and a hallway that led to several other rooms in another direction. He started toward the living room, quickly clearing it before finding Molly in the family room. They started down the hallway together, checking a bathroom and a master bedroom, along with the closets.

"Just the upstairs left," he commented quietly as they started toward the stairs off the living room and near the front door.

Making their way to the top level, they cleared two bedrooms, two bathrooms, and a home office space rather quickly. Breathing a sigh of relief, the pair went downstairs, gathered what few belongings they possessed from the truck, and secured the house once they settled inside. A search through the pantry revealed some canned goods, and a Jeep Grand Cherokee inside the garage provided a second transportation option. Before they explored the house more thoroughly for any firearms or ammunition, they plopped in different seats in the family room for a breather.

"You need to eat," Molly insisted as Bryce rubbed his sore shoulder.

"I need to show you how to use this device," he insisted. "Once the sickness sets in, I'm not going to be any use to you."

"I've used a smartphone," Molly said, somewhat insulted. "How hard can it be? Don't they dumb things down for you military types?"

"Ouch," Bryce said, finding the statement accurate in his line of work much of the time. "While that may be true, there are a few tricks to calibrating this thing."

Military personnel specialized in fields to keep things simple because they were cogs in a larger wheel, but that didn't mean all of their jobs were simplistic. Running the day-to-day operations on a ship as a lieutenant commander kept him busy, and proved stressful occasionally, but he supposed it seemed easier than other jobs he carried out as a young officer in the Navy.

"You not a fan of us military types?" Bryce asked, putting an emphasis on the last two words.

"I'm indifferent," Molly replied. "None of you were around in my recent time of need."

"Things are stretched a little thin with ninety-nine percent of the population walking around without heartbeats."

"How did things get so bad so quickly?" Molly asked, though the question wasn't directed at Bryce in particular.

"An act of terrorism can do that."

"How did no one figure out Nadeau sooner? There *had* to be signs."

"For years he made his company reliable, indispensable almost. In a world where things became more expensive and less timely, he met deadlines and provided excellent customer service. No one suspected a thing, and his products probably went through checkpoints without a second thought after so many flawless deliveries and inspections."

"Your people learned this when?"

"We've done a couple of missions collecting data from known buildings where Nadeau operated. It's been tough piecing together his days, weeks, and years leading up to the event. And the brass don't tell me everything."

"You could've left anytime you want to," Molly noted aloud. "What made you stay with an employer that offers limited information and sends you into danger, personally, on two occasions?"

"First off," Bryce said, his tone a bit more stern than he anticipated, "they didn't force me to take either mission. I volunteered because I could make a difference, and because the people I work for protected and fed my family while I was at sea. They didn't have to risk life and limb to protect our families, but they did."

Molly stood, walked to the front window, and stared outside a moment, as though unable to settle in and feel safe in the house she once knew.

"I'm not sure they have the right to ask so much of you," she finally said, still looking outside. "It's unlikely Nadeau knows how to reverse any of this, and even if he does, he probably wouldn't be in a sharing mood."

"If there's even a chance to return the world to normal, it's worth putting our lives on the line."

Both realized the heavy nature of Bryce's words, because he certainly made the ultimate sacrifice when a zombie attempted to make him a hot snack.

"Your crew didn't have much of a problem leaving you," Molly said with a neutral tone. "Any chance they'll be back this way for another mission, or to recover you?"

"I knew the risk when I drew the undead away from that plane," Bryce replied. "They had valuable information with them, and I had to ensure Dan made it home safe. They all saw what happened, so there isn't a chance they're coming back here for me."

"They could've waited a few more minutes and helped us clear the dead," Molly said firmly.

"I was compromised," Bryce said, internally wishing he could have at least said a proper goodbye to his brother, if no one else.

"Isn't there some way to reach them?"

"Well, I had a sat phone with me, but it was broken in the tussle at the airport. The only thing I have left, for as long as I'm able, is to track Fournier."

Bryce stood, looking at several of the family photos hanging along the main wall, as though this particular house somehow remained exempt from the chaos that took over the rest of the world those first few days. A family of five, consisting of a mother, father, two daughters, and a son, adorned several posed and vacation photographs.

"What happened to them?" he wondered aloud, considering the house gave the impression they simply packed a few belongings and left on foot.

"Who cares?" Molly asked indifferently.

Bryce realized how much he missed during those first few weeks, when people like his brother and Molly fought tooth and nail just to survive each day.

"Does it ever bother you that so many average, everyday people died because of one man?"

"Dwelling on it doesn't better our current situation," Molly countered. "We've *all* lost people. And Nadeau certainly didn't act on this alone. We've seen evidence to the contrary already."

"You know, you can talk about it," Bryce offered. "My job required me to be a good listener."

"Maybe some other time," Molly said.

"I may not have much of that, you know."

"I'm aware," she said, her expression softening a bit. "Maybe we should spend what time we *do* have getting a few things done."

Bryce continued to stare at the photographs momentarily, wishing for one last chance to address his family before the sickness settled in and claimed him.

Pulling out the electronic tracking device, he spent about five minutes going over the finer points of using it, how to reset it, and using the charger.

"They chose a vehicle charger," he said, holding it up after pulling it from his gear. "They figured car batteries will still be charged for months, whereas electricity everywhere else would be sketchy."

"Right," Molly said. "I think I've got the hang of it."

She took hold of the device, locating the red dot making progress in a westerly direction.

"Where do you suppose he's going?" she asked.

"Hard telling. Nadeau owned property in the States and Canada, so there are a number of possibilities."

"If it were me, I'd stay isolated, but in a centralized location where my allies could all reach me."

"Dear God. Do you suppose he's doing some kind of Noah's Ark plot where he and a select few will repopulate the Earth?"

"One sure way to prevent that would be a bullet between his eyes," Molly said.

Bryce sighed through his nose.

"Hopefully this works," he said, holding up the device. "So many things can go wrong."

Eventually the daylight faded, and dusk overtook the neighborhood. Both Molly and Bryce took steps to secure the house, eventually finding two revolvers and a shotgun inside the house with some ammunition. They also located clean bedding and decided to sleep on nice beds for a change. Despite living in completely different conditions, both were subjected to cots, sleeping bags, and whatever else they could find for bedding much of the time.

Bryce used a bucket of water to clean blood particles from his hair before rinsing his forearms and hands over the bathroom sink. He removed the top of his uniform and the white shirt beneath it, wondering how a zombie bit through both so quickly before he responded. Using a washcloth, he cleaned the wound, wiping his own dried blood away from the teeth marks that remained in his shoulder. Thus far, the wound didn't appear swollen, particularly red, or infected, but Bryce knew the timeline for such things varied between each infected person. He felt fortunate he didn't lose a chunk of flesh and tissue, though he wished his military brethren had taken a risky shot to prevent his fate.

Staring into the mirror, he questioned how much of a productive future remained for him. Dying in his hometown area felt somewhat natural, but he felt alone without Isabella, Dan, and Nathan, his son whom he'd already missed so much time with during the boy's young life.

"How are you feeling?" Molly asked when they took a few minutes to relax, sitting in the family room with only a candle to provide lighting.

A few flashlights from the kitchen and garage could aid them, but they decided to conserve the batteries. They also ate a few of the canned goods found in the kitchen to maintain their strength.

"Surprisingly, I feel alright," Bryce replied. "That being said, I'm sleeping with my door shut tonight just in case. I'm sure you know what to do if I pass in my sleep."

"I do," Molly assured him, looking away because she'd obviously put the undead down a number of times.

Once they went their separate ways for an overnight sleep, Bryce used a piece of stationery and a matching envelope he located earlier to pen a note to his wife. He hadn't spoken to Molly about delivering any messages, because he doubted the chances of Molly ever meeting Isabella, but he wanted some closure if he was due to expire soon.

Words didn't come easily, because he'd never truly expected to know death was coming. Military life taught him to hope for a swift death because anything else was torture, simply delaying the inevitable. He penned a few paragraphs, signed the letter, and sealed it, writing Isabella's name across the envelope before placing it on a dresser.

Bryce fell asleep that night hoping a can of cold store-bought chili wasn't his last meal.

Two

Daylight helped rouse Bryce from his slumber in the morning, but he felt sweat across his forehead and light wetness in the sheets beneath him. Fearing the worst, he jumped out of bed and wiped his forehead, feeling no fever. He remembered having strange dreams throughout the night, and the temperature dropped outside, causing him to sweat. His body and mind finally gave in, letting him sleep peacefully the second half of the overnight. Detecting no physical ailments other than the soreness around his right shoulder, he stepped to the mirror, seeing little change in the wound. Minor redness appeared near the bite mark, and he threw on a white undershirt and his pants before stepping into the hallway.

"Looks like you've been busy," he commented, seeing their cache of firearms all around Molly as she sat in one of the chairs.

"I've been cleaning them. Their owners did a subpar job of upkeep."

"I'm surprised you didn't check to see if I was alive," Bryce commented, walking into the living room for a look outside the front picture window.

"I figured if you turned, you would've been thumping against walls and woke me up," Molly called, half-teasing. "Seriously, though, how do you feel?"

"Surprisingly good," Bryce answered, seeing no activity outside, undead or otherwise.

He returned to the family room, checking on the tracking device which occupied part of a coffee table. His target continued to move west, along the northern part of the United States without crossing into Canada.

"I wonder where he's heading," Bryce pondered under his breath.

"If he wants isolation, Montana or Wyoming wouldn't be a terrible destination," Molly said, obviously hearing him. "Wide-open spaces, and the dead probably don't much care for snow and cold."

"We'll know about their preferences soon enough. Winter starts early up here, probably in a month or so."

Molly walked over to him, peeling back the shirt for a look at the wound.

"It's as though you were bitten by a dog, and not one of those *things*," she commented.

"I'm still not optimistic."

"You should be. Most people are breaking out in a sweat and running a fever within hours. After a while, they can barely hold down food or water. Their body begins to shut down and they're bedridden until they pass."

"You have an unusual way of cheering people up."

"I'm trying to tell you the sickness may pass you by, skipper."

Bryce ignored the nickname, partly because it wasn't accurate, and also because he didn't share her cheerful outlook.

"I feel as though Dan told you a little bit about me," he said instead. "What's your story?"

"He didn't tell you?"

"Not in detail. Does he even know your last name?"

Molly returned to her seat.

"I go by Pembroke now."

"What does that mean exactly?"

"It means there aren't Social Security numbers these days, or computers to look people up, so I'm choosing to use my grandmother's maiden name on my mother's side."

"To everyone their own. Any particular reason?"

"She was strong-willed in a time when that wasn't the norm. In her day, she saved a lot of lives as a nurse in the military, but she also saved me and my mother from my father."

Molly seemed to harbor a mild, general resentment towards men, but Bryce wondered if he was about to learn why.

"My father wasn't good to my mother," she revealed. "My grandmother took us away from all that, and put us up for over a year until the divorce could be finalized."

"Your mother and grandmother were close?"

"Not particularly," Molly said. "This is my paternal grandmother I'm talking about. She alienated her own son when she found out what he was doing to us."

"That had to be tough."

"It was an adjustment to say the least. I learned a lot from her, like how to stand up for myself, and patch the occasional wound."

Bryce suddenly felt a bit guilty.

"I'm sorry if it feels like I'm dragging you along," he said. "You're free to tell me to go fuck myself and go wherever you need to."

"It's no trouble. Besides, my options are a bit limited at the moment. I can't fly to Virginia, I don't have a home to return to, and all of my allies are dead or far away from here."

"I appreciate you stepping up to help me at the airstrip."

"When your own military brothers didn't lift a finger?"

"I have to believe they had their reasons."

"They restrained your brother, or he would've come down that ramp."

"I know," Bryce said, his mind recalling the events of the previous day. "I stayed behind for his sake, so I'm glad they kept him up there."

"One thing bothers me, though."

"What's that?"

"Two or three of them restrained Dan, but they let Fournier jump off that plane without batting an eyelash. What gives?"

"I'm not sure," Bryce admitted. "They didn't have identical orders to mine, and I doubt they knew about the tracking device. It was almost like protecting Dan was more important than bringing in that piece of shit."

"You sure they were protecting him? That Marine received that phone call and his demeanor changed."

Bryce recalled the moment, and how the Marine who received the call refused to share any details to the group. At first, he considered the man didn't want to reveal military orders with two civilians nearby, but the more he thought about the moment, the more Bryce contemplated the orders might have been about him or his brother specifically.

"I'm not sure about anything right now," Bryce admitted.

Both sat silently a moment, contemplating the past, and the immediate future.

"When do we start following Fournier for real?" Molly finally inquired.

"The device will tell us his precise location," Bryce said, "but we need eyes on him to make certain he doesn't pull a fast one, or end up a rotter."

"You didn't exactly answer my question."

Bryce smirked.

"We pack what we can, and leave later this morning."

***

Over the next week, the pair personally spotted Fournier three times through binoculars without giving away their position. He continued west, obviously possessing a destination he'd committed to memory, possibly given to him by the gatekeepers in Canada where he stopped for a short time before the military caught up with him.

He switched vehicles several times, and it appeared he changed shirts, but Bryce guessed he either wore the same pants, or kept the first pair with him during his travels because the tracker remained with him. Clean pants or blue jeans that fit well weren't easy to come by in the apocalypse, and Fournier made at least as many stops as the duo tracking him.

Like the man they pursued, Bryce and Molly stopped to rummage through houses and apartments for food and supplies, changed vehicles a few different times, and even found changes of clothes. Bryce hadn't worn civilian clothes on a regular basis in years, so the concept felt foreign to him at first.

Without the means to shave, Bryce felt an itchy beard coming in, and most of his face felt unaccustomed to having hair. During his years in the Navy, he remained well-groomed, getting weekly haircuts and keeping his mustache neatly trimmed. For the first time, Bryce found himself away from the blanket of the military, and its rules and regulations.

He grew to believe some kind of miracle spared him from joining the ranks of the undead as his wound began to heal, rather than infect him from within. Bryce wanted to believe the wound wasn't deep enough to infect him, or Molly's bottled water washed away any infection before it entered his bloodstream, but Molly reached a different conclusion.

She insisted Bryce, and possibly his brother, were somehow immune to the virus that wiped out much of the world's population. Perhaps he simply didn't want to believe it, but the more he thought about the way the military whisked his brother back to Buffalo, the more he began to question the circumstances. Either way, he didn't want to receive another bite to test Molly's theory.

"He must have received some information from that stop in Canada," Molly insisted as the pair drove through a town along the northeast portion of Ohio.

Drives that once took hours, now took days due to gridlock, hiding from the undead, stopping to syphon gas, locating food, or swapping vehicles. Being confined to a vehicle for hours on end left time for discussions, including why they were tracking Fournier if the government could do so themselves, and what they would do if they located the secret lair where Nadeau presumably hid from the world.

Bryce shared Molly's fear that Fournier might discover the tracker or leave his pants behind, leaving them as the only real means to follow the man to his destination. If they discovered the location, Bryce wasn't certain how he'd communicate with anyone in the military unless he discovered a sat phone or a reasonably quick way to travel to Virginia. Part of him wanted to give up the search and return to the base to reunite with his wife, son, and brother, but a sense of duty, and the memory of his parents, drove him forward.

"Where are we?" Molly asked when they stepped from their current car, a black Chevy Spark, as dark clouds rolled overhead.

A threat of storms reared its ugly head some miles back, but the pair was forced to drive into the heart of the severe weather. Bryce knew from the spattering rain they were about to get drenched, so he parked in front of a row of houses that offered shelter.

And possibly danger.

"I don't even remember this place's name," Bryce said as they made their way toward a row of four houses.

Possibly not even appearing in their Atlas, the town possessed little of interest to the pair. Without so much as a fire station or town hall, it appeared rather bland. On the plus side, Bryce figured the undead weren't much of a threat in such an unpopulated area.

"There isn't even a store here," Molly stated as she tried the front door on the first house, finding it locked.

Now the rain began pouring, soaking them both instantly, despite Bryce wearing a green slicker he'd found in another town. He and Molly carried a practical wardrobe with them in small suitcases, preparing them for each inevitable weather situation.

Bryce tried the front door on the second house, finding it locked as well. "What the hell?"

Molly walked ahead, finding the third house accessible, turning the knob and beginning to take a step inside.

"Wait," Bryce said loudly enough that his voice carried over the pouring rain.

"What?"

"Clear it first," he said, just as anxious to escape the elements, but not willing to throw caution to the wind.

Molly knocked on the door frame several times, staying put and listening for activity as Bryce took her side. He pulled out a flashlight, aiming the beam inside after switching it on, finding much of the furniture piled to one side.

"Well, that's odd," he stated.

"Definitely."

"Watch for traps," Bryce said as he purposely stepped inside first, shining his light at the floor.

He didn't consider the house an ideal place to stay almost immediately because the ceiling had begun to collapse, the walls were stained with several holes in various places, and the floors appeared messy. He questioned whether the house was condemned *before* the apocalypse, because even as an overnight squatter, he'd never perpetrated such destruction in *any* house.

Odors of fecal matter and urine reached his nose, and seemingly Molly's as well, because she winced when they reached the halfway point in the first room.

"Maybe it's time to break down a door," Bryce proclaimed as they turned to exit the way they came, finding several undead stumbling around near their car.

Both reached for their knives, opting to deal with their slow adversaries quietly. Bryce kicked one against the car before thrusting his blade into its skull, while Molly clasped a male zombie dressed in street clothes by the throat, holding it back at a safe distance before stabbing it through the left eye. After several days in an undead state, their skulls began to soften just enough that blades penetrated them with far less effort.

Molly managed to pull the knife free before the zombie slumped to the ground, turning to face Bryce. Walking in unison, they approached the fourth house in the line and tried the front door, finding it open and far more accommodating inside.

"At least it doesn't smell like shit," Molly commented as she stepped inside, using her flashlight to illuminate the main room of the ranch style house.

After a few minutes, they cleared the house and shut the front door, leaving the downpour outside.

"It's been a few days," Molly said as they rummaged through the kitchen cupboards for food and supplies. "We need to lay eyes on Fournier."

Bryce didn't like getting too close to the man, for fear he might spot them and alter his course purposely. Even so, he understood they needed to make certain Fournier hadn't caught on to them and placed the tracker on someone else, or a zombie. He might have left his pants somewhere, only to have them picked up by a different survivor. Any number of issues might lead them into danger for no reason, and Bryce could simply return to Virginia if his quest suddenly ended.

"We aren't far behind," Bryce said, finding a few canned goods and some boxed food inside one cupboard. "We'll make up some miles and see if we can spot him around dusk."

"I'm not trying to back out of this partnership, but the odds of us tracking him to some secret bunker are pretty slim."

"How so?"

"So many things can happen to this guy, or your tracking device, along the way. I hope what's left of our government has some kind of backup plan."

"I'm not sure they do," Bryce said, stuffing his finds into a backpack he'd picked up in a house a few days prior. "I wasn't privy to whatever information they located on the hard drives we confiscated. If they even found anything."

Both of them froze in their tracks when the sound of an approaching vehicle entering the neighborhood reached their ears. Days often passed without them encountering another human being, and the risky proposition of speaking with other survivors often weighed on their minds. Neither felt overly concerned until the vehicle stopped near the house they were currently exploring, and the motor continued to run. To Bryce, the motor sounded like a diesel pickup truck, possibly the kind farmers once drove, and now troublesome people tended to pick from the vast selection of four-wheeled transportation.

Without uttering a word, Bryce pointed to a nearby closet where he and Molly stowed themselves momentarily while the vehicle parked outside, continuing to run. Bryce and Molly breathed only when necessary, and for his part, Bryce felt guilty, as though someone outside of the house might hear him breathing and discover his location. As a rule, no one searched closets when entering a house, so he felt reasonably safe.

He heard a door open from the truck, and a few footsteps followed that, sounding rather loud, like some sort of boots. Barely audible through the rain and the open front door of the house, the noise concerned Bryce, because he didn't particularly want to shoot someone when Fournier remained his primary concern. Apparently, the driver, or passenger, of the truck found little of interest, because the person returned to the vehicle and it drove away a few seconds later, allowing them sighs of relief.

Neither spoke a word, but the sensation of danger, coupled with their close proximity, drew them an inch or two closer before Bryce opened the door, releasing them from the confines of the tiny space. He walked to the front door, checking to make certain the truck had moved along, seeing and hearing no sign of it.

"That can't be good," Molly said, joining him at the door.

"They might have spotted our car and stopped for a look."

"In that case, we should get moving."

"Yeah," Bryce agreed.

A few minutes later they cautiously stepped outside, hearing the truck in the distance moving slowly along a parallel street.

"They must be looking for something," Bryce commented, assuming the driver's seat.

Over the course of the past week, he and Molly had collected a number of firearms and boxes of ammunition during the times they stopped to raid homes or businesses. He felt confident that shooting the front of any truck with a shotgun would disable it, hoping to avoid any shootouts with random strangers.

Although they managed to leave town without encountering the person or people inside the truck, the close call reminded Bryce that he wasn't the only person on the road, and other people could impede his mission to track Fournier. He also knew the lengths he would go to just to ensure his mission didn't fail.

Later that evening, the heavy rain let up to a steady drizzle when they stopped half a mile short of where the red beacon led them on the tracking device.

"See him?" Molly asked as Bryce peered through a set of binoculars at a house down the road where a red Mazda car of some kind was parked.

Fournier opted to take a state highway, rather than the occasionally impassible interstate, which suited the lieutenant commander just fine. Bryce found a small hill just high enough to overlook the houses while providing cover.

"Not yet," Bryce answered. "I think he went inside. He might be holing up for the night."

Based on the red dot's movement on the screen, the pair knew Fournier must have been driving, and not walking, which indicated he, or whoever wore the pants with the tracking device, was indeed alive.

"When we finally get answers about Fournier what the hell are we going to do with the information?" Molly asked.

"What do you mean?"

"I mean neither of us is a pilot, we don't have a sat phone, and the postal service isn't exactly operating these days. It could take a month or more to get any information back to Virginia."

"I have some ideas about that. We may still have some allies in New York who can help."

Molly was about to inquire further about his statement, but both heard the sound of a vehicle approaching. Bryce felt certain the truck that stopped outside of the town they scavenged took the same route, because the engine sounded much the same. He didn't feel as though they were followed, because they had been settled into their position for nearly half an hour. He did question, however, if someone in the truck knew Fournier, or put him at risk, which endangered everything Bryce wanted to accomplish at the moment.

Fournier hadn't been stupid enough to leave a vehicle parked out front, so if the truck parked at his location, he likely knew the person, or possessed the worst luck known to man.

Feeling his body tense, Bryce stared through the binoculars, hoping the truck simply passed by, alleviating both of his potential concerns. It slowed down, as though the driver was looking at the houses, possibly for somewhere to bed down for the night.

"What the fuck do they want?" Molly questioned aloud.

"Hard telling. We can't have them hurting Fournier, though."

"Helping the man out would pretty much ransack our stealthy efforts."

"A dead Fournier is no use to us. We'd have to switch to Plan B at that point."

Both watched momentarily as the truck's brake lights went dim and the truck moved down the road. Bryce remained concerned that they hadn't laid eyes on the man since their arrival, but a few minutes later, Fournier poked his head out the front door, like a groundhog making certain every predator had left the area.

"Our target is alive," Bryce said, handing Molly the binoculars.

"Let's hope he stays that way."

"Well, now that we've verified Fournier's well-being, it's time for us to find shelter."

"Those houses a few miles back looked decent."

Bryce groaned, knowing that checking a house for zombie activity after dark wasn't an ideal situation. Sleeping outside felt less appealing, so he stood from his spot on the hill, remaining hunched so Fournier didn't spot his silhouette if he nervously peered through a window.

"I'm sure you remember how brisk autumn in New York can be," Molly said. "Any shelter is good shelter if it gets close to freezing, because we aren't that far removed from the Great Lakes yet."

"Oh, I recall," Bryce said with a sigh, thinking back to what seemed like mountains of snow in the Buffalo area during his childhood. "Let's hope Ohio is accommodating during our housing search. We'll fall back tomorrow and track Fournier from a distance while we start getting winter supplies."

"We need a hybrid," Molly suggested, "so we don't have to keep switching vehicles."

"We're going to need a snowplow before long. Hopefully Fournier doesn't drag out this little adventure too much longer. I'd like to get south before the lake effect snow hits."

Molly grinned.

"In that case, you'd better hope he's heading to Indiana, or we're going to be adding snowshoes to our shopping list."

Three

Dan Metzger couldn't believe he was standing beside virtually everyone he cared about at one time. When he left his friends to stay on a military base with his brother, he figured his chances of seeing them again were remote at best.

Unfortunately, time wasn't on his side, because he'd left the base with his sister-in-law, nephew, and a Navy captain who agreed to fly them to New York to find his brother. Colby Sutton, an ally from his former group, coaxed him into leaving before Isabella, his sister-in-law talked him into fleeing the base for a different reason.

Because Metzger remained under the watchful eye of military personnel at all times, they didn't exactly walk through the front gate with the blessing of the military brass.

Now the two reunited factions stood in the middle of a highway, mere miles from the Navy base Metzger chose to leave behind.

"Where's Juan?" he asked aside to Jillian Varitek, who stood beside him.

"We ran into a group," she replied. "He didn't make it."

Metzger hated hearing that one of the people who helped him survive the trek from New York to the base in Norfolk, Virginia hadn't survived. He'd already seen what the current worldly situation did to the living, either taking their lives, or transforming them into monsters. He felt lucky to have found a group of good people who leaned towards mercy and compassion, though they weren't afraid to do battle with anyone who threatened their lives.

"I hate to break this up," Scott Timmons said, taking Metzger's side. "It won't be long before the guards realize you're gone, so we need to form a plan and keep moving."

Metzger realized his straightforward plan suddenly became more complicated. Sutton wanted him out of the base to help mend fences, because Sutton had gotten himself excommunicated from the group. Isabella and Timmons wanted to fly him to New York to search for his brother, which immediately became his personal priority. He still wasn't convinced, like Isabella, that Bryce might still be alive, but it wasn't as simple as picking up a phone to find out.

"Sounds like we're parting ways again," Sutton said, somewhat deflated. "I have to keep looking for my boys."

Jillian didn't speak a word, but Metzger could tell she was still fuming over whatever rift he created between them. To hear Sutton tell the tale, he hadn't committed a heinous crime against humanity, but Metzger knew the man acted abrasively at the worst of times. His decisions sometimes saved the group, and almost nearly as often led them into hazardous situations.

"I have to put my family first as well," Metzger said to everyone around him. "And, unfortunately, that means we have to travel light on our way to New York."

"You're going *back* there?" Gracine Tucker asked, not bothering to hide her surprise.

"I don't have much choice," Metzger replied. "My brother didn't come back from a mission up there, and we have to find him."

"A lot's happened in two weeks, apparently."

Metzger forced a grin.

"More than you know."

He turned his attention to Jillian.

"Do you want to come with us?"

She glanced at the group, obviously torn about parting ways with them, but she couldn't stand the thought of traveling with Sutton, or forcing the group to take sides.

"Yes," Jillian answered before turning to the others. "I wish you all the best in your travels, and hopefully we'll meet up again."

"We will," Metzger said assuredly. "Do you still have the sat phone I left you?"

"Yes," Jillian answered before digging in her pack and producing the phone Metzger found shortly after the apocalypse at the home of his parents.

"Take this," Metzger said, tossing it to Sutton. "I found another one, so this way we can keep in touch."

"*Him?*" Jillian questioned, openly unhappy regarding his choice of a responsible party to carry the phone.

"If anyone's going to survive, it's him," Metzger answered just above a whisper.

"You know the number?" Sutton questioned.

"I've got it memorized. Just keep everyone else safe until we get back."

Sutton nodded, his dog Buster taking his side, wagging his tail and looking happy to be around so many friendly humans.

"I have to admit, I was expecting more of a happy reunion if we found one another," Luke Johnson said.

He stood beside his adopted daughter, Samantha, who appeared a bit sad that the adults were parting ways almost immediately.

"We'll be back," Metzger promised. "We're going to find Bryce, and hopefully we'll get some answers about that douchebag Fournier."

"Who?" Luke questioned.

"The guy who tried to run us down at the airport in Lancaster."

"He's *alive?*"

"Not only that, but he's tied in with the guy who started the apocalypse."

"All the more reason to hate him," Sutton stated.

Timmons cleared his throat, indicating their short conference in the middle of a highway needed to wrap up soon.

"We really have to go," Metzger said to everyone before him. "You guys need to make yourselves scarce as well, because the military will surely be on the warpath."

"Why?" Gracine asked. "What did you *do?*"

"It's not what he did," Isabella said. "It's what they want from him."

"Which is, exactly?" Metzger asked, because a sequence of events had kept her from disclosing the full truth about his use to the military, and why she believed his brother was still alive.

"We're among friends, obviously," Isabella said, clapping her left hand into her right. "You and Bryce both have immunity to whatever virus turns the rest of us into the undead."

"What?" Metzger asked incredulously, knowing in the back of his mind his blood might hold some importance, but never suspecting full immunity to the contagion.

Everyone else appeared stunned as well.

"He could hold a cure to what's going on out there and you're whisking him away?" Luke asked, directing his question at Isabella.

"There's no cure once you turn," Isabella answered. "They were working on a vaccine to slow or stop the disease altogether once someone was bitten."

She opened a pouch and produced several vials, handing two of them to Gracine, who stood the closest to her from the faction that wouldn't be traveling to New York. Gracine accepted them, eyeing them momentarily before placing them in a bag already lined with a few clothing items.

"They were keeping him prisoner," Isabella explained to Gracine and the others. "Even worse, they didn't tell Dan the truth, even though they knew my husband might be alive."

"Is this true?" Luke directed his question at Metzger.

"Yeah. They wouldn't let me roam the base without armed soldiers following me everywhere."

"I would kill for protection and three square meals."

"Full disclosure, life was a lot better with all of you than on the base," Metzger confessed.

"None of us will be able to return after this," Isabella said. "But it's our one shot at finding my husband and this one's dad."

She held Nathan, Metzger's nephew, close to her.

Metzger went to everyone in his former group and gave them a quick hug. He stopped at the stranger in the group.

"Dan Metzger," he said, introducing himself as he shook hands with the man who possessed a few days of stubble on his face.

"Steve Driscoll," the man replied. "I've heard quite a bit about you."

"I'd say if it's bad, not to believe it, but these days everything we hear is bad."

"Ain't that the truth?" Driscoll replied with a raised eyebrow.

Metzger saved Sutton for last, having something specific to tell him.

"I'll be back," he promised. "Don't lose that phone."

"I won't. See if you can get your girlfriend to forgive me."

Metzger nodded, making no verbal commitment.

"Keep an eye on that pilot," Sutton warned so only Metzger heard.

In return, Metzger gave a questioning look.

"There's something about him I don't trust."

"You don't trust anyone in the military, Colby," Metzger replied, keeping his voice equally low.

"He didn't leave that base out of the goodness of his heart," Sutton added with a slight shake of his head. "Just watch your back."

Metzger nodded, bending over to scratch Buster's head before returning to the people he intended to travel with to New York.

"We really do need to go," Isabella urged him.

She'd been standing by quietly, but Metzger could tell she shared Timmons' desire to distance themselves from the base.

"Okay," he said, giving a quick wave to Sutton and the others before addressing them. "Take care. Hopefully I'll see you all soon."

Slowly, the group walked back to the dark blue Ford Expedition they found outside the base shortly after leaving. Although low on fuel, the vehicle held their gear, and Metzger hoped it might run long enough to get them to an airport. He felt confident if they could find a plane large enough to hold their group, Timmons would get them to the area where he last saw his brother alive. Pilots tended to discuss missions with one another, so the captain likely knew the spot already.

"Where do we go from here?" Metzger asked Timmons, knowing the man possessed knowledge of local airports outside the Navy base.

"We just left three perfectly good airports near the base," Timmons replied. "Our next closest option is Norfolk International. But it won't be the safest."

"They're going to follow us," Isabella said.

"Possibly," Timmons replied. "I'm more concerned about the airport being overrun with the infected."

"Possibly?" she questioned his first statement. "They were watching him day and night."

"They don't have the resources to send search parties after us," Timmons said as he opened the rear hatch and rummaged through his bag until he located a pistol that he stuffed in his jeans along his lower back.

"A few thousand people live on that base, and inside Norfolk city limits," Isabella argued.

"A third of them are civilians, and the military is about to have a host of new problems when they can't feed all those people this winter. Those soldiers and sailors are about to go searching for food supplies, not hunt us down."

By now, Metzger's former group had drifted away, likely carrying out their own disagreements after Sutton caused them problems and broke into the base to find Metzger.

"You're saying they won't come after us?" Metzger questioned as he climbed into the front passenger's seat.

Isabella, Nathan, and Jillian occupied the back seat with all of the gear behind them.

"Oh, I'm sure they'll search," Timmons said, starting the vehicle, "but they'll keep it quiet, and they won't send a whole platoon after us. It's not exactly a Scooby Doo mystery where we're going."

"You're awfully calm about this for someone who just went AWOL," Metzger commented.

"I lost my last reason to stay when I found out I was flying decoys into the base so they could keep up appearances."

"The President was a decoy?"

"Yeah," Timmons said bitterly. "All this time our politicians have been living in secret bunkers, safe as can be, while the rest of us scrounge to survive and fight off the infected."

"I'm not sure you've had it that bad," Isabella said from behind them. "You've been eating three square meals behind secured gates most days."

Timmons put the vehicle into drive, turning to get them facing south.

"A little gratitude would be nice," he said. "I didn't have to agree to leave three square and fences behind."

"Why did you?" Metzger questioned.

"In this case, it's the right thing to do," Timmons answered. "And your sister-in-law promised a secluded paradise once we find your brother."

Metzger turned to give a questioning stare to Isabella, who simply provided a knowing grin that didn't provide an answer to his silent inquiry.

Over the course of the next hour, Metzger navigated the Navy pilot along a series of roads that kept them away from the busier state highways and interstates where vehicles and the undead tended to clog the path.

"I hope we find something that'll fly," Timmons said when the fences surrounding the airport became visible in their headlights.

"That doesn't exactly instill confidence," Metzger said, putting the map down momentarily.

"This place is mostly commercial, son," Timmons responded, looking out the window for a way into the airport that didn't involve climbing, ramming through fences, or dealing with dozens of undead. "Flying a 747 isn't practical where we're going, so I'm praying someone left something a little smaller behind."

"Wow," Nathan commented from his middle seat. "This place is huge!"

Metzger's major concern was soon realized when he saw the undead lingering behind chain link fences, clawing at the metal when they spotted the SUV. Although Norfolk International Airport wasn't exactly JFK or O'Hare in terms of size, it received a reasonable share of traffic along the East Coast when it was operational.

Any generators that helped light the grounds had long since failed, and the dead were simply blurs in the headlights as Timmons drew close to the fence, looking for a way inside. Metzger couldn't imagine flying out of the airport blind, knowing debris and the undead likely blocked any runways. Unless Timmons knew some trick to navigating in sheer darkness, they weren't leaving the area until at least dawn.

"We can't be the first people to try snatching a plane," Jillian commented from behind Metzger.

"It's just a matter of finding how they entered," Timmons said with strain in his voice as he made a sharp turn to avoid striking a metal pole that supported the fence.

"There's no chance of us clearing them like this," Metzger commented, having already spotted a few dozen undead inside the airport property.

"As an added bonus, we're running low on fuel," Timmons said. "Leading them away from the airport could be risky."

"We'll find other vehicles inside," Isabella said with confidence. "It's an airport, after all."

Timmons soon found he'd been driving the wrong way, as taxiing lanes came into view and buildings began disappearing behind them. He turned around, doubling back to find an entrance closer to the main terminal, or a parking area where they might locate a vehicle with sufficient fuel.

After another five minutes of driving, a light appeared beyond the steering wheel, indicating low fuel. Timmons found the main entrance completely open with no crossbars or gates to impede their travel. He drove inside, and the undead immediately surrounded the vehicle and began pawing at the windows. Metzger turned to see Isabella pulling Nathan close, shielding him from the noise and even scarier visuals of the decaying undead that wanted to make warm meals of the SUV's inhabitants.

"This is better," Timmons commented just above a whisper once the group was inside the fence, now given multiple options for entrances and parking lots.

"There won't be any thinning this herd," Metzger said. "We don't have enough ammunition, and it's dark as fuck out there."

"Right now, I'm more concerned about getting us another ride," Timmons said. "Going to be hard to window shop for aircraft if we run out of gas."

"There," Jillian said, spotting what appeared to be an employee parking lot, based on its small size and proximity to the main building.

Close to a dozen undead remained near their vehicle, threatening to overrun the group if the Explorer came to a stop. Metzger knew from experience he could deal with that number, so long as more didn't appear suddenly from behind vehicles or shrubs. Eliminating those around them might draw additional undead to their location if not done quietly, so he looked for an ideal area to park the Explorer.

"There," he told Timmons, pointing to a corner where no vehicles or threats were visible. "If I can pop the hatch and get my sword, I can deal with this many."

"I'm not letting you do this alone," the Navy captain said.

"Yes, you are."

"I can help," Jillian volunteered, touching his shoulder from the back seat. "Let me be your eyes."

Metzger hesitated only a second before answering.

"When I get my sword, grab a flashlight and spot them for me. Light will blind them, just like it does us, so you can shine it in their eyes."

"Okay."

"You're going to need help out there," Timmons insisted, driving to the spot Metzger indicated and putting the vehicle in park.

"We're going to need a pilot," Metzger countered. "We've got this."

Timmons hadn't seen Jillian in action, and perhaps he felt a need to step up and protect the women, but Metzger wasn't about to let the captain risk their one opportunity to return to Buffalo in a timely manner. Tracking Bryce wasn't going to be easy, whether his brother sought shelter, visited the home of their parents, or attempted the arduous journey back to Virginia.

Without another word, he and Jillian exited the vehicle, went to the back and opened the hatch long enough to grab the sword and a flashlight. Closing the hatch for safety, they turned to confront their virtually mindless enemies. Jillian used the beam to illuminate the threats closest to Metzger, and he went to work, cutting through the skulls of three of them before stepping back to assess the situation and suck in a deep breath.

"You good?" he asked.

"Yeah," Jillian answered, shining the light on a female stewardess less than ten feet from them.

"This couldn't be much more cliché," Metzger commented, stepping forward to swing his blade through her skull with practiced ease.

"You spoke too soon," Jillian said as a man dressed in mechanic overalls stumbled into view, too slow to defend himself against the sword.

A splat noise reached Metzger's ears when the top of the zombie's head struck the pavement, and he looked beyond the collapsing body to another four approaching threats. By now, Timmons, Isabella, and Nathan stepped from the vehicle, staying behind him.

"You can start looking for vehicles," Metzger said to none of them in particular without turning around. "Be careful. The dead sometimes lie under cars."

Thanks to Jillian, he dealt with each of the undead individually, and in two instances, she blinded them with the flashlight, making his job incredibly easy because they turned their attention to her, never seeing his sword's blade. When the last body fell, Metzger expected to hear and eerie calm, but a universal groan reached his ears instead. He couldn't tell if a vast number of them stumbled inside the fencing, or worse, inside the terminal. Without adequate lighting, he couldn't see the threat, and he hoped someone managed to locate a suitable vehicle before additional threats discovered their location.

Metzger kept his sword in a ready position as he stepped over to help check the vehicles for accessibility and spaciousness. He didn't particularly care about cleanliness at the moment because they weren't traveling far. The group simply needed to stash their belongings and remain safely encapsulated as they drove around looking for aircraft.

"How is this place so undisturbed?" Metzger asked Jillian as she took his side, checking for danger inside and around the cars before opening several doors.

A few lacked keys, some remained locked, and one didn't have enough fuel to instill confidence in Metzger. He looked up, seeing Timmons and Isabella getting farther down the row without protection. About to call over to them about the danger of getting too far away from lighting and protection, Metzger heard a piercing scream from his nephew. Nathan had taken a few steps away from his mother, attracting the attention of a zombie lurking beneath a car that grabbed his foot. Metzger started sprinting to Nathan's side, realizing he couldn't possibly reach the boy in time to save him from having his ankle bitten.

Four

Metzger stopped in his tracks when he saw Timmons reach his nephew and calmly kick the zombie's head, breaking Nathan free from its grip. When the zombie lurched forward again, basically crawling along its stomach from beneath the car, the pilot stomped on its skull twice, ending the threat completely.

"Yuck," Timmons commented, raising his right foot to have a look at the blood and brain matter dripping from his government-issued shoe.

Metzger and Isabella checked Nathan for any wounds, finding none.

"Sweetie, are you alright?" Isabella asked, dropping to one knee to address her son.

"I'm okay," Nathan said, putting forth a brave face.

"The noise will attract more infected," Timmons said. "We can't stay here."

"Thank you," Isabella said to Timmons as she stood, pulling her son close. Saying nothing, the captain simply nodded.

Metzger appreciated his sister-in-law being frank with him, and he wanted to know his brother's fate, but he hated putting Nathan in the least bit of danger. Obviously, Isabella considered the risk worth their time, or she wouldn't have taken such a personal risk.

"Check their pockets," Metzger said, nodding in the direction of the bodies. "If they worked here, maybe they have car keys."

He walked over to one of the bodies after Timmons finished checking it, wiping the blood from his sword along both sides on the faded clothing.

Jillian found a set of keys on the mechanic's body, struggling momentarily to pull them from his pants underneath the overalls. Pulling them free, she hit a button on the key fob, causing a nearby vehicle to chirp and emit marker lights that indicated its location. Everyone turned to look, and Isabella caught the location of the vehicle, leading everyone to it, taking Nathan by the hand.

"This one, I think," she said when they drew close to a dark blue truck with a shell over the bed.

Jillian pressed the button again, causing the truck to respond. She opened the door, stepped inside, and turned the key just far enough to check the fuel level.

"It's nearly full," she reported.

"Let's get our stuff transferred," Metzger suggested.

Timmons fetched the Explorer and parked it beside the truck, allowing everyone to quickly throw their belongings into the covered truck bed.

"You want to ride up front?" he asked Jillian, wanting to protect his family personally.

"No," she answered. "Get the captain to a plane so we can get the fuck out of here."

Metzger nodded and helped the women and his nephew safely climb into the truck bed before securing it. He walked to the passenger side of the truck, sliding into the seat before addressing Timmons.

"We can't fly until we have daylight, right?"

"If we want to survive takeoff, yes."

"What are the chances we can raid that terminal for supplies?"

Timmons grimaced at the thought.

"I picture wall to wall undead inside."

Starting the truck, Timmons paused a moment before looking directly at Metzger.

"You still want to check, don't you?"

"Not while it's this dark outside, I don't. A quick peek inside will let me know if it's safe or not."

"We still have a few hours before daylight," Jillian called from the enclosed truck bed, barely audible. "Surely some survivors would've cleared the inside, right?"

"Or died trying," Isabella countered. "There could be hundreds of them."

"Just get me close," Metzger suggested to Timmons. "I'll jump out, look through one of the windows with a light, and see what's what."

Timmons nodded, driving over to one of the large panel windows that loomed over their new vehicle. Looking around to ensure no undead were within striking distance, Metzger opened his door, jumped out, and darted to the window. He pulled the small flashlight from his pocket that he'd learned to carry early on, shining it inside.

Immediately, he found several staggering zombies, possibly survivors who tried to make a stand. Beyond them he spied some shelves inside a small store where passengers could almost certainly purchase soft drinks or snacks for the wait between security checks and flights. He couldn't tell if food items remained because the flashlight's beam couldn't reach that far. The undead began to take notice of him, however, turning to confront him from the other side of the thick glass.

Hearing them approach from behind the truck, Metzger quickly counted five in plain sight before turning around. A few drew close to the truck, so he pulled his sword from its sheath, making a clean cut through the first one's skull. The second, a woman wearing business attire with half of her left cheek bitten off, growled and hissed at him before raising her arms and lurching forward only to receive the pointed end of the short sword through her forehead.

Quickly wiping both sides of the sword off along the fallen zombie's clothing, Metzger slid it into the sheath before returning to the truck.

"Well?" Timmons asked.

"About five that I can see. Might be doable once we can see better."

"You'll have some time while I do a preflight check, assuming we can find a decent aircraft."

"Preflight check?" Metzger asked skeptically of the man anxious to get off the ground.

"It'll be brief," Timmons assured him. "I've at least got to check the vital stuff to make sure we don't crash and burn a few miles from here."

Putting the truck in reverse, Timmons scoured the nearby fencing until he found a hole that led to the portion of the airport where the runways and taxiing areas were located. A few mammoth planes appeared like freighter ships in the truck's headlights, looming massively over the truck when it drew close. Metzger craned his head to see the logos painted on the planes, finding them familiar, but they might as well have been visiting an aircraft graveyard, because he knew they couldn't possibly land one of them safely.

"No good," Timmons muttered, looking ahead where two large planes had collided off to the side of one runway.

"Rough landing?" Metzger questioned.

"People probably tried to leave," Timmons surmised. "Had no idea what they were doing."

"That doesn't bode well for us, does it?"

"No."

Unfortunately, the fence that granted them entry to the airstrip also permitted the undead to stagger around the area, though their numbers appeared manageable to Metzger.

"Maybe we don't need to raid the terminal," Metzger thought out loud.

Timmons looked at him quizzically.

"If we can access these planes, they're going to have snacks on them."

"You sure are thinking about food a lot."

"And you haven't been on the road, Captain. A few days of not knowing where your next meal is coming from gets you focused on food."

"Son, I've become a master of going without in this lifetime."

"That's well and good, but we're all going to need our strength when we face the dead, and the living."

Timmons remained silent a moment, likely giving little thought to the dangerous survivors lurking in every corner of the world.

He drove around the terminal, finding another large plane Metzger believed was a 747, as a few smaller options presented themselves in the distance. Feeling both nervous and excited, Metzger's heart raced momentarily as Timmons stepped on the gas, striking an ambling zombie along the left fender. When they approached the first aircraft, it looked much like the Cessna that Metzger and members of his group flew from New York to Virginia, but he didn't need to step out from the truck to spy the damage along the wings and tail that likely grounded the aircraft forever.

"That's disappointing," Timmons grumbled, driving around the right side of the plane to the next aircraft parked in the open.

It stood some distance away from the traditional terminal area where passengers boarded larger planes.

When they approached the next aircraft, Metzger tried to avoid getting his hopes up, because the plane looked intact. With white coloration along the top half of the plane, including the wings, and a dark blue underbelly, the plane certainly appeared large enough to carry their small group. Headlights didn't reveal every detail about the aircraft, particularly its fuel level, but Metzger felt it could take to the air at first light.

"What is it?" Metzger inquired.

"A Cherokee Six," Timmons answered. "If she can fly, she'll get us there."

Timmons navigated around the plane with the truck, much the way submersibles might circle a sunken ship, inspecting every inch possible without stepping outside. A zombie stepped in the path of the truck, and the pilot mowed him down without even realizing it until everyone heard the thump from the truck's grill. Barely acknowledging the vehicular homicide, if it could be called such a thing, Timmons continued to lower his head for a good view outside his side window.

"She looks solid," Timmons finally stated. "I can't imagine why anyone left her here unless she's out of fuel."

"That could be a problem," Metzger said.

"But not a deal breaker."

Metzger saw looming daylight along the horizon, providing them a slightly better view of the airfield and the danger around them. He noticed several holes along the fence that granted access to the undead to come and go as they pleased. Fortunately, it appeared the airport failed to hold their attention, because only a handful wandered inside the actual flight areas.

"You're going to have to watch my back while I check the plane," Timmons said as he parked the truck behind the Cherokee Six.

"Okay," Metzger said, jumping out his side of the truck and opening the back to free his family and Jillian.

He helped Isabella and Nathan down first, and then Jillian, who gently took hold of his hand as they shared a brief tender moment that didn't include words. Only when Timmons cleared his throat did their hands separate, and Metzger looked to the captain who returned a stony glance.

"We can check inside for food and water," Isabella suggested.

"You want to leave Nathan here?" Metzger asked, thinking the boy would be safer outdoors, instead of enclosed in a large, dark airport terminal.

Isabella nodded, and Metzger tossed her his flashlight before she and Jillian left to search for a way inside.

"Want to see the inside of a plane?" Metzger asked of his nephew, who excitedly nodded several times. "When Captain Timmons gets the hatch open, you can go inside, but you can't touch anything."

"Okay," Nathan promised.

"*Anything*," Metzger insisted.

Timmons opened two doors on the left side of the plane, one that flapped upward, and another that opened just like a car door. He helped Nathan into the aircraft before turning to Metzger.

"You can quit with the 'Captain Timmons' shit anytime now."

"Aye, aye, Captain."

Metzger turned and drew his sword, hearing only a groan from Timmons before the pilot set to work, examining the Cherokee Six. A few lingering undead had taken notice of their truck traveling around the airstrips, beginning to walk their way. Metzger surveyed the area, and began stalking towards the two zombies closest to him, daring them to get through him if they wanted to bring harm to his nephew and the man who could get him to his brother the fastest.

***

Jillian found a door nearby that led into the central hub of the terminal instead of the chutes heading out to where planes normally docked for passenger loading or unloading. She found it unlocked, opening it for Isabella who stepped inside, immediately searching for nearby danger. Jillian slipped in behind her, seeing only a few undead wandering around the lounge furniture and nearby counters.

"I'm surprised anyone stayed here long enough to die," Isabella said just above a whisper.

"Maybe some of them died trying to get out of here," Jillian suggested, drawing the knife she kept sheathed at her side.

Jillian stepped forward, using her blade to stab one zombie in the skull before it could lurch forward with grasping fingers. It fell, and she turned to kick another dead soul in the gut, knocking it to the floor before looking around.

"We only have a few minutes," she said, seeing a few vending machines that wouldn't function without electricity.

Shooting them might provide food, but that strategy offered a new set of problems when the undead all turned to locate the origin of gunfire.

"They must have a kitchen, or employee lounge," Isabella said, also scanning the area with her eyes.

Both of them crossed the large terminal to an area marked for employees only, and Jillian opened the door, cautiously peering inside before proceeding. She turned on the flashlight as the area was enclosed, without the benefit of mammoth windows like the main terminal. Hearing a hiss behind some kind of desk or counter, Jillian turned with her knife and rammed it through the skull of a loyal airline employee who never left work after the fateful day when the world turned upside-down.

"You seem well-adapted to this," Isabella commented.

"It doesn't take long."

Using what little light the flashlight provided, the women went through the employee lounge, finding little of use until they reached the area where bulk supplies were stored. Grabbing a few rolls of toilet paper, Jillian stuffed them into her backpack, while Isabella looked through some boxes for additional useful items. A moment later, she came across some packaged snacks used to replenish the planes when they landed, and several cases of various booze.

"Tempting," she said, though she ultimately left them behind.

"What's that?" Jillian asked, shining the light's beam on a stack of boxes in one corner.

"Looks like candy bars," Isabella replied, ripping open a few cases and helping Jillian load the snack-size candy into her pack.

Both of them heard the sound of the undead pawing at the door where they first entered the employee area, remaining perfectly still a moment.

"If Dan doesn't get to them, I have an idea," Jillian said, thinking it might be far easier for Metzger to deal with them if they remained distracted.

"I take it you and Dan are more than friends," Isabella said without any judgment in her tone.

"We've traveled together," Jillian answered without giving away details of her history with Metzger. "We're good friends."

"But he didn't bring any of his other friends along on this trip."

"I had my reasons for wanting to separate from the others."

"He speaks highly of all of you," Isabella stated. "I think he had some regrets about staying on the base, especially after they started treating him like a prisoner."

"Things might have turned out differently for the rest of us if he hadn't stayed," Jillian said, thinking about her father, who might be alive if Metzger had been there to avert the crisis that claimed his life.

"Are we stuck here until he comes to get us?" Isabella asked.

"No," Jillian answered, unwilling to wait for any man to save her from danger.

She aimed the flashlight toward the single entry to the room.

"Hold that door open and stand behind it. If any of them are out there, let them come to me."

"You sure?"

"Yes."

Isabella held the door open, but none of them came inside, because they were trapped behind the next door that led back to the main terminal.

"This may be a bit more challenging," Jillian stated, finding fewer things to hide behind or maneuver around in the office area.

Isabella reached for the doorknob, clutching the knife at her side in case she could help Jillian in any way once the undead poured into the room. She yanked the door open, standing behind it and counting the number of zombies that entered the room until four made it inside. They took a path directly to Jillian, seeing the light and hearing the noise as Jillian pounded her palm on the nearby countertop.

Choosing to close the door before too many more entered, Isabella got the jump on one of the undead stabbing it in the skull and finding the tip of her blade stuck only about an inch into the skull while failing to subdue the zombie.

"Crap," she muttered, trying to pry the knife free as the zombie tried pivoting its head to munch on her wrist.

Its teeth clamped shut several times, missing her wrist by inches as she led it around the room. From what she could tell, Jillian dealt with the other three zombies swiftly as several stabbing sounds reached her ears. Isabella could barely see as the flashlight beam danced up and down while Jillian defended herself. Finally given enough light to operate safely, Isabella used the knife to direct the zombie against a nearby wall, where she used both hands to plunge the blade into the center of its skull, putting it to rest.

"You okay?" Jillian asked, taking her side as the zombie slumped to the floor and Isabella wriggled the knife free from its head.

"Fine. Sorry about that. Just didn't want too many of them in here."

"Smart thinking. How many more?"

"I couldn't really tell. Maybe three just outside the door?"

"Okay," Jillian said as a bead of sweat dribbled down her cheek and her knife dripped blood from the zombies. "Same thing. You're going to get the hang of this."

"You got it," Isabella said, walking to the door, looking to Jillian, and receiving a nod before opening it once again.

***

"What's taking them so long?" Timmons asked as he checked some items on the plane's exterior while Metzger guarded him from all sides.

"They'll be fine," Metzger assured him. "Jillian knows what she's doing."

"Is she the girl you had relations with?"

"I think you already know the answer to that."

Metzger had shared certain details of his past with the pilot when he never thought he'd see his former group again. He hadn't brought up the subject, but Timmons inquired, and he felt comfortable enough talking to the captain to reveal certain details.

"Well, I have mostly good news," Timmons said after completing his visual inspection of the aircraft.

"So, what's the bad?"

"We are very low on fuel."

Metzger simply raised an eyebrow, waiting for an elaboration.

"Like we aren't going to make it to New York, low."

"Options?"

Timmons looked around, seeing the same limited resources as Metzger.

"We could try and syphon from the fucked up Cessna over there," Timmons said with a nod, "or we might get lucky and find a fuel truck around here. Even gas from an automobile would get us there, but it harms the valves over time."

Metzger checked the area around them for danger, seeing half a dozen zombie corpses lying on the ground from his handiwork. For the most part, cloudy skies had moved east, leaving them the beginning of a sunny day. Except for one crashed aircraft along one particular runway, the remaining routes appeared mostly clear. Lines of concrete intersected with small fields of grass, appearing to go on forever because the larger planes required lengthy runways. If time permitted, someone would probably take a vehicle down the chosen runway and make certain no bumps in the road might literally derail their trip.

He walked over to check on his nephew before making any decisions about their fuel situation.

"You being good?" he asked, looking up to Nathan, who sat in one of the passenger seats that faced one another behind the cockpit.

"Yup."

"Don't touch anything up front, okay?"

"Yup."

Metzger turned to Timmons, reasonably convinced his brother had raised Nathan to obey commands from familiar adults.

"I'm going to check on them," he informed the captain, nodding toward the terminal. "You be okay for five minutes?"

"You've giving me babysitting duty?"

"Would you prefer zombie stabbing duty?"

"Go have your fun," Timmons said, airily aiming one hand in the direction of the building. "We'll be fine for a few."

Metzger knew the captain was far from defenseless, but he didn't want to hear gunshots when they were so close to leaving Virginia. Scores of zombies could easily derail their plans to use the mostly vacated runways to reach the friendly skies.

Finding the same door Jillian and Isabella had used, he stepped inside, finding several corpses lying along the floor. Seeing little activity around him, he called out to them each by name, receiving no response.

"Jillian?" he called again, marching down the terminal to his right, trying to figure out where they might have traveled.

Traveling to the right, he found several zombies lingering near a door. As they turned to confront him, he sliced through both of their skulls before they could even raise their arms. He dared turn the doorknob without much thought, finding a dark, empty room before him.

"Anyone in here?" he called without raising his voice too much.

No response returned, so he closed the door and went to the end of the hub where several doors led to the boarding gates. He couldn't imagine Jillian and Isabella went exploring the chutes that didn't lead to planes in most cases. Turning around, he returned to the central portion of the terminal, spying a vending machine along one wall. He quickened his walking pace, and made his way to the machine, wondering if the Plexiglass might shatter if he tipped it over. Thinking better of it, he gave a testing jab with the sword, puncturing the substance, though not all the way through.

"Damn," he muttered, knowing he couldn't use the sword as some sort of makeshift jigsaw.

Looking around, he didn't see any undead, so he decided to rock the machine back and forth several times until it landed on the floor with a crashing sound that echoed throughout the facility when the front of the machine shattered into dozens of pieces. Contained beneath the machine itself, the glass couldn't harm Metzger when he attempted to raise it from the ground. He tried lifting the top first, but only got it about a foot off the ground before the weight of the device forced him to drop it.

"What the hell happened?" Isabella asked when she and Jillian appeared from a nearby door that Metzger hadn't checked.

"Trying to get us a few supplies," he answered, looking down to the vending machine.

"We found some stuff in back," Isabella answered.

"You two okay? I yelled for you."

"We're fine," Jillian answered. "Had to lead some of our dead pals out of the terminal."

"A little help and I can lift this thing if you want," Metzger offered.

"Sure," Isabella replied, helping him roll it along its longer end until it sat on one side, offering them every candy bar, cookie, and potato chip options inside.

No glass remained in the front display window to cut them as the three hastily grabbed snacks and stuffed them into their packs.

"That'll get us through," Metzger said before leading the way to the nearest exit.

A moment later the three stepped outdoors, breathing in clean morning air without any sign of wandering zombies in the area. Timmons continued to check the plane, taking notice when they approached.

"Nice of you three to take your sweet time coming back," he commented with moderate sarcasm.

"You're not even ready yet," Isabella stated.

"Fuel," Metzger said before the pilot could state the one thing holding them back.

"Oh," Jillian said, pulling out a set of keys and jingling them. "Like the kind a nearby fuel truck might carry?"

"Where'd those come from?"

"We found them after we raided the pantry," Isabella answered.

"Then where's the truck?" Timmons grumbled.

"We've been a little busy," Metzger said. "Jillian and I can take the truck and search for it. It can't be far."

"Neither can my employers," Timmons noted. "By now they're bound to realize their favorite asset is missing."

Metzger nodded, walking with Jillian to the truck where he opted to jump in the driver's seat. After a few weeks of being confined to the military base while everyone else got to wander into the city, or go wherever they pleased, he wanted the freedom of driving. Despite being surrounded by fences once again, he knew these wouldn't hold him.

"You sure you want to come with me?" he asked once he started the truck, putting it into gear before driving around the previously unseen areas of the airport.

"What's that mean?" Jillian asked uneasily.

"Scott's right. The military probably isn't going to let me go without a fight."

"I'll take my chances. I can't be around Colby right now. Not after what he did."

"He didn't make it sound so bad."

"He *would* lie just to save face, you know. Colby only went to you because he had nowhere else to turn."

"His sons are still out there. He's going to look for them."

"But he's not going alone, is he? Chances are he'll get someone else killed during his search."

"Someone else? Is he the reason Juan died?"

"No. Him and his new friend are the reason my father got killed."

"Jesus," Metzger said, focusing his attention on the road, looking for the fuel truck in between stalled planes and boarding terminals. "I'm so sorry."

"He got separated from us, and he hooked up with another group, bringing them straight back to us," Jillian explained. "To say they were shitty people is an understatement."

"So, the bad folks didn't make it?"

"No. After one of them shot my father, Colby managed to finish off three of them and spare his buddy Driscoll."

"There has to be an explanation," Metzger reasoned. "Colby wouldn't have brought them to you if he thought they were a serious threat."

"Yet he did. Are you taking his side?"

"No," Metzger said defiantly. "I'm just trying to understand."

Metzger thought of Sutton as a lot of things, but not an outright murderer, and certainly not someone careless enough to purposely bring danger to the rest of the group. People who killed other people might also threaten Buster, and he wouldn't take such a chance with his family or his canine. For the meantime, he decided to simply listen, and let Jillian vent.

"I'd already lost Mom, and didn't even know it," she said. "She went into town one day, looking for my dad, and got bitten. She took steps to make certain she didn't harm anyone by turning."

Metzger got to the end of the terminal and failed to find the truck. It occurred to him that they wouldn't likely keep it in the open, and he recalled what looked a bit like a service area when they entered the airport. Being dark at the time, he couldn't make out details, but he figured a fuel truck wouldn't be in the open until its services were required.

"Did the keys, or their location, say where we might find the fuel truck?" he inquired.

"There were a bunch of keys inside a mounted lock box," Jillian replied. "These had a tag for the fuel truck, so I just grabbed them, knowing we'd need the fuel. The office where we found them had been ransacked, so there was nothing left to indicate where the truck might be."

Metzger turned the truck around, heading to the area he remembered from earlier that morning. A few minutes later he pulled up to a lengthy building where some mechanical equipment, including tools and an air compressor were left outside, as though the people using them had simply taken a morning break.

Jumping from the truck, Metzger approached the area, spying several vehicles, and lots more equipment inside the lengthy garage. He didn't initially spy any undead walking through the area, but that didn't mean they weren't around. Carefully opening the main entrance, he peered his head inside, and motioned for Jillian to join him once he didn't find immediate danger awaiting them.

Only one garage bay deep, the building held the equivalent of approximately eight bays in length. Metzger quickly spotted what he assumed was a fuel truck, looking like a small gas tanker with a panel that mirrored those of fire trucks. He walked over, found a release for the garage door opener that no longer functioned without electricity, and looked around for a ladder tall enough to reach it.

"Ladder," he said quietly to Jillian in case any undead ears listened for activity.

Finding one in the back of the building, they quickly set it up, allowing Metzger to climb and release the bar. They teamed up to lift the garage door, and Metzger managed to start the truck and drive it outside. Jillian drove their other truck back, while he brought the fuel truck to the plane, parking it nearby.

"This work?" he asked Timmons.

"It should. Hope I remember how to use one of those things. It's been a few years, and it wasn't exactly my job to refuel planes."

After a few minutes of trial and error, Timmons figured out how to get the truck's pump system activated, and they stretched a fuel line to each of the wings to fill the tanks. He informed them that each wing held two tanks, and that he was filling them to capacity for a potential return trip. While the captain worked on getting the plane ready, everyone else moved their gear from the passenger truck to the plane, getting ready to depart.

Everyone took a breather for just a few seconds while Jillian drove the truck along the main runway to check for obstacles with Timmons riding shotgun in the truck. Metzger moved the fuel truck while they were gone, leaving it near the terminal for someone else to use. He figured much of the fuel would go bad before long, especially in a bulk container.

When the group finally got settled into the plane, Timmons checked a few things over along the control panel and with just a few flips of switches, he brought the plane to life. Metzger sat beside him in the copilot seat, feeling a bit tense because he expected the military to show up any moment and threaten to shoot them down if he didn't return peacefully to the base. No such thing happened as Timmons brought the single propeller to life, carefully aiming the plane in the correct direction for takeoff.

"Ever flown before, kid?" the captain asked Nathan, who could barely stay in his seat from the excitement of flying, and possibly seeing his father again.

"When I was little, but I don't remember it."

"Buckle up. You're about to get a great view out your window."

Timmons took a moment to memorize the controls, and Metzger knew from personal experience that every aircraft wasn't laid out exactly the same.

Once the captain felt comfortable with everything around him, he throttled up the Cherokee. Gaining momentum over the next thirty seconds, the plane built up enough speed to easily clear the fence at the end of the runway, well in advance.

"Wow," Nathan whispered in awe as objects below grew smaller, like doll houses and toy cars.

Metzger wanted to speak further with Jillian about her ordeal, because she obviously hadn't gotten over it, but he felt compelled to stay near Timmons and continue his piloting education. He imagined they would have time to talk in private at some point, but for the next few hours, Metzger needed to remain focused on getting home to Buffalo and searching for his brother once again.

Five

When Metzger and his current group neared the Buffalo-Lancaster Regional Airport several hours later, Metzger began scouring the ground for familiar landmarks. Timmons possessed familiarity with the airport, but without military hardware at his disposal, finding their destination wasn't so easy thousands of feet in the air.

"This is a far cry from what I'm used to," Timmons grumbled, taking a look at the tablet-sized screen that displayed a generic GPS reading of the area below and slightly ahead of them.

Driven by satellites instead of computer software, the GPS system would remain reasonably accurate for years to come, providing them with a trustworthy roadmap.

"Are we going to crash?" Nathan asked out of nowhere.

"Why would you ask that?" Isabella scolded.

"I dunno."

Timmons studied the map on the screen momentarily, making several adjustments that began to slow the plane as he descended slowly enough that Metzger barely noticed. Metzger couldn't imagine a civilian plane built before he was born could challenge the Navy captain, and Timmons hadn't appeared intimidated once during the flight. He calmly studied the controls and dials every so often, but never once seemed perplexed.

"We're about to land as smooth as a baby's bottom," Timmons said, turning to Nathan, who giggled.

"Unless we smack a few zombies in the runway," Metzger commented.

"There is that," Timmons muttered, arching one eyebrow.

Unlike the runway they departed from, the Lancaster airport possessed more debris than ever in the form of rotting bodies, random belongings, and a few cars. Part of Metzger felt relieved that more survivors had visited the airport, but disappointed that they may have ended up adding to the ranks of the undead. Timmons took notice as well, trying to figure out where to stick the landing so he could avoid some or all of the debris.

Continuing to slow, the plane wobbled slightly as they drew closer to the ground, but Timmons kept it steady enough that Metzger harbored no concerns about a disastrous landing. He turned long enough to see both Jillian and Isabella staring ahead, trying to avoid showing anxiety, while Nathan leaned forward, staring with awe as the ground drew closer.

"You buckled in?" Metzger asked his nephew.

"Yeah," Nathan answered almost absently, his eyes unblinking.

Isabella put an arm across his chest to keep him restrained, but Nathan refused to sit back or look away. Metzger turned to focus on the runway as it drew closer, spying several items that might cause a bumpy landing. He almost started to say something and begin pointing them out, but he quickly decided not to distract Timmons, who possessed a perfectly good set of eyes.

When the plane touched the concrete for the first time, everyone aboard felt a little bump that wasn't hard enough to jar them. The plane coasted another thirty yards smoothly until one of the wings clipped a wandering zombie who turned just in time to get sacked. Timmons turned briefly to look at the wing, which looked as though someone had thrown a small can of red paint across the metal. He quickly brought the plane to a stop as several more undead took notice of the noisy, large object that landed conveniently near them.

"Time to depart," Timmons reported once the aircraft came to a stop.

Isabella managed to open the dual side doors, granting them freedom from the cramped plane, though it placed them in immediate danger. Metzger undid his restraints, scrambling behind his seat to locate his sword and deal with any threats.

"You might want to hurry with the luggage," Jillian called as he reached the back of the plane, tossing backpacks and duffel bags to his companions.

Finding his own pack, Metzger grabbed it and exited the plane before pulling his sheathed sword from inside. He turned, finding two members of the undead community closing in, so he unsheathed the weapon, studying them a moment. Not recognizing either the male or female zombie before him, he sliced off the tops of their skulls in two swift motions. Metzger stood over them momentarily, questioning how large a grid he needed to search before feeling content.

"There'll be more," he proclaimed.

"We need a vehicle," Isabella stated.

"I may have that handled," Metzger replied, thinking of the key fob in his pocket that went to a Toyota Prius halfway across the small airport.

He left some belongings, including family photographs and memorabilia in the trunk of the car, locking it before he struck out for Virginia with part of his last group.

"You got a secret stash of vehicles?" Timmons asked, casually pulling his duffel bag from the plane.

"Not exactly," Metzger answered, nodding toward the Prius in the distance.

"Oh, that is peachy," Timmons said sarcastically. "We might as well be a group of clowns squeezing into that thing."

"Start putting our stuff into the car," Metzger told Isabella. "I'm going to start looking for clues along the runways."

"You okay?" she asked, and Metzger realized he wore his emotions outwardly, feeling a bit nervous about searching for his brother.

Or his remains.

"We need to know," he replied, walking away so he could begin the search.

Metzger hadn't studied the migratory patterns of the undead, so he didn't know how far his brother might have wandered if he indeed joined their ranks.

Seeing no other immediate threats to him or his fellow travelers, he walked in the direction where the military plane left with him and a number of Marines aboard, leaving his brother and Molly behind. Images of that day ran through his mind, and he felt the panic of losing Bryce all over again, fighting to stay in the moment and concentrate on discovering clues.

As he walked, scanning the concrete and grass around him, the runway felt like it went on forever, but he soon located the spot where his brother was assaulted by a number of the undead. Their rotting corpses were now lying atop the concrete in close proximity, no longer a threat to anyone. A tiny stain from dried blood remained embedded in the runway for Metzger to see, and he knew without a doubt his brother and Molly left the airport alive.

"What is it?" Isabella asked, approaching from behind.

"This is where it happened."

"None of these corpses is Bryce," she assured him.

"I know," Metzger replied, recalling exactly what clothes his brother wore during the mission.

He tried thinking of where his brother might go after leaving the airport, but Bryce reasoned with a logical mind, leaving emotion out of the equation.

"Where would he go, Izzy?" Metzger asked. "I don't think he would go to Mom and Dad's house."

"Unlikely. You're assuming your friend didn't have somewhere safe to go."

"I think the school was all she had, and it was compromised."

"Bryce would either find his way back to us, or he might track that guy from the school," Isabella reasoned aloud.

"Fournier."

"Yeah. That guy."

Metzger knew his brother's sense of duty, suspecting Bryce would never let Fournier escape cleanly. He would either interrogate the man, or trail him to locate additional answers regarding Nadeau. It occurred to him that he possessed no earthly idea what course his brother took, and hazarding a guess meant placing the lives of those around him in danger.

"If he completed his mission, or was forced to give up, he might head for safety," Metzger thought aloud. "He couldn't possibly know what happened at the base, so he might try contacting his superiors."

"He'd need a sat phone, or military equipment to reach them," Isabella deduced.

Metzger felt dazed, because he never expected to find anything except evidence his brother died at, or near, the airport. He felt certain Bryce or Molly would have left some kind of note about his fate, or perhaps an indication where they were heading.

"Did they have a contingency plan?" Isabella pushed.

"Not that I'm aware of," Metzger answered, knowing they shared very little information with civilians like him, particularly about sensitive missions.

Any shred of information went back to Virginia on that transport plane, and Metzger recalled being too stunned to ask questions or remain vigilant about his surroundings.

"Are there any vehicles missing that might have been parked nearby?" Isabella asked.

"I don't know," Metzger answered a bit more firmly than he intended. "I thought I had just witnessed my brother's death, Izzy. I wasn't exactly at the top of my game."

He knelt beside the fallen undead, seeing red holes in each of their skulls. His final images of Bryce took place when the cargo hatch began closing on the plane, giving him an obscured view of his brother's struggle to live. At one point, Bryce reloaded, so Metzger assumed Molly had assisted him with the remainder of the zombies, putting down the herd.

"Those two cops talked like they were positive the group they encountered were heading west," Metzger spoke his thoughts. "I can't imagine Bryce would've captured Fournier and forced him to talk. Those Marines let the man go pretty easily, which leads me to wonder if they were tracking him via satellite."

"Where to in the west?" Isabella inquired. "Did they know which state?"

"They didn't. Probably Wyoming, or Montana, where there's lots of real estate. That's assuming Fournier didn't return to Canada."

"I expected more than this," Isabella admitted, the movement of her arms encompassing the area that yielded little information.

"So did I."

For a few additional minutes the pair scoured the area, finding nothing of value to them. After two weeks, Bryce could be virtually anywhere, and both of them understood the near impossibility of locating him.

"We're never going to find him moping around here," Timmons said with the passenger side window rolled down when he pulled beside them in the gray Prius. "And this car is not my idea of a sweet ride."

"It'll get us further than anything else around here," Metzger responded.

"Sure. I found your little stash in the trunk, too."

"And it's still there?"

"It is."

Jillian and Nathan were already crammed into the back seat of the vehicle, and Isabella joined them to sit beside her son. Metzger got into the passenger seat, finding a few maps already stowed between the seats for his use.

"I'm going to do a lap around this place to make sure we don't miss any clues," Timmons said. "If we don't find anything, where are we going?"

Metzger looked back to Isabella.

"Don't your parents live around here?"

"No. They moved east of here to run a small resort."

"Does Bryce know about that?"

"We visited a few times. Why?"

"Assuming he's alive, and finds the answers he's looking for, Bryce would have to find somewhere to hole up during the winter. Making it back to Virginia would be nearly impossible unless he took to the air. Where is the resort?"

"It's near Blue Mountain," Isabella answered.

Metzger figured her parents wouldn't have moved far from the Buffalo area, but apparently they found life more appealing in the Adirondack Mountains.

"Are they alive?" Metzger asked quietly, trying to avoid upsetting his nephew, who already felt confused about whether his father might be alive or not.

"Last I knew they were making a stand at the resort and doing just fine."

"Are we going to see Grandma and Grandpa?" Nathan asked. "Will Dad be there?"

"We don't know where Dad is, Nathan," she answered. "He's still on a mission for the Navy."

"Thoughts?" Metzger asked of Timmons, who'd begun driving along the inside of the security fence, finding no clues about Bryce's whereabouts.

"Anywhere we go, it's a one-in-a-million shot at finding your brother in the open. If this is somewhere he might go, I say we head there and get shelter. It's either that, or go back to Virginia and take our chances with the military until he returns."

Metzger didn't plan on returning anywhere without his brother.

"The mountains aren't exactly open highway," he cautioned his sister-in-law. "We could get stranded there."

"They're isolated," Isabella said. "Protecting Nathan is my priority, and we'll be safe there."

"Sounds like that's decided," Timmons stated. "We'll do another lap around the outside of this place, then we'll take this rugged, off-road vehicle my good buddy Dan selected for a trek up some mountains."

"We could always fly there," Metzger suggested sarcastically.

"That would be nice," Timmons replied, "but I doubt they'd have a runway, and we need the plane in one piece if we're going fly anywhere else."

"Is this place sustainable?" Jillian asked, breaking her silence. "Food? Water? Shelter?"

"You'll have to see it to believe it," Isabella answered.

Metzger considered their immediate and distant future as a group, and decided to make a request.

"Can you drop me by the main building when we get done searching the outside?" he asked of Timmons.

"Need a bathroom break?"

"No. I can only assume we're coming back here to fly out at some point, and it doesn't make sense to lug my box of heirlooms with me."

Isabella shot him a questioning look.

Within a few minutes, the Prius stopped in front of the building, and everyone indeed took bathroom breaks inside the dark confines of the building, because some old habits were hard to break. While some of them propped doors open to see within the small restrooms, Metzger removed a photo from the box of family photographs and keepsakes before hiding the box. He was able to slide a ceiling tile aside and place the box above the ceiling where vandals and the military alike wouldn't be able to find it.

"Thanks," he said to Timmons, who saw the last of his actions.

"You're welcome. Still think we should've made this trip? Your nephew is about to get an eyeful."

"That's what I'm afraid of."

"If I can drive a hybrid half as well as I fly, we'll be okay."

Metzger chuckled.

"I can't wait until we find a gas-guzzling SUV so I can stop hearing about the Prius."

"You're never going to hear the end of it. Believe me."

Metzger rolled his eyes, ready to get on the road and see more of his home state and the dangers it presented.

A few minutes later, when Isabella joined him at the front door, he handed her a recent family photo of her, Bryce, and Nathan posed at a studio. Bryce wore his uniform, and Metzger wasn't positive his brother owned a regular suit after being in the service for so long. Isabella stared at the image momentarily before a tear formed in one eye.

"Thank you," she said, giving him a quick hug. "Now we just have to find him."

"We will," Metzger responded, not sure he believed his own words.

***

When General James McCall of the United States Army was tasked with creating a joint base at Naval Station Norfolk, he never imagined the difficulties associated with merging the military personnel and civilians. Surrounded by high-ranking officers from each military branch, the collective managed to get creative, first by powering the town to give the civilians a safe haven, while allowing the military to conduct business on the base. Rules and regulations were drafted to arm civilians while they worked and lived in town, but they weren't allowed to bring firearms inside the base perimeter.

Beginning his military service around the time of the Gulf War, McCall went through an ROTC program, starting at the rank of second lieutenant. He spent many of his years in sandy countries, learning the culture, and the tactics associated with winning wars in the area. As he rose through the ranks, he spent more time stateside, advising the CIA, Congress, and even the President at times.

Eventually assigned to an intelligence team when he reached the rank of colonel, McCall excelled, finally making time for marriage and a family. He spent more than a decade studying an enemy abroad that now suffered the same afflictions as his own country. No country remained safe from the infection that caused the dead to rise.

While the military created emergency plans for wars, even holocausts, it required a few days to adapt their plans to the undead crisis while political leaders were whisked away for their own safety.

At first, leadership hoped that finding Jean Pierre Nadeau might lead to a cure for what caused the apocalypse, but after scouring confiscated computers and reading through mounds of paperwork, they realized the man covered his tracks. Finding him, much less getting him to produce the formula for a cure, seemed improbable, if not impossible.

A small miracle fell into his lap when it turned out blood samples taken from the first mission to Buffalo were compared to blood drawn after the mission. It turned out Dan Metzger possessed a marker in his blood that showed immunity to the substance that killed much of the world's population. What seemed even stranger was the fact that the chemical was present before the plane touched down in Lancaster, meaning Metzger was exposed to the biological agent *before* he stepped foot on the base.

By all rights he should have gotten sick, died a slow, painful death, and passed away to eventually return as a zombie.

McCall still believed in civil rights for all persons, so he kept Metzger guarded, not wanting to imprison the man simply because he proved useful to their scientists. Unfortunately, his decision allowed the civilian to exit the base sometime in the middle of the night, likely with help as his sister-in-law and nephew were nowhere to be found. While Metzger wasn't the only person in the world with immunity to the outbreak, he was the only local case.

"You were right," Admiral George Eagan said as he walked into the small conference room where McCall and Colonel Jack Tarrell of the Marines were already seated.

"About?" McCall pressed.

"It seems Captain Timmons is missing as well. He was scheduled for a flight this afternoon and a check of his quarters revealed some missing personal effects."

Eagan took a seat at the table, removing his hat and setting it down.

"This is a disaster," McCall stated. "Our people are close to synthesizing a vaccine for this plague and our one good test subject walks out the front gate."

"We could create a search grid," Tarrell suggested.

"No," McCall said, knowing the runaways had a five-hour head start. "We have three airstrips nearby, and none of them have reported any unusual activity. We have a team heading out to the civilian airport a few miles away. They'll either find them there, or we'll know where they've flown. Lieutenant Commander Metzger's brother has to assume he's alive, much like we do."

"Timmons wouldn't have leaked that information," Eagan said adamantly.

"Your pilot wasn't privy to those details," McCall said, "but the wife was snooping around the base yesterday. She must've found some answers and convinced Metzger to leave with her."

"We know where they're going," Tarrell said. "We have the means to intercept them."

"There's still some guesswork, Jack. There are a *lot* of airports in the Buffalo area."

"But only one where his brother was bitten."

"Yes, the one where your men left his brother behind because he wasn't playing nice with them. We explicitly contacted your team leader and told him to bring *both* of them back."

"They've been disciplined," Tarrell assured him. "In their defense, they said things were chaotic at the end."

"I've heard the recordings and reviewed the plane's footage, Colonel," McCall said gruffly. "A little more effort would have brought our Navy man home with his brother."

Tarrell said nothing, his lips pressing together in a silent protest.

"I can't afford to send entire platoons after the brothers," McCall continued. "I've got several thousand people living on base, and in town, and we're about to hit winter with an impending food shortage. It's going to be everything we can handle to feed and clothe these folks."

"What do you suggest, General?" Tarrell asked.

"If Lieutenant Commander Metzger is loyal to God and country, he's going to use the device we provided to track Fournier," McCall thought aloud.

"Tracking him was always a contingency plan in case the man escaped. We've been following Fournier's every move since he left the airport, and there's every reason to believe he's leading us straight to Nadeau."

"What are you proposing?" Eagan asked.

"We send one man, armed with a tracking device, to follow Fournier. This may net us Fournier, and both Metzger brothers, should they reunite."

"Sounds like a win-win situation," Eagan stated, rapping his fingers against the conference table. "Did you have someone in mind?"

"It'll have to be someone with piloting skills who can handle himself," McCall replied.

"I may know someone," Tarrell said thoughtfully. "He's one of our Marines."

"None of the men from the Buffalo fiasco, I hope."

"No," Tarrell said, barely able to suppress his annoyance about the partially-failed mission. "He's one of mine, but he knows how to fly civilian aircraft from his teenage years."

"That works out nicely," McCall added with a cagy grin. "If that's the case, we send him north, posing as a civilian until he finds one, or all of our targets."

Eagan appeared concerned.

"What is it, George?" McCall asked.

"What about the others, including my pilot?"

"We aren't looking to harm anyone, George, if that's what you're asking. That being said, however, our primary concern is the three targets, and not civilians, or your AWOL pilot."

"Dragging either of the brothers back here without the family probably won't work."

"What do you recommend?"

"If possible, have your man use a little deception."

"Maybe have him take out the pilot so they have to rely on him for a flight home," Tarrell suggested, drawing an uneasy look from Eagan. "I didn't say to kill him, George."

"You didn't have to," Eagan said. "Is this what we've come to? We're willing to murder our own, and civilians, to manufacture a cure we might not even need?"

"What is that supposed to mean?" Tarrell asked, furrowing his eyebrows.

"It means if we haven't breathed this stuff already, what are the chances we're going to?"

McCall leaned forward, looking sternly between both officers.

"Who's to say Nadeau is done?" he asked no one in particular. "I'm preparing for our worst-case scenario, and I plan to keep everyone on this base alive."

He drew a deep breath.

"Even if it comes to a little collateral damage."

"Would you like me to fetch him, Jim?" Tarrell asked.

"Yes. Bring him to me, so we can lay down some ground rules."

Six

Four Days Later

"I can't stick around," Steve Driscoll said from the passenger's seat of the box truck Colby Sutton drove down a Virginia highway.

Buster occupied the seat between them, sleeping peacefully after growing bored from their conversation, or lack thereof, nearly an hour ago.

"Any particular reason?" Sutton asked.

"There are a few things I need to deal with."

Sutton found it strange that Driscoll always sought the company and security a group provided until this particular trip. When Sutton found, and ultimately saved the man, Driscoll had taken up with some men who didn't possess good moral character. Sutton wasn't convinced that Driscoll didn't have a bit of a racist streak in him, but the man helped them during several scraps with other factions.

"This detour to my old camp won't take us long," Sutton said. "If you have somewhere to be, we can help get you there."

"It's not that," Driscoll replied. "I just feel there are better fits for me out there."

Sutton imagined he was referring to the three people behind them in a recently discovered car with half a tank of gas. Even before the apocalypse, Sutton didn't trust others easily, and anyone wanting to leave a perfectly sound group gave him reason for pause.

"We aren't the best with firearms as a whole, but we stick together and defend our own," Sutton said. "You know what's out there, and not everyone takes to strangers."

"I can make it on my own," Driscoll said. "At least for a while."

"Can you?"

"What's that supposed to mean?"

"I've just never seen you on your own."

Sutton weaved through a pair of cars parked awkwardly in the middle of the road. Driscoll didn't appear comfortable with his last statement, though he kept his thoughts to himself.

"You know I don't talk a whole lot," Sutton said, "but I've let these folks down a few times now, and I'm willing to do whatever it takes to make it up to them."

"Looks to me like you're making them travel with you to your old stomping grounds."

"I feel you're not the parenting type, so I'll let you in on a little information. Even though my one and only marriage failed, it left me with two sons. I'd walk to the ends of the Earth to find them, and there isn't a single person, living or dead, who could stop me."

"Haven't you been here once?" Driscoll asked without judgment.

"We all stopped by the camp, but there wasn't any sign of them."

"Then why go back?"

"Because I hold out hope," Sutton said, putting an edge to his voice. "My boys had a long way to travel, and it's been a few weeks, so I'm checking again."

Both of them remained silent a few minutes as Sutton passed a few individual zombies along the highway. He knew they were drawing close to their destination, and soon the isolated highway would become a county road that eventually led to several dirt paths. He felt a little bit surprised to see zombies at all, because cars and residences dotted the area, but he supposed nearly two months into the end of the world they found plenty of time to wander.

"I'll stick with you through your search," Driscoll said. "I'd like to see you find your boys before I head out."

"Don't feel obligated."

"Well, it'll be dark soon. Probably best I stay until morning."

"Suit yourself."

When Sutton turned onto the county road, he felt a sense of relief, as though immersing himself in the nature around him put aside the darkness of the apocalypse momentarily. He'd prepared for the end of the world for quite some time, but never anticipated sharing his life with strangers, or having to find shelter every night.

"I miss the little things," Driscoll admitted. "Hot dogs at a campfire, popcorn, even using a toilet in peace. Now I've gotta clear an area before I squat to take a dump."

Sutton said nothing, focusing on the road, even though the concrete offered a very dull view, devoid of vehicles, zombies, or trash.

"There has to be something more than this," Driscoll continued. "Maybe the government is working something behind the scenes to restore the planet."

"I wouldn't put much faith in them."

"The gay dude said they turned you all away at the base."

"They did, without a second thought."

Sutton recalled how the guards who met them allowed Metzger inside to see his brother, but denied access to the others, despite a child traveling with them. His second experience at the base gave Sutton some insight to future problems. Strength in numbers was always beneficial against the undead, but feeding, clothing, and protecting thousands would eventually lead to shortages. He pictured the fat cats from Washington living it up in their protected bunkers, eating canned food and drinking filtered water for years while ordinary citizens suffered.

When the group finally reached the camp about half an hour later, the sun provided its last rays as dusk approached. Sutton pulled into the campsite with lowered expectations after the initial visit went so poorly. Many of the cabins had burned to the ground, and a large plane stuck out of the lake at a strange angle with its nose buried below the water's surface. As he pulled to a stop near the entrance, Sutton saw the sign he left for both of his sons that contained a message specifically for them to remain in the area.

To him, the sign appeared undisturbed when he stepped from the box truck. He picked it up, looked at it, and set it on the ground. Saying nothing, he motioned for his fellow travelers to follow him further into the campground.

When they reached the area where his cabin once stood, he saw the remains among the blackened grass where the fire had ravaged virtually everything in the area. He stepped from the truck, staring out at the lake where the plane had finally succumbed to gravity, falling into the water, belly-down. Only a few feet of its white paint remained visible atop the water, like an elongated boat turned upside-down and grounded. Buster walked around, using the charred grass as his personal restroom after a few hours of being trapped inside the box truck.

"This is depressing," Gracine said when she took his side. "Any sign of your boys?"

"Not yet," Sutton answered, looking around.

Several zombies floated in the water, breaking the silence as they provided throaty growls. They managed to float without effort, and Sutton wondered what made them so buoyant. Fortunately, they couldn't muster brainpower enough to remember swimming techniques, so they simply floated in place, occasionally flailing their arms at the people on land. Sighing, Sutton felt overcome by grief because he felt certain something tragic befell both of his sons, leaving him without any family.

Virtually every survivor knew their family was gone, either deceased, or too far away to realistically ever see again. Metzger proved the exception to the rule, and one simple trip to Buffalo might have robbed him of his brother. Sutton hoped his ally began to understand that the military wasn't the benevolent group they appeared to be. After all, they still answered to men who lived in bunkers like rats.

"What's this?" Luke asked, walking over to a tree where a plastic bag hung by a tack, swinging in the breeze.

He yanked the bag from the tack, cautiously taking a peek inside before pulling a sheet of paper out and unfolding it. After a few seconds of reading the note, he walked over to Sutton and handed him the paper.

"Definitely for you," Luke said, providing a warm grin.

Sutton took the note, anxiously reading it for clues, finding that one of his sons had addressed the note to "Dad" and put "C.S." after that in parenthesis to let him know the note was for him. He read the words carefully, his eyes darting back and forth across the page as his oldest son provided him with an update.

"What does it say?" Gracine asked after a moment.

"My oldest, Sean, says he's in the next campground over."

"Does he say anything else?" Luke inquired.

"Not much," Sutton answered. "He wrote in a code of sorts so only I'd know what he meant."

"How far is it?" Driscoll asked.

"Less than a mile. We can be there in a few minutes."

Without another word, everyone climbed into their respective vehicles, and Sutton patiently waited for Buster to finish sniffing the grass and marking it with his urine before he jumped into the box truck. Sutton followed, almost afraid to see what awaited him at the other campground, which contained more privately-owned cabins. All of them varied in size and features, remaining far enough apart that their occupants enjoyed privacy during their visits, but close enough that help wasn't unreasonably far.

"Does it seem legit?" Driscoll asked him once they reached the dirt road that accessed the next set of cabins.

"It does," Sutton answered. "I just hope he's still there."

When he located the grounds, Sutton drove through an open iron gate with rock walls on either side. Strangely, a jack-o-lantern was perched atop the rocks on the right side, it's face illuminated from within by a candle.

"That's not creepy or anything," Driscoll muttered. "Would your kid do that?"

"Not likely," Sutton answered, concerned that his son wasn't the only person residing on the grounds.

Now growing dark outside, Sutton passed a few cabins, spying no activity in either. He stopped at the third cabin, which he recalled being rather central to all of the others, despite being over a hundred yards away from them. Parking the box truck, Sutton stepped out, scouring the area for any movement. He knew if his son spotted him, he'd cautiously approach the group only after making certain no traps awaited him. Sutton raised his boys to exercise caution, teaching them how to shoot, and how to survive if and when the world turned bad.

"We're stopping?" Gracine questioned when she emerged from the car.

"For now," Sutton answered. "No sense in driving around all night. We'll build a fire and let Sean know we're here."

"You *did* see that freaky pumpkin at the gate?" Luke asked, openly concerned.

"It means we're probably not alone," Sutton answered. "We stick together at all times. We don't want a repeat of what happened to Juan."

Using flashlights, the group explored the cabin, finding food and supplies inside. They built a fire within the brick pit outside, able to cook while receiving warmth on a rather brisk evening. Several large logs surrounded the firepit, but they also found webbed folding chairs that Sutton preferred after hours on a stiff seat inside the box truck.

Two beds and two cots awaited everyone inside, but Sutton wouldn't be able to sleep until he received some answers. He stayed by the fire for over an hour, attempting to appear casual while he scoured the grounds, hopeful his son would emerge any moment to greet him. Ordinarily, he might worry about the undead wandering through the woods, but they seemed thin in this particular area, and he kept firearms close by. Buster's senses detected unfriendly people, and the undead, and he, in turn, let his owner know of any impending danger.

One by one, the others turned in, leaving him alone with his thoughts, which he admitted weren't good company. He heard animal sounds throughout the evening, both on the ground, and even several different birds in nearby trees. Sutton began to wonder if wildlife would continue to act normally if danger lurked nearby. A branch snapping behind his chair startled him, but when Sutton whirled around, he found Gracine trying to quietly approach from the cabin.

"I thought you might be sleeping," she said just above a whisper.

"Were you going to sneak up and tackle me if I was?"

"Nah," she answered with a smile, assuming the folding chair next to his.

Both sat a moment, listening to the crackle of the fire as embers floated and danced in the air above the flames.

"You're worried, aren't you?" she finally asked.

"A little. Sean's note said he hadn't found my youngest. I wonder if he got antsy and went out to search."

"If he's practical, like his old man, he's waiting patiently around here until the coast is clear."

Sutton said nothing, fiddling with a stick by tracing the dirt with it. Buster walked over to him, seeking attention, so Sutton scratched his head a few seconds.

"He minds well," Gracine said. "I've never seen a more loyal dog."

"You obviously haven't seen his less perfect moments," Sutton said as he tapped Buster's side, sending him over to Gracine for additional affection. "He's usually pretty good though."

"What do you make of that creepy-ass pumpkin at the entrance?" Gracine asked as she patted Buster's back and scratched his neck.

"Obviously someone's been here."

"I'm saying someone's *still* here. Candles only burn so long."

"Not much we can do about it tonight," Sutton decided. "We'll stay in the cabin, keep ourselves safe, and do some exploring in the morning."

"Might want to bring in some of your guns, too."

Sutton lifted the right side of his shirt, revealing a sidearm tucked away. He also planned on bringing in his sniper rifle with the thermal vision scope and a fully automatic AK-47 he'd found during his travels.

"My hero," Gracine said, sarcastically looking thankfully to the heavens.

"Thank you."

"For what?"

"For your discretion about how we originally met."

"Those soldiers were up to no good," Gracine said. "Lord knows what they were going to do to me, but they had you by the balls when they threatened your dog."

Sutton recalled the day in question, feeling vulnerable all over again because five soldiers held Gracine at bay, possibly about to rape her, possibly just wanting to toy with her before they moved on or shot her. As a weary traveler, he simply wanted to get past them and go about his business, but as fate would have it, one of the soldiers spotted him. Likely a group of wayward National Guardsmen, they didn't seem to have any scruples about what it took to remain alive and fed. Sutton raised a rifle at them when they approached, leaving Gracine kneeling on the ground behind them with her belongings.

All five of the men appeared ragtag in nature, only two of them wearing helmets, and none of them wearing body armor in the warm weather. Their uniforms appeared dirty and in some cases, torn from their travels.

Buster, sensing his master's tension, growled at the men, showing his teeth. This served only to have one of them take aim at the canine. Why they didn't fire, Sutton never knew, but he immediately moved in front of his dog and pled for Buster's life after laying down his rifle.

"Let's waste the whole lot of them and take what they got," one of the men suggested.

"We don't have to kill them," another suggested. "They ain't got much anyway."

Sutton possessed his box truck at the time, but he kept it hidden, usually driving a different vehicle locally, or walking sometimes with his dog.

"But now they've seen us," the first soldier said.

"What are they going to do? Call the cops?"

Buster started to take a step forward, but Sutton placed a hand against his snout, keeping his pet behind him.

"We need to kill the dog," another said. "He's probably been trained for those underground fighting rings. I don't want him attacking us down the road."

"Please," Sutton said, feeling his eyes well up from emotion. "Come on."

"What's the dog worth to you?" the first soldier asked. "We need supplies. Hook us up and we might let him live."

Sutton couldn't lie, because Buster's life depended on him complying with the soldiers. He felt a tear dribble down his right cheek because he couldn't lose his last companion in addition to everything else.

"I've got a truck. It's full of supplies. Food, toilet paper, bedding, the works."

Every one of the soldiers looked at him skeptically, because no one in the apocalypse traveled so well-prepared.

"What kind of truck?" one of the soldiers asked, his expression perplexed.

Sutton never got to answer, because a bloody hole appeared along the left shoulder of the man when a bullet pierced his flesh from behind. Knowing immediately that their potential victim decided not to wait and see what fate awaited her, Sutton reached for his sidearm as the soldiers all turned to confront Gracine. He fired two shots, striking two men along their upper backs, downing them immediately. The two uninjured men took shots at Gracine, missing their mark, and as one turned to confront Sutton, he was shot along the left side of his neck. Blood spurted from the wound immediately, and even as the man went to clasp it with his free hand, his legs betrayed him, allowing him to topple like a detonated building to the ground.

Not backing down for one second, Gracine marched forward, firing a shot at the soldier that missed completely. He went to fire at her, and in desperation she squeezed the trigger again, striking the man in his forearm that clasped the firearm. He yelped in pain, dropping the gun as she got close enough to swing her own sidearm against his temple, dropping him in a heap.

Their initial encounter never left Sutton's mind, and as he sat beside her in the present, he felt thankful to have Gracine and most of their group nearby. He never expected forgiveness from Jillian, and wasn't optimistic about seeing her or Metzger again in his lifetime. Even so, he planned on finding a vehicle charger that worked with the satellite phone Metzger gave him, just in case he received a call.

"For the record, I'm glad we didn't lose you," Gracine said, the glow from the fire reflecting in her face as she turned to speak to him.

"If Jillian hadn't run off with Dan, me and Buster would've hit the road."

"She's going to forgive you," Gracine said with a soft, knowing grin.

"I don't know. I could've done a lot of things differently that day."

"Those creeps were heading that way whether you were with them or not. Because of you, the rest of us didn't get shot."

Sutton supposed she had a point, but he still hated that Jillian saw her father so briefly before his death.

"Well, I'm turning in," Gracine said, raising her hands over her head while she yawned a few seconds.

Standing, she placed a hand on his shoulder and leaned down to kiss him on the cheek, which Sutton didn't refuse. After she walked into the cabin, Sutton stared at the fire momentarily before looking out to the trees, admiring the stars between their branches and leaves. The setting might have made for a beautiful painting, or even a nighttime photograph if properly shot. He preferred the rural setting to all of the dangers that lurked inside the cities and towns. Still concerned about his sons, he turned to Buster.

"You about ready to crash, boy?"

Buster turned his head sideways in response.

"Me, too."

Sutton kicked dirt on the fire to extinguish it, not wanting stragglers or the dead to find their position. While the campground area appeared reasonably clear of the undead, he knew at least one living person remained in the area, and it concerned him not knowing the person's identity. He looked around, seeing and hearing nothing, wishing his son would emerge from the woods and end his anxiety. Instead, he turned to walk inside with Buster and see what answers daylight brought him.

***

After a night of tossing and turning before finally drifting off to sleep, Sutton heard birds chirping outside, along with other woodland noises the next morning. Throwing aside the blanket, he swung his legs out from the wood-frame bed, ready to step outside for some answers. Buster remained lying beside his bed, showing no inclination to eat, or run outside during the early morning hour, so Sutton tiptoed around him before putting on the hiking shoes he found at a house the previous week.

Everyone else appeared to be asleep as he stepped quietly through the house, unlocking the door to confront the morning. He smelled the burned wood from the previous evening, and several other pleasant odors only found in nature. Far removed from smog, landfills, and even undead masses, he remembered why he loved being isolated from the world so much. When he stepped onto the front porch, he heard his new footwear clop against the wood planks, but as he stared into the open area along the front of the building, Sutton spied something unusual near his firepit and beyond the two parked vehicles.

Instinctively reaching to his right hip, he realized he hadn't grabbed a firearm in his haste to look for signs of Sean. Taking only a few steps forward, down two steps, he confirmed the two objects he saw were bodies, both blackened from being thoroughly burned, and neither appearing to be undead in nature. Sutton knew the difference, and these bodies weren't severely skinny like most of the undead, nor did they appear ragged, or decomposed, in the few areas that hadn't suffered burns. He felt sick to his stomach, because he feared for the lives of both of his sons if they'd returned to the site and some maniac got to them.

Despite the sounds of nature, he heard a different noise behind him, and when he turned to look at the end table set on the porch by the cabin's previous owners, he spied a lit jack-o-lantern staring back at him.

Seven

“This is a terrible idea,” Timmons grumbled while the group gathered their few loose belongings inside a house the travelers had borrowed for the night.

“What are you complaining about now?” Isabella asked, folding a sleeping bag as her son followed her example with his own bedding.

During their travels, the group discovered that the gray Prius worked incredibly well because they didn't have to deal with fuel issues nearly as often. So long as they thinned the undead numbers, and didn't have to plow through them, the car held up nicely. Along the way, they found a blue Prius, allowing them to divide their group and carry more belongings as they discovered weapons, bedding, and clothes they could use during their journey. Metzger often rode with the pilot, because the women thought he complained too much.

Metzger informing the captain that the color of their new ride was Seaside Pearl did nothing to improve the Navy man's disposition.

“If I had known our destination was *this* far away, I could've crash landed us closer to the lodge,” Timmons said.

“It's half a state away,” Metzger stated. “Back in the day, probably a six-hour drive.”

“We're now into day four, son,” Timmons retorted. “I honestly can't imagine your brother is going to hike all this way when he's finished with our terrorist conspirator.”

“You obviously haven't seen winters up here,” Jillian chimed in. “If Dan's brother gets pressed for time, his options will be limited.”

Timmons grunted, likely thinking how easy it would be for him to grab a plane and fly south to escape winter.

Once his friend stepped outside, loading the second Prius, Metzger approached him after making certain everyone else remained occupied inside.

"What's up with you these past few days?"

"What?" Timmons asked, appearing genuinely surprised at the question.

"You're acting like something crawled up your ass and died, especially after you found out where we're headed."

Timmons placed a few items in the trunk before turning to Metzger.

"Maybe this isn't what I signed up for when I agreed to fly you back here."

"What did you expect exactly?"

"I expected your brother to leave us some kind of road map if he survived. We found nothing, so now we're risking life and limb to go climb some mountain?"

"It's not exactly Everest," Metzger countered. "If I didn't think this was Bryce's next stop, I wouldn't go. I'd head west and look for him."

"If your brother is alive, he's carrying out an assignment. It may be unofficial, but he wants answers about what happened, and he's pissed that guy killed your parents."

"So am I," Metzger added sternly.

"You know you can't go back to Virginia, but that's exactly where your brother will go."

Metzger exhaled through his nose, wondering if the captain made a valid point. Bryce had no idea about the happenings at the base, or that he might walk through the gates of the military installation only to be a captive blood donor.

"I expected this to be over immediately, Scott," he finally admitted. "I'd steeled myself against finding him walking around with those glazed eyes. A hundred times I envisioned myself putting a knife in his skull to end it, and I was prepared for that."

Metzger felt a wave of emotion strike him, and he turned away from the military man briefly because he wasn't sure if he could maintain his composure.

"But you know he's alive," Timmons said, putting a compassionate hand on his shoulder.

"I know he left that airport alive," Metzger said, looking the captain in the eye. "What do we know besides that?"

"You know he shares your blood. And that means more than being immune to these things," Timmons said, almost scoffing at the notion. "It means he's a survivor like you."

"Lot of good that'll do if we don't find one another."

"That's not on you," Timmons said assuredly. "Izzy took you from that base, hell, that shitty life they had planned for you. You're protecting them, now, and abiding by her wishes."

Metzger took a few deep breaths, calming himself.

"And that's why we're going to see her parents. Even if we don't find Bryce, she needs to know they're okay, and it's our best shot and providing a safe haven for Nathan."

"For the record, I don't think your brother will step foot in New York again, unless it leads him back to Virginia."

Timmons spoke his peace and closed the trunk.

"I wouldn't blame you if you had somewhere else to be," Metzger said, trying to give the pilot a way out.

"I'm not sure you understand why I agreed to all of this," Timmons said while slowly shaking his head.

Spying the others emerging from the house, Timmons apparently didn't feel comfortable speaking the words he felt in front of them. Metzger supposed he might find the time, or the courage, to say them during the next lengthy portion of their journey.

While Isabella helped Nathan load their stuff into the gray Prius, Jillian walked over to Metzger while Timmons decided to make a last sweep for items inside the house.

"Everything okay?"

"I'm not entirely sure," Metzger said, his eyes following the military man into the open door of the house. "Sleep well?"

"Well enough. How far are we from the resort?"

"We're going to be hitting some lesser traveled roads, so hopefully we can make it by noon."

"Time is a foreign concept to me anymore," Jillian admitted.

"I just guestimate time by the sun's position," Metzger said. "It's nice not living by an alarm clock, or worrying about Daylight Saving Time."

"Not exactly a fair tradeoff, though."

"No," Metzger said, thinking of the losses in his life. "It isn't."

Jillian drew a little closer to him.

"Maybe we should let the captain take a shift with your family. We could catch up."

"Izzy might kill him, but I guess that's a chance we can take."

After a few minutes, everyone convened around the two vehicles, and Metzger decided to bring up Jillian's idea.

"If it's okay with everyone, Jillian and I need to catch up, so we'd like to carpool a while."

Isabella looked to Timmons, trying to keep her expression neutral.

"That's fine," she said. "The captain and I have a few things to sort out as well."

Metzger couldn't imagine what his sister-in-law needed to discuss with the military man, but he suspected their conversation might revolve around their agreement to depart the base. For his part, Timmons looked more frustrated than angry or disappointed, and Metzger realized he needed to speak with the older man about his loyalties at some point.

Within a few minutes, both cars were loaded and the new pairings drove toward the Adirondack Mountains, and the hope that safety and some creature comforts awaited them.

"I wish you had been with us these past few weeks," Jillian said after a few minutes of travel where Metzger followed his sister-in-law's lead, driving a few car lengths behind.

"Me too, at this point."

"No, I mean the whole thing with Colby might have been avoided if you were around."

Jillian quickly caught the way her words came out.

"I don't mean it's your fault, but I'm sure you wouldn't have let things escalate to the point that people got killed."

"I'm not exactly a pacifist."

"I know, and the worst thing is that Colby started off with the best of intentions. When we dropped you off, he found a few soldiers rummaging through his box truck, so he tied them up and left them there. The officer didn't take it so well, and from what we could tell, he murdered his own man and tried to pin it on us, or at least Colby."

"Holy shit," Metzger said. "You really did have a full plate."

"It gets worse. Once we found out the National Guardsmen were following us with a drone, of all things, Colby volunteered to stay behind and deal with them so the rest of us could continue onward."

"That doesn't sound very Colby-like, but still very noble of him."

Jillian appeared conflicted.

"I thought he was turning a corner, and we went ahead without him to my hometown. I found my mom dead in the house. She'd been bitten, and left my sister and I a note before taking things into her own hands."

"I'm so sorry," Metzger said, looking to her as a tear formed along the corner of her right eye.

From personal experience, he understood how it felt losing parents to the apocalypse, or the aftermath of the initial event.

"Thanks," Jillian said. "I ended up finding my father alive, still cleaning up the town and dealing with the undead in the area. The whole town looked like something out of a commercial, with manicured lawns in some of the neighborhoods, and cars parked in driveways. It looked more like aliens swooped down and took everyone away, rather than people he knew were dying and turning into ravenous monsters."

"What did he do with the bodies?"

"He found the means to dig a few mass graves and bury most of them. Some, he burned, but as they died, he dealt with them. After he found my mom, I think he just threw himself into his work, not wanting to return home and deal with her body."

"That's terrible," Metzger muttered.

"But that was my dad. He just soldiered on through tasks all his life."

"Where does Colby fit into all of this?"

"I figured he would have told you his slanted side of things."

"He told me a little," Metzger admitted, "but I want to hear your version."

Jillian removed her seatbelt, prepared to get comfortable before telling her tale, but the Prius began beeping incessantly because she ignored its warnings.

"It's thinking of your safety," Metzger commented, having to nearly shout his words to be heard over the rhythmic beeping.

Jillian groaned before snapping the seatbelt into place once again.

"Just when you think the apocalypse frees us from everyday cares, this happens."

"It can always be worse. We're lucky to have two hybrids."

Jillian waited a moment before continuing her story.

"So, Colby came barreling into town with these four other guys, and there was a confrontation at the place where we were staying. My dad remained calm, but he wasn't going to give into their demands."

"And what did Sutton do?"

"He stayed quiet. These guys didn't know we knew one another, and I think he was trying to keep it that way."

"Like, in a malicious way?" Metzger questioned.

"No. He was keeping the element of surprise, and when the shooting started, we all backed up and fired back. In the middle of it all, my dad was shot by one of the men."

"By Colby?" Metzger asked, knowing better, but trying to coax more information out of Jillian.

"Of course not," she said, though her emotions bordered on anger. "He shot three of them dead, and knocked Driscoll to the ground. He didn't think Driscoll was the same as the other three."

"What did you think?"

"I think they were both guilty of running with terrible people for their own protection."

Metzger said nothing a moment, drawing a suspicious stare from Jillian.

"You're thinking he's in the right, aren't you?" she asked, openly fighting to avoid sounding judgmental.

"I think Colby is going to do what's best for Colby," Metzger answered. "I also think he appreciates our group enough that he broke into a military installation and asked me to smooth things over with you."

"Which benefits him, or he wouldn't have done it."

Metzger smirked, drawing a smack on his arm from Jillian.

"It's *not* funny."

"Look, Colby puts on this tough guy façade, but he wants to stick with us. If he wanted to hang out with military prepper types, he would."

"He stays with us so he can assert his dominance and save the day every once in a while."

"I recall him saving our bacon with those rednecks who moved tractor trailers in our way," Metzger said. "He could've cut and run, but he got us out of that situation. And he volunteered to deal with the military folks, which, granted, is a problem he likely created."

"*Did* create," Jillian affirmed.

"I can't tell you what to do, and you certainly have a right to be angry with him, but I don't think Colby is a villain. He's a guy looking for his kids who's made a few mistakes along the way. He probably wasn't the most socially acclimated person before the apocalypse."

"I know," Jillian said, sounding as though she might be accepting an alternate take on her position. "It's just that I had more than I expected to find in my home town, and in a matter of two days my last living family member was gone."

She paused a moment, reflecting on something.

"Here I am droning on about my problems and you're probably worried sick about your brother."

"My brother can take care of himself," Metzger said as a matter of fact. "It's just nice to talk to someone and take my mind off the situation for a while."

"I'm sure the captain gave you sagely advice during your drive time."

"He doesn't exactly carry a conversation," Metzger replied. "And Colby gave me this cryptic warning to keep an eye on Timmons."

"Colby is paranoid about everyone and everything. You can't buy into that."

"That's what I thought, but Scott has acted differently ever since we reached the airport in Lancaster. It's as though he didn't get something he'd bargained for."

"He's seen the undead before, right?"

"Yeah. It's not that." Metzger paused. "I can't really explain the feeling. Part of me wonders if he's experiencing culture shock. For the first time in years, he's not around his pilot buddies, and he's dealing with civilians. Maybe it's like when prisoners get released after serving hard time, and he's not adjusting well to the outside world."

"Could be."

He trusted Timmons, mainly because the man risked his career, even his life, to transport the crew out of Virginia. Pilots seemed a different breed, from what Metzger experienced during his time on the base. They didn't seem to conform to the extent that typical military personnel did, though they followed orders.

Isabella saw something in him that prompted her to ask for his help, despite not knowing him very well. Her only knowledge of Timmons came from her husband, or Metzger, when he spoke of his time around the pilot and his aircraft.

"You missed something else, too," Jillian said as though slightly ashamed to speak about the incident.

"Oh?"

"We encountered some people who once operated the rides and games in my town during the annual festival."

"Carnies?" Metzger questioned.

"Yeah, but they wanted the town for themselves."

"Why do all these people think they're entitled to just make themselves mayors and take over towns?"

"It's more than that," Jillian said. "One of her group was thrown in jail for touching a child, and the lady in charge of the group wanted some kind of retribution."

"I see," Metzger said, though still waiting for an explanation.

By the time Jillian relived the entire story about the confrontation with Dark Lady and her people, speaking about how they kidnapped and murdered Vazquez, the group drew close to a rest stop along the right shoulder of the road where several cars, a semi with trailer, and a school bus occupied various spaces. With some parked more appropriately than others, Timmons and Metzger found spots to park along the left side of the abandoned vehicles before everyone stood to stretch their legs.

Metzger wasn't sure what he thought about Jillian letting the undead tear Dark Lady apart, but he understood the two women shared a history that couldn't be entirely revealed in a single car ride. Just before he pulled in behind Timmons, Metzger listened as Jillian asked if he could forgive her actions. He didn't immediately answer, thinking the previous court system might have labeled her choice as second-degree murder, or perhaps voluntary manslaughter.

He didn't intend to leave her hanging, but Timmons swerved into the parking area rather suddenly, so Metzger followed, forced to concentrate on the road as debris lined the concrete. On either side of the divided highway, trees ranged as far as the eye could see.

"I'm not going to judge you," he told her before they interacted with the others. "We've all had to do things we might regret later. Things we wouldn't have done before."

He paused a bit before speaking the last words on the subject, letting his eyes meet hers so Jillian understood his sincerity.

"Maybe I should be judged," Jillian said, her eyes reflecting the pain of recalling the experiences in Virginia. "Maybe I'm no better than Colby, and here I've been acting high and mighty."

"You've been running on emotions," Metzger said, taking hold of her hand. "I know that feeling pretty well."

Jillian obviously recalled what happened to his parents, because her expression shared his pain.

"It may be time to switch driving arrangements," Isabella said, approaching Metzger and Jillian as Nathan explored the area nearby.

"Stay where we can see you," Metzger called to his nephew, knowing Nathan had very limited experience around the undead.

"Sorry," Isabella said, addressing Metzger directly. "I'm about ready to tell your buddy to fly himself wherever."

"What's the trouble?" Metzger asked, suppressing a smirk.

"He's unbearable," Isabella stated, and Metzger looked over her shoulder to find Timmons strolling further up the lane momentarily. "The second we didn't locate Bryce at that airport, your buddy turned into an asshole."

"I'm not sure he approves of our plan," Metzger said casually. "I agree with him to the extent that I don't think Bryce will attempt this trip."

"We're almost there," Isabella said. "We have to finish the trip."

"It's your parents, Izzy. I get it. You need to know they're okay."

"They're the only extended family Nathan has left. It kills me whenever he asks about Grandma and Grandpa Metzger."

"Maybe it's time he learns the truth," Metzger said, personally unwilling to relay the demise of his parents to his nephew.

"After we make it to the lodge," Isabella assured him.

Before their conversation could continue, Metzger heard a noise coming from the woods to the right side of the rest stop. Everyone else appeared to hear the sound as well, which reached his eardrums in the form of snapping twigs and a low, constant growl of some sort. Before the first zombie reached the edge of the woods, rearing its ugly head with a growl as it searched for prey, Metzger was already darting towards his nephew. He scooped Nathan off the ground before ducking behind a vehicle, hiding them both from ravenous eyes.

Peering above the car, he spotted Isabella and Jillian doing much the same, but Timmons remained some distance away from them, though obviously aware of the danger. As the first member of the undead appeared, the noise grew to a constant rumble of footsteps and moans before multiple zombies appeared, walking in a line about five or six bodies deep in some parts of the chain. Timmons managed to scurry beneath the bus, and though Metzger had never seen panic in the pilot's face, he saw it now.

"Don't make a sound," Metzger said to his nephew, seeing they remained in danger because the parade of zombies showed no signs of ending anytime soon.

He was able to maneuver, despite staying low, and motion for everyone else to remain close to the ground, and to take cover under the larger vehicles. Carefully grabbing his nephew's hand, Metzger led him in a crawl over to the trailer hooked to the semi parked in the rest area. By now the string of undead had begun crossing the rest area, making their way onto the state highway. If a single zombie spotted Metzger, or his nephew, it might deviate from the herd and lead every one of its kind straight to the small group of survivors.

Sounds of branches snapping, grass being trampled, and shoes clopping against the pavement, almost in unison, reached Metzger's ears. He felt the tension in his nephew as the boy clutched his arm, but he didn't dare say a word at first. Based on the noise, and the amount of weight stepping on the blacktop at once, he expected to feel tremors beneath him. Instead, he only felt the trembling of Nathan, who tried to burrow his face against the paved surface.

"Just stay still and don't say a word," Metzger whispered to the boy, giving a reassuring squeeze to his arm.

Metzger managed to look out from his position, finding his sister-in-law and Jillian hunkered beneath a pickup truck, hiding them from sight. Timmons remained in place, but a few of the undead began breaking away from the pack, possibly hearing or seeing something that distracted them from blindly following the herd.

Nathan looked up, seeing the mindless enemies walking in his direction, and gave a whimper.

"Be brave," Metzger whispered. "They won't see us."

More and more undead broke away from the pack, and at least a dozen passed the vehicles where everyone hid without taking notice. Metzger tried formulating a plan in his mind, but keeping five people away from a massive group of the undead wasn't easy. The dead didn't tire, they possessed no sense of fear, and as hunters they remained relentless once they spotted prey.

Unlike Nathan, he dared not close his eyes for one second. His heart pounded, and he felt naked without his sword, because it rested on the floorboard behind the driver's seat. Pulling out a pistol and opening fire would basically sign a death certificate for everyone he cared about. Instead, Metzger slowly maneuvered his body, and Nathan's, to the opposite side of the trailer where the shadows and a large tire helped conceal them from the pale eyes of the zombies.

He noticed several wet spots along the blacktop once they reached their destination, and Metzger realized his nephew had wet his pants from the traumatic experience. With more pressing things to concentrate on, Metzger ignored the accident, saving Nathan a bit of humiliation in the process. From his position, Metzger could see everyone else in his party. Like him, Timmons had managed to wriggle to the far side of the bus, making him virtually invisible to anyone unless they knelt down for a closer examination. Jillian and Isabella remained under the truck, far enough away that the undead wouldn't spot them unless something drew their attention.

Metzger felt as though he could hear his own heartbeat over the moaning and growling of the undead, afraid his nervous breaths might draw them to him. He dared take a peek ahead, seeing no letup to the string of undead crossing the rest area. Feet with various footwear passed by, sometimes with a foot at a sideways angle, barely slowing the zombie it belonged to, because their purpose seemed singular in nature. Much like a classic horror movie, Metzger half-expected a pair of feet to stop before a zombie peered under the trailer and located its victims.

At one point, a male zombie dressed in black riot gear that appeared more police than military, dropped to the ground. Metzger stiffened as the zombie angled its head in the direction of where Metzger hid his nephew. His options for defense were his firearm or a pocketknife, and neither felt as practical as his sword. His heart pounded, but he remained perfectly still, waiting to see if the zombie crawled his way, surely bringing friends with him if he did so.

Perhaps because the face shield was obscured by dust, or something else caught its attention, the predator turned its head away as though it hadn't seen them. It struggled to stand, like a newborn fawn, apparently more interested in catching up with the herd. Metzger surmised it couldn't see very well, because it seemed to turn its head, listening for the sounds of multiple feet walking, and he wondered how well sound traveled through the riot helmet. As it moved on, he breathed a sigh of relief, pulling Nathan a bit closer.

After a few minutes, the portion of the herd that broke off, passing dangerously close to the living, tapered off, and the remainder of the dead continued across the highway. A few of them appeared to have issues walking, like mangled legs or feet, or found themselves slowed for some other reason.

Enough minutes passed that Metzger felt certain he was going to urinate in his pants as well, because nature beckoned for him to relieve himself soon. A few close calls terrified the group when the undead slowed down in front of the vehicles, as though something drew their attention, but they eventually moved along. Several times, Metzger reminded his nephew not to make a sound, and though Nathan hadn't spent much time with him, he seemed to trust his uncle.

Metzger looked ahead, seeing no undead crossing the blacktop, and each zombie that deviated from the main group walked down the road in a different direction, forming their own staggered parade.

He slowly crawled out from beneath the trailer, gently tugging Nathan.

"It's okay," he assured his nephew. "They're gone."

Thus far, Nathan experienced the undead in minimal numbers within reasonably controlled environments where Metzger dealt with them handily, a few at a time. Being thrust into a mob of them provided everyone with a jolt of terror, and Metzger felt as though he'd run a triathlon because the adrenaline coursing through his body during the entire experience left him exhausted.

Everyone met up in the center of the parked vehicles, each expressing their fatigue and relief. Nathan ran over to give his mother a hug, and she knelt down to embrace him. No one seemed to notice he'd wet his pants during the march of the undead, and Metzger wouldn't say a word. His nephew had enough to worry about in the new world without feeling ashamed of being frightened.

"What the fuck was that?" Timmons asked.

"Language," Isabella scolded him quickly, but the pilot simply shrugged an apology.

"I've never seen them in a pack like that," Metzger confessed. "If one of them would've spotted us, we couldn't have escaped. At least not together."

"Is it safe to start driving?" Jillian questioned.

Metzger looked behind him, seeing only a few undead in the distance, and to his left, only a handful seemed to linger before crossing the highway to catch up with the others.

"We should give it a few minutes," he answered before heading to the Prius to retrieve his sword, not taking anything for granted.

"Where did they come from?" Isabella asked. "There aren't any major cities in the area."

"They could've come from anywhere," Timmons suggested. "They've had two months to grow in number."

"That was a thousand or more," Nathan said with youthful enthusiasm, now that the danger had passed.

"A couple hundred, maybe, Nate," Metzger said, giving a wink and a smile to his nephew.

"You could've killed 'em, Uncle Dan!"

"Maybe," Metzger said, though he knew a few hundred would overwhelm him sooner than later.

A handful of stragglers emerged from the right side of the parking area, and their glossy eyes immediately spotted the five survivors.

"Well, there's your chance, Uncle Dan," Timmons said with an air of sarcasm.

Metzger counted five of them, with a sixth zombie rounding a tree, stumbling along the soil before reaching the blacktop.

"I can handle these in under a minute," Metzger said confidently, pulling his sword from its sheath.

"Manchester," Timmons said, causing everyone to stare at him with confusion.

"What?" Metzger asked, stopping short of charging the zombies, beckoning for an elaboration.

A cursory glance indicated the undead remained a safe distance away from the group.

"It's a challenge, a dare of sorts," Timmons explained. "In our briefings, when a pilot would say he could do something that sounded unreasonable, we would say 'Manchester' to call him out on it. And when the pilot failed to deliver, he got a slap from the person who called him out at the next briefing."

"That sounds very one-sided," Metzger noted, furrowing one eyebrow. "What if I get this challenge done as promised?"

"You get to slap me instead," Timmons said as though he felt confident he had little to fear.

"Sounds fair," Metzger said, stepping forward and slicing through the skull of the first zombie.

He turned briefly to see Timmons tapping something on his wristwatch, likely starting a timer, and in turn, their challenge.

Metzger dealt with two more in short order, but another two rounded the corner, causing him to sigh internally because he didn't have the energy to fight off a small cluster of the undead consecutively.

In all, nine appeared from the trees, and Metzger either stabbed them through their skulls, or sliced them cleanly from ear to ear, but he required two quick intermissions to catch his breath and draw strength he didn't know he possessed.

Feeling somewhat like a zombie himself, he stumbled back to the group, holding his sword with the pointed end down, dripping blood onto the blacktop.

"How long?" he dared ask his friend.

"One minute, eleven seconds," Timmons said, maintaining a neutral expression.

"That's really not fair," Jillian pointed out. "More of them appeared after Dan started killing them."

"What do *you* say, son?" Timmons asked, addressing Metzger directly.

Knowing he could fight the bet on a technicality, Metzger decided he needed to let Timmons have the victory because the captain seemed disgruntled about their trip at every turn.

"Fair's fair," Metzger said, approaching Timmons and looking him in the eye.

"Good lad," Timmons said with a nod. "What did the five fingers say to the face?"

Metzger was about to think of an answer when the Navy man provided him with a moderate slap across his right cheek that stung for only a few seconds.

"Slap," Timmons answered his own question.

"I hope you're happy now," Metzger said.

"Happier," Timmons said, providing his first grin of the day.

Timmons walked away to grab something from the other Prius, leaving Metzger rubbing his cheek momentarily.

"What's his problem?" Isabella asked, shaking her head.

"He needed that," Metzger answered. "He was just as scared as the rest of us. And don't worry, because I'll definitely get him back."

Jillian slipped her fingers between his, taking his hand before he consciously realized it. Thrilled that everyone survived the ordeal, he squeezed her hand lightly, exhaling in relief.

"I need to answer the call of nature before we go," Metzger said, releasing Jillian's hand so he could use one of the nearby portable toilets.

"Me, too," he heard Isabella say.

Once everyone took a bathroom break, they met up near the cars, finding Timmons staring at a map.

"I hope that little parade isn't an indication of what to expect in the mountains," he said, appearing a bit concerned.

"I wouldn't think so," Metzger said. "It's almost like they were trying to reach a destination."

"They're attracted to sound and sights," Jillian stated. "Animals hunt in packs, so why would it be any different with these things? They're probably all looking for the next populated area together so they can overrun it."

"You're giving them too much credit," Timmons scoffed.

Metzger looked up to the sky, trying to gauge direction by the sun's location. He determined most of the undead appeared to be heading west, where his brother might be dealing with problems of a different nature.

"What's wrong?" Isabella asked.

"Nothing," he answered. "We should probably get going."

"Agreed," Timmons said. "We keeping the seating arrangements the same for now?"

"Sure," Metzger answered.

A few minutes later, both of the cars left the parking area, and as Metzger pulled onto the road, he saw a few zombies lingering behind the herd. He put the car in park momentarily, waiting to prove or disprove Jillian's theory.

"Everything okay?" she asked.

"Yeah," he answered. "I just want to see something."

One of them turned to look at the Prius, and he wondered momentarily if they were drawn to some unseen force far removed from New York, but the zombie stared, emitted some throaty noise Metzger couldn't hear with the windows up, and began walking toward the Prius in search of prey. Feeling a bit relieved, Metzger put the car in drive and began following Timmons to their final destination.

Eight

"Wake up!" Sutton yelled when he stepped into the cabin, stirring everyone inside after their initial shock to being awoken like boot camp recruits.

"What is it now?" Gracine asked, sitting up and wiping her eyes.

"There are bodies outside," Sutton reported.

"What?" Luke asked, wiping the sleep from his eyes, despite the surprise registered in his voice.

Everyone slowly got up from their beds, cots, or sleeping bags and gathered in the cabin's main room before Sutton led them outside. There, the two bodies remained in the yard, and the jack-o-lantern flickered its toothy grin at the group.

"What the hell?" Driscoll asked upon seeing the gutted vegetable.

Gracine stepped down from the porch landing, shaking her finger at the bodies and muttering some Ebonics under her breath that Sutton thought might be voodoo in nature.

"Colby, you rolled in here last night all nonchalant," she said, turning around to shake her finger at him. "This ain't some Halloween prank your kids pulled. This is some real shit. Those bodies be burned to a crisp and they ain't around to party this year. You feel me?"

"At least one of my boys has been here," Sutton said. "I can't leave until I know."

"That doesn't mean you should drag us into your deathtrap," Luke said. "Those bodies didn't crawl over here in the middle of the night. Someone *really* doesn't want us here."

Driscoll stepped off the porch, sauntering over to the body on the right, examining it as he drew closer.

"Dear God," he said with disgust. "I think this person was alive when he was set on fire."

Everyone stood by momentarily, trying to digest the situation before them.

Driscoll circled the body, looking for additional clues by Sutton's estimation. Sutton decided to walk over, mainly to avoid the wrath of his companions. He confirmed what he already knew, seeing the mouth fully ajar as the man probably screamed his last words while on fire. Just enough of the body remained intact that he knew it wasn't either of his sons.

"This has to be the work of one person," he surmised aloud.

"How can you be so sure?" Luke questioned. "Didn't we just deal with an entire clan of sick and depraved individuals?"

Buster approached his owner, sniffing around the area of the bodies as though something intrigued him.

"Stay," Sutton ordered him before he drew any closer to the smell of death.

Very little odor reached his nostrils, causing Sutton to wonder if the bodies weren't fresh. Although the entire incident felt strange, like a cat and mouse game, he wasn't in a playing mood.

"I can't ask any of you to stay for this," he said. "I'll deal with this sick asshole and find my boys."

"That sounds like a terrible idea," Luke stated.

"There are five cabins in this area. His base of operations has to be in one of them."

"Or he lingers just outside of the area and waits for unsuspecting victims to arrive," Driscoll suggested. "I don't see any drag marks, but I do see some tire tracks."

He nodded up the path where the tracks began or ended, far enough away that anyone in the cabin might not have heard a vehicle in the overnight.

"How far do they go?" Sutton inquired.

"As far as the eye can see," Driscoll said, pointing the way.

"Don't do this," Gracine said before Sutton could take a single step. "You know this is probably a trap."

Trees prevented the light of dawn from illuminating the woods well enough to spot details clearly. Sutton knew he needed better daylight to spot any potential traps, but he couldn't linger too long if he wanted to locate the madman responsible for burning people alive. He walked to the second corpse, finding similar circumstances, knowing this person wasn't dead when his body was set ablaze. He also knew this wasn't either of his sons, but if the murderer kidnapped victims and held them before killing them, his sons might be on borrowed time if they indeed reached the area.

Looking down, he saw two fingers severed at the second knuckle. Appearing as though they were deliberately cut, and cleanly with precision, the ends appeared charred as well. Sutton knew the wounds took place before the gruesome burning ceremony occurred.

"How are we sure they weren't zombies when this happened?" Luke questioned, taking his first step down from the porch.

"They'd still be zombies," Driscoll answered. "There aren't any marks on them that indicate fatal wounds."

"If this guy is keeping prisoners and torturing them, there's a chance he has Sean or Jacob," Sutton surmised. "I can't let this go."

"We have Samantha to think about," Luke said. "It's not safe staying here."

"You all need to go," Sutton offered. "Me and Buster can deal with this."

An awkward hesitation kept everyone from speaking momentarily.

"I'm not sure we're any better off out there," Luke said. "What if this psycho laid traps in the woods, or along the roads?"

"That's a concern," Sutton admitted. "If you aren't going to leave the campground, you should all stay here and arm yourselves."

"You're really going to check all those cabins by yourself?" Gracine questioned.

"I've got Buster."

"This would go a lot faster if we all went with you," Driscoll reasoned. "He left those bodies to scare us. He doesn't want us to come looking for him, because we might fuck up his little game."

"Fine," Luke agreed, "but we have to protect ourselves. This one doesn't get out of the car."

He referred to Samantha, who looked a bit frightened by all of the adult talk.

Sutton spent about half an hour drawing a rough map of the area, and explaining how to get to each cabin. Everyone agreed driving was the best bet, because it provided them protection, but only one traditional vehicle sat in the driveway for their use. Sutton said he didn't mind using the box truck, but it wouldn't traverse very well through any dense foliage. It also made for a terrible getaway vehicle if anyone came after them.

After making certain everyone had weapons locked and loaded, Sutton led the way on foot with Buster and Driscoll at his side, while everyone else followed in the most recent car the group acquired during their travels. He kept looking for traps along the way, carrying the long-range rifle that provided him with a thermal vision scope. In the woods, it might provide him with an advantage so long as the sun didn't bathe the woods with morning rays.

"How well do you know these cabins?" Driscoll asked.

"I'd only stepped foot in one before last night."

"We don't even know if this guy is holing up in one of them."

"I'm beginning to get the impression the plane crash had nothing to do with my cabin burning," Sutton said. "But even a pyromaniac needs somewhere to stay, and any one of these cabins beats sleeping with bugs and snakes."

"I hate to say it, but in the scheme of things, you picked a fucked up place to buy a cabin."

Sutton grunted, agreeing, and no longer wanting anything to do with either campground location once he located his sons.

"I have to imagine this guy is going to see us coming," Driscoll stated.

"He probably will, but I don't care about that."

"Shooting him in the head is preferable to letting him circle around us in the woods."

"Agreed, but we're screwing up his plan, so he'll probably come to us."

Driscoll started to say something else, but Sutton held up his right hand, stopping them both in their tracks. Kneeling down, Sutton found a thin wire in the road he figured might be a boobytrap of some sort, but as he examined it more closely, he wasn't so sure.

"What is it?" Driscoll asked quietly, squatting down beside him.

"It's low to the ground," Sutton replied, "so I'm not sure it's a tripwire. Might be an early warning system. Walking or driving over it probably rattles some cans, or makes a noise to alert him that strangers are near."

"Or the dead," Driscoll reasoned.

"Either way, one end or the other should lead us to him."

Sutton walked back to the car the others were piled in, speaking to Gracine when she rolled down the driver's side window.

"There's some kind of tripwire in the middle of the road," he said. "Driving over it might alert him that we're nearby."

"You expect us to skip through the woods?"

"Give us a few minutes and we can track it down in both directions."

"You're splitting up?" she asked with skepticism. "This is how you white folks get hacked up in the slasher flicks."

"Aren't the black people usually the first to get chopped up in those things?" Driscoll asked, trying to get a rise out of Gracine.

"Only 'cause dumb crackers bring that shit down on them."

Sutton cleared his throat before their conversation grew any more intense.

"I'm asking that you stay here while Steve and I check both ends of this thing," he said. "I'm going to leave Buster here, because I don't want him spring-ing any traps or alarms."

"That's not very reassuring," Luke said.

"You have guns," Sutton pointed out, tilting his head. "Besides, we'll be back in a few minutes."

"That's what white people always say in those movies right before they get a hatchet to the face," Gracine said with a bit of sass.

Sutton turned to Driscoll.

"Let's get this over with."

Sutton chose a direction and began following the line through the woods, finding it barely lingered more than an inch above dirt and foliage the entire duration. Carefully stepping around the line the entire walk, Sutton finally discovered the end wrapped around a tree and secured in place with some kind of tack that penetrated the bark.

Since the discovery required only a few minutes of his time, Sutton walked back to the road and signaled to his friends in the car that he was going to follow Driscoll's path. Buster looked to him anxiously, wanting to leave his post beside the driver's side of the car.

"Stay," Sutton said firmly.

He followed Driscoll's path in the other direction, suspecting the other end of the wire led to either a cabin, or some remote camp in the woods. Unable to determine his new enemy's mindset, or motivations, Sutton imagined he was dealing with a psychopath who no longer felt required to hide behind pretense. Once the rules of survival changed, some people let out their inner inhibitions. Like a trapdoor spider, the man simply hid in the woods and waited for his prey to arrive before springing his trap.

Although Sutton knew of the five cabins in the area, he couldn't recall their exact locations, leaving him at a disadvantage. He carefully walked nearly a hundred yards through dense shrubs, weeds, and trees, hearing little in the way of insects and birds. Strangely, the predatory undead were nowhere to be found, causing him to wonder if the man kept the area clear so only his chosen prey would venture into his world. Plant life grew less dense as Sutton saw the blue sky through the branches above him, just before a small clearing emerged, revealing his destination. Sutton stood by a tree momentarily while he observed the small cabin before him, seeing no activity. His stomach tightened, because he didn't see or hear any sign of Driscoll, leaving him gravely concerned.

Daring not call out, he stepped forward, finding the end of the wire attached to a thin aluminum pole that looked a bit like a misshapen silver Christmas tree with cans and bells hanging from it. Sutton suspected it provided the cabin's occupant with numerous false alarms, but also alerted him to unsuspecting travelers in his area. He obviously knew a group of people took up residence not very far from him, and Sutton wondered if they were now doing exactly what the man wanted.

Treading as lightly as possible, Sutton approached the cabin, seeing no open doors or windows from the rear. He took a few steps to the side of the structure, seeing no evidence of Driscoll until he looked down and spied a trail of recent footprints in the moist soil. Following the footprints to the front of the cabin, he stopped just short of the veranda that held one chair and a small, round table. Eerily, the front door stood wide-open, inviting him inside. Unfortunately, the footprints led to the front steps where wet footprints from the morning dew completed the trail and went inside.

Unnerved by the fact that Driscoll hadn't shown his face, or said something, Sutton felt concerned that his fellow traveler found trouble.

Or trouble found him.

Knowing he couldn't enter the cabin silently, no matter how hard he tried, Sutton slid the sniper rifle around his shoulder by its strap, opting to pull the sidearm from his belt. He hadn't found a holster that fit the .40 semi-automatic, so he'd stuffed it inside his belt that morning. Holding the firearm in a ready position, he ascended the stairs, making little noise as he did so, stepping inside the cabin a moment later.

Less than a thousand square feet, the cabin presented little in the way of exploration. Virtually an open-floor concept throughout, the space consisted of a kitchen, complete with an island that doubled as seating for meals, that tied into living quarters. That area contained only few pieces of furniture, and no mounted animal heads or rural décor one might expect inside a genuine log cabin. Only a bedroom behind a closed door remained a mystery to him, so Sutton carefully walked over to the door. He kept his gun trained on the door as he opened it, hearing a pained squeak that lasted two seconds while the door slowly opened inward. Sutton felt like he waited an eternity for the door to come to a stop, but a window inside the room revealed an unmade bed, a dresser, and some strewn clothing.

Not exactly a luxury cabin, the structure didn't have closets or sealed off spaces, other than the bedroom. Sutton wondered where the hell Driscoll had gotten to, if not inside the cabin. Every clue indicated that the man preceded him in checking the space, but no evidence of him remained. Carefully stepping into the living room, Sutton checked the ceiling first for any attic access, finding none, before he scoured the floor for some sort of hatch leading below. He knew he wasn't the only person preparing for the end of the world before it happened.

As though intentional, the cabin didn't have a rear door, though a porch occupied the back portion of the cabin. A carpet remnant was evident along the opposite side of a loveseat in the living space. A plain tan color, the remnant appeared stained, filthy almost, and no respectable cabin owner would bring it inside, before or after the apocalypse.

Unless the fragment served a purpose other than interior decoration.

Sutton walked over, lifting one corner to see a metal circle with a twist lock about the size of his fist. Careful to stand back while doing so, Sutton aimed the gun at the square space about a foot-and-a-half square while he turned the twist lock counterclockwise about a quarter turn before it released, allowing him to pull up on the hatch.

He hadn't seen basement windows along the cabin's exterior, meaning the cabin certainly wasn't built to modern architectural codes. This likely meant that a hermit or prepper chose to build the cabin in such a fashion. Sutton threw the carpet fragment aside, allowing the hatch door to open fully as he looked inside. Light from the outside didn't prove enough to give him a full view of the cabin's lower level, and he didn't have a flashlight with him, so he peered down, trying to get his eyes adjusted to the darkness, hoping someone didn't have a gun trained on him. He found a ladder attached to a wall, or perhaps a support beam, but about halfway down the ladder's bottom half was swallowed by darkness.

Maneuvering to the other side of the hatch, Sutton tried pulling it all the way back, hoping the hinges might snap, meaning the door couldn't seat correctly and lock again. He quickly discovered the hinges were thick, too much so for him to snap or bend, so he began looking for a nearby tool to use for striking them.

Using what little early morning light penetrated the cabin's few windows in the common area, Sutton began looking through cupboards for anything useful when he heard a cry for help from the basement area. Inside the cupboard he currently had open, Sutton noticed a flashlight, which he switched on before returning to the square opening.

"Hello?" he called.

"Help!" the voice said in reply.

"Sean?" Sutton asked with bewilderment, recognizing the voice.

"Dad?" came the equally shocked response.

"I'm coming," Sutton said as he scurried down the ladder, finding a body on the dirt floor at the base of the ladder.

Absolutely no light penetrated the lower level, because no windows existed in the area, which appeared just as large as the main level in square footage.

He shined the light downward, discovering Driscoll immobile on the floor.

"I think he's dead," Sean Sutton said from behind a set of bars crafted before the apocalypse, but modified afterwards to be a jail instead of a safe room. "He threw him down the ladder like a sack of potatoes."

Sutton went to his son, clasping the bars that went from floor to ceiling, with wooden planks covering them about to his waistline along the front. He saw no key to the lock along the door, and no good way to force the bars open. His son appeared a bit haggard, dirt covering portions of his familiar face, and Sutton noticed Sean had grown his hair nearly to his shoulders since the last time they met in person. He and Sean touched fingers through the bars for only a second before both realized the unseen danger still lurking nearby.

"Where is he?" Sutton asked once he discovered he couldn't free his son without a key.

"I don't know. He threw that guy down here and locked the hatch a few minutes before you got here."

Sutton turned around, realizing the ladder was mounted to a thick support beam, and behind it was a prepper's dream with dry goods and other supplies lining shelves that wrapped around the other half of the basement. Even in front of the stocked walls were free-standing shelves with more goods, including what looked like tools and a small generator.

"How did you wind up down here?" Sutton inquired, not looking to his son, but up the ladder because he sensed a trap.

"Long story," Sean answered.

Sutton's instincts proved correct when a hand holding a Molotov cocktail appeared above the opening. Sutton immediately saw the open flame at the end of the bottle, dancing on some sort of soiled rag, and aimed his firearm, taking two shots before the bottle landed beside Driscoll, setting some of the man's clothing on fire.

"Fuck," Sutton muttered, confronted with a decision to make regarding three lives as the fire began to spread, and the hatch above him slammed shut.

Nine

Waking suddenly, Driscoll began screaming as the fire spread along his left arm and torso where the bottle had shattered. He started to stand and shake his arm, but Sutton grabbed him and helped smother the flames before they spread any further.

"Glad to see you're alive," Sutton said.

"What the fuck?" Driscoll asked in shock. "Last thing I remember is walking into the cabin before everything went black."

"Well, now we're trapped in the basement of this sick fucker's fantasy cabin," Sutton answered, climbing the stairs to find the hatch's handle twisted and secured from the other side.

He found a mechanism on the underbelly of the hatch that would move the latch away from the steel plate that kept the square hatch from swinging upward. Grabbing it with his fingers, Sutton couldn't move it by finger strength alone because of the weight from above. He quickly descended the ladder, holding the flashlight, so he could search for some kind of tool that might assist him.

"Steve, meet my son, Sean. See if you can get him out of that cell somehow."

Driscoll still appeared stunned when Sutton turned to face him after locating a pair of pliers that might provide leverage enough to swing the latch away from the metal plate.

"Good to meet you," Sean said.

"Yeah," Driscoll said. "Likewise."

Driscoll began looking for a key, or some sort of tool that might help undo the lock on the cell. Sutton used the pliers, freeing the latch and pushing upward on the hatch, discovering the entire cabin around him on fire. He smelled some kind of accelerant, kerosene perhaps, and the flames appeared around the living quarters of the cabin where the chemical was poured, beginning to ascend the walls to create a blanket of fire. Even worse, the entry door remained open, allowing fresh air from outside to feed the fire.

It sounded and felt like a hundred logs around him were placed in a mammoth fireplace as the crackling sounds reached his ears. Furniture, curtains, the kitchen island, and even the floor appeared to be saturated with flames, and the intense heat immediately radiated to his skin, as though he'd stuck his face inside an oven and not pulled back in time.

"Fuck!" Sutton yelled as he let the hatch drop down, descending the ladder to search for more useful tools.

"What's wrong?" Sean asked.

"He set the entire cabin on fire. He's trying to bring it down on us."

"Well, that's not good," Driscoll said with concern, obviously having no luck finding a key or other means to open the cell.

"Dad, if you can get out of here, save yourself," Sean offered from behind the bars.

"Sean, I didn't come back here just to find you and bail," Sutton said, turning briefly to his son. "We're all getting out of here, and we're going to find this asshole and rip his dick off."

Driscoll continued to search for useful items, but without a flashlight, and Sutton's light providing intervals of illumination, his efforts were slowed. He finally found a second light and switched it on, though the warmth from above began creeping downward from radiant heat. All three men looked above, seeing the orange glow flickering between the beams in the floor, providing a grim warning about their imminent future.

"Did you see where he might have put the key?" Driscoll asked, turning to Sean.

"I never even saw the dude," Sean replied. "He sucker-punched me when I came over here, and the next thing I knew I was in this cell."

Along with tools and food supplies, the basement also contained some random items that Sutton considered useful. He pulled three blankets from a bundle stacked along the right side of the storage room before locating a fire extinguisher on the floor that appeared unused. It certainly wasn't going to contain the inferno raging above the three men, but it might buy them safe passage out of the cabin if used correctly.

"There's a reciprocating saw here," Driscoll reported, popping the case open to pull out the saw.

He examined it briefly, popping in a rechargeable battery from the case before pulling the trigger. It didn't sound fully charged, but Driscoll walked over to the cell, prepared to begin cutting.

"It'll never make it through all of the bars," he stated.

"The lock," Sutton and his son said simultaneously.

"Oh, yeah," Driscoll said, catching his error. "Guess the idea of burning alive got me a little distracted."

"Then snap out of it," Sutton said as he continued to use his flashlight to examine every shelf for additional items.

Hearing the saw's motor fire up did little to distract him from the job at hand, because he knew the fire upstairs would eventually bring the ground floor into the basement. Such heavy timbers would crush everything in their path, including shelves, the panic room, and human beings. Sutton knew the thick flooring would hold out long enough to buy them reasonable time, but in the recesses of his mind he wondered how the fire grew so intense, so quickly.

Finding nothing else after a quick sweep, Sutton joined Driscoll outside of the cell, finding the saw struggling to cut through the cell door's thick bolt.

"Stop," he said to Driscoll, who immediately complied.

Sutton shined the light's beam on the blade, finding the teeth worse than those of a meth addict.

"That blade is shot. I'm not even sure it's a metal-cutting blade."

"Pardon me for not analyzing its specific properties," Driscoll said testily.

Sutton located the case, finding three other blades inside. Two of the blades were designated to cut metal, so he plucked one from the case, taking it over to the saw. Fortunately, the saw possessed one of the quick-change systems where no tools were required to swap blades. Hearing the crackle of wood burning above him, Sutton hastened to switch the blade out, barely able to see as he cradled the flashlight under his armpit.

"Here," Driscoll said, taking the device and holding it to assist him.

"Thanks."

Sutton finished changing the blade and cut into the bolt where Driscoll had already managed to get it halfway severed. Extremely dense in nature, the bolt began to wear on the blade as Sutton neared the end of the cut. He worried about changing blades once more, because seconds counted when the floor above might collapse, or the fire grew more intense in nature. He knew fires eventually touched their highest point and rolled across ceilings. Smoke would begin to bank down to the floor, filling the lungs of anyone trying to crawl to safety, and flames would dance along the ceiling, reaching temperatures too high for human survival.

Several times over the course of the apocalypse Sutton had seen his life flash before his eyes, but the thought of his offspring suffering such a torturous death bothered him. As the blade began to fail, he pressed down on the saw, willing the blade to provide Sean an escape route. When the bolt finally gave in, the blade snapped in two, as though a fitting end to its sacrifice.

Sutton and Driscoll pulled the door open, and Sutton led the way to the blankets and the fire extinguisher as a thought crossed his mind.

"Wait here," he told them as he walked to the back of the storage room, grabbing three jugs of distilled water from the shelves before returning. "These will be toast in about five minutes, so we might as well use them."

Each of them doused a blanket with the water, providing them with a protective barrier when they charged through the flames above. It occurred to Sutton that neither Driscoll, nor his son, knew the layout of the cabin.

"When we exit through the hatch, we need to run to the left," he explained. "The cabin isn't very big, and I'll lead the way, trying to douse what I can."

"Can't we just make a break for it?" Sean asked. "Without the extinguisher? It'll slow us down."

"It's fucking hot, kid," Sutton replied. "This'll give us a fighting chance."

One at a time, they tossed the blankets around their bodies, creating a wet robe of sorts to protect their bodies from the intense heat about to attack them. Toting the extinguisher, Sutton ascended the ladder, pulling it close to his body as he pulled the pin. Throwing the hatch open in one swift motion, he felt the heat through the blanket, but he aimed the extinguisher in the direction of the open door, blasting the flames with the chemical agent from within the red device. He hadn't even bothered to look at what type of extinguisher he held, because any type of extinguisher would help deaden the flames long enough for the three men to escape.

"Come on!" he shouted to Driscoll and his son, who waited their turns below him on the ladder.

He climbed out, helping pull Sean out of the hole, giving him a gentle shove toward the open door before assisting Driscoll through the hatch as the fire began to regroup. As though trying to block their path and claim their lives, it began encircling them until Sutton used the last of the extinguisher's chemical to shove it back.

"Go!" he urged Driscoll, following close behind the man as they ran through the open door to the outdoors, stopping to catch their collective breath as they panted from the near-death experience.

Sutton immediately realized they hadn't gotten far enough away from the burning structure as the heat continued to penetrate his skin. He received a small taste of what being burned alive felt like before leading Driscoll and his son away from the cabin. Although the thick timber withstood the flames, crashing noises from within indicated that furnishings, and perhaps the floor, didn't fare as well.

Each of them dropped the blankets to the ground, and Sutton checked to make certain his firearm remained tucked in his pants. Finding it secured, he wanted to press forward, dealing with their new adversary before the man got very far.

"I want a piece of that asshole before he escapes," Driscoll said, echoing Sutton's thoughts.

"I think we all do," Sutton said, looking around the ground.

He found trampled grass and snapped twigs along the ground, indicating the direction in which their adversary fled. Sutton assumed his son's attacker didn't feel confident the fire would finish the job, or he had other affairs that urgently required his attention.

"We can't afford to lose him," he said. "He may have other prisoners, and we don't want to be springing any other traps."

"I'm good," Driscoll reported.

"Me, too," Sean said. "Let's track this bitch."

***

"I feel like a sitting duck," Luke said from the passenger seat of the car.

"Me, too," Gracine admitted. "I know these cabins can't be *that* far apart. They've been gone a while."

"We should look for them," Samantha suggested.

"We definitely should *not*," Gracine said, turning to face the youngster in the back seat.

"But why?"

"Because there are creepy things like spiders and snakes out there. And your guardian here doesn't like creepy, crawly critters."

Gracine referred to Luke, who simply played along, acting as though he didn't want to venture outside the car.

Luke opened his door a moment later.

"What are you doing?" Gracine questioned.

"Just stepping out a minute," he answered. "It's stuffy in there."

"I'll roll down the windows," Gracine said, turning the key just far enough to allow her to roll down the two front windows.

"I smell smoke," Luke said, sniffing the air before licking his forefinger to test for wind direction. "It's coming from the way Driscoll and Colby went."

"Great," Gracine muttered, shaking her head.

"Are they in trouble?" Samantha questioned.

"Knowing Colby, probably," she answered before putting forth a pretense grin, a front that Samantha only sometimes believed.

Luke took a step forward a second before someone emerged from the woods in the direction of the smoke. Gracine didn't recognize the man, and instead of appearing shocked, like Bigfoot being taken by surprise as he was photographed, the man looked their way with disdain. She pegged him as under forty years in age, with black hair and a reasonably fit build. He gave them only a few seconds of his time before moving on, and Gracine sensed something foreboding occurred at the cabin.

"That son-of-a-bitch," Luke muttered.

"Language," Samantha said, not understanding the gravity of the confrontation.

"We don't know what happened," Gracine said, addressing Luke directly. "Let him go, and we'll deal with him later."

"What if we're the only ones left?"

Gracine looked over to Luke, across the roof of the car, knowing they were handicapped until they discovered what happened to Sutton and Driscoll.

"We head to the cabin," she said, making up her mind.

"Are you insane?" Luke asked.

"Did that man look like someone you want coming after us in the middle of the night? We need answers, and obviously they made it to the cabin."

"That man was running from something," Samantha said almost under her breath.

"Sweetie, that was a bad man."

"He was afraid of something," Samantha insisted. "I saw it on his face before he noticed us."

Samantha got out of the car, shutting the door behind her.

"We have Buster," she said. "Let's go find Colby."

Gracine looked to Luke with a bit of admonishment, and he rolled his eyes in return.

A few minutes later, the trio followed the worn path where feet had displaced the grass and shrubs, providing them a safe trail. Dark gray smoke became visible less than a hundred yards away from the road, and they could see black embers floating through the air like small burnt kites, occasionally caught by the wind, floating lazily in midair.

Growing more concerned by the second, Gracine felt relief when they encountered Sutton, Driscoll, and a younger man coming their way along the same trodden path. Before she even thought about it, she wrapped her arms around Sutton and gave him a hug.

"Don't scare me like that again," she whispered to him.

"I don't plan to."

"And who is this?" she asked when their embrace ended, referring to the stranger.

"This is my oldest son, Sean," Sutton replied. "Our new friend was holding him captive before he tried barbequing us."

"We just saw him," Luke reported.

"Oh?" Sutton asked, intrigued. "Where?"

"He crossed the road in front of us," Gracine answered. "Looked at us all stone-cold, too."

Buster maneuvered his way over to Sutton, getting his head petted and scratched for his efforts.

"This is ending today," Sutton promised. "I'm going to find that son-of-a-bitch and get some answers."

Luke looked to Samantha, who said nothing about Sutton's language.

"Why didn't you admonish him for curse words?" he asked the girl.

"Because he's Colby," she said, cupping her hands in front of her waistline and twisting from side to side.

Everyone shared a chuckle, but Gracine knew the group had some business to conduct before they left the area.

Ten

Metzger couldn't believe his eyes when the two cars struggled to ascend the final hill to the group's destination, where he hoped safety and serenity awaited them. Like a classic painting, the autumn trees surrounding the group provided orange, yellow, red, and some green coloration, though some of the leaves had begun to fall, covering the road from the lack of regular traffic. The sun's rays occasionally struck the windshield in the late morning light, causing Timmons to squint as he struggled to watch the road.

Before him, the thicket of trees gave way to a resort that contained much more glass than he felt comfortable staying behind during the apocalypse. In all, he assumed the resort took up several acres, but only the main building came into view, standing proudly on two stilts, overlooking the thousands of area trees. Much of the building rested on leveled ground, helping to support the back half of the structure, though it appeared a bit worn and neglected, causing him to wonder if they were going to find friendly faces, or a dead-end.

"It looks terrible," Timmons said from the driver's seat. "Is she sure her folks are alive?"

"Last she knew," Metzger answered. "Maybe they don't have a chainsaw to clear the debris."

Parking the two vehicles next to one another in the small parking lot to the side of the main building, everyone stepped out to stretch their legs.

"Are you worried?" Metzger asked Isabella.

"A little," she admitted. "This is tough to get to, but Mom said the place was incredibly self-sufficient, even before things went bad."

"People who know that might want it for themselves," he said, echoing the thoughts she didn't speak aloud.

"I can't assume we're safe," Isabella informed everyone. "Keep your weapons close until we know for certain."

Metzger followed her up to what appeared to be the primary entrance located along the side of the main building. Everyone else grabbed a few things from the vehicles before following them. As he drew closer, Metzger saw that a few collapsed trees hadn't actually made contact with the building, and the cracks in the window actually looked fake. He stared at them momentarily, trying to decipher what exactly didn't look right about their appearance.

"What's wrong?" Jillian asked when she reached his side.

"Nothing. I think my brother's in-laws may be pretty damn smart."

"At least there aren't any infected up here," Timmons said, his mood openly more positive.

Strangely, the parking lot remained empty except for their cars, as though anyone staying at the resort heard the horrible news and immediately left to find friends and loved ones. Residing in the mountains sounded safe due to the remote nature of the compound, but limited food and water could only hold out so long, and finding civilization wasn't like driving down the road to the grocery store.

Metzger smelled nature in the form of trees and a few remaining flowers, finding the aroma intoxicating compared to dust, trash, and death in the cities. Birds chirped overhead, and a few random animal noises echoed from somewhere in the woods. It felt as though the resort might have become one with nature, reclaimed by the land after humans abandoned it, but Metzger wasn't positive every human moved on. If Isabella's parents said they were going to make a go of it on the property, he had little reason to doubt they were either living there, or deceased due to the greed of others.

Isabella bypassed the main entrance, reaching a plain beige door along the back of the building that looked as though it might be an employee entrance. Turning the knob on this door, she found resistance.

"Locked," she said when she turned to the others.

She tried the main entrance with similar results, and Metzger felt encouraged that someone cared enough to secure the building.

Only when the group walked up some decorative stone stairs behind the main building, did the resort's entire form begin to reveal itself. Behind the building they found ten cabins, set a reasonable distance apart, an outdoor swimming pool that nature had reclaimed with leaves floating in the green water, and a barn farther back on the hill, behind the cabins. Although one might call them cabins, the buildings before them appeared more like miniature houses with windows, paint, and chimneys. Metzger thought they looked like upscale summer camp buildings, painted conservative colors like powder blue, yellow, and a tasteful lime green.

Everyone stood at the edge of the rear property, observing the setting before them. No one dared speak, fearing they'd made a trip for nothing, and Isabella's parents might be buried somewhere behind the barn, or worse, walking with the dead.

"We have guns," Timmons noted, looking to Isabella. "Call to them and see what happens."

Isabella looked to him as though uncertain she wanted to know the truth. From experience, Metzger could relate, but he also didn't want them wasting time while his brother's location remained uncertain.

"Mom?" she called, loudly enough that anyone in the cabins or main building could hear. "Dad?"

Everyone waited a moment, drawing deep breaths until a door opened in the green house on the left side. A couple stepped outside, each toting a shotgun, and it required mere seconds for them to recognize Isabella. Lowering their defenses, they ran over to give both her and their grandson a hug, almost in unison. Metzger noticed they both sported graying hair as the apocalypse didn't allow for trips to a stylist for hair coloring or routine trims.

Isabella finally turned to the group once hugging and kissing ended to make formal introductions.

"Everyone, this is my mother, Phyllis, and my father, Harold."

She then introduced Metzger, whom they remembered from the wedding, and one other family occasion, Jillian, and Timmons.

"Captain Timmons is a Navy pilot," she added.

"Do you know Bryce?" Phyllis inquired.

"We met only briefly, ma'am," he answered politely, drawing stares from everyone around him.

"Phyllis," she corrected him.

Timmons nodded courteously.

Phyllis Padgett possessed only a few strands of strawberry blonde hair, though her figure had given way as she neared the age of sixty. Appearing healthy, she carried a few extra pounds that most people in the apocalypse weren't afforded. She wore comfortable sweatpants and a floral top, undoubtedly a public faux pas before the world changed. Bryce always seemed to like her, though she'd rubbed him the wrong way a few times, saying her only daughter was chained to the military because of her husband.

As for Harold Padgett, he seemed very laid back by comparison to his wife, with only a handful of red strands left to his graying hair. He wore dark work pants, his choice before and after the apocalypse, and a button-up shirt with long sleeves. Metzger recalled him often wearing baseball caps of New York sports teams, like the Bills, or the Bisons out of Buffalo. Today, up in the mountains, he donned no such headgear despite the cooling temperatures. A tall, wiry man, he possessed strength enough to hoist his grandson off the ground at will, and always displayed excellent work ethic.

"Why the hell are you staying out here?" Isabella questioned her parents once everyone had settled down, referring to the green cabin.

"It's safer, dear," her mother replied.

"Safer?"

"Everyone wants to target the main building," Harold added. "They don't give a shit about the cottages."

"How many visitors have you had?" Metzger asked.

"Not many," Phyllis answered. "We've scared off one or two live ones, and Harold dealt with the few braindead vermin."

"Let's get them inside, dear," Harold suggested. "They're probably half-starved and ready for hot showers."

"Hot showers?" Timmons questioned, as though asking for clarification if they were pulling his leg or being truthful.

"We have solar panels," Harold answered proudly. "And the barn up the hill has real animals. This place was created to be self-sufficient, even before all of this, because we couldn't just hop in the truck and shop. And no one wanted to deliver all the way up here to us."

Metzger looked beyond the main building, and down the mountain where he felt like he could roll for days before stopping if the trees weren't in his path. It felt a bit dizzying knowing how high he was above civilization, and it became readily apparent why former guests wouldn't attempt the trek, even if they knew the secrets harbored by the resort.

"Blue Mountain Resort," Metzger read the large wooden sign aloud, spying it in the parking area near the main building.

"The lake and the museum aren't incredibly far from here," Phyllis noted as she walked past him to unlock the side door to the building.

"Museum?" Nathan questioned. "Neat! I wanna see it!"

"There'll be time for that later," Phyllis replied. "You're going to have plenty to keep you busy up here."

Over the course of the next hour, everyone unpacked what clothing and weapons they possessed from each Prius. Part of the main building was a front desk area for check-ins, some offices, and a residential area for the manager of the grounds. In the end, it turned out Phyllis and Harold ran the resort and stayed in the main building.

"What happened to the owners?" Timmons asked when the entire entourage gathered in the main lobby, some opting to stand after the long drive.

"We heard from them twice," Phyllis replied. "They were going to drive up here, knowing the safe haven they'd created, but they never arrived."

"A few of the kids that worked for us went off to find their families, but they never came back either," Harold added. "We've been alone much of the time."

"No offense," Timmons said, "but I'd be much obliged if you'd point the way to the hot showers."

"Go to the back and upstairs," Harold said with a chuckle.

Timmons gave an informal salute and headed that way, leaving the others to converse in the lobby that provided all kinds of natural light because the resort sat above most of the trees. With the front being floor to ceiling windows, with only a few support columns in between the panes, light flooded the room during daylight hours.

"I have to ask the burning question, dear," Phyllis said to Isabella. "Where is your husband?"

By the time Isabella caught her parents up on the entire saga of Bryce's return, the missions to Buffalo, and the issues at Naval Station Norfolk, Timmons had returned from a refreshing shower. With his hair still wet, the pilot wore clean blue jeans and brown cowboy boots, which he packed specifically for the trip. Metzger didn't understand much about the pilot, except that he remained stuck in his ways, regardless of how much the world changed.

"So, we're waiting it out with you until he travels here, or the situation changes," Isabella concluded.

"Why would he volunteer for that mission a second time?" Phyllis questioned.

"Because we got close to finding the prick responsible for all of this," Metzger answered, failing to disguise his discontent. "We got them all of the information and they turned on both of us."

"I hate to tell either of you this, but the chances of him coming all the way up here are slim to none," Phyllis said.

"We know," Isabella said. "I just needed to keep Nathan away from what's out there."

Metzger excused himself from the conversation a few minutes later, opting to head upstairs for a hot shower. Amazed at the cleanliness of the main building, he couldn't believe they possessed electricity, hot water, and the means to create food on a daily basis. Part of the conversation revealed a greenhouse just beyond the barn that produced fruits and vegetables. Winter might hinder the process a little, but they could still maintain an ample food supply.

On his way through, he found a common area in the back, complete with an indoor pool and a hot tub that appeared fully functional and clean. Drawing a deep breath, he sighed and chuckled happily to himself, knowing he wanted to experience each of them at some point. Shaking his head in amazement, he ascended the stairs to a more private area that Phyllis and Harold graciously let their guests use.

In the hallway near the bathroom he found a stackable washer and dryer that looked brand new. So long as Harold and Phyllis could locate appliances and supplies when their current stash began to break down, the couple could live out the remainder of their years in the scenic Adirondacks. Compared to his life since the week preceding Labor Day, Metzger felt as though he'd found utopia. Contemporary fittings, elegant design, and appliances surrounded him as though he'd just won a sweepstakes for a new house. He walked into the bathroom, plucked a fluffy white towel from the pile, and held it up to his nose with no expectations. Greeted by a lilac odor that mimicked what he remembered from his childhood, and even some adult laundry days, Metzger shut the door behind him.

"Phyllis, you've outdone yourself," he said under his breath.

Searching the medicine cabinet, he found a variety of medications, both prescription and over-the-counter. Ignoring those, he opened drawers in the vanity, coming across a rechargeable hair trimmer. Contemplating his appearance momentarily in the mirror, Metzger finally decided to use a guide comb to adjust the length of his hair, running the trimmer across his head numerous times. He liked his new look, and it felt rather comfortable having less hair. Considering he hadn't shaved since the day the world fell apart, however, Metzger felt his beard gave him the look of a burly biker. He held up the trimmers, removed the guide, and looked in the mirror.

"Why not?" he asked with a shrug.

A few minutes later, the beard was reduced to stubble, which suited him. Metzger wanted to start growing the beard anew, but he didn't ever want it long enough to reach his nipples. With scraps of loose hair covering his body, he started the shower, and a few minutes later found the hot water both relaxing and invigorating simultaneously. He used shampoo, body wash, a soap bar, and even the conditioner just to relive each experience after going without for so long. Metzger felt a bit selfish for doing so, but silently vowed not to consume so much of the limited products again if he was allowed another shower.

So much of the experience felt unreal, as though the past few months were a nightmare and he found his conscious mind returning to reality. He dried his body, put on the cleanest clothes he possessed, and returned to the lobby downstairs to find everyone still deep in conversation.

"Shower's free," he announced when he entered the room, "though I'm not sure how much hot water is left."

Phyllis laughed momentarily.

"We've been living it up, up here, while you've all been on the road."

"Some of us more than others," Jillian noted, though she didn't aim the remark at any present company.

"What's with the windows and the fallen trees outside?" Metzger inquired, taking a seat in one of the available lounge chairs.

"Halloween decorations in the windows," Harold replied. "Those vinyl stick-on things. We wanted the place to look broken down so people wouldn't think the place was safe."

"Aren't the lights a dead giveaway?" Jillian asked.

"We shut this building down before dark," Phyllis answered. "It would be like a beacon up here, so we shut off the lights and stay in one of the cabins. Anonymity is how we survive."

"There's a little tractor out back I used to move trees in front of the building," Harold said. "I've been considering filling in the outdoor pool since it'll never get used again. It adds to the feel that this place is unlivable, though."

"If someone gets this close, they're going to know the truth," Metzger said. "Better to fill it in, so no one here gets hurt."

"Does anyone know you're here?" Phyllis asked.

Metzger sensed she was asking for the sake of caution, and for everyone's safety.

"No," Isabella answered. "It wasn't in the plan all along, and I'm not even sure Bryce will guess we traveled here."

"You're welcome to everything we have," Harold said. "However, we'll probably have to make some trips to town if you're all staying through the winter."

"Winter?" Timmons questioned as though he hadn't planned on staying for more than a few days to a week.

"Once the snow falls, it'll be pretty much impassible on these roads without snowplows. This place will keep us warm, but we'll need food and supplies to make it through."

Timmons spent the entire conversation standing, leaned against the door frame of the extra-wide entrance into the lobby. He appeared stiff, as though unwilling to commit to staying at the resort for an extended time.

"You make it sound as though you can go to the market whenever you want," Jillian commented. "Are there ample supplies in the area?"

"Oh, there are supplies," Harold answered with a chuckle. "Several local stores were isolated, and we get creative with the stuff we find. Most times, I could only grab a handful of things before the dead started to surround me."

Metzger fully understood the situation from experience.

"I'll gladly lend a hand on your next trip."

Timmons walked over to a seated Metzger, putting a hand on his shoulder before looking down to him.

"A word?"

"Sure," Metzger said, standing to follow the captain wherever he wanted to hold a conversation out of earshot.

Ending up near the exterior pool, the captain didn't appear especially happy when he turned to face Metzger.

"We can't stay up here all winter," he stated, shaking his head.

"What exactly did you think you were signing up for, Scott?"

"Not this, son."

"You figured we were going to find my brother stumbling around with a hankering for human flesh, didn't you?"

"You've already admitted that's what you expected."

"I have. You knew when you left the base this could be an extended trip. Yet you've been nothing but a horse's ass the entire time."

Timmons suddenly turned serious.

"I took you to the airport, risked life and limb to steal an aircraft and fuel, and brought you exactly where you said you left your brother."

"There's something more to this," Metzger said, beginning to realize Timmons wasn't simply irritated because he was inconvenienced. "Were you on some kind of timetable?"

"What?" Timmons questioned indignantly.

"You almost told me something once before," Metzger pressed. "What was it?"

"They knew your sister-in-law was poking around," Timmons admitted.

"*They?*"

"The brass. They didn't want to lock you up completely, because manpower was already thin, and they figured eventually you'd try and escape the base."

Metzger considered that train of thought reasonably accurate, because the only thing keeping him at the base was the thought of being close to his last remaining family members.

"So how do you figure into all of this?" he asked without hiding his irritation.

"An admiral approached me the morning we left, before Isabella made her request," Timmons began. "He admitted they fucked things up when it came to your brother. Both of you were supposed to be brought back."

"That way they'd have two guinea pigs," Metzger muttered. "The Marines *did* fuck that up, because they could've gotten Bryce to safety, even after he'd been bitten."

"If you watch someone get bitten, that's a death sentence," Timmons said. "They didn't see any point in bringing a dead man back to a military installation."

"On more than one occasion, Bryce had to put them in their place," Metzger said. "I'm not so sure they didn't leave him for dead out of spite."

"We don't think like that," Timmons said. "We have beefs in the military, but we settle them and move on."

"Fine," Metzger said, still not certain of what happened at the Lancaster airport. "So an admiral approached you for what reason?"

"He wanted me to bring you and your brother back, *if* I was privy to some escape plan on your part."

"So that's what this is? A scheme to get me and Bryce under military control?"

Metzger raised a fist and took a step toward Timmons, who retreated a step.

"No, no," the captain said quickly, holding up his hands. "Just because I agreed, doesn't mean I intended to follow his orders. I don't even know that he asked me in an official capacity."

"Bringing me and my brother back would certainly give you some leverage, though."

"Look, they asked me to betray your trust in me. I wouldn't do that. I didn't befriend you just to stab you in the back."

"Then why didn't you tell me about this sooner?"

"It was unnecessary. I didn't want to take a chance of you getting pissed."

"So, brooding around all of us seemed like a better option?"

"I'm sorry," Timmons said sincerely. "The outside world isn't what I thought it was going to be. And I certainly wasn't expecting to wind up in the mountains."

"Can I trust you, Scott?" Metzger asked flatly, beginning to question the captain's sincerity. "If not, you're welcome to head back to Norfolk while you still can."

"My loyalty is to *you*," Timmons said with a serious expression, pointing directly at Metzger. "I'm not following leadership that hides in some bunker, or admirals and generals who haven't even been face-to-face with the infected. I know that me asking to stay by your side means I have to protect your family as well, but *you're* the one who's going to lead people out of this, whether you know it or not."

Metzger grew concerned that Timmons regarded him as some kind of messiah.

"Why? Because I'm immune to the disease?"

"No, because you've confronted it head-on, and you have the best intentions of all of us," Timmons replied. "I'm willing to follow you to the ends of the Earth because I've been around you long enough to believe in what you're doing."

"I'm going to find my brother, Scott."

"I believe you." Timmons' face etched a bit of his concern before he added another comment. "I also believe the right thing for you and Bryce to do is return to the base when you're ready, but I'm in no position to make that happen. If that was my intention, I would've made a move before we came to maple syrup country."

"Why would I return to the base?"

"If they didn't develop a cure or vaccine from what samples they took from you, thousands of people will remain at risk. What you do is your choice, because the only thing I'm asking for is forgiveness for my secrecy, and the chance to stick around."

Metzger thought about his position a moment, knowing he wasn't going to kick the pilot out of a safe haven for keeping a mostly harmless secret.

"If you haven't experienced a winter up here, you're about to get a number of chances to prove yourself," he finally said.

"That's all I'm asking."

"You taught me a little about piloting, and you're about to get some lessons in return. New York is in winter ninety percent of the time compared to normal states."

Timmons gave an uncertain grin, and the two men shook hands, prepared to confront several different hardships in the apocalypse.

Eleven

"You can't go after this guy by yourself," Gracine told Sutton when they returned to the central cabin where they'd stayed the night.

Both bodies remained in the yard as a stark reminder of the adversary they faced. Luke had taken Samantha inside, but everyone else stood on the front landing, near the creepy jack-o-lantern with the candle that finally burned to the bottom.

"He's one person," Sutton said. "He can only lay so many traps, and he probably destroyed his one stockpile of resources by torching that cabin."

"Then why wouldn't he run?" Driscoll asked. "We should be hitting the road ourselves right now."

"There are three cabins left to check," Sutton reasoned aloud. "I want answers, and while I'm at it, I can disarm any traps he left for people who don't know any better."

"Dad, you're fully capable," Sean stated, "but you're no trap expert. You could still fall into something."

"I'm not going to spend another night looking over my shoulder," Sutton insisted. "One way or another, this ends today."

"You're not going alone," Sean insisted.

"I work better alone."

Driscoll cleared his throat.

"Whatever you two decide, I'm leaving. Now."

"That seems like the opposite of safe," Gracine said with a raised eyebrow.

"And all of you splitting up, either chasing this guy, or waiting for him to come burn you alive, sounds better?"

Gracine looked at him, placing her right hand on her hip.

"You sound scared."

"It's hard enough to survive with things the way they are, and you throw a serial killer in the mix? This sounds like as good a time as any to move along."

Sutton had heard enough.

"If you're going to go, go already. We can't afford to have you take either of the vehicles."

"I'll be fine," Driscoll said. "There were cars between here and the other campsite. I can walk that far."

While Driscoll gathered up what few belongings he could take with him, Sutton turned his attention to his son.

"I don't want you going with me."

"You can't do this alone. We take Buster, and we stick to the main roads."

"And we're just supposed to sit here like targets?" Luke questioned.

"You have guns," Sutton stated, giving him a sour look. "The guy isn't brazen enough to come after a group."

"He just tried to set three of you on fire," Gracine noted.

"I was there!" Driscoll called from the other room where he continued to gather items.

"You were unconscious," Sutton rebutted. "And you're about to be this guy's target again."

"I'm pulling my ass out of the fire," Driscoll said, returning to the group, holding a pack that contained a few firearms and some supplies. "Pun intended."

"This isn't the time to leave," Gracine said directly to Driscoll. "You're panicking."

"Sister, I was ready to go before we encountered this psycho," he replied, wincing as he put a hand up to his head as though he felt pain.

"I'm not your sister," Gracine said, "and you might as well paint a target on your back if you leave now."

"You all said it earlier. He's one person. He can't track all of us at once."

"Don't do this," Sutton said, his tone just short of uttering a plea. "You can't make it on your own."

"I have before," Driscoll said, slinging the pack over his shoulder. "I'll find others."

Gracine shook her head.

"What the fuck is wrong with you?" she asked. "We aren't your ideal companions because I'm not the right color, and he's gay?"

She nodded in the direction of Luke, who said nothing, but didn't look appreciative of Driscoll's actions if he was guided by prejudices. Driscoll started to say something, but turned away, exiting through the door with a dismissive wave without looking back.

"That went well," Luke said sarcastically.

Sutton knew he needed to deal with the main project at hand to keep everyone safe.

"You're staying," he said to Sean. "We'll talk when I get back."

"Where are you going?" Sean questioned.

"I'm going to keep us all alive," Sutton replied. "Keep Buster safe while I'm gone."

Sean started to step forward, but Sutton placed his palm against his son's chest.

"Stay."

"I don't know these people," Sean said so only his father could hear his words.

"They're friends," Sutton assured him. "Better friends than I've deserved these past few weeks. So keep them safe for me."

Sutton made certain he possessed the weapons and tools necessary to track the murderous stranger before exiting the door, seeing no sign of Driscoll when he stepped outside. Just once, he wanted to make a stop with the group that didn't include them running into dangerous or deranged individuals.

***

"We can't let him go off alone," Sean said less than a minute after his father's departure.

"Have you met your father?" Gracine asked, knowing better than to talk sense into the man hellbent on locating their latest nemesis. "Has he always been this stubborn?"

"Yes."

As concerned as she was for Sutton, Gracine also worried about Driscoll. He didn't appear entirely in control of his faculties when he left.

"What happened to Steve?" she asked of Sean, who returned a quizzical stare. "How did he end up in that pit with you?"

"It was a basement. And I think he was conked over the head before he was thrown down there."

"He wanted to leave before all of this happened," Luke said. "I say we let him go."

"He wasn't in his right mind," Gracine said. "Head trauma is making him loopy, and Colby is on a mission, so he just let him go."

Buster whimpered at the front door, hating being left behind. He went to the windows he could reach, either by standing on the floor, or on furniture, to look for his owner.

"He tried to help me," Sean said. "The least I could do is make sure he's okay."

"We can't take Buster," Gracine thought aloud. "He'd try and track your dad."

"He can stay with me and Samantha," Luke said. "I'm not taking her out there while that maniac is on the loose."

Gracine gathered a few firearms, handing a semi-automatic pistol to Sean.

"I take it you're well-versed?"

"My father would disown me if I wasn't."

"I suspected as much. Let's track down Steve and make sure he's of sound mind before he gets too far."

"Beats going stir crazy around here and worrying about my dad."

***

Driscoll started off by following the road out of the campground, not wanting anything to impede his progress. The farther he walked, however, the more he worried about someone tracking his movements. He'd wanted to leave the group, because he felt conflicted being around a person of color, and a homosexual, which went against everything his upbringing taught him.

His father, a fire and brimstone preacher, presided over several congregations during his three decades of preaching. In his early days, he preached his true thoughts, about how homosexuality sent people directly to hell. He also put out vibes that people who weren't Caucasian were inferior people in every sense of the word. For years, Driscoll knew nothing different, and he tended to associate with like-minded individuals throughout his school years, ensuring his father liked the friends he brought home.

Before he knew it, Driscoll found himself in the middle of the woods, not certain where he was because he lost track of time.

Or rather lost time altogether.

He didn't recall why he chose this particular direction, and possessed no clue about which direction he currently faced.

His skull felt as though it was on fire, a condition that came and went ever since he fell victim to the lunatic rendering him unconscious.

Finding a tree with cleared ground surrounding it, Driscoll slumped against the thick stump and sat on the dirt with his back against the tree. He remembered the times his father jokingly talked about how nice it would be to own slaves, and how wrong the country became after the Civil War and the civil rights movement.

Even in the apocalypse, Driscoll traveled with people who shared the same thoughts as his father. Not until he met Sutton, and the rest of the group shortly after that, did he begin to get to know people who weren't just like him. He couldn't say he knew them much beyond their names and their recent actions, but they took care of one another. They acted like family in every sense of the word, even though they didn't share a bloodline.

If not for Sutton, Driscoll would have died in the shootout in South Hill when his group acted irresponsibly and tried to bully survivors for no good reason.

He knew they were bad seeds, but back then Driscoll knew no other way to survive. Losing his friends and family early on when the world ended, he made a stand at the house where his folks lived, even with their bodies buried in the back yard. Eventually, the stored and gathered food and supplies ran low, forcing him to leave the area. He dealt with the undead when they staggered onto the property, but the survivors became a larger issue. Driscoll began to realize he couldn't fend them off alone, and wherever he chose to travel, he needed people with him, or he'd perish.

Continuing to sit against the tree, Driscoll took in the sounds of nature with squirrels chattering, birds chirping, and an unusual sound he couldn't quite distinguish. He closed his eyes for a moment, then when he opened them again, the lighting had somehow changed, as though time had passed. He spotted someone walking directly towards him, but his mind didn't instinctively make him reach for his firearm, or stand in preparation of defending himself. He felt oddly at peace, as though he was exactly where he needed to be.

"Son, what are you doing sleeping on the job?" a slender man with a strong build asked him once he drew closer.

"Dad?" Driscoll questioned almost sleepily. "Aren't you-"

"Don't sass me, son," his father said with his drawl that originated in Georgia. "I asked you a question."

"But, Dad, I didn't mean to-"

"Staying with niggers and faggots has made you weak," his father said as Driscoll clamored to his feet, only to receive a poking finger in his chest. "I told you to stick with your own kind."

"I didn't have a choice."

"I don't want excuses, Steven. You need to get your ass to steppin' before I tan it."

"Yes, sir."

Driscoll's mind still felt hazy, and he couldn't explain how the father, whose death he personally witnessed was speaking to him, but Driscoll felt obligated to comply. He found little time to dwell on his situation, because his father walked by his side, constantly monitoring his every move, much like his teenage days.

His father always wore his hair short, almost military by nature, and in this instance, his temples appeared gray, mixed in with otherwise black hair. A thick vein always protruded from his neck, as though he perpetually remained angry at something. His voice carried, like a drill sergeant, or an auctioneer perhaps, and Driscoll remembered jumping to attention whenever Alvin Driscoll raised his voice around his children.

"Did you sleep with her, Steven?" his father asked with fire in his eyes.

"Who?"

"The nigger lady. Did you have sexual relations with her?"

"No," Driscoll answered defiantly. "I would never."

"Because she isn't your wife, or because she's colored?"

"Well, both," Driscoll answered.

Driscoll continued walking, feeling a bit more certain of his course now, though his father remained at his side, except when he needed to step around a tree. From the corner of one eye, Driscoll thought he saw his father move through a tree, like a ghost phasing through a solid object, or a wall. He said nothing, however, because there wasn't much he could say to the man who shaped him during his formative years.

"I raised you better than this," his father said, shaking his head. "I would rather see you strike out on your own and get bit than stay with these people."

This isn't real, Driscoll began to think, recalling how overbearing his father could be with his mannerisms, voice, and that hard strut he did when something lit a fire under him. Despite all of that, his father never ranted, even during sermons, and this entire conversation felt false to him. He stopped suddenly, still surrounded by trees, feeling as though he wasn't making any headway to the destination he thought he knew. Suddenly, he couldn't remember where he was heading.

"Steven, you need to snap out of this funk you're in," his father said. "Wake up."

Driscoll continued to stand, uncertain of where to go next. His father grabbed him by the shirt collar with both hands, drawing his face within inches of his son before yelling at him.

"Wake up!"

Driscoll felt his body jolt awake as he found himself still seated at the base of the same tree. He somehow dozed off, or lost consciousness, and his head still ached. He saw a figure walking directly at him, and he wondered if he was experiencing an unrelenting wave of déjà vu. When this figure drew close, however, it hissed and growled, revealing itself as a member of the undead before dropping down with its jaws aimed at his neck.

***

Sutton chose the path of least resistance when it came to tracking down the mysterious murderer. He followed the road to the cabin where the man was heading when the group last spotted him, believing he might have set up shop in the building farthest from the campsite's entrance.

When he drew closer, he stepped off the dirt road, trudging through the shrubs and overgrown grass instead. He monitored a few steps ahead of him the entire way, searching for traps that might alert the predatory man, or ensnare Sutton, leaving him defenseless. Despite being motivated by revenge of his son, and wanting to prevent others from falling victim to the man, Sutton maintained incredibly calm, not rushing into action.

He didn't like that Driscoll felt so determined to leave, because the man, in turn, placed the others in danger. Banding together always kept them safer, and Driscoll could become a victim, or he might get captured and used as bait. For all Sutton knew, the man who burned others after torturing them might be tracking him at the moment, but he kept his firearms handy. Occasionally, he turned to scour his surroundings through the thermal scope of his sniper rifle. He spotted a deer one time, and a few birds perched in trees, but no shapes that resembled a human being.

Sutton wanted to catch up with his son, and keep him safe, but he knew this particular action kept far more people alive if he succeeded. Buster's assistance would have been a benefit as always, but he didn't want his canine falling into a trap, or giving away their position. Leaving him with Sean also kept his son safer from harm, because Buster protected anyone he considered an ally.

When the cabin finally came into view, Sutton pulled the sniper rifle around his shoulder where it was strapped and had a look directly at the cabin. Thermal imaging couldn't penetrate solid surfaces, but he hoped to find a trace of warmth from where the killer had placed a hand against the wood, or a door, as he entered. Seeing no signs of the man recently stepping outside, he slowly moved forward, listening for any distinctive noises. He felt a bit disturbed by the fact that the animals around him suddenly had little to say, possibly meaning they sensed danger.

He began to doubt his adversary's ability to create traps. The wire he encountered earlier was simply an early warning device. Also, the man didn't elaborately ensnare the people he captured for his sick games, instead knocking them cold with tools or blunt objects. Sutton's only sighting of the man looked more like a blur than anything, and he mainly focused on the fiery bottle about to be thrown his way in the cabin cellar.

Trying to avoid breathing too loudly, Sutton felt his heart pound as he approached the cabin. He didn't feel particularly fearful, exercising caution during the moment he hoped to get some measure of revenge. Several pumpkins lined the ground along the front of the porch, still intact, and likely waiting their turn to be carved as a creepy warning to people who dared come near the cabins.

Assured the rifle was strapped over his shoulder, he stepped on the first step of the cabin's small porch, pulling the sidearm from his pants, keeping it in a ready position. He attempted to peer inside the windows, and the glass of the front door without making himself an easy target, finding it difficult to see details inside.

Because the porch only lined the front of the cabin, Sutton needed to step down to check around the back. Along the side of the cabin, he saw half a dozen lengthy mounds of dirt where he could only assume bodies were buried in shallow graves. He stared only a few seconds, daring not linger, though he couldn't fathom the man's motivation for harming human beings in such a way. Something *had* to be wrong with him before the apocalypse, and now the world was his playground where he could hunt and maim.

In back, Sutton found little to help his search because the windows were seated too high for him to safely look into, and no porch, parking spot, or otherwise smooth ground existed to offer assistance. Sutton imagined the structure held a few bedrooms, and possibly a large kitchen or living area based on the square footage.

Returning to the front, he noticed an area trampled by footsteps recently that he hadn't noticed when approaching the first time. He felt positive the man who caused his son so much grief entered the cabin, and perhaps felt he possessed all five cabins. Standing still a moment, Sutton listened intently to everything around him, finding the animals remained silent while no noise came from the cabin.

He walked up the front steps once more, knowing he was made if the mysterious man remained inside, or ever stepped foot inside in the first place.

Drawing a deep breath and exhaling, Sutton opened the door with his left hand, keeping his sidearm gripped in his right. When the door opened inward, he spied a younger man standing before him, feeling certain it was the killer because no one else would hole up inside the cabin. Taking aim quickly, Sutton took half a step inside and fired at the man's shoulder, not wanting to kill him.

Yet.

Instead of seeing the man flinch in pain, however, Sutton witnessed a mirror shatter in front of him, leaving him stunned momentarily. In less than a second, Sutton felt his entire body tense because the man had crouched along his hiding spot to use a stun gun on him. Completely defenseless, Sutton dropped his firearm before collapsing to the floor, completely at the mercy of a man who had already proven he held little regard for human life.

Twelve

Driscoll felt certain he'd been in and out of consciousness a few times when he awoke to find gray, cloudy skies overhead. He sensed it might be early afternoon, but he wasn't certain. In fact, he didn't feel certain about very much as he spied an immobile zombie to his left that wouldn't re-animate based on the bloody stab mark in its skull. Beside his right hand, he found a knife covered in blood, and several feet to his right, a female zombie put down permanently in some fashion.

"Looks like you had a little skirmish, son," Driscoll's father said, appearing to him again as a few raindrops pelted Driscoll in the face from the towering trees.

"Striking out on my own was a grand idea," Driscoll commented sourly, grabbing the knife before wiping it against the ground to remove the blood.

He attempted to stand, but a pain along the right side of his stomach caused him to wince. He looked down, finding blood soaked through his shirt. Hesitantly, he reached down, pulling up his shirt to find teeth marks centered in the blood stain.

"Oh, looks like one of them got you," his father said with barely an ounce of empathy in his tone.

"I see you let me fight my own battles as always, Dad," Driscoll said, letting his shirt drop down.

He dared not process what the bite meant, knowing if death was coming for him, he didn't want to be alone. Even worse, he didn't want to turn and have the people he knew finding him staggering around. He especially didn't want to be a mindless entity tracking them down for food. Closing his eyes momentarily, he decided to walk back to the cabin, finding his head continued to ache, even after taking a few calming breaths.

Taking up the sidearm he'd dropped at some point, Driscoll tucked it along his back. He began walking toward the cabin, wondering if the others left the grounds, or decided to help Sutton.

"You can't go back to them," Alvin Driscoll said, walking alongside his son, a disgusted look on his face.

"You'd rather I die out here alone in the woods? Like a wounded animal just waiting to bleed out?"

"Better to be one with nature than go against its intended purpose for you."

Driscoll continued walking, ignoring what he felt certain was a side-effect of whatever plagued his mind following the head injury.

"Don't walk away from me, boy," his father said.

"I'm just walking, Dad. But while we're strolling out here, can you answer me one question?"

"Shoot," his father answered casually, walking around a tree while keeping his eyes locked on his son.

"We moved quite a bit when I was a kid," Driscoll stated. "You always had reasons for why we moved from town to town, or a new state, but I never felt like you shot straight with us."

"There isn't a question in there, son."

"Okay," Driscoll said testily. "Why did we really move all the time?"

His father drew a deep breath, likely framing the words in his mind before speaking them.

"Sometimes the congregations didn't like what they heard," he finally said.

"Meaning?"

"The truth hurts sometime, Steven. I didn't preach my opinions about inferior folk, but squeaky wheels always seemed to find out."

Driscoll found his way back to the path, not feeling like trudging through the heavily wooded areas because it sapped his strength. He wasn't feeling the effects of the bite yet, but knew his future, based on witnessed events over the past few months.

"Maybe you should've stuck to biblical stories in your sermons and your personal life," Driscoll noted.

"I should take this belt off and smack you, son."

He reached for the buckle, and Driscoll recalled numerous times as a child when he or his siblings received whippings for wrongs, or perceived wrongs. The moment passed, and his mind returned to the present reality, which presented a wide variety of dangers instead. Perhaps his father prepared him for some of those dangers, teaching him to shoot firearms and live off the land to a certain extent.

"We both know you can't hurt me," Driscoll said. "I'm going crazy, or just resolving some stuff, but you're just a memory to me now."

His father fumed, looking ahead momentarily.

"That's real," he said, pointing to a zombie heading directly for Driscoll.

Drawing his knife, Driscoll approached it, swinging wide with his right hand when he usually shoved the undead first, or restrained them with his free hand. Finding its mark just the same, the blade punctured the zombie's skull, ending its diminished life.

He wiped the knife off once again, using the zombie's clothing, before returning it to the sheath.

"Happy?"

"I'm not happy with the direction you're headed."

"You mean literally, or philosophically?"

"*Both*, if you're heading back to those people."

"You talk about them like they're animals," Driscoll noted. "They're pink on the inside, just like you and me. I've seen proof of that."

His father drew close, an angered look crossing his face.

"If you go back to them, they're going to cast you out. They can't help you, son. Only the Lord above can help you now."

"I agree," Driscoll said. "You know, it took me years, but I finally listened to other preachers at church, and they were nothing like you. I realized maybe it wasn't all of them who were wrong, but-"

"Don't you say it," his father warned.

"Because the truth hurts?"

His father said nothing, choosing to brood and huff instead.

"You led me astray for years, Dad," Driscoll said.

"I toughened you up, Steven. Who bought you your first business right after high school?"

His father bought him a mowing business, which Driscoll eventually sold to venture into a bait and tackle business, which later expanded into a camping and wilderness shop. The business barely stayed afloat during some tough economical periods, so Driscoll was forced to ask his father for help when tacking on gun sales to the shop.

By this time, he realized his father kept him and his siblings within reach, almost manipulating them into requiring his advice, or his financial backing. His father had a way of making ideas seem like those of his children, but in the end, he was a puppet master who got them to do things his way. And Driscoll couldn't say things turned out badly, at least until the apocalypse. His father always provided for him, taught him right from wrong, mostly, and never abused him.

"I guess it took this head injury to make me realize what really matters in the world now, Dad," Driscoll admitted. "Your way just doesn't hold up anymore."

He paused momentarily as his mind returned to the day when he returned home, shortly after the start of the apocalypse, finding his father turned, and his mother bitten because she refused to leave.

"I buried you, Dad," he said aloud, as though expelling the demons that plagued his mind for the past few months. "In the end you didn't take care of us, and you allowed yourself to take Mom with you."

"Deflecting your troubles won't help you through the problems you've got now," his father said. "You'll be seeing me soon enough."

"Assuming we both end up in the same place," Driscoll said with a chuckle.

"You know I couldn't have killed myself, son. Suicide is a mortal sin."

"I'm aware. You could've taken measures, though, like tying yourself down, or asking Mom to shoot you. Maybe that's what I'll ask these people to do for me in the end."

Alvin Driscoll looked at him, not with anger, or understanding, but rather disappointment in his eyes.

"It hurts your head even worse to hold a conversation with me, doesn't it?"

"It does," Driscoll admitted.

"Good."

With his parting word, Alvin Driscoll stepped behind a tree and disappeared from view. Reliving part of his childhood, Driscoll felt alone and abandoned, because he fought and struggled to earn his father's love, realizing too late how misguided some of his father's beliefs were in the modern world.

His skull and his side ached, but Driscoll wasn't about to give up. If his life was measured in hours or days, he wanted to go out being of help to those who assisted him. They provided for him after his family died and other groups left him with empty promises.

Several minutes passed as he followed the trail, and when he finally spied people ahead, he started to instinctively head off the dirt road into the brush, but stopped short when he recognized them.

"Are you okay?" Gracine asked from a distance as she, Luke, Sean, and Samantha headed toward him with Buster by their side.

"I've been better."

All of them looked at him warily when they drew close, spying the wound along his right side.

"I've been in and out of consciousness," Driscoll admitted. "I got all of them, but one of them got a piece of me first, apparently."

"I'm sorry," Gracine said sincerely.

"It's my own fault," Driscoll said, surprised he felt and sounded as calm as he did. "I shouldn't have left like that. I probably got a concussion when that guy attacked me, and I haven't been right since."

"How are you feeling?" Sean asked, fishing for information about his overall condition.

"Not bad, except the bite mark hurts," Driscoll answered.

"You should come back with us," Gracine said.

"Where's Colby?"

"He went after the guy who attacked you."

"Where did he go?"

"To the cabin across from the one where that douchebag tried to fry us," Sean answered.

"He hasn't come back?"

"We've been out looking for you this whole time," Gracine said.

"He shouldn't deal with that guy alone," Driscoll said, stepping forward.

"You need to rest," Luke said, putting a hand up.

"I have an expiration date that's coming due. My last few hours should be spent doing something worthwhile. Let's go see if Colby made it back."

***

Sutton shook his head when he regained his faculties, and instinctively tried moving his appendages to avoid the danger that had already subdued him. Unable to move, he quickly noticed his hands and feet were bound to a wooden chair by synthetic rope that wasn't about to give. An old, sturdy chair with wooden planks facing forward secured his arms because they were resting atop the planks. His feet were tied to the thick chair legs below, preventing him from kicking or maneuvering the chair.

He thought about working his hands back and forth to try loosening the bindings, but his eyes noticed his captor standing across the room, sharpening a knife with a revolver sitting on the kitchen counter beside him. Sutton could already tell his firearms and blades weren't on him, and he regretted being deceived by the mirror trick.

While the younger man appeared to know that Sutton eyeballed him, he said nothing, simply continuing his work.

Not much of a talker in his own right, Sutton decided he needed some answers if he wanted to attempt an escape at some point. Because the killer showed no mercy to his other victims, Sutton certainly wouldn't waste time trying to reason with him. Any information he gathered might be of use, because he hoped to break the chair or slip through the bindings the minute the killer stepped outside. Sutton looked around, unable to spy his weapons, even though he knew he hadn't lost consciousness. In fact, he remembered being dragged along the floor to the chair, even as his body convulsed, feeling helpless, like watching from inside an empty vessel that didn't respond to his commands.

"This cabin isn't yours," he said, trying to initiate a conversation.

He needed to stall for time, even if information wasn't forthcoming.

Instead of replying, the man continued working with the knife, eventually stuffing it into a sheath along his right side before placing the revolver in a holster that sat along the front of his waistline on the left side for an opposite-sided draw. Sutton watched him get into the drawer of a desk along the wall to his right, rummaging for something specific. Because the chair was against the back wall of the living room, Sutton could see most of the cabin except for any bedrooms behind him. He began maneuvering his wrists in circular motions, trying to slowly get the ropes to loosen, monitoring his captor carefully.

"You should be running," Sutton said. "More people are coming to these campgrounds."

Without so much as looking back, the man continued to sort through the drawer, picking out a few items, looking at them, and replacing them carefully. He finally turned to Sutton, taking a precise two steps forward before stopping and studying his prey momentarily.

His dark hair appeared disheveled, as though he attempted to give himself haircuts without the benefit of a good mirror. Although not thick or muscular, the young man looked fit. His weathered face displayed two scars, likely created by blades. Sutton pictured innocent people protecting themselves, or loved ones, from this monster, using whatever knives they possessed. A particularly long gash lined his forehead, mostly horizontal, while a vertical streak ran down his right cheek. This scar appeared fresher, as though received within the past week or two, looking particularly red as though it might be infected.

"You didn't strike me as the type who talked much," the younger man said when he finally spoke.

"I'm not."

"You chose a bad time to start. I'm going to kill your friends now."

Sutton watched him turn about-face as though he'd just graduated a military academy, too stunned to say anything for a few seconds.

"You can't kill them," he finally said. "They outnumber you."

Stopping abruptly, the man waited a few seconds before turning around slowly.

"They're going to die," he said assuredly. "And you're the bait."

***

"He's not here," Driscoll said when they returned to their cabin, finding no sign of Sutton having returned.

"We have to find him," Sean insisted. "I can't lose him now."

"It's a risk we can't take," Luke said, speaking on Samantha's behalf.

No one wanted to place an eight-year-old in harm's way.

"I'll go alone," Driscoll volunteered. "I'm already compromised, but I can still use a gun."

"And what if you both wind up dead at that cabin?" Luke questioned.

"Then you all need to leave while you can, and don't look back."

Driscoll checked both the pistol and knife at his side momentarily before looking up to see concerned eyes looking his way.

"It'll be okay," he said. "And I'm sorry I was an ass earlier. Well, pretty much this entire time, I suppose."

"You weren't that bad," Gracine said. "We didn't exactly give you the warmest welcome."

"Thanks."

Driscoll prepared to leave when Sean clasped his arm.

"You should take Buster."

"Your dad wouldn't want that."

"If something happened to Dad, Buster would never be the same. He'll protect you."

"I know he will."

"One more thing," Gracine said as Driscoll was about to summon Buster.

"What's that?"

"Come back to us. Don't get yourself killed out there."

Driscoll gave a perplexed look, since he considered himself a dead man walking.

"There's a chance we can take care of that bite for you."

"Nothing can stop the spread."

"No, but Isabella gave me something they were testing at the base. I'm just saying there's a chance."

Driscoll nodded.

"Forgive me if I don't hold out much hope."

He whistled to get Buster's attention.

"Come on, boy," he said, and Buster perked up at the opportunity to head out.

"Be careful," Gracine said.

"Always."

***

Sutton waited mere seconds after the murderous young man stepped outside before openly rolling his wrists to loosen the grip of the ropes.

Bound tightly, the ropes began cutting off the circulation to his hands, but he fought them, trying to get some play between them and his wrists. While the prospect of dumping the chair on its side and attempting to break it sounded more beneficial, Sutton suspected his captor hadn't gone far, and he needed to save such a move as his last resort.

He began to regret coming alone, but he didn't want anyone else, particularly the one son he'd found, and his dog, getting hurt. He knew their hearts, however, and when they didn't hear from him, they'd come, and likely get hurt nonetheless. Vowing to improve upon his people skills if he survived the experience, Sutton managed to get a little wiggle room for his wrists, though a far cry from escaping the bindings.

Less than five minutes after stepping outside, the young man returned, immediately heading for a drawer in the kitchen where he produced a hammer and two long nails.

"Can't have you trying anything while I'm away," he said, carrying them over to the chair that held Sutton in check.

Sutton tensed, realizing the young man intended to hammer nails through the top of his hands, into the chair's arm planks, making escape far more difficult.

And painful.

He reached Sutton, carefully placing a rusty nail between two of the middle bones on the backside of his hand, prepared to hammer the nail through flesh when something caught his attention. Sutton didn't hear a thing, but he would be the first to admit his mind was preoccupied with the pain about to ravage his nerve endings. Walking to the window, the killer peered outside, acting paranoid that someone else was already tracking him to the cabin.

Putting the hammer and nails on a table, much to Sutton's relief, the young man grabbed a rag covered in motor oil and what appeared to be animal hair, quickly tying the cloth around Sutton's mouth, keeping him from uttering more than muffled cries.

"Can't have you warning your friends, or screaming," the man said as he cinched the gag. "And it sounds like they're close. They'll be joining you soon enough."

Even before the young man made his way out the door, Sutton tested the filthy cloth wrapped around his head, finding his muffled voice incapable of making enough noise to leave the cabin. He tasted used motor oil as the pet hair irritated the inside of his mouth. Even breathing through his nose did little to better either predicament. He wasn't sure what the killer heard, or thought he heard, but Sutton wasn't about to dawdle. Fortunate that a second chance came to him without death or additional injury, he fought the chair by twisting his body several ways until it crashed hard on its right side.

Although it didn't break apart, he heard something crack behind him, meaning the backing or one of the legs was compromised. Sutton attempted to back it into the wall behind him, but a lack of physical momentum kept the chair from further damage. He turned the entire chair so his back faced the ground, using his legs to hoist himself and the piece of furniture off the ground several inches before letting everything collapse against the hardwood floor. His first three attempts yielded no results, and he immediately felt winded because the gag kept him from breathing normally, or through his mouth.

Propping his head against the wall, Sutton managed to get more height by balancing the lower half of his body by putting strain on his neck and head. The maneuver hurt like hell, but he managed to get more than a foot off the ground before he slipped and sent all of his weight and momentum onto the chair as it hit the ground, fracturing along the molded, glued joints of the old chair. With the wind knocked from his lungs, he rolled to one side, able to spit out the gag as it somehow loosened from the fall. He found his arms and legs freed, but struggled to truly free himself as they remained tethered to the pieces of wood.

Sutton continued to spit out hair as he fought the ropes, managing to stand so he could look for a blade and his firearms. He looked like an odd, homemade Halloween costume with wooden planks and chair legs draped from his appendages. He trudged to the kitchen, opening a few of the drawers to find pot holders, silverware, and some paperwork before finding a medium, sharpened knife in the last one. He plucked it, able to cut the ropes from one arm, freeing each of his limbs in less than a minute without cutting himself.

Next, he set to finding his firearms, or anything useful in the cabin. If his friends had come for him, they placed themselves squarely in danger and he wasn't about to let anything happen to them. He carried one of the chair arm planks with him, figuring it could be swung in self-defense, or held up to take a bullet, like a shield, in a pinch. Sutton searched a few random drawers, finding nothing of use, but he felt drawn to the drawer the man rummaged through before leaving the first time, wondering what interesting weapons or trinkets were hidden there.

He pulled on the handle, immediately finding an assortment of items like jewelry, driver's licenses, and Polaroid photographs staring back at him. Some of the photos on the surface showed victims bound, likely in their final moments of life, and some of them depicted the bodies after being thoroughly burned. Feeling terrible that he hadn't found this man sooner, and saved some lives, Sutton drew a heavy sigh. Though he wanted to leave and search for his weapons, Sutton couldn't help but pick up a few of the items, immediately realizing the items belonged to people this man captured and tortured. Without doing an exact count, he estimated at least three dozen items occupied the drawer. He doubted any of the victims meant any harm, likely stopping for a rest and a place to sleep, only to have their lives stubbed out instead.

Feeling sickened and choked up at the same time, he discovered more photographs depicting victims either bound and looking helpless, or already burned by the killer. Sutton was about to close the drawer out of disgust when an item toward the bottom caught his eye.

"No," he muttered, seeing the photo on a driver's license partially obscured by the other items inside.

Hesitant, he started to reach for the object several times, balking from fear of the truth he already knew in his heart.

Finally, he plucked the license from the bottom of the pile, finding an image of his youngest son staring back at him.

"Jacob," he said under his breath as tears welled in his eyes.

Sutton choked up immediately, feeling emotion overwhelm him as tears rolled down his cheeks without hesitation. Finding Sean was a blessing, but he held out hope of finding both of his sons alive and well. Knowing all too well he would have reunited with both of them if not for a murderous intervention, Sutton pocketed the license, knowing he needed to save the mourning process for later if he wanted to protect the people left in his life.

He choked back his sobs, wiped his eyes with his sleeves, and began searching the remainder of the cabin for his firearms and knives. It occurred to him the killer might be planning something heinous, because leaving Sutton bound to a chair all alone seemed foolhardy. Perhaps he wanted Sutton to step outside, even chase him through the woods, but Sutton had a better idea. He felt emotionally compromised, fighting to keep his wits about him as he entered the rear bedroom, finding a stack of items that included clothing, suitcases, some supplies, and a collection of firearms that included his own.

"Time to end this," Sutton vowed, taking up his weapons, prepared to put his plan into action.

***

Driscoll stayed along the main road until he drew closer to the cabin in question. Buster remained with him, and Driscoll felt impressed by the canine's intelligence, both in judging people accurately and doing what humans wanted from him without being told.

Feeling the sting of the bite along his side, he pressed onward, feeling certain he was about to carry out his last good deed on Earth. From what he gathered, the government tried creating a variety of vaccines or medication for whatever caused the dead to rise. He knew the sister-in-law of their friend grabbed a handful on her way out of the base and gave a few to Gracine. Without being tested in *any* kind of conditions, much less a variety, the medicine was a gamble that Driscoll didn't expect to pay off on his behalf.

Concerned that he hadn't seen the first sign of Sutton, and Buster hadn't indicated locating any living person, Driscoll kept monitoring the area around him. Odors of recent burning reached his nostrils, and he couldn't tell if the campfire Sutton started in the overnight blew from their camp, or something more sinister wafted his way.

Buster perked up, hearing or smelling something to his left, and dashed off without warning into the woods. Driscoll stood in place, stunned momentarily, to see if the canine returned to him, or found something nearby. As though tracking something hurriedly, the dog was swallowed by the fall foliage almost immediately. Driscoll heard the sound of the brush rustling until the dog vanished from sight, leaving him feeling very alone and vulnerable.

"He'll protect you," Driscoll repeated Sean's words to him mockingly, under his breath, feeling very much the opposite of protected.

He momentarily considered returning to the main road, knowing the killer wouldn't be as apt to hear him coming, but he'd easily be spotted without any cover. Being on the wrong end of a scoped rifle wasn't how Driscoll planned on leaving the world.

Cautiously stepping through the woods, Driscoll kept shifting his eyes to the ground on the lookout for traps, and then upward, knowing he was drawing closer to the cabin. Wishing the group had the means to use and charge some kind of walkie talkies or higher-end radios, Driscoll envisioned them communicating better and knowing the status of everyone in the group with the push of a button.

Finally finding his place in the group, and coming up with ways to improve their lives made him regret keeping everyone at arm's length for so long. His father set him on a path that brought him to such people after avoiding them for so many years. He wanted to start over with them and be a true member of their clan, and not just someone who toted a gun and occasionally pitched in.

Driscoll stopped to address the constant pain at his side, pulling up his shirt, which resisted him because blood and sweat caused it to adhere to his skin. He finally got a look at the bite mark, which appeared more inflamed than before with a darker shade of red circling the wound. Releasing the shirt, Driscoll looked to the side where Buster ran off, seeing no sign of the dog. He was about to continue the last leg of the walk to the cabin when the distinct sound of a branch breaking behind him alerted him to the presence of another person. Turning too late, Driscoll discovered the trigger was already being pulled on a weapon aimed at his chest.

Thirteen

Driscoll found himself on the wrong end of a taser, which rendered his muscles useless as they tensed from the electrical current paralyzing him and sending him into a heap to the ground. He felt his weapons quickly stripped from him as the man who assaulted him tied his hands behind his back with efficiency. To ensure success, the man zapped Driscoll a second time with the taser, providing him time enough to hogtie Driscoll's feet, effectively neutralizing his prey in every way conceivable.

Feeling himself hoisted over the man's shoulder, Driscoll knew he was being taken to his death, one way or another. He struggled against the man, able to shake his body and kick slightly with his legs.

"Quit, or I can skin you alive right here," the man threatened in monotone.

Driscoll stopped fighting, taking a few deep breaths as the woods passed by from a strange vantage point. He noticed a bag being towed behind the man carrying him, and it looked as though the lengthy bag carried his firearms and blades, along with some other items.

"Doesn't matter," he said. "I'm dead already."

"That makes sense on no level."

"I was bitten."

"Interesting."

"Interesting?" Driscoll questioned, beginning to struggle once more against the callous, sociopathic young man who held human life in a completely different regard than the average person.

"Stop."

Driscoll opted to quit squirming once again, trying to buy time for Buster or the others to find him, if they had even decided to search.

Halting where he stood, the man held many options over Driscoll, including dropping him on nearby rocks, slitting his throat, or using the taser again.

"I'm taking you to your friend."

"Is he alive?" Driscoll questioned as the man began a steady walk through the woods once more.

"He is."

"Keep me, and do whatever you want," Driscoll volunteered. "Let the rest go."

"They've seen me. That cannot happen."

"They're not going to come after you."

"Two of you already have. This is what happens to people who trespass in my territory."

Driscoll couldn't imagine what shaped this killer to end up the way he had, though he felt surprised to hold any conversation whatsoever with him.

"I may keep you as a pet," the man said out of nowhere, and Driscoll felt certain they were drawing closer to the cabin. "I may even let you change and bite your friend so I can keep you both."

Trying to wrap his mind around such a bizarre concept, Driscoll couldn't imagine what motivated him to murder people, experiment on them, or keep the undead like pets. He seemed almost detached, in some ways like a scientific mind, but in others, a troubled person with some hang-ups that weren't addressed before the apocalypse.

Perhaps the solutions simply didn't take.

"You can't keep doing this," Driscoll said.

"Doing what?"

"Killing people for no reason," Driscoll replied, struggling to get his words out as he bobbed up and down slightly on the man's shoulder.

"I have my reasons."

Driscoll felt his mind wander a bit, knowing his life measured in hours regardless of what this man did to him. He hoped being reunited with Sutton might provide them with a way to team up and escape the madman's ploy.

Allowing this individual to hunt down the remainder of the group simply wasn't an option in Driscoll's mind.

When his captor came to a stop, Driscoll sensed they had reached the cabin. He wondered if the man sensed danger, or perhaps savored the moment before enjoying the torture and dismemberment of his two prisoners. He saw the thin rope used to tote the bag of weapons drop to the ground, meaning the guns and knives were there for the taking. Driscoll wished he could hold a firearm for two seconds and bring the cat and mouse game to an end.

Feeling the man struggle to ascend the stairs while carrying him, Driscoll heard a few grunts before they reached the small porch. He figured the man might set him down before opening the door, but the man turned awkwardly with Driscoll still perched atop his right shoulder, turning the doorknob before lugging him inside.

Less than two seconds passed before Driscoll heard some words being spoken by someone other than his captor, a gunshot ringing out, and him being dropped to the floor like a sack of potatoes. Still trying to gather his wits, Driscoll saw two feet from ground level leaving the cabin, darting for the woods. He wasn't sure if he was about to be finished off, rescued, or left for dead, because everything happened in a blur.

***

Sutton decided after viewing the photos that he didn't want to trudge through the woods looking for the killer, because the man wasn't going to attack his entire group at once. Most likely, he wanted to scout the area and make certain no one set out to search for Sutton. Temporarily hardening his heart, Sutton put aside tears and mourning after deciding exactly how he wanted to deal with the deranged young man.

He spied the man carrying what appeared to be Driscoll over his shoulder almost a hundred yards away, through the front window. Him not being alone didn't alter Sutton's plan very much, but he knew his aim needed to be a bit more accurate.

During the half hour the man left the cabin, Sutton formulated his plan after several attempts that didn't feel vengeful enough. Simply shooting the man when he walked inside didn't feel right, because he wanted the killer to feel some form of fear first. Sutton wanted the man to know he was bested before a bullet penetrated his skin. The fate of some three dozen victims, including his youngest son, demanded that the man suffer, feeling tortured in one way or another, before being put down like a rabid dog.

When he stepped outside to clear his head and listen for the man's return, Sutton found inspiration when he noticed the pumpkins for a second time.

He spent the next five minutes gutting a pumpkin and carving a face into it, all the while monitoring the outdoors through the window facing the same direction as the door. Not particularly concerned with the quality of his work, Sutton carved a face in the vegetable after scraping the bottom just smooth enough to steady a candle. He'd located candles and a lighter in his earlier searches, so he set the jack-o-lantern on the table, facing the door, and placed a lit candle inside. Part of him wanted to be seated, facing the door when the killer arrived back at the cabin, but he needed to keep watch and anticipate any issues before the man stepped inside.

Not usually one for theatrics, Sutton felt surprisingly spirited about enacting precise revenge against the man. Basing his murders on intimidation and a sense of foreboding, the man needed to experience a few of his own tactics before meeting his end.

Reunited with his firearms, Sutton waited behind the kitchen table he'd placed about five feet in front of the main entrance. He waited patiently, holding the gun, simply waiting for the events to unfold as they may. Because the man carried Driscoll on one shoulder, he wasn't going to be able to quickly go for a weapon. Standing back from the window so he couldn't be seen, Sutton observed Driscoll struggling a few different times against the young man. Each time, the killer spoke, and Driscoll stopped wriggling, allowing the man to carry him to an undetermined fate.

Humming the tune of Neil Diamond's "Solitary Man" while waiting, to keep his nerves steady and his mind occupied, Sutton found his idea of solitude different than those in the lyrics. He kept pushing people away from him during the outbreak of the infection, but over the past few weeks he realized he needed trustworthy people by his side. Sharing his supplies wasn't an issue, because Sutton now felt confident that he would find more supplies or settle somewhere and begin anew with his current group. He wasn't foolhardy enough to believe survival was easy in any future scenario, but they could find somewhere safe, with land and water, and make a go of it.

But first, he needed to deal with the situation at hand.

When the killer reached the front door, he turned his body somewhat sideways to reach for the doorknob, carrying Driscoll inside without much effort. It wasn't until he'd fully stepped inside that he noticed the carved jack-o-lantern staring back at him, displayed atop the dining table. Sutton stepped into view, pointed the gun at the young man, and waited for a clear view.

"Trick-or-treat, motherfucker!" Sutton uttered angrily, squeezing the trigger and clipping the man in the shoulder because the killer turned to put Driscoll in harm's way.

Without hesitation the killer ran out the door, and into the woods, but Sutton stepped forward, anger from within fueling his steady hand as he took aim at the back of the man's knee. At nearly forty feet from the cabin, the young man likely believed his escape inevitable, so he could return to haunt the group, or others, at a time of his choosing. Assuming his shooting stance from the porch, his breathing calm and collected despite his expression showing his anger outwardly, Sutton required only a few seconds to line up the shot before firing.

Blood spurted from the side of the man's right knee as he fell forward, hitting the ground without the benefit of breaking his fall. Sutton calmly walked down the porch's front stairs, hearing Driscoll get to his feet behind him, despite the ringing in his ears from firing a gun without hearing protection. Without looking back, the young man struggled to his feet, like a wounded deer, before continuing to run forward. Although the younger man couldn't run very fast with a significant limp, Sutton didn't feel like tracking him through the woods. Some dark thoughts ran through his mind as he raised the pistol and shot the man in the back of his upper left leg.

Crying out in pain, the man dropped to the ground once again, but Sutton didn't feel an ounce of remorse. He continued marching forward, stalking his prey, his eyes unblinking as he stared holes in the man who murdered his youngest son. No form of punishment felt severe enough for the man, regardless of whether he experienced a troubled childhood, couldn't take medications in the apocalypse, or he was simply born a psychopath.

By the time Sutton reached him, the man was crawling, using only his arms, because both of his legs were deemed practically useless by Sutton's precision aim.

Stealing a glance behind him, he found Driscoll waiting on the porch, leaning against a railing for support due to some kind of injuries, patiently waiting for events to unfold. Returning his attention to the injured killer, Sutton looked skyward, finding the gray sky getting darker. A few drops of rain struck his face, and thunder rolled in the distance.

"You should've killed me when you had the chance," Sutton said with a growl.

"Kill me and be done with it," the man replied, his left hand grasping at a nearby shrub to pull himself forward.

"That would be more than you deserve," Sutton retorted. "After all, you killed someone I loved very much."

All of the sudden both of them were motionless, and the man acted as though he wanted to hear the story, even if to relive the crime in his mind.

"Who?" he asked without trying to turn his body for a look at Sutton.

"My son."

"Oh, I remember him," the man said with a deranged chuckle. He wanted Sutton to pull the trigger and end his life, so he intended to play the part until the end. "He even looked a little bit like you."

"Where is he buried?" Sutton pressed.

"They're all near the cabins."

Sutton couldn't imagine why the man buried so many people outside of all five nearby cabins, except that he wouldn't want the smell of death, or burned flesh, turning away potential victims.

Taking not particularly good aim, Sutton fired into the man's lower backside, hoping to strike parts of the intestine, or perhaps a kidney. Yelping in pain, the young man seemed to accept the reversal of fate, because he didn't try escaping or pleading for his life.

"Do you want to know why?" he asked instead.

"Not particularly," Sutton answered, firing another shot that struck the back of the man's left leg around the knee, cutting off realistic means of escape by running, walking, or limping into the woods.

Sutton looked ahead when he heard growls and throaty hissing emerging from the woods. Three members of the undead spotted him, and he slowly backed away, hoping they might discover the young man lying on the ground and provide him with a fitting end. All of them kept their eyes locked on Sutton, and he continued to walk backwards toward the cabin, prepared to defend himself against them if necessary.

As they were about to pass the killer, however, Sutton decided to try something. He took aim and put another bullet in the man's right leg, causing him to yelp once again. The noise attracted the undead like piranhas to blood, and they dropped down immediately, sinking their teeth into various parts of his body. He screamed at first, then began laughing uncontrollably. Sutton's expression went from relief to horror as the man made an effort to turn and face him, even as the zombies went about ripping portions of his skin and tendons from his body.

"You're just like me," the man said, continuing to laugh while his eyes locked on Sutton. "You're poison."

A few seconds later, the young man couldn't help but scream as the undead dug deeper into his body, and two more appeared from the woods to help them feast. Sutton saw blood spurt from the man's neck at one point, and he knew mere seconds separated the killer from death. He turned, walking back to the cabin where Driscoll waited on the porch. Only the sounds of the zombies feasting reached their ears at this point.

"You okay?" Sutton inquired.

"Not entirely," Driscoll said, lifting his shirt to reveal the bite mark from earlier.

"Oh, God," Sutton said, hoping he hadn't caused anyone else in his group more suffering. "Was it one of these?"

"No," Driscoll answered, forcing a smile. "I left with a head injury from earlier and got attacked between bouts of consciousness."

Both sat silently a moment, watching the undead feast on the former killer of trespassers.

"You never pushed him for where your son was buried," Driscoll noted aloud. "And I'm sorry for your loss, by the way."

"Thanks," Sutton replied. "I didn't want to know, because I want to focus on the people I have left. Right now, that includes you, so maybe we should get you back and try one of those miracle cures."

Sutton reached to assist Driscoll down from the porch, but the man waved him off.

"I'll be okay. You going to take care of the dead so they don't come after us?"

Without a word, Sutton drew his knife before walking over to the five zombies still munching on portions of the serial killer. He stopped about halfway to his destination because something else emerged from the woods running at top speed, coming straight for him.

"Buster!" Sutton exclaimed, dropping down to greet his dog, rubbing both sides of his head before scratching his ears

Buster seemed delighted to see his master as well, but he quickly turned to growl at the undead that took notice of his nearby run.

"*Now* he shows up," Driscoll lamented, approaching them from behind.

"Where was he?" Sutton asked, stepping forward to stab the first approaching zombie in the skull.

"He walked with me out here until he spotted something in the woods and took off."

"He probably smelled these things," Sutton said.

Only one of the five continued to snack on the young man's fresh corpse, and Sutton dealt with the remaining three that approached him in order of proximity. As usual, he exercised caution, stabbing them from the side so they couldn't snap at him easily with their teeth. His blade got stuck in the third one's skull, but he kicked the fourth one back while working the knife free, like a logger getting an axe unstuck from a fallen tree.

"Why was he with you?" Sutton asked a bit pointedly to Driscoll.

"Your son told me to take him. He said he'd protect me, which he did, until he didn't."

"Probably a good thing he took off," Sutton commented. "The asshole probably would've shot him to make sure he could get to you."

When Sutton approached the final zombie, which ignored him to gnaw on some unfolded intestines, he plunged the knife into the back of its skull, retracting it before the zombie dressed like a painter fell to the ground. His white coveralls, long since covered in blood and muck, began to match the graying skin along his face. Wiping his blade off along the already dirty clothes, Sutton knelt down, hearing a gasp of some sort beside him. Knowing the killer couldn't have already begun his second life, Sutton stood quickly, taking a step back.

Staring down at the young man, he realized the killer hadn't even died. Somehow the undead missed his vital organs, eating at various muscles in the arms and legs for the most part. Nearing the end now, however, the cold-hearted man no longer seemed to consciously understand anything around him as he stared blankly to his left, away from Sutton. He began choking on his own blood, which bothered Sutton, only because he believed the man deserved to be cognizant of his slow, painful, impending death.

He drew his sidearm, starting to take aim because Driscoll required medical attention, and drawing out the process endangered him all the more.

"Knife," Driscoll said. "We don't want more of them."

"Probably more fitting anyway," Sutton said, tucking the firearm behind him before his right hand reached for the blade.

As he did so, the young man took one final gasp, looking skyward at the dark clouds. Along his face, he almost appeared to be grinning, as though satisfied with his death. Sutton shook his head, not wanting to allow the man any of his final wishes. He swiped his hand along the man's eyes, closing them, before using the knife in the side of the killer's skull, ending the ordeal once and for all.

He thought about the trinkets inside the cabin, and all of the victims left in the wake of this man's destruction. Sutton possessed his son's driver's license, having pocketed it before the killer returned. Leaving the trinkets in place might provide answers for friends or family of the deceased, if any were fortunate enough to make it alive to the campgrounds.

"Let's get back," Sutton suggested as Buster took his side, happily wagging his tail.

When they arrived back at the central cabin, everyone stepped outside to greet them. Sutton didn't give them much in the way of highlights, but assured them the killer was dead, and wouldn't be harming anyone again.

While Gracine took Driscoll inside to weigh his options, Sutton took Sean aside, and even Buster seemed to sense impending bad news, opting to walk away from the pair to check the perimeter and use the woods as his personal restroom.

"What is it?" Sean asked, evidently seeing concern in his father's eyes.

"It's Jacob," Sutton answered.

"Oh, no," Sean said, his eyes immediately welling up because he knew the news before even hearing it.

"I found some things inside the cabin, Sean. This guy had been doing this since the apocalypse began. Jake probably didn't have a clue when he got here."

Sutton used his son's nickname, given to him the day he was born.

"What happened to him?" Sean asked, his tone indicating he might not really want to know.

"I don't know exactly. There wasn't a whole lot of conversation between me and the fucker who killed him."

"We should search. Maybe the killer didn't throw away all of their belongings."

"What good would that do?" Sutton asked, thinking that dwelling on the matter only served to add to their anguish.

"I don't want Jake to be just a memory that fades with time," Sean said. "Our cabin is gone, and my cell phone has pictures, but it won't last forever. I don't have anything to remember him by."

Sutton dug into his pocket and produced the driver's license, handing it to his only remaining son.

"We'll search all of the cabins before we leave the area," Sutton assured him. "But we can't stay here, Sean. Not after this."

"I know," Sean said, tears running down his cheeks one at a time.

Sutton pulled him into a hug, feeling his own tears forming at the corners of his eyes. He'd lost one of the reasons for battling the undead, and the living, for months on end. If not for finding Sean, he might have changed his perspective, or gone crazy after dealing with the serial killer.

Leaving Sean to process the information after a few minutes, Sutton went inside to find Gracine holding two syringes in front of Driscoll. One appeared pink, and the other a lime green color, indicating they were different sample batches. Luke and Samantha were in the other room where it looked as though Luke read a book to her to keep her mind occupied.

"It's one or the other," she said, holding a syringe in each hand. "Using both might cause one to counteract the other."

Driscoll groaned at the decision, which might literally mean life or death.

"I hate pink," he said, "but my gut tells me it's the better shot for some reason. Maybe it's the days of pink lemonade as a kid, I don't know."

Gracine pulled the cap off the needle.

"Pink it is."

"Aren't these things usually refrigerated?" Driscoll questioned.

"Isabella didn't say shit about keeping them cold, so I think we're good," Gracine said. "And I'm not sure you have the luxury of being too picky."

Driscoll accepted his fate, allowing Gracine to inject him with the pink serum. She placed a bandage across the puncture mark after that, since they didn't have much in the way of medical supplies.

"Should we have waited for him to show symptoms before doing that?" Sutton asked Gracine once they were alone in another room a few minutes later.

"He was already sweating, and he was warm," Gracine said. "Finding someone else who's immune like Dan is one in a million, and I'm not sure the planet still has a million people."

"It does," Sutton said. "But most of them are assholes."

"I hope he pulls through," Gracine said, shaking her head somberly.

"You've all been giving him the cold shoulder since he joined us," Sutton noted. "He's not perfect, but he's better than most people we've run across."

"He apologized to us before searching for you. Seems he had some regrets."

"Don't we all," Sutton said, his voice trailing off as he thought about losing a son, and costing Jillian her father because he didn't act sooner.

"We'll get through this," Gracine said, taking his hand. "We always do."

Sutton looked into the other room at Driscoll, wondering if her words would hold true. Too many times he'd been disappointed by outcomes since the end of the world. He hated when people knew they were going to die, and inevitably turn, because no words felt right, and there wasn't much to say or do that comforted them.

He supposed soon enough they would learn if the formula was enough to save Driscoll. Even if it worked, how the hell would they let anyone know without compromising themselves?

And Metzger?

Fourteen

Four Days Later

During the first three days following the experimental vaccine's injection into Driscoll's system, Sutton held out hope that it might take. Driscoll remained in a flu-like state with sweating, fatigue, nausea, and body aches. Everyone kept a close eye on him, and Driscoll didn't speak about burning up inside, or the extreme body chills that some people experienced when the end drew near.

On the third evening, Driscoll finally said things were changing in his body, and he didn't think they were for the better. He had remained completely honest with them for their safety, and just before bed, he reported his body feeling incredibly cold inside, and hot along his skin at the same time. The group had remained at the same cabin because Driscoll wasn't well enough to travel, and their needs were fulfilled for the time being.

Sutton found more of his son's belongings in one of the other cabins, and he managed to salvage a few items from the recently burned cabin where the interior collapse had put out some of the fire by cutting off its oxygen supply from the outside. Every so often a few undead showed up, and he dealt with them as necessary. A few occasionally washed ashore from the plane crash in the nearby lake, and Sutton wondered if the plane harbored any supplies that might warrant an underwater search. He thought he possessed some diving equipment in the box truck, but without adequate lighting, such an expedition would be highly dangerous.

During the third evening, the group stayed inside because a cold front made it uncomfortable to sit near the firepit, even with a fire. They remained unusually quiet, as though everyone sensed this might be their final night with Driscoll, because the vaccine managed to stall the inevitable, but not cure him.

"I'm going to close the bedroom door," Driscoll said when he decided to turn in. "And I'm going to tie my leg to the bedpost."

"There's no need," Gracine said.

"I know you can all take care of yourselves, but I don't want to take any chances."

Driscoll had revealed to them that he didn't want to kill himself at any point because Christians considered the act a mortal sin. For the same reasons he didn't want any of them shooting him before he truly died because he didn't want that on their consciences, or their souls. He told them a little bit about his overbearing father, and that, despite some of his father's questionable teachings, he took away the messages in the Bible and believed in scripture.

"I appreciate everything you've done for me," Driscoll said, appearing somber, yet at peace with what he seemed to think was coming. "If this is it, I wish you all safe travels."

Everyone nodded, but not another word was spoken as Driscoll shut himself in the bedroom, likely wrapping himself in blankets to curb the chills that consumed his insides.

Sutton couldn't speak for the others, but he didn't sleep particularly well that evening. Luke kept Samantha in the other bedroom for safe keeping, and the others found their own spots in the main living quarters. Gracine stayed up to read by candlelight, finally blowing out their final light source a few hours after the sun's light left the woods.

After a night of tossing and turning, Sutton stood from his sleeping bag shortly after dawn, quietly making his way over to the room where Driscoll slept. He stood outside the closed door a few minutes, listening intently for throaty growls, snoring, or anything except the silence he received. Knocking didn't feel right, in case Driscoll actually fell into a restful sleep and his body began to heal, fighting through the horrible symptoms that plagued him.

Sutton was about to return to his sleeping bag, but when he turned, he bumped into someone.

"Shit!" he said just above a whisper, discovering Gracine shared his thoughts and curiosity about Driscoll's fate.

"Well?" she asked as Sutton caught his breath from the jump scare.

"I can't hear anything," he whispered. "Maybe he's resting."

"Maybe he's transitioning," she said with a pessimistic expression.

"If he turns, we can deal with that later," Sutton said, beginning to fear they might wake Driscoll with their conversation if he was indeed sleeping.

About to depart the area, they heard the door open from the bedroom behind them, revealing a sleepy-eyed Luke.

"What's going on?"

"We're debating what to do," Gracine answered, keeping her voice down.

Closing the door most of the way behind him, Luke took the few steps required to reach the other bedroom door, listening momentarily with a perplexed look. When he turned to face his friends, he gave a shrug to indicate he didn't hear anything inside.

Sutton motioned for them to move away from the door, and a few seconds later they all stood in the living space, remaining quiet so they didn't wake Sean or Samantha.

"I'm going to get a flashlight and go in there," he said. "This is ridiculous, us standing around like a bunch of school kids about to get caught."

"Fine," Gracine said softly, not objecting since they were all curious about Driscoll's physical state.

Sutton grabbed a functioning flashlight from the kitchen counter and quietly made his way to the room, turning the knob slowly. He stuck his head inside first, trying to listen for any sounds, and sniff the air for the distinct odor of death. His senses detected no abnormalities, so he stepped inside, finding the double bed loaded up with blankets as Driscoll likely struggled to get warm enough. He was about to feel like a complete heel if the man awoke from a good slumber and found Sutton standing over the bed.

At least four blankets created a hump over Driscoll's form, and Sutton couldn't see the man's face because the blankets covered every inch of him. Sutton started to reach for the blankets, but guilt kept him from lifting even one from Driscoll. Calling the man's name seemed equally cruel, so he stood over the bed momentarily, debating what action to take.

Finally, he reached down and carefully removed a few layers of blankets to reveal the side of Driscoll's head, and the man had rolled on his side at some point during the night. Unfortunately, he'd turned the opposite way, so Sutton couldn't get the answer he wanted. Momentary observation of the blankets indicated he wasn't breathing, because they weren't moving up and down as one might expect, but Sutton needed to make certain Driscoll was dead before taking a course of action he couldn't take back.

Using the flashlight to guide him around the bed, Sutton stepped over several articles of clothing, a duffel bag, and a few other objects before reaching the other side. Upon reaching his destination, he shined the light toward the front of the bed, but not directly at Driscoll. Even without bright lighting, he immediately discovered his worst fears had come true. With his jaw partly agape, and his eyes locked in a death stare, Driscoll faced the covered window, recently deceased, but not turned quite yet.

Drawing a heavy breath, Sutton reached for his knife, stepping forward to complete his friend's final wish when the eyes suddenly took notice of him with new life.

"Fuck," he muttered as Driscoll's undead form stood to attack him.

Sutton tried backing up, but the cluttered room tripped him up, and he fell backwards, his back striking the wall hard enough to knock the wind from his lungs. His attacker clumsily stood from the bed to attack him, but tripped as well because his right foot was tied to the bedpost, landing him awkwardly on his back, with his teeth dangerously close to Sutton's feet.

Hearing the noise of teeth gnashing together, like dentures clapping over and over, Sutton pulled his feet back, taking up the knife that fell beside him. His other hand clasped the flashlight so he didn't leave it behind, and he made his way to his feet slowly enough to assess his sore body for injuries. Unable to take the growls and hisses any longer, he bent over beside the shell of Driscoll's former self, which continued to reach and grasp for any part of Sutton it could grab. In one swift move, he plunged the knife downward, penetrating the back of the skull and putting Driscoll out of his misery for good.

"Sorry you had to do that," Gracine said from the door, having just opened it.

"For a second there, I thought it would be easy," Sutton confessed.

Sutton walked to the door, wanting a breather before dealing with burying Driscoll and officially planning their next move. He had discussed some options with Gracine the past few days when the others weren't around, because he didn't want Driscoll to feel they were ready to move on without him. He also wasn't certain that Driscoll wouldn't recover until the previous evening when it became readily apparent the vaccine no longer held back the infection.

After a few minutes, he walked outside, grabbing a shovel from the small tool shed located behind the cabin where a push mower and a few basic tools were kept. Sean approached him once Sutton found a suitable place to dig a hole, not far from the cabin.

"This was our plan," Sean said. "Where do we go now?"

"I have a few ideas," Sutton replied. "My job took me to a lot of interesting places, so I've got some ideas that other groups probably haven't considered."

Sutton caught up with his son when time permitted, but he felt guilty whenever he left Driscoll alone for too long. No one quite knew what to do when Driscoll didn't recover after a day or two. They hoped his body was battling the symptoms, but the pink vaccine appeared to be a dud in the end.

"The others *are* coming, right?" Sean inquired.

"Of course," Sutton answered, as though surprised at such a question.

"You were never much for other people, Dad."

Sutton continued to dig, reaching about a foot deep in the ground at this point, in a rectangle large enough to hold a body.

"Things have changed a bit. I've lost people I cared about along the way."

"Did you have any idea about Jake? Do you think that guy had killed him before your first stop here?"

"I don't know," Sutton answered without trying to sound testy, though he didn't like his son drudging up the past. Personally, he still felt raw about the entire ordeal. "The first time here, things were a little messy. The cabins at our site were gone, there was an airliner in the middle of the lake, and zombies roaming everywhere. Sticking around didn't sound like the best plan."

"But you left the note."

"I did, because I held out hope for both of you."

Sutton continued to dig, feeling sweat begin to drip from his forehead, despite the cooler fall temperatures. He wore a flannel shirt, and the t-shirt beneath it began to collect perspiration.

"Feel like taking a turn?" he asked his son.

"Sure," Sean said, taking the shovel when it was offered.

Sutton rested a few minutes, watching his son continue to deepen the hole.

"I'm going to get Steve's body and wrap it in something. Doesn't seem right just throwing him in the ground."

"You two were close, weren't you?" Sean asked.

"We were," Sutton admitted. "After what happened to Jake, I was holding out hope for some good news. But I guess that wasn't in the cards."

Sutton walked inside, spending a few minutes grabbing one of the blankets from the bed and wrapping Driscoll's body in it. He ended up grabbing a second blanket, because he wanted to keep the worms at bay for a little while longer before they devoured his friend. He supposed even the undead were part of nature, simply eating and keeping the new, unprecedented food chain moving. Everyone else spent their time gathering up what few belongings they brought inside the cabin the first night the group arrived. He carried Driscoll outside, alternating turns with Sean to dig the hole deep enough. They got a little deeper than three feet before rocks and some tree roots hampered their efforts, so Sutton decided the depth would suffice.

Once the body was covered with dirt, the group stood silently over the unmarked grave a few minutes, reflecting on how Driscoll changed their lives during the brief period he traveled with the group.

Not exactly a funeral service, they each paid respect in their own, silent way. After the group departed the grave, they turned their attention to packing what they could into the latest car they'd found, and the box truck, which could barely hold more items. Sutton had decided to bring Buster and Sean with him in the truck, while Gracine would drive Luke and Samantha to their next destination, following his lead as they checked out housing prospects.

Even as the sun emerged from the clouds, rain from the overnight continued to drip from tree leaves all around them. By late morning, everyone appeared packed and ready to travel. Sutton watched Sean usher Buster into the box truck's cab before seating himself. Sutton was about to slide into the driver's seat when he felt a vibration along his right pocket, followed by a ringtone, catching him by surprise.

"What the fuck?" he questioned, pulling out the sat phone Metzger had given him, surprised it continued to maintain a charge since he hadn't plugged it in recently.

He stared at the number before chastising himself for thinking he'd know anyone's sat phone number, because no regular phone worked in the apocalypse. Giving a shrug, he decided to answer it to see if Metzger was checking in with his former group.

***

Over the past week, Bryce continued to trail Fournier through all of Ohio, and into the northeastern portion of Indiana. Fournier stayed along Interstate 90, heading west, and Bryce still didn't know if the man sought a final destination, or another stop along the way. It stood to reason Nadeau set up several outposts to guide his people to him, but he couldn't imagine how Fournier would know about another stop unless he'd committed one to memory and disposed of the original document.

"I'm amazed he hasn't discovered us yet," Molly said as Bryce walked with her along the interstate.

Dotted with vehicles, the interstate presented drivable options, yet Fournier seemed to ignore them for the time being.

"*I'm* amazed he hasn't lost the tracking device," Bryce said. "He throws away a few clothes and we'll be forced to make a decision."

"*You'll* be forced," Molly corrected him. "I'm just your hired muscle."

Both shared a chuckle.

Pulling out the tracking device, Bryce located Fournier's dot a few miles ahead of them.

"He's going south," Bryce noted. "A little place called Goshen."

"Off the interstate?"

"It appears so."

Bryce looked at the device, which kept accurate time because it worked from satellites.

2:34 p.m.

"I'm ready to see a town again," Molly confessed.

"Me, too. This is starting to feel like a wild goose chase, though."

"He's heading somewhere specific. No one takes the interstate for no reason."

"Between cars and the dead, it's a death wish."

Fournier handled himself well during the trek across several states, avoiding the dead when possible, and using weapons when necessary. On a few occasions, Bryce felt certain he would lose track of the man when Fournier commandeered a vehicle and he and Molly remained on foot, unable to locate transportation in a timely manner.

For the most part, they managed to eat regularly, and find vehicles before they actually needed to use them. Molly didn't complain, nor did she speak much about her past before the apocalypse. She implied her life was mundane before zombies came along, as though they gave her a purpose.

During the past few weeks, Bryce felt guilty being away from his family for so long, knowing they expected him to be dead, or wandering as a mindless monster. Poor Nathan probably didn't understand much about the undead, and for that matter, Bryce couldn't wrap his mind around the science of it. Volunteering for the more recent mission wasn't necessary, as the device in his hands proved, but he always liked being at the forefront of the action. Although he was in line to command his own ship one day, Bryce didn't go above and beyond for accolades or promotions. Learning the truth behind Nadeau's plan ate away at his soul, and he wanted to confront the man personally one day, and learn the truth about why the tycoon wanted to murder millions of people.

When he and Molly neared an exit ramp, Bryce heard an odd noise that hadn't reached his ears in over a decade. Standing on the highway, over a road that ran perpendicular to the interstate, Bryce spied a horse pulling a black buggy. Hearing it as well, Molly took his side, looking down at the vintage mode of travel and a man dressed in black pants with a blue shirt, and a wide-brim black hat.

"The Amish," Bryce muttered, having seen them only a few times since childhood.

When he passed beneath them, the man glanced up at them, and for a moment Bryce thought he might act as though he didn't see them, but his eyes locked with Bryce's, and he gave a courteous nod. Bryce nodded in return, and the encounter struck him as odd. He wondered if this man still had to locate supplies for his family, or perhaps the sickness ravaged his people, leaving him alone to fend for himself.

"If anyone is built for this, it's them," Molly said.

"True, but they'd come to rely on people like us, with machinery, to help them out. And gardens are seasonal, so I hoped they canned enough goods to last through winter."

"Let's hope *we're* not here by winter."

Following the directions of the GPS device, Bryce led them down the exit ramp as the clopping sounds of horse hooves trailed in the distance. He detected the odor of manure, which actually seemed refreshing compared to death and random garbage. Unfamiliar with the city of Goshen, Bryce and Molly started south on U.S. 33, wondering where Fournier needed to be. From what they saw when they spied on him in person, he possessed ample supplies, and didn't appear to require much to keep going.

"I feel like this is an important stop," Molly said, echoing the thoughts in Bryce's mind.

"He doesn't deviate like this very much," Bryce surmised. "I wonder if there's some clue, or maybe another safehouse here."

When they reached the city limits, the pair exercised caution because Fournier wasn't visible. The main drag appeared updated, though the buildings were built in the past century when business was booming and world wars occurred. Literally touching one another, as though they were one large building occupying a city block, the businesses were only distinguished by their various colors and signage on their particular brick building. What life the owners once breathed into them now appeared dingy and drab without backlit displays and signs incapable of being lit from within.

Sticking to the alleys, Bryce and Molly kept out of sight since they weren't exactly certain where Fournier was heading. The tracking device put them close, but Bryce knew he needed to stay at least a city block away.

"I wonder if any of these buildings have a fire escape in the back," he said to Molly. "A higher vantage point would be handy."

Looking at the device quickly, Molly got an idea of where Fournier was located before backing down the alley to fulfill Bryce's request. Fournier continued to move along a street ahead of them, possibly searching for a specific location. Bryce couldn't imagine the man needed food, and it felt too soon to search for shelter. A few hours of daylight remained, and Bryce knew the man's habits well enough to know this wasn't a normal stop.

Molly returned a few minutes later, appearing optimistic.

"No roof," she said, "but I gained access to one of these buildings. The downstairs is clear, and there are stairs leading to the second and third levels inside."

Bryce nodded affirmatively, and the pair made their way into the building a minute later, carefully ascending the stairs to the second floor. Bryce didn't need the entire floor cleared, but rather the area facing the front side so they could spy on Fournier. Not hearing anything unusual on the second floor, he pointed upward, asking Molly to lead the way to the third floor for an even better view. She headed up, guided by natural light from a few windows in the common hallway of what appeared to be an apartment building. Both expected a zombie to attack them from either direction in an instant, but no surprises awaited them as they stepped foot on the top level a moment later.

A complete lack of the undead worried Bryce a bit, as though survivors, or another of Nadeau's followers, might have cleared the city and stuck around.

Dust covered the window of the open apartment Bryce chose, so once they cleared the three rooms in the humble living quarters, he propped open the window for a better look outside. He spotted Fournier walking down the street in their direction, so he ducked back from the opening, and Molly took the hint, doing the same. Fournier, however, appeared to be reading some form of paperwork in his hands, searching numbers on the buildings, and street signs to make certain he reached the correct location. His destination was directly across the street, which Bryce considered good fortune if they could see and hear everything the man did, but disastrous if he spotted them.

Fournier reached the front door of a building in the middle of a row of three-story buildings that all ran together, and Bryce couldn't tell how one would guess which door was correct. Carefully peering around the sides of the window, with semi-transparent curtains blowing in their faces, Bryce and Molly watched Fournier knock on the door twice, hesitate, knock once more, hesitate again, and knock three times.

"Interesting," Molly said quietly.

"Indeed," Bryce said, putting the sequence to memory.

Less than a minute passed before an armed man answered the door. A few inches taller than Fournier, he appeared rather intimidating, holding a sidearm in one hand, with a rifle slung over his shoulder. Bryce wondered how tedious life in one of the apocalyptic safehouses must have been, and why the people continued to show loyalty to Nadeau.

"I need passage," Fournier said to the man.

"Name?"

"Xavier Fournier."

Now the man gave him a quizzical stare.

"What's wrong?" Fournier asked.

"We heard about the fiasco up north."

"I had nothing to do with that," Fournier practically pleaded.

Bryce found it interesting that this group, more accurately this network, kept in communication with one another. Nadeau possessed the means and foresight to organize hundreds, possibly thousands of people for a single goal. Perhaps he fed some of them a slanted truth about his scheme, or the lack of options after the apocalypse sealed their allegiance to him, but he certainly didn't plan to decimate the world on a whim.

"The boss isn't happy with you," the man blocking the front door added. "He said you should've laid low and bided your time, not created a slave compound."

"Those people were expendable," Fournier argued. "In the ultimate scheme of things, they were dead anyway."

Bryce felt his blood boil because his parents were among the people termed expendable. He exercised enough calm to surprise even himself, because his mind constantly manufactured new, creative ways to torture the man before ultimately killing him, but he refrained. Above all else, Bryce upheld his commitment to the government that employed him. They wanted to find Nadeau, and very few realistic means of locating him existed.

"I don't think you grasp the situation," the man guarding the door said. "The boss doesn't want any of us attracting attention. You were supposed to lay low and await further orders."

"Things changed," Fournier said. "People wanted shelter, so we put them to work."

"That's not what we heard. Some of your people got here first and told us what happened. The boss isn't happy."

"I can make it up to him," Fournier said. "And where are *my* people?"

"They moved ahead to the next destination," the safehouse guard answered. "Like the rest of us, they know there's a war ahead, and they followed orders."

"I've been loyal," Fournier said, fighting to avoid sounding desperate. "I kept our people safe."

"Safe? You let a ragtag group infiltrate your facility and wipe out most of our people because of the trouble you caused. You aren't going to slip anything past the boss."

Bryce looked over to Molly, who provided a knowing smirk.

"They were jealous of the facility," Fournier said. "They were after what we had, that's all."

After a few seconds of looking doubtful about anything Fournier told him, the man held up a hand.

"I'll make a call," he said before ducking inside, slamming the door behind him.

Fournier shook his fists, openly distraught about being treated in such a way. He'd walked and fought his way to this destination for days, only to have the safehouse's keeper question his loyalty and methods. Bryce watched the man pace up and down the block for just over a minute before he looked to Molly, who wore a scoped rifle over her shoulder. The pair located it in one of the houses they raided, and she told him about how her grandfather taught her to shoot in her younger days.

"You might want to get that ready," he said quietly. "I have a feeling our target is about to make a move, and I won't be surprised if guns are involved."

Molly carefully slid the rifle from her shoulder and stood back from the window to take aim, keeping the barrel back from view. The last thing the pair could afford was to be spotted from across the street when they had remained so discreet thus far. She laid the tip of the barrel down against the base of the window to support the weight of the gun, knowing she might be holding her position a while.

"Where would you like me to aim?" she inquired.

"At the door," Bryce answered. "I have a feeling our guard may bring some friends. We can't afford to lose Fournier now."

Less than a minute passed before the door opened and the safehouse guard emerged, still holding his sidearm.

"Well?" Fournier asked impatiently, as though he wanted to get started on whatever path was now chosen for him.

Without a word, the man raised his firearm, and though Fournier started to say something when the gun was pointed at his forehead, the words never emerged. The shot rang out through the city, sure to attract the undead, but as Fournier's body collapsed, Bryce felt his jaw drop from the pure shock of the situation. If anyone should have killed the man, it should have been him or his brother, and now weeks of walking and scrounging were wasted.

Molly looked to him, equally surprised, but awaiting his next directive. Bryce fought the numbness overtaking his body, forcing his mind to concentrate on the present.

"Shoot to wound if he tries to go inside," Bryce told her. "I'm going down there, so cover me."

"You got it," Molly said.

Bryce raced down the stairs, not particularly concerned about how much noise he made because he felt confident Molly could cover him effectively. As he rounded the stairs from the second story, descending to the ground floor, he drew his sidearm, prepared to get what few answers he might from the man guarding the safehouse.

As he reached the ground floor, Bryce yanked the front door open as a shot rang out, and he spied the man dropping to the ground, clutching the area around his knee as his sidearm dropped to the ground. Bryce held up his pistol, crossing the street while keeping the gun aimed at the man.

"Don't move!" he ordered.

Appearing shocked, the man looked between Molly and Bryce, unable to believe his position was compromised. His eyes shifted to the gun lying beside him.

"Don't try it," Bryce said firmly. "I want answers, but I can have a look inside if you have a death wish."

"Who are you?" the man asked, still clutching his leg.

"Molly, come on down," Bryce said without letting his eyes shift from his prisoner. "I'm with the government. We've been following this man across four states."

"Figures," the guard scoffed. "He's been nothing but trouble for us."

"So I heard. Where is Nadeau?"

Now the man chuckled, which erupted into a light, choppy laugh laced with pained groans intermittently.

"There are so many protective layers between this place and him. You'll never find him."

"I'd be obliged if you provide me with the next safehouse location," Bryce ordered more than requested.

"You won't get them from me," the man stated without falter. "And you won't get them inside, either. We're asked to commit things to memory and destroy the originals. Unlike Fournier and some of his people, I know how to follow orders."

"As do I," Bryce stated. "You can either tell me, or we can keep putting holes in you."

"And risk bringing the dead around? I don't think so."

An awkward silence filled the streets of Goshen momentarily, mainly because Bryce felt he'd entered a stalemate.

"We both know this ends with me dead," the sentry said.

"It doesn't have to," Molly said, crossing the street to take Bryce's side. "You work for a man who did an unspeakable evil. It's not too late to rectify that."

Now the man gave another pained laugh.

"What you just said is from a certain point-of-view. One that's wrong by the way. He didn't do this in the name of religion, or because he suffered some kind of mental breakdown. Whatever you people were told, it isn't true."

"Maybe you should enlighten us," Bryce said.

"I don't think so," the man said, quickly reaching for the gun beside him.

"Stop!" Bryce said, knowing what the man intended to do.

Molly took aim with the rifle at the man, ensuring he didn't endanger her or Bryce. Both watched as he put the gun to his head and pulled the trigger, taking his own life.

Bryce watched the opposite side of the man's head explode outward, spewing blood and brain matter on the building and sidewalk nearby. He drew a heavy sigh, because words couldn't express the emptiness he felt after so many weeks on the road ending in failure. He stared momentarily at the bodies lying at his feet, wondering if any answers awaited him inside, and the sentry lied to him to stall for time.

"I wasn't going to let him hurt us," Molly said evenly, as though the bodies and weeks of travel didn't faze her one bit.

"I know."

Stepping over to Fournier, Bryce searched his pockets until he located the tiny tracking device that allowed him to follow the man across state lines. Placing it in his own pocket for the time being, he suspected another scenario requiring its use might eventually cross his path.

As though inviting them inside, the door remained open, and Bryce had little reason to believe anyone else was holed up with the dead guard.

"We need to check, despite what he said," Bryce muttered numbly.

***

Nearly an hour later, the duo had gone through every inch of the business building converted into a makeshift apartment. It didn't contain an underground lair, like the safehouse in Canada, but the man wasn't lying when he said it contained no paperwork leading them to Nadeau. Instead, they located books, electronic tablets, a laptop computer, and many everyday items one might expect to see before the apocalypse.

Atop the roof, a solar panel provided electricity for the sentry, giving him hot showers, electricity, and creature comforts most people envied in the present. City water would have failed in approximately a week after the apocalypse, so the sentry had a device rigged on the roof to catch water. From what Bryce could tell, he used gravity to filter it down to a water heater, essentially making it well water from the sky.

Although they felt a bit guilty, each of them took a hot shower within the hour while the other continued searching the apartment for useful items or clues. While drying off, Bryce noticed an electric razor sitting beside the sink. He wasn't about to use another person's personal grooming accessories, so he left his beard untouched for the time being.

Having all three stories for one person felt a bit much to Bryce, but he realized guest bedrooms existed for travelers deemed worthy of Nadeau's benevolence. Bryce located dirty magazines while Molly showered, and he didn't mention his find to her, or the books he found about survival and prepping, mainly because they didn't warrant extra attention.

Strangely, the living spaces appeared in disarray, because the man seldom cleaned up the areas, but the guest rooms looked as though they were barely touched during the past few months. Either he kept them presentable, or very few people made it as far as this particular safehouse. All sorts of questions ran through Bryce's mind about how the organization worked, and why Nadeau cared enough about these particular people when he heeded little mind to murdering millions that fateful weekend.

In the kitchen, they located a pantry stocked with some canned goods, but a lot of sealed packets of rations. Bryce recognized them as being the types of food the military and NASA might use because they provided basic nutritional needs and required little space for storage.

"This guy was fanatical," Bryce noted when they found the food and his small stash of firearms and ammunition in another room.

"Enough to kill himself," Molly added. "Who *are* these people? And why such devotion to a maniac like Nadeau?"

"If we knew, we wouldn't be beating the bushes like this."

While they continued the search, finding an older videogame console, and games that could be played offline, along with a few Blu-ray and DVD players, they didn't find evidence of the man keeping anything of use in tracking Nadeau. Even the computer and tablets turned up no information, and though they found a two-way radio, neither dared to use it because they didn't want to give away information that the safehouse was compromised. Because neither of them knew the lingo used by Nadeau's people, code words, or how the process worked, they wouldn't gain anything useful from a radio conversation.

Bryce doubted anyone would answer if he got on there and initiated a conversation or asked for assistance.

Satisfied the converted business offered them nothing else, the two grabbed some rations and a few canned goods for the road. They stepped outside and moved the bodies aside, not concerned in the least about covering them, much less putting them in the ground. Bryce knew Fournier deserved to be picked apart by birds and scavenger animals after his part in genocide. Both of them possessed full packs, and a few extra firearms as they stared at the bodies one last time.

"Where do we go from here?" Molly inquired.

"I'm not entirely sure," Bryce answered. "Nadeau is somewhere west of here, but we stand no chance of locating him now. I guess we head east and see what happens."

"Maybe I can help with that," a voice said from behind them, halfway across the street.

Both Molly and Bryce trained their guns on the man, who held his hands halfway up, not appearing overly concerned.

"And who might you be?" Bryce asked, studying the man.

Reasonably clean cut, the man wore blue jeans and an old New York Islanders sweatshirt. He toted a few firearms, and carried a pack, but Bryce immediately recognized the man's mannerisms, placing him as military in nature because he carried himself well and seemed very self-assured, despite his surroundings. His blond hair was cut very close to the scalp, and even through the bulky clothes he appeared quite fit.

"Sergeant Eric Linderman," the man answered. "I'm with the Two-Six out of Camp Lejeune, and I've been sent to bring you home."

Bryce looked at him, slightly perplexed about a few different things.

"How do you know who I am?" Bryce asked, his eyes scanning his own body from head to toe since he wore civilian clothing.

"I think most of the personnel at Norfolk know who you are now, sir."

"Why would they send anyone for me?" he questioned, "and how on God's green Earth did you find me?"

"You're not the only one with a GPS system, sir," Linderman answered. "They provided me with one, assuming I could track you by tracking Fournier if you were still alive."

"And why would they think I survived? They would obviously know I was bitten by the infected."

Bryce made certain to speak the military terminology, rather than the term 'undead' that so many civilians tended to use.

"They ran some blood tests," Linderman confessed. "Our medical personnel believed if you survived the attack, you'd recover."

"And they told you all of this?" Bryce questioned. "That kind of thing is usually above your paygrade, sergeant."

Even Molly now looked at Bryce, openly wondering why he grilled the young Marine about details. After all, the man offered to get them back safely to the base.

"Sir, it's not exactly a secret at the base. The fact that you survived means they could develop a cure from your blood."

Linderman looked to the bodies on the street.

"Looks like you had a skirmish."

"Not so much us, as them," Molly said. "We got close to locating Nadeau, but he chose the easy way out."

Linderman nodded, though he didn't appear very concerned about Nadeau or the events taking place in Goshen.

"How did you get here?" Bryce questioned.

"I took a civilian aircraft," Linderman answered. "I learned to fly crop dusters before enlisting, so they asked me to come find you."

"Evidently I don't rank *that* high on their list of priorities," Bryce acknowledged.

"How so?" Linderman questioned with an arched eyebrow.

"One man. One plane."

"Sir, they wouldn't deploy a lot of manpower and valuable equipment on a hunch. Limited numbers prevent us from doing things like we used to."

"I know," Bryce said, finally cracking a grin and lowering his firearm. "I'm just giving you a hard time, sergeant."

Linderman appeared relieved.

Fully aware that the Marines would send an elite squad of two to four men during normal operations, Bryce wondered why they hadn't sent at least a few more if he was so important to them. Perhaps the Marine wasn't being completely straightforward, and they sent individuals, or pairs, to track him in various directions from the airport.

"I'm across the Ohio border," Linderman said. "Been following you by foot or car the past few days."

"You ditched the uniform awfully quick," Bryce noted.

"Fatigues," Linderman said. "Call it self-preservation. Some people would just as soon shoot *us* as they would the infected."

Bryce looked to Molly.

"Doubtful we're going to get far before dusk," he commented before directing his attention to the Marine. "The lady comes with us, sergeant."

"Of course, sir," Linderman said without hesitation.

"This aircraft does have more than two seats?" Molly questioned.

"Yes, ma'am," Linderman answered. "Cessna with room for four."

He turned to Bryce momentarily.

"If I may say so, you look like hell, sir."

"Being out here, you tend to go native," Bryce stated. "There aren't exactly packs of razors and hot showers around every corner."

Bryce motioned for Linderman to lead the way toward the plane.

"We can probably get a few hours in before dark," he stated.

"Yes, sir."

"Have you seen my family, sergeant?"

"No, sir," Linderman answered. "From what I understand they're anxious to see you, sir."

"They're still safe at the base?"

"Last I heard, sir."

Getting a good start, the trio walked to the edge of town before spying the first pack of undead ambling their way after hearing the gunfire. What often started as one or two became a mob when something caught their attention and they grouped up, following whichever one took the lead. Bryce counted seven undead, separated by several feet, heading directly for them. He never understood how they could tell the living apart from their own kind, but he supposed the living didn't drag their feet when they walked, or shuffle so slowly.

"You want a crack at this, sergeant?" Bryce asked, cupping the top of his sheathed knife with his left hand.

"I can handle it, sir."

Linderman pulled his own knife out, and Molly assisted with a few of the zombies, keeping things quiet by stabbing them in the skulls. Bryce measured the Marine, observing the man's peak fitness in action, and why he was selected to bring the Navy officer back to Norfolk. Bryce realized he didn't have time for more conflict as the younger man took down five of the seven zombies within a matter of seconds. Bryce waited until Linderman stabbed the final zombie in the skull before swinging the butt of his sidearm against the younger man's head, knocking him cold in an instant.

"Why the fuck did you do that?" Molly asked in bewilderment.

"To avoid springing the trap," he answered a few seconds later, taking a few deep breaths as he scoured the area for more undead, or worse, the living.

Fifteen

Three Hours Earlier

Deciding they were too close to Fournier, Bryce asked Molly to have a look at the rest stop on their right while he checked a few of the cars for useful items. She agreed, and both knew they would need to deal with a few of the undead meandering around the parking lot. Bryce quickly dealt with two in his proximity, spying at least four more that took notice of him. Because they weren't about to reach him quickly, he checked a few cars and found two duffel bags and a backpack in the back of a hatchback that hadn't been disturbed. Unfortunately, a preteen zombie remained in the back seat, determined to keep anyone from getting inside.

"Where are your parents?" he questioned aloud, seeing no evidence of an attack near the car.

He spied a bite mark on the girl's neck, wondering if her parents stayed with her, only to suffer the same fate. If so, they might be wandering in the parking lot, or heading inside the small building where Molly was about to check for supplies. While looking into the rear glass, Bryce caught a glimpse of his reflection, noticing his beard began to look like his brother's because he hadn't shaved since leaving the base in Virginia.

Opening the door, Bryce watched the girl lurch at him and fall forward, striking the concrete with her skull. Taking advantage of her misfortune, Bryce reached down to thrust his knife into her skull, ending her misery. He then turned his attention to the back of the car, popping it open and pulling the first of the duffel bags out for inspection. Strangely, he found mostly maps and family photos in the two bags, though one held a box of ammunition. Some credentials that identified an adult woman as working with the CDC were also stuffed in the second bag. Bryce wondered if she was going to, or escaping her workplace when whatever unfortunate circumstance left the family stranded.

He set the bullets aside, figuring at least one of the parents that left took a gun with the intention of returning. Putting any terrible images aside, Bryce pulled the backpack to the bumper, unzipping it for a look inside.

Sounds of the undead drawing closer reached his ears, and he peeked around the open hatch, finding two a few car lengths away. Bryce sifted through the pack, finding a few granola bars, which he pocketed, a small towel, two unopened water bottles, and clear plastic packaging of some kind. He pulled it out, along with a small box taped to it, finding a small miracle in his hands.

"Could it be?" he questioned, believing he'd found a satellite phone, still in its original packaging, along with a car charger.

He quickly put down the two zombies endangering him, cleaned off the blade, and set to opening up the phone by cutting the plastic packaging. A sticky note contained the phone's assigned phone number, so he stuffed the paper into his pocket with the granola bars. Bryce then slit the seal on the charger, saying a little prayer that the phone was indeed activated before these people met their untimely ends. Once he had everything out of the packaging, he slipped into the driver's seat of the car, plugging the phone into the charging port, trying to get the phone a minimal charge so he could turn it on to see if it worked.

Early in their quest to track Fournier, Bryce attempted to be chivalrous and assist Molly with the undead when they did sweeps for food and supplies. He soon realized she required no help, and she actually grew cross with him when he dealt with the undead in her vicinity. Now he hoped she wasn't in need of assistance, because he powered up the phone, which warned him of low battery power, and dialed the number from memory of the phone his father kept in the kitchen in case of emergency.

Bryce never understood why his father purchased a sat phone, but it worked out, because his younger brother ended up taking it when he visited the family homestead.

Ringing twice before someone picked up, Bryce felt certain it wasn't his brother's voice on the other end.

"Hello?"

"Who's this?" Bryce asked.

"Who's this?"

"Bryce Metzger," Bryce answered, using his real name because it wasn't likely anyone could track him down in the apocalypse.

"Dan's brother?"

"You know my brother? Is he okay?"

"Yeah, yeah. Well, last I knew. I'm Colby Sutton, a friend of his. He gave me this phone before he headed back to Buffalo to look for you. I'm guessing he didn't catch up with you."

Bryce felt stunned that his brother would leave the safety of the military installation to look for him, when he knew damn well Bryce would want him to stay with Isabella and Nathan.

"Why would he come look for me? And why did he give you that phone?"

"He found that other phone in Canada, so he gave me this one because he remembers the number. And it was your wife's idea to come look for you."

"What?" Bryce demanded, raising his voice. "She left the base, too?"

"Yeah," Sutton replied. "They figured out that you two had immunity to the infection and they were keeping your brother prisoner to draw blood samples."

Bryce couldn't believe his ears. People he worked with left him for dead and used his brother as a guinea pig for their experiments.

"Have you talked to Dan?" Bryce inquired.

"He hasn't called, and I don't have the number to that phone. I can relay a message if he calls, though. I'm sure he'd be thrilled to know you're alive."

"That would be great," Bryce responded. "It's unlikely I'll see him again for a while because I'm in Indiana."

"I figured you would've been on your way back to the base," Sutton said.

"Under normal circumstances, yes. Look, I need to get off here and help a friend. Did Dan say where he'd go if he didn't find me?"

"No, but he won't return to the base, and you shouldn't either."

"I don't plan to at this point."

"New York is your home state. Would Dan have a safe spot in mind?"

Bryce considered the possibilities, knowing Isabella wouldn't leave Nathan exposed to the dangers of the undead and impending winter conditions.

"Look, I need to go," Bryce said. "If you talk to Dan, please tell him I'm heading back to New York."

"I will," Sutton assured him.

"Thank you. For everything."

"Good luck."

Both severed the connection at the same time, and Bryce looked up in time to see Molly emerge from the building, stabbing an inattentive zombie in the skull. She searched the parking lot for Bryce, and he felt guilty for not being more help. Taking the phone and the charger, he stuffed them into his own pack, planning to explain the find to Molly later.

He emerged from the car, catching her attention.

"Everything okay?" she asked, tossing him a generic candy bar made of peanuts and caramel that sounded much like a PayDay.

"Yeah," he answered. "Found a few little things."

"These were hiding in a supply room under some other boxes. All the good ones were picked over."

Bryce plucked one of the granola bars from his pocket, tossing it to Molly.

"Found these and some sealed water," he said. "Not much else."

"You sure you're okay?" she asked with a quizzical stare. "You look a little shaken up."

Bryce nodded to the body beside the car, not willing to share the news about his brother and the base just yet. Molly spoke skeptically of the military and the government, despite the position Bryce held within the Navy.

"It's always weird putting down the young ones," he stated. "I can't imagine if anything ever happened to my boy."

"Understood." Molly paused to give him a moment before speaking again. "You ready to roll out?"

Bryce nodded, afraid of being alone with his thoughts while they trailed Fournier. Sutton provided answers, and good news for the most part, but Bryce didn't like the thought of his family being on the road. He also felt betrayed by his employers. Overlooking why he was left behind at the airfield was one thing, but knowing they didn't do right by his brother was another issue completely.

"You want a fresh car?" Molly asked.

Bryce saw five eligible prospects in the parking lot, suspecting at least one might start. They didn't require fast transportation at the moment, but if Fournier swiped a vehicle, they might be hard-pressed to catch up.

"Let's see what we've got," he answered.

Stepping into the car where he discovered the phone, he found keys in the visor, and upon trying them, he discovered the car held less than a quarter tank of gas. He turned the key completely, and the car roared to life.

"Guess we'll save our feet a few miles of walking," he said, forcing a smile.

"We will indeed," Molly said, climbing into the passenger's seat.

***

Now Molly looked at Bryce as though he'd lost his mind.

"This guy was the ticket back to your base," she stammered. "Why would you do that?"

"Norfolk is the last place I want to go right now," Bryce answered, searching his pack for a zip tie.

He located one and used it to secure the Marine's hands behind his back.

"Did I miss something?" Molly asked, looking at Bryce shrewdly.

"You did. I located a sat phone at the rest stop we hit a few hours ago and someone gave me a heads up. I'd rather talk about it once we get moving, because I don't want to risk this kid hearing anything I have to say."

Molly shot him a look that indicated she didn't appreciate being left out of the loop. Because she trusted him, however, she shook her head, not doubting his words for a second.

"We can't just leave him like this," she said.

Bryce realized a subdued person in the middle of a street was a delectable treat for the undead, and fair game for unruly survivors.

After checking a few vehicles in the streets, they found a car that might get them a few miles down the road, and a van already open and cleared of the undead. Bryce located the GPS tracking device on Linderman, taking it so it couldn't be used against him. Bryce then searched him for additional items, finding no sat phone, and only a few weapons. He heaved the Marine into the van and made certain all of the doors were shut tight. He left the man his weapons, but in the front seat where he wouldn't immediately find them to free himself. Bryce felt reasonably certain Linderman possessed a sat phone when he left the base, likely stowing it inside the plane he flew, or somewhere along the way.

Considering he took the emitting device from the body of Fournier, Bryce didn't want to be tracked personally. He knew the military would have other GPS trackers, and other people they could send after him. He figured he might use the device to lead them astray later. He might also be able to find a container capable of blocking its signal until he found another use for it.

"What was that all about?" Molly asked from the passenger's seat once they were a few miles down the road.

Bryce explained the phone call, and what Colby Sutton told him.

"And you trust this guy?" Molly asked without any judgment either way.

"He knew things about Dan, and he wouldn't have a reason to lie. He said Dan gave him that phone and kept the one he found in Canada."

"If that phone was purchased in Canada, would it be able to call phones from other countries?"

"They work worldwide," Bryce answered. "At this point, the only concern is how long the subscription plans will last."

"So, your people sent that guy after you because Dan left the base, didn't they? They're working on a cure."

Bryce nodded.

"At the expense of my brother. But I feel as though my wife was the driving force, because Dan would've stayed near them to keep them safe. Isabella probably guessed I was immune and conned him into escaping to look for me."

"She sounds tough," Molly said with admiration.

"And far more intelligent than me. Now I'm just hoping I can calculate her next move."

"Where could she go once they realize you're not at the airport?"

Bryce hummed in thought a moment.

"Dan would realize you weren't there as well, so he'd assume we got out. Knowing my pragmatic wife, she'd go halfway across the state to see my in-laws."

"Do you think they survived?"

"More than likely," Bryce answered. "While Isabella would want to check on them, she'd be more concerned about reaching the area where they lived."

"What do you mean?"

"They maintained a resort in the Adirondacks. Very isolated, very hard to reach during certain times of the year. And the perfect place to keep my son protected."

"Ah, so she *is* a mama bear."

"And Nathan is her cub."

Heading east felt good to Bryce, knowing he might see his family again. Despite his disappointment that tracking Fournier ended up a complete waste of time, he felt worse that his employers treated his brother so poorly. His future appeared uncertain, but he'd already begun formulating some ideas where they might go if the resort was compromised. He also knew he was realistically a few weeks away from the resort, at best, and winter weather didn't wait until the official start of winter to strike central New York.

Molly glanced in the mirror on her side, squinting as though questioning something she saw behind them.

"What is it?" Bryce asked.

"I think we have company," she answered.

"Ah, fuck," Bryce said as he looked in the rearview, spying a large black Dodge pickup barreling down on them.

"How did he escape so quickly?"

"Apparently the military brass didn't send a chump after me," Bryce answered. "We're going to have to deal with him here and now."

Bryce pulled the car to the side of the road, stepping out and reaching for his firearm in one move. He took aim at the driver's side of the truck, firing without hesitation, but intentionally missing the driver. Now the truck screeched to a halt, and idled momentarily as though the Marine wasn't sure how he wanted to proceed. Superior officers weren't present to give him orders, and he wasn't about to listen to anything Bryce might say.

Stuffing his sidearm behind him, Bryce turned to Molly.

"Cover me," he mouthed the words with barely any sound, so Linderman didn't overhear him. "And if he does something stupid, take out a kneecap."

Bryce stood, waiting for the younger man to exit the truck, which he did after about thirty seconds. When he did, the two men eyeballed one another, and Bryce could tell the Marine wasn't accustomed to failing an assignment.

"Failure is an option," Bryce informed him. "You can tell them you couldn't find me, or I had a group that outnumbered you."

"I'm afraid that isn't going to happen," the Marine replied. "You're coming with me, even if I have to break both of your legs."

"That might be frowned upon," Bryce said. "And I would certainly fight back."

"They said I had to bring you in alive, but they didn't really provide too many guidelines about your condition when I did."

Bryce stepped to his right a little bit, trying to determine if the young man found the knife and sidearm stuff in the front of the van. He didn't immediately see any weapons, meaning the Marine likely hurried to find a vehicle, putting his own safety behind his determination to track Bryce.

"What makes you think you're going to touch me without taking a bullet?" Bryce asked, knowing Molly already had her firearm aimed at the Marine.

Because he hadn't stepped closer to the truck, Bryce left enough distance between him and his adversary to give Molly ample time to aim and fire. Even so, the determined, gritty look etched in the Marine's face indicated he wasn't going to simply give up and walk away.

"I'm ordering you to stand down," Bryce said, playing his last available card before someone received injuries.

"My orders come from far above your paygrade, lieutenant commander," Linderman said before he charged without any warning at Bryce.

Molly fired a shot, which clipped the young man in the leg, but Bryce immediately figured it was a flesh wound, because it didn't slow Linderman one bit. Bryce prepared to strike the Marine in the jaw when he drew closer, but Linderman ducked low and scooped the Navy man up in one fell swoop, dropping him hard atop the concrete with a tackle.

Following that, he immediately went for Bryce's sidearm, reaching around his waist, but Bryce slammed an elbow into the Marine's jaw, buying him a few seconds. Unwilling to be taken hostage, or force Molly to take a shot she might not be willing to make, Bryce reached and snagged the sidearm, tossing it to the side so he and Linderman could duke it out without weapons. His maneuver angered the Marine, only causing the man to strike him several times. Bryce blocked a few punches that would have bloodied his face, but Linderman settled for a few good body shots that bruised his ribs instead.

While Linderman was incredibly fit, having been through boot camp and seen live action far more recently than Bryce, he let his anger get the better of him. Wrapping his hands around Bryce's throat, he attempted to subdue his target by rendering him unconscious, but he also lost sight of Molly, as though she posed no threat at all.

Bryce knew he couldn't reach Linderman's face, or anywhere that might help him out of his predicament, so he tried prying the Marine's strong hands off his throat, managing only to slow the process of him losing consciousness. He struggled to breathe, and Linderman appeared intense, as though he might not stop once he put the Navy officer out. Bryce continued to battle, but he retained the worse of the two fighting positions on his back.

"Stop!" he heard Molly scream as he began to fade.

His vision blurred, and his hearing felt as though earplugs muted every noise around him. It almost sounded like listening to a conversation underwater, unable to make out distinct wording, and Bryce knew he was fading fast.

Molly swung something at the back of Linderman, knocking him away from Bryce momentarily. Sucking in a few desperate breaths while the Marine focused on Molly, he spotted her holding a metal pipe of some sort, and Linderman clutching the back of his head. A few trickles of blood ran down his hand, and Bryce had no idea why the man wasn't atop the concrete unconscious.

"Bitch," Linderman muttered, standing to confront her, giving Bryce a few necessary precious seconds to recover.

Linderman took a few calculated steps towards Molly before his mind apparently realized a firearm remained ripe for the taking, mere yards away from the trio. Bryce's mind reached the same conclusion a split-second earlier, but he couldn't beat the Marine to the discarded gun. Instead, he sprung to his feet and tackled the man when he went for the gun. Both hit the ground hard, but Bryce used Linderman to break his fall, driving his head into the man's chest, knocking the wind from him just long enough to create separation and keep the Marine from assaulting him again.

Bryce got to his feet to discover Molly had already recovered the gun, taking aim at Linderman, who slowly rose, feeling the effects of his various new injuries. He stared at both of them with a mix of anger and determination.

"It's not worth it, kid," Bryce stated. "We don't want to kill you, and shooting your knees won't help your cause. The dead love a warm meal that can't run away, and you'll never get back to your plane."

"They need you back," Linderman said through clenched teeth.

"They sent *you*," Bryce reiterated. "Just you. If I was *that* important, they would've gassed up one of those cargo planes and sent a squad."

"Resources can't last forever," Linderman said. "They're being cautious."

"No, they know someone else with this immunity of mine will come along. They're gambling with your life, sergeant."

"I'm just following orders," Linderman said as though he still wasn't about to give up.

"And I'm going to find my family," Bryce said. "After that, there's a good chance I'll head back to the base, because I want to do my part. Do you have any family left, sergeant?"

"No, sir," Linderman said with some bite on the second word, as though he thought Bryce might be verbally poking him. "Last I knew, they tried reaching kin in Alabama and I never heard from them again."

"Don't give up," Bryce said. "Not until you know for certain. "You married?"

"Not yet, sir."

"Marriage, kids, it changes your world, Linderman. In a good way. I don't want to hurt you, but neither you, nor a hundred of the infected can stop me from seeing my wife and son again. I was a moron for volunteering for a second mission, hoping to find the man who caused all of this. Sometimes it's better to stick around and protect the ones you love instead of playing the hero."

Bryce meant his words, and he could tell that Linderman didn't doubt him. After a few seconds of thought, the Marine relaxed his shoulders, apparently knowing he wasn't going to outmaneuver the duo that spent more than two weeks on the road together.

"What do I tell them?" Linderman asked, forming a sour smirk.

"You've got plenty of time to come up with something," Bryce answered. "Don't tell them I was dead, or that'll look strange when I do return."

Linderman fought off a grin, holding his hands up defensively.

"Fine. I won't follow you again."

Molly took aim with the sidearm at the Dodge, shooting one of the tires, impeding the Marine's ability to follow them if it turned out he lied. The noise would also draw the undead, which might keep him occupied if he didn't find shelter or another vehicle.

"Thanks," Linderman said sarcastically.

"You've got a spare," Molly said. "The next round won't be in a tire if you follow us."

Linderman dismissed the notion with a submissive wave of his hand.

"Good luck, sergeant," Bryce said before turning with Molly to head for their car.

"You too, Commander," Linderman said, addressing Bryce by rank as well.

A moment later, Bryce had the car heading east once more, and Molly turned to him.

"I still don't trust him," she said.

"Can't say I do either, but I think he might have realized a losing cause when he saw one."

"I wonder if his plane even had room for three," Molly contemplated aloud.

"Probably not," Bryce surmised. "And thanks for saving my bacon back there."

"You're welcome," Molly said. "Now, just get our asses to New York before Mother Nature catches up with us."

"Yes, ma'am."

***

For the better part of two weeks, Brad Weir and Mike Mullins headed south, traveling the highways and roads that appeared safest. Former police officers, the two men had kept their uniforms out of a devotion to those they

183

served with who didn't survive the apocalypse. Although they had switched clothes several times over, they kept the uniforms in the packs they carried as they headed for South Carolina.

Weir didn't tend to deviate too far from the course given to him by the people from his church who loaded up a bus and promised to take his family to a safe haven in South Carolina. He remembered hugging and kissing them all goodbye, taking it for granted that a dozen other people could band with them and keep one another safe. One of them was a fellow cop, and two were former military, or he would never have let his wife and kids travel ahead of him.

In truth, he needed to find answers for a colleague he hadn't known incredibly well over the years, but Weir believed in an unwritten code that stated he needed to help his brother in blue.

Even after the answers, several other predicaments kept the duo in Buffalo, and then a random encounter ate at their moral compasses until they detoured to a Navy base in Virginia to provide information to the military brass. Some terrible truths came out during their travels, but they stuck it out, seldom arguing about much of anything.

"I wish I knew something more," Weir confessed as they neared the state border between North and South Carolina.

"What do you mean?" Mullins asked from the passenger seat of the Ford Fiesta they found in a garage at the last house they cleared before a good night's sleep.

"So many things could've happened. They could've changed vehicles a dozen times like we have, they could've gotten lost, or-"

"Don't think like that," Mullins said, trying to calm his friend.

"I've been thinking like this the whole time. I just haven't said very much about it."

Mullins stared out the window momentarily as a frail, male zombie dressed in a tattered suit swiped a hand at the passing Fiesta.

"We'll be there soon enough."

"And what if they're not there? Backtracking all this way would take forever."

"You left them in good hands, Brad, or you wouldn't have left them in the first place. And you're making me feel like shit because I held you back."

Weir sighed weightily.

"I'm sorry. Look, you didn't force me to stay. In fact, you really didn't even ask."

"Just the same, I'm eternally grateful you stayed behind. If I'd have found my family and I was all alone, I might not be here right now."

Weir said nothing, getting the gist of what his friend meant. Now he found himself in the exact same position, and not knowing tore him apart from the inside.

He felt as though he and Mullins had discussed virtually every topic from their former careers to the military involvement, or lack thereof, in the post-apocalyptic world. Mullins had served four years in the Army, and felt more could be done than simply having military personnel reside at a base and re-store the adjoining town. With their stored weapons and ammunition, he argued, they could begin to eradicate the threat and put the world back together before civilization fell backwards, literally centuries, to an age before electricity and functioning motor vehicles. Without fresh fuel, the vehicles they currently drove and dumped, would be roadside museums in his opinion, within the year.

"When we find your family, are we staying down here for certain?" Mullins asked, as though some different ideas ran through his mind.

"I guess it depends. Why do you ask?"

"I don't like the way the military is handling things."

"Planning a one-man coup, are you?"

"Nah. Those kids are following orders."

"So are their leaders."

"And their leaders are following orders blindly, from a hierarchy that barely exists. They're probably hidden away in some bunker, unaware of the struggles we have up here."

Both Mullins and Weir neared fifty years in age, so both knew about life-long struggles and obeying orders, even when the orders weren't sound.

"I don't know what difference it would make, but I'd like to go back," Mullins said as though his notion felt unrealistic.

"You were military," Weir noted. "I know you don't think they're mindless robots just following orders. They need good people on their side, because pretty soon wearing a uniform isn't going to make a difference."

"How so?"

"That Nadeau guy obviously has followers, even now. Until he's found and dealt with, there's always going to be a threat."

"You saying I should go vigilante and hunt him down?"

"I'm saying," Weir started to reply when his eyes locked on something that concerned him ahead in the highway. "Oh, shit."

"What?" Mullins asked, obviously not spotting the same issue.

"That's the bus," Weir said, his eyes wide with apprehension because the royal blue bus with yellow lettering was parked at an awkward angle along the slow lane and the highway's shoulder.

He drew close enough to read the side of the bus, just to be absolutely certain.

Williamsville Baptist Church.

"Has to be," Mullins muttered, taking notice of the New York State plate on the rear bumper.

When the car came to a stop, both men exited hurriedly, approaching the bus on either side, looking and listening intently. On the left side, Weir thought he heard a growl from inside that sounded like the undead, but he took notice of the thin, dusty layer covering the paintjob. He wondered how long the bus remained stranded along the road, and what happened to the passengers inside the vehicle.

Reaching the front, he and Mullins locked eyes, both knowing what needed to be done next. Mullins led the way to the hinged door on the right side, and gave the door a few knocks, noticing it wouldn't take much to push it aside and step into the bus.

A single growl reached their ears, but it didn't come toward them. Weir wondered if someone died on the bus before or after the other passengers departed. The sole zombie, assuming there really was only one, might be strapped to a seat, or trapped beneath a heavy object.

"Step back," he warned Mullins before giving the door a moderate kick that caused the hinges to move the door slightly to one side.

He finished moving the door, sweeping it aside with his left arm and his right hand brought a Glock 22 from his work days to his side.

Still, nothing dangerous emerged, and reasonably sufficient sunlight pierced the windows, despite the dusty coating, so he stepped inside, cautiously looking around. He quickly noticed the source of the noise near the back of the bus, restrained by a seatbelt that barely allowed her to grope in Weir's direction and growl at him.

He stepped down the aisle as Mullins entered the bus, both men looking to the floor for any initially unseen hazards. Once he cleared the aisle and reached the woman wearing a pink windbreaker and fashionable glasses, he studied her face momentarily.

"Recognize her?" Mullins inquired.

Weir thought back to everyone making their way onto the bus. He wished he knew more people from the church he and his family attended before the world fell apart, but he truly knew a handful of churchgoers who weren't in his everyday life, and recognized almost as few.

"I can't be sure," Weir said. "A *lot* of people attended our church."

"This isn't a bad thing," Mullins said, drawing closer to study the bite mark on the woman's arm, which penetrated the material of her windbreaker. "She probably got bitten and strapped herself in so she didn't hurt anyone."

"I hope."

"We keep looking," Mullins urged. "They ran out of gas, or had a malfunction, and picked up another vehicle. We're just a few hours away from their destination."

"A few hours under ideal conditions in the old days," Weir corrected him. "We're at least a few days out, but you're right. There's no evidence that anything terrible happened to them."

Mullins drew his knife, swiftly stabbing the zombie in the skull, ending her torment. He pulled the blade out, letting her body slump toward the bus window where it would begin to disintegrate, adding to the food supply for bugs and rodents that feasted on dead flesh.

"Well, we keep going until we find your people," Mullins said, holding out his fist, as he wiped the blood from his knife onto the closest seat.

Weir forced a grin, forming a fist with his left hand as he holstered his firearm. He bumped his buddy's fist with his own, forming a pact with Mullins, even if he harbored fears in the back of his own mind.

Only time would tell what fate had in store for the two officers at the tail end of their quest.

Sixteen

For one reason or another, none of the buildings and communities Sutton and his small group checked seemed to work out. Some were overwhelmed with the dead, a few appeared in complete disrepair, and some were occupied by other survivors. It appeared residents of Virginia thought alike when it came to their dream apocalypse abodes.

"This isn't working out very well," Gracine informed him as Sutton drove the box truck down the road toward another small town she found on the map.

Small towns, it seemed, were also plucked clean of supplies, which meant they relied more and more on the goods stored in the back of the truck. Sean decided to ride with Luke and Samantha in their most recent vehicle acquisition, a Nissan with good gas mileage. Although he didn't say it, he appeared smothered by his father over the past few days as Sutton tried to reconnect with his eldest son. Several moments passed where one of them wanted to bring up Jacob, but neither dared start the conversation about Sutton's youngest son or his untimely passing.

Unfortunately, Sean took Buster with him when he switched vehicles.

"What isn't working out?" Sutton asked.

"Finding a new home."

"There are tons of places out there. We just need to be creative."

"It's too bad your cabin burned down. We could've lived on fish forever."

"Yeah," Sutton said thoughtfully. "There's something to be said for food and water."

Gracine sat quietly a moment, and Sutton could tell that her mental gears were moving when he glanced over. He navigated the truck around a few stopped cars, along with a few staggering dead, and decided to ask what she was contemplating.

"What is it?"

"What?"

"You're thinking about something."

Gracine grinned without looking in his direction.

"I'm thinking about this place where I did a very high-end delivery back in the day. It was part of a small, gated community with some incredible houses."

"The same kind of houses we've had no luck securing so far?"

"The same kind."

Already tired of dead ends, and frustrated that his own apocalypse plan was likely done in by a fire bug serial killer, Sutton debated whether he could stomach another waste of time. He really couldn't, but he also knew that every nice house and community in the greater Virginia area couldn't be claimed by the living.

"How far?" he inquired.

"That's the thing. I'm trying to remember which town it was near."

"How do you not remember something like that?"

"I can remember the community like it was yesterday," Gracine said, "but I took thousands of trips in my days as a truck driver."

"Maybe the map can refresh your memory?"

"Thanks," she replied. "I hadn't thought of that."

Sutton caught her sarcasm, but she did pick up the map for another look just the same. Sutton continued driving, wishing he could stop every few miles to relieve his frustrations by dealing with some of the undead meandering in the highway. While he didn't mind Metzger's credo about every dead zombie being one less threat, he certainly didn't live by it. He wasn't some weirdo who got his jollies by toying with the undead before killing them, but Sutton did consider them a great form of stress relief.

"It might be here," Gracine said, pointing to a spot on the map.

Sutton stole a glance, finding the destination west of their current location. "Lynchburg?"

"It sounds right. Unfortunately, I won't really know until I see the town."

"Big factory and Civil War town," Sutton said, throwing out a few general facts.

"That doesn't exactly give me a visual, Colby."

"I can't call up images on my phone. Sorry."

"Guess we're going to Lynchburg then."

"I guess we are."

***

When Sutton drew near the small city, coming in from the east, he found a threat in the form of undead wandering the streets in mob form. For some reason, their numbers hadn't been thinned, or something attracted them to the city.

"I'm not sure I'll be able to get you that visual," he told Gracine. "This is too thick to drive through."

Gracine stared ahead momentarily, not focusing on the undead as she concentrated to remember the landmarks and which way she went through town.

"It's southwest of town," she said, her eyes immediately diving into the map. Follow 460 as long as you can."

Sutton headed west on the indicated highway, working his way around the undead. Their travel appeared to draw the zombies toward them, meaning he needed to pick up speed at some point to lose them.

Once they made their way along the outskirts of town and exited the south end of Lynchburg, Sutton put a safe distance between the box truck and the undead before stopping. Behind him, his son stopped the car because he had taken over driving duties to allow Luke and Samantha some rest.

Sutton opened the back of the box truck, digging a few feet inside the stacked boxes until he located what he wanted, hoping to lead the undead away from them.

"What are you doing?" Gracine asked, her face drawing a perplexed expression.

"This," Sutton answered, drawing a lighter from his pocket before lighting some fireworks and angling them so they shot into the air, noisily exploding.

Gray clouds left the fireworks barely visible in the late afternoon sky, but the undead were easily distracted, and the noise might be enough to keep them occupied. Sutton found a different type that launched higher and farther, so he lit them and let them fly behind him. They exploded almost directly overhead from the undead.

"A few more," he said, "and hopefully they'll keep looking skyward."

"This won't work unless we make a clean getaway," Luke commented.

"We should," Sutton said. "The road ahead looks clear for the next mile or so."

Lighting off the last of the fireworks, Sutton urged everyone to get into their vehicles before he and Gracine led the way down the highway. His plan worked, and the undead remained distracted long enough for them to get a head start. Gracine began looking for familiar landmarks again, but a few miles passed with no word from her.

"Nothing yet?" he asked.

Gracine groaned as though perhaps something appeared familiar to her, but she couldn't quite narrow it down.

"It just isn't clicking," she said just above a whisper.

Nearly another two miles down the road, Gracine stared at a sign beside the road, even when Sutton passed it. Beyond the sign, a double iron gate sat nearly fifty yards off the road, and behind it, several large houses barely appeared over the shrubs and the gate. Trees surrounded much of the property, hiding it from view and likely deadening any noise from within. Hitting the brakes, Sutton slowly turned around so Sean had time enough to follow his lead.

He stopped in front of the sign, providing Gracine additional time to determine whether this was the place she visited during her trucking days.

Sutton finally looked at the plate, which identified the community beyond the closed gate, and he wondered if any of the houses had vacancy.

"Maplewood," he said the name aloud.

"That's it," Gracine said, openly confident about the discovery. "There was a collector in there who purchased a motorcycle and it was one of my stops."

"I thought you did long haul trucking."

"I did a little bit of everything," Gracine said. "I had different employers over the years."

Parked near the sign, everyone exited the vehicles, taking a look around as gray skies above threatened snow. Temperatures remained near freezing, which left them in peril of driving through freezing rain if they continued down the road, or didn't find shelter behind the gates.

"Not exactly welcoming," Luke noted, seeing the gates shut and foreboding.

"Leads me to think someone might actually live here," Sutton said.

A few undead staggered down the road in their direction, and as one emerged from some nearby trees and growled at the group, they turned their attention to it. Sutton slowly reached for his knife when a woman emerged from the trees, stabbing the zombie in the skull with a most unusual weapon.

In fact, everything about her appeared unusual, considering she was dressed like a Catholic nun. For a moment, everyone in the group stared at her with curiosity, and Sutton noticed her olive complexion, as though she might be from overseas.

"What?" she asked, looking at the group, speaking with a thick Spanish accent. "Haven't any of you seen a woman of faith before?"

In her right hand, dripping blood from the zombie's skull, she held a sturdy metal crucifix with a sharpened end. As though the scene before them weren't odd enough, a man stepped from behind her, wearing the black clothing and the white collar of a priest. Appearing to be in his early forties, at least ten years older than the nun, he bore a full, thick beard of red hair that matched the fringe of hair around his head. He looked from her to the group with anticipation in his brown eyes, as though waiting to see if they made a move.

"Do you folks live here?" Gracine asked, breaking the momentary silence.

"We do," the priest said slowly, as though compelled to speak the truth at all times.

"Oh," Gracine said as though their hopes of getting through the gates were suddenly dashed.

"We have room," the nun said, drawing a concerned look from the priest that escalated to a bit of anger.

"It's not our place," he said, addressing his colleague, though loud enough that Sutton and the others heard.

"We aren't looking for trouble," Sutton said, attempting to get them through the gates via peaceful means. "We're just exhausted after so long on the road."

"I'm not trying to be rude," the priest said, his expression softening. "Behind those walls is a community, and they were kind enough to invite us in. I'm sure we can get the leadership to meet with you. If nothing else, we can probably put you up for the night."

"Thank you," Gracine said before Sutton could reply. "That's very kind."

She turned to look at Sutton, openly wondering if she prevented him from saying something that might lead them to trouble.

"I was being diplomatic," he said just above a whisper. "I swear."

"What is that?" Luke asked the priest, who held a rather long staff in his right hand, with a sharpened point at the end.

It appeared metal in nature, and as he looked at it, Sutton believed it might be a display crucifix from a church.

"It's what it looks like," the priest answered. "I took it from my church and did a little modification."

"That's one way to use the body of Christ," Gracine commented so only Sutton heard.

He said nothing, simply shaking his head a moment.

Excusing themselves with little more than a word, the religious duo headed toward the dual gates where they were allowed inside. Sutton and the others waited less than five minutes before the gates opened once more and they saw people inside waiting for them.

No less than a dozen people from the village stood at the gates, studying Sutton and the group as though judging them for a crime. Each of them held a firearm, pointed downward, sending a message that Maplewood was occupied. Both the priest and the nun stood near the front, and the priest stepped forward.

"I suppose introductions are in order," he said. "I apologize for not doing so before. I'm Father Paul, and you already met Sister Rosa. Folks, this is Robert McAllister, and his wife Nancy."

He nodded toward an older couple standing in the forefront of the group, appearing experienced and not intimidated in the least by strangers standing at the threshold of their quaint village. Both possessed white hair, appearing to be in their early seventies, and dressed in rather clean, contemporary clothing considering they stood in the center of an apocalypse.

Robert sported a full head of white hair, looking as though he belonged in Beverly Hills with his riches, because he somehow maintained a tan despite the recent turn in the weather. His wife maintained a short haircut, practical in the current times. She dressed a bit more conservatively, blending in with the people around her, though she appeared unfazed by the strangers before her. Wearing blue jeans and a green flannel shirt, Nancy's face displayed a few dirt streaks, as though she'd been doing some outdoor work when the religious duo spread the word about strangers at the front gates.

"Our scouts spotted you down the road," Robert McAllister stated, his eyes unblinking. "You don't appear to be harmful people, but we've been burned before."

"You seemed to have survived whatever issues you had," Sutton said.

"This place has been standing since the start of things. We've endured a number of things."

"So have we. We're a bit weary of the road."

Nancy stepped forward.

"What's in the box truck?" she inquired, as though it might be an incendiary device meant to bring down the entire community.

"Supplies," Sutton answered. "I had a camp by the water, but the entire complex was wiped out by fire. We were turned away by the military at Norfolk, so we're running out of options."

Silence filled the air a moment, and Sutton felt certain they were about to experience life on the road again.

"We're being rude," McAllister finally said. "Leave your weapons and the truck outside the gates, and we'll discuss this over dinner."

***

Within a few hours, the group was shown around the gated community, though they weren't allowed inside any of the buildings. Members of both groups interacted, and it became obvious they were being tested, if not groomed, for occupancy within the gates. At first, Sutton tried to frame all of his responses accordingly, but he finally decided to be a bit more forthcoming, because the residents appeared to want a true depiction of the new group.

He spoke with several people, but none of them gave answers that varied much from other residents. Sutton began to believe they were coached to give only surface information that revealed nothing about the inner workings of the community. Being pragmatic as usual, Sutton observed that only half of the community appeared to carry firearms. Some of them worked outside, and he began to notice a pecking order of sorts where some people did certain jobs that suited them, or assignments given in exchange for some unknown favor.

He counted twelve houses in all, with a few smaller, common buildings along the grounds. A pool and workout facility were likely built with home-owner association money before the apocalypse, but now the pool looked only halfway full with fall leaves floating atop its dreary water. Sutton estimated the price of the large houses before the world collapsed, knowing he could never afford one with his previous salary. By no means destitute, he knew the limits of his means, and a community where people purchased exotic vehicles and pets online wasn't in his price range.

"Can I ask you something?" Sutton asked when Father Paul took a turn showing him around, though the group had been informed dinner was nearly ready.

"Sure."

"How did you come up with that?"

Sutton referred to the long crucifix the priest carried with him to deal with the undead. It separated into two parts, both iron, making them easier to carry. They screwed together when Father Paul required their use, resting in a modified backpack when he didn't need them. Sutton likened the pack to the one Metzger used to carry his swords, both practical and sturdy.

"My father was a machinist," the priest answered. "He taught me quite a few things growing up, including how to work metal and customize it. I followed Sister Rosa's lead and saw the potential in this as a weapon, both for stabbing, and as a spear."

"You divided it into two parts?"

"Yes. Part of me feels bad about using a religious prop as a weapon, but there's a story behind that for another time."

Sutton heard children laughing, and when he glanced, he found Samantha playing with two other neighborhood children as they chased one another around one of the houses. He grinned, hoping against the odds that they might be welcomed into the community.

"You care about them, don't you?" Father Paul asked with a comforting grin, accented by rosy cheeks brought on from the cold.

"I suppose," Sutton answered, trying to fend off emotions because he needed to be scouting the grounds.

"You're their leader. There's nothing wrong with saying you care."

"I'm no leader," Sutton scoffed.

"They look up to you. Gracine says you've saved them on several occasions."

"I'm a father who's been looking for his sons. Not like the kind of father you are, because I've done it before."

Father Paul looked at him curiously with arched eyebrows as they stopped walking momentarily.

"Isn't that a thing?" Sutton asked almost defensively. "You're not allowed to-"

"You're correct," Father Paul answered, breaking into a smile. "We aren't allowed to have sex."

"Ever?"

"Ever."

Sutton began to realize the group had been handed off to different people several times over, which meant they were looking for inconsistencies in their stories. He actually admired the caution they exercised, which caused him to like the group even more. He took notice that all four corners of the grounds possessed recently constructed towers just as tall as the trees surrounding the property. Any higher and the towers would be easily spotted from down the road, which would certainly alert travelers to the existence of the community.

"Dinner's ready!" Nancy McAllister called from the largest house in the gated community.

"You said you were taken in," Sutton said as he and the priest strolled toward the house. "You had no affiliation here?"

"Not really. A few residents knew me from church and thanks to their generosity, Sister Rosa and I were welcomed inside."

"Do you still hold church services?"

"We call it mass, and yes, we do."

Sutton tapped his right hip, feeling naked without the weight of a knife or gun. Looking around, he saw everyone from his group approaching with different tour guides, or chaperones in this case, anxious to see what the future held.

Almost like a football huddle, their original group met outside the front door momentarily while everyone else went inside, or to their respective houses if they weren't invited to dinner.

"If there's any chance of us staying here, we can't blow this," Gracine said, her attention focused on Sutton more than the others.

"This is too good to be true," Luke said. "I haven't felt this secure since I left my house in New York."

"I don't want to get anyone's hopes up," Sutton said. "They were incredibly cautious while showing us the grounds."

A few seconds passed and no one thought of anything else to contribute to their conversation.

"We're being rude," Sean finally noted, nodding at the open front door since everyone else awaited their presence inside.

A few minutes later, they were seated at a table for twelve with the community's power couple, the priest, and the nun. A fire in one of the two downstairs fireplaces kept the house warm, and candles provided the light atop the table. Sutton immediately smelled something delicious, thinking it might be a roast of some sort, but he couldn't imagine where the community might find beef.

"You must be famished," Nancy said as everyone took a seat.

Platters with potatoes, carrots, gravy, and the meat Sutton smelled occupied the long table. He felt certain they were about to be murdered, or initiated into the community, at least for the evening. In a pan, atop the nearby counter, Sutton felt positive he spied brownies, causing his mouth to water.

"You're probably wondering what the roast is," Nancy said as she cut it into manageable slices before distributing them. "One of our better hunters shot a deer yesterday, and allowed us to reap the rewards with you folks."

Sutton began to question the excellent treatment, not in a suspicious way, but rather his group possibly filling a need. While they might have found residents capable of shooting animals, he wasn't convinced they possessed people skilled in dealing with the living. He felt as though the people he strolled with around the grounds conducted a rather informal interview, and for his part, he answered honestly. Yes, he had killed the living during their travels, but Sutton didn't consider himself a murderer. In each instance he defended himself, or the group when he took a life.

Everyone received a plate full of food and dove in, enjoying their first truly good, warm meal in quite some time. Not until they were about halfway through the dinner did the conversation pick up again.

"I hear you've had your struggles out there," McAllister commented, directing his words at Sutton and Gracine, who sat beside one another.

"It hasn't been easy," Gracine answered. "We were lucky to find one another."

"And I'm sorry for your losses," McAllister said genuinely.

Everyone ate in silence for another minute or two.

"Not to be rude, sir," Sutton said, breaking the silence, "but this whole thing feels like an interview, or a test."

"Very astute, Mr. Sutton," McAllister said. "We can't have dangerous people walking around our community. I'm sure you understand our caution."

"Fully. I wouldn't want strangers knowing the layout of my community either."

"We have a tightknit community," Nancy said. "It's amazing how the end of the world turned some people into monsters. We don't want those kind of people here."

"You've been very quiet," Sean said, addressing Father Paul and Sister Rosa. "You obviously like it here, right?"

"It certainly beats being out there," Father Paul answered. "It amazed me that when social constraints were removed, some people reverted back to primal instincts."

Everyone paused to take a bite from their meals.

"Does any of this make you question your faith?" Sean asked the pair.

"If anything, it's strengthened my beliefs," Rosa answered. "God has provided for both of us by protecting us within these walls."

"We're hoping to create a church in the community," McAllister said. "One thing we need in this world is faith."

Sutton wasn't entirely sure faith would carry the day against the threats that lingered outside of the walls. He didn't want to bring a negative cloud over their heads at an otherwise festive dinner, so he remained quiet.

"What happened to your congregation?" Gracine asked Father Paul directly.

"When things went bad, it seemed the church was the last place they turned," he answered solemnly. "Most of them scattered to find their families and protect what little bit they owned. "Sadly, I didn't see most of them again."

"We stayed at the church several days," Rosa added. "We only saw a few familiar faces, and some of them weren't as we remembered."

Sutton realized he didn't need to bring pessimism to the table, because such a sad tale took care of that for him.

"I think we've all seen those faces," he said, recalling the early days when he struck out on his own, before he left his home area.

McAllister cleared his throat.

"That being said, you have a child, a friendly dog, and an interesting blend to your group. We were initially going to provide you with a hearty dinner and shelter for the overnight."

"And now?" Gracine asked curiously.

"We took a look in the box truck."

Sutton felt his blood boil, because no one asked his permission to unlock and search his truck. He began to shove his chair back, but McAllister sensed his hostility, quickly holding up a hand.

"Rest assured, we merely looked, Mr. Sutton," he said. "Should you choose to move along, we'll supply you with a new lock and key. Nothing was touched or removed."

"What is this all about?" Luke asked, speaking his first words at the table. "This whole thing feels like a background check."

"In a way, it is," Nancy replied.

She looked to her husband, who provided a nod of agreement.

"If you're interested, we'd like to offer you the last of our houses here on the grounds."

"It isn't grand," McAllister said quickly. "We have water from the well. All of the houses have woodburning fireplaces. There isn't any power, but we're working on a solution for that."

"That's generous of you," Sutton said, "but I feel as though this offer isn't simply out of the goodness of your hearts."

"I'll be blunt," McAllister said. "We would expect you to share your supplies with the community, and we ask that you assist us with keeping the place up and running. You have experience with the dead, and deadbeats of the living variety. We have books, we have firewood, we have running water, and we have walls. It's not an unfair trade, but we aren't going to force your hand. You're welcome to spend the night and sleep on the decision."

"I don't think there's a need to ponder the decision," Sutton said, drawing wide eyes from his group, mainly because they expected him to flatly turn down the offer.

In the past, when his future appeared far less clear, Sutton might have gathered his family, and his dog, and lived as long as the box truck allowed. After the events at the Navy base, and later his former campsite, Sutton no longer desired to travel. He wanted to keep Sean and Buster safe, and he'd grown to care for the others who traveled with him, even if he seldom admitted it. Additionally, Gracine kicked him in the foot several times, indicating she didn't want him to act as he'd done in the past.

"How about we toast to our new partnership with some of those brownies over there?" he asked, drawing relieved smiles and laughs from everyone at the table. "If that's alright with my cohorts here."

"Yes, it's okay," Gracine said, and the others nodded in agreement, outwardly ecstatic about the thought of staying somewhere more than a night or two.

Seventeen

Early December

Metzger grew accustomed to knowing the date and time on a regular basis thanks to Isabella's parents and their use of clocks and calendars in every building on the property. Phyllis and Harold grabbed the necessities whenever they raided a store or abandoned home, but they also took items that kept their lives a little more normal.

"Keeps us sane," Harold sometimes said.

Winter came early in the mountains, and Metzger had volunteered to take over the duties of scouring through nearby towns, particularly businesses and homes that hadn't been looted yet. People didn't tend to gravitate to the Adirondacks, because both creatures and the undead occupied the woods, ready and willing to devour the living.

Travel up and down the mountain proved challenging, despite having paved roads, because snow removal no longer existed on a larger scale. Harold occasionally used his tractor to clear paths between buildings, and around the start of the road downward, but he couldn't spare the fuel to travel very far down the road.

On this particular morning, melting icicles dripped water from tree branches onto the ground as a warm front swept through the area. Metzger knew snow remained a possibility between the months of October and April for much of the state, so he decided only a few trips remained to forage for goods down the mountain. After dressing for the weather, he stepped outside and cleared off the gray Prius, prepared to take it into some areas Harold marked on a map that hadn't been checked.

"I'm going with you," Timmons said, joining him in the parking lot and wiping an arm across the windshield of the car, pushing the snow away.

Timmons wore an insulated parka and a pair of duck boots he found during one of their earlier runs, to shield his feet from cold and wetness.

"This should be a quick run," Metzger said, wiping off the driver's side window and seeing his own bearded face after a month without shaving or trimming it back. "There's no need to risk it."

"You wanted me to prove my intentions, right? This is how I do it."

"You've been doing your fair share around here, Scott. And you know I trust you."

Timmons continued wiping down portions of the car with his parka sleeve. Snow throughout the parking lot became a white mush in the early morning hours, easy to step through, but not ideal for driving certain vehicles.

Within a day of their arrival, everyone was provided with sleeping quarters in one of the cabins behind the main building. During daytime hours, everyone utilized the building for cooking, gatherings, or reading. Harold converted one of the smaller rooms in the main building into a pantry, and sometimes a member of the group cooked for the others. Metzger questioned how their life off the grid compared to a vacation in the area before zombies roamed the planet. Never in his life had he listened to so many compact discs, or read so many novels. Like the others, he sometimes perused books that helped with their situation by telling them how to build, grow, or cook certain items. He vowed that if he found animals in the wild that could be caught or tamed, he would attempt to, so they could expand their farm on the mountain.

No one knew exactly how long such a large group could exist on the property without growing their own food and finding replacements for the appliances and machines certain to break in the future.

Between the two of them, Metzger and Timmons wiped off the Prius in under a minute as the car's dark paintjob helped soften the snow that fell on it the past two days. Sunlight warmed Metzger's skin, and he sensed the temperature might reach the low fifties at some point. He wasn't willing to wait because descending the mountain roads in the snow wouldn't be an issue. His plan involved making three or four stops if time permitted, and by then the roads might be clear of the elements. If snow and ice remained, however, Metzger knew he might need a hand pushing the Prius out of any snowdrifts.

"I have to go," Timmons insisted once the Prius became fully visible. "I'm going stir crazy around here."

Metzger chuckled.

"Fine," he said. "But what I say, goes. We can't be wasting time out there and heading back after dark. The last thing we need is people spotting us."

"Understood."

Metzger walked inside, finding everyone gathered in the main building, finishing a breakfast of eggs and some sort of salad.

"Want some?" Isabella offered.

"I'm good, thanks."

"You're up early," Jillian noted.

"The captain and I are making a run. The sun is out and the snow is melting. We may not get many days like this before spring."

"Need some extra hands?" Jillian offered.

"I appreciate it, but I've got a few things to discuss with Scott."

"Suit yourself," Jillian said, rising from the bar stool style seat where an island and kitchen table combination butted up against the kitchen, making it easy for everyone to converse.

She planted a quick kiss on his lips, considering any secrecy to their blossoming relationship died a few days after their arrival to the mountain. More often than not, the pair shared a cabin, and they began to learn more about one another's past lives because the tranquility of their setting allowed for more communication.

"Anything else for the wish list?" Metzger asked, holding up the sheet of paper with more than two dozen items scribbled on it since the last supply run.

Food and toilet paper always went without saying, so everyone wrote down personal preferences or other needs.

"Chicken feed if you come across any," Harold said. "We can always use it."

Metzger shrugged helplessly, doubtful about his chances of finding any.

"Oats or birdseed will do in a pinch," Harold added.

"No one else?" Metzger asked, receiving no answers after everyone looked to one another. "Okay. With luck, I'll see you all by suppertime."

Before heading for the door, he walked by Jillian, running his fingers gently across hers without saying anything. She squeezed his forefinger for luck, and Metzger never broke stride, grabbing his short sword and his father's old .357 before heading outside where Timmons waited beside the car for him.

"We good?" the pilot asked.

"Yeah. It's unlikely we'll find half the stuff on the list, but we can try."

Metzger wore a thick blue jacket, something like mountain climbers might don before scaling a steep target, and regular boots that didn't have much insulation, because he didn't want sweaty feet later in the day.

He drove them down the hill, mainly because Timmons complained he didn't want to be caught dead driving a Prius. Metzger simply rolled his eyes and began navigating them to the first location the captain read to him from Harold's map. A sheet of paper gave them directions, and the location was circled on the map, giving them a few methods by which to locate the country store a bit farther out than other businesses the group had raided during the past month.

Although the drive was nearly two hours away from the resort, the four destinations Harold marked on the map were close in proximity, meaning less wasted time once they arrived.

"What are we going to do when this doesn't hold out?" Timmons asked half an hour into their journey.

"What do you mean?"

"Supplies aren't going to last forever, especially with five of us infringing on Isabella's parents."

"Supplies won't hold out wherever we go," Metzger countered. "But you're right, because this won't get any easier."

"I'm sure the base is feeling the same crunch right now," Timmons figured aloud. "They planned to build greenhouses, and find animals to breed, but none of that is an overnight fix."

"Will our illustrious leadership come to the rescue?"

"If you're referring to the politicians, the answer is no," Timmons virtually growled. "We pilots are free thinkers, which is why I saw the writing on the wall and followed Isabella to you."

"Only after you agreed to subdue me and bring me back to the base."

"Son, that was self-preservation, and I haven't made one solitary attempt to strip you of your freedom."

"I know," Metzger chuckled. "I just like giving you a hard time."

Snow along the roads proved hit and miss once the Prius descended the road that led to the resort. Fortunately, no heavy drifts bogged down the area in general, allowing the car to navigate normal roads fairly easily.

Except for navigational directions, Timmons said very little the remainder of the way. When they reached a country store, looking a bit overgrown with several rusty bikes lying in front of it, Metzger questioned why such a place was on Harold's list. One window was broken, and the two other visible glass panels appeared dingy. Vegetation blocked their view beyond the intact windows, but Metzger could tell the building extended further than he could see, into the woods. A broken-down truck sat beside the building with one flat tire, and several shrubs appeared to have taken control of the property well before the apocalypse.

"When did this place go out of business?" Timmons asked as he stepped from the Prius. "1989?"

"Harold must know something we don't," Metzger surmised as he took a few steps around each side of the building, trying to figure out their best access point.

"We're going to have to boost a truck if we find half the stuff on this list, Dan. Your car that runs on gerbil power won't hold a whole lot."

"Then let's find some stuff," Metzger said, finding a door along the right side that appeared to be held up by a single hinge.

He provided a swift kick, sending the door inward, and he knocked on the frame several times, hearing no familiar undead sounds in return.

Inside, he found a counter with an old cash register, several beverage coolers that hadn't seen use in years, and several shelves, both mounted and free-standing, that no longer held goods.

"This was a waste," Timmons muttered, taking Metzger's side within the store.

Metzger looked around, finding a door along the far wall that might lead to additional storage, so he tried the knob, discovering it opened with ease, but into a dark, cool corridor. Despite the dampness, a variety of pungent odors nearly made him turn back. He took the flashlight from his pocket, clicking the button to illuminate the hallway ahead. It led to several additional doors, and it appeared that perhaps the previous owner lived behind the store itself.

Stepping cautiously inside, Metzger found a bathroom on the left that appeared untidy enough that he felt certain no one had occupied the living quarters in a decade. He saw dark mold along the sink and tub, and the shower curtain covering half of the tub appeared complete, but dingy. Strangely, the floor didn't look nearly as dirty, as though someone stepped across the laminate regularly, keeping it clear of dirt and grime. No window existed in this room, keeping it dark, even as his flashlight beam crossed the mirror on the medicine cabinet, reflecting back at him.

"Take a look at this," Timmons said grimly from across the hall.

Metzger stepped across, into a bedroom where the pilot shined his own light on a body with a shotgun next to it. By no means a coroner, Metzger could only guess the body had been there for a month or more, because decomposition took hold, and it appeared very blackened, possibly from warm spells in the late fall. While the body put off a putrid odor, it wasn't as overwhelming as a recently deceased corpse. Metzger shined his beam near the neck, finding the head wasn't attached, and remnants on the wall and floor indicated various pieces of skull and brains landed throughout the room.

"I'm saying this guy was a hermit," he surmised.

"Your friend could've clued us in," Timmons complained. "Living hermits don't take too kindly to trespassers."

"We can ask Harold about that later. Let's hope our buddy here didn't decide to check out because he ran out of supplies."

A check of the kitchen revealed it remained only slightly better than the bathroom, and Metzger decided the former occupant wasn't in great health when the apocalypse began. Perhaps he was bitten, ran out of supplies, or asked for help that never came. Any number of scenarios might have led to the man's decision to blow his head off, but Metzger figured that mystery might never be solved.

Only one room remained, and the door hadn't been opened in quite some time based on the dust along the floor and atop the doorknob. Metzger figured it might be a guest room, or perhaps an excessive hoarding situation, but he opened the door, hoping to find something that justified the trip to the old store.

"Wow," he muttered, finding shelves of dried goods inside the room, including powdered potatoes and milk, dried rations that includes everything from trail mix to biscuits and gravy, and even flavored drink packets. "It's like he shut down shop, knowing the end was coming."

"We can barely fit a fraction of this in the hippie mobile," Timmons said, shining his own flashlight inside.

"We don't have to take it all today," Metzger noted. "And if we find a truck, we'll get everything we can."

"It's a waste of time and resources if we don't bring all of this back, kid."

Metzger gave the notion a moment of thought, coming up with a solution that worked.

"The rest of the list can wait if we get short on time," he suggested. "We find a truck or van, and we pack up this load. We can't afford for someone else to find it before our next run."

"I can't count how many people we had to fend off to get in here," Timmons said sarcastically before breaking into a grin. "Yeah, I know it only takes one lucky person to stumble on this place."

Metzger imagined a person might want to sleep in the store overnight for shelter, and accidentally discover the cache located in the back.

"There aren't many vehicles left in these parts," Timmons said. "And I don't remember seeing any along these roads."

After requesting the map and receiving it from Timmons, Metzger opened it, looking at their location, knowing towns were sparse in the area.

Stops near the Adirondack Mountains, including towns and hamlets, were tourist traps before a fateful day that changed the world. Winding roads meant taking hours out of their way around mountains and wooded areas, and Metzger didn't want to spend the night in a strange area.

"How well do you know the area?" Timmons asked.

"We vacationed here a few times as a family, but I can't say I know it well. I just remember it taking forever to drive from place to place."

"Forever, huh?"

"I was a kid. Everything seems like forever at that age."

Metzger studied the map momentarily before his eyes landed on a potential area that might net some vehicles, and possibly additional supplies.

"Lake Placid," he said, pointing to the small town.

"Like the movie?"

"No, like where the Winter Olympics were held in 1980. It's a tourist trap, but a decent number of people lived there."

Both men secured the building as best they could before entering the Prius and heading for the small town. Timmons navigated once again, and only a few minutes passed before they conversed about some different topics. For a while, they discussed things they missed from their former lives, like sporting events, draft beer, and their dating scenes until Timmons steered the conversation into their present situation.

"So, you and the girlfriend getting serious?" the Navy man inquired.

"We're getting a little closer, yes."

"I noticed you two are sharing cabins more often than not. I hope you're being cautious."

"I appreciate the advice, Dad," Metzger said with a bit of sarcasm.

Timmons cleared his throat momentarily before speaking again.

"I realize we have these exchanges sometimes, but how old do you really think I am?" he asked.

Metzger paused before answering, because he never possessed good instincts when it came to guessing ages. He always figured Timmons might be in his early to mid-fifties, but he recalled hearing someone who knew pilots say they were typically retired or promoted by that age.

"I'm going to insult you with whatever I say," Metzger finally answered.

"I turned fifty this year," Timmons answered, making certain to look him in the eye. "Younger than your real dad by a good five years or more."

Metzger wasn't certain if the captain was genuinely upset with him, or simply proving a point, so he said nothing, which created an awkward silence.

"I have nothing but your best interest at heart," Timmons finally said. "Having a baby in these times is the last thing you want."

"I'm aware," Metzger said. "We've been careful."

A moment of silence passed again.

"How old did you really think I was?" Timmons pressed.

"No comment."

Timmons sat back as Metzger obviously knew the route for the next few miles.

"When you reach my age as a pilot, the Navy tends to force your hand," Timmons said reflectively. "I was looking at having to retire, or take a promotion to rear admiral."

"That sounds kind of cool. Admiral."

Metzger spoke the last word with enthusiasm, which caused Timmons to wince.

"Desk job."

"They can take you out of the cockpit just like that?" Metzger asked.

"It's the nature of things," Timmons replied. "Statistically, bad things can happen with older pilots."

"I'm pretty sure you wouldn't have been unemployed very long."

"Oh, there were always airline jobs after a little training, or jobs flying rich types. I just wasn't ready to leave military life."

"Yet here you are, far away from your base."

Timmons sighed.

"Things changed, kid," Timmons said thoughtfully. "We went from a nation with enemies to a broken military with no real leadership."

"You still have admirals and generals."

"Who listen to politicians hiding in bunkers. I don't see them battling the elements and the infected, do you?"

"But you were okay with taking orders when they were safely tucked away behind fortified government buildings?"

"It wasn't perfect, but it was the America I knew."

Metzger wasn't sure how he felt about the military or the government. He wished he could ask his brother, because Bryce had every reason to feel betrayed if he survived the undead attack and realized what his government had done to him.

"There's something I've been wanting to ask you," Metzger said.

"Shoot."

"We always talk about me and my family, but you've never really told me much about your past, other than your Navy adventures."

Timmons sucked in a breath and held it momentarily, as though debating where to begin, or whether he wanted to delve into his marital life.

"That may have to wait," he said, nodding ahead to the small town that began to come into view.

"You're not getting out of this," Metzger promised. "By the end of the day you're going to spill the beans."

"Or?"

"I'll disown you, and you'll have to spend every waking moment with Phyllis and Harold."

Timmons grumbled at the thought.

"Fine. Once we get what we need, I'll talk."

When Metzger drew near the town, he noticed the main drag, which looked much like other upstate towns with its brick buildings and awnings that didn't appear apocalyptic. Strangely, much of the town looked as though the power had gone out, and it simply waited for the power company to come restore it. Debris and stalled vehicles didn't clutter the streets here, though Metzger spotted a problem because dozens of undead roamed the area, and they had already spotted the Prius.

"See any trucks?" Metzger asked, trying to count the number of adversaries walking in their direction.

"A few," Timmons answered. "We'll be hard-pressed to reach them with this wall of infected in the way."

"I have some ideas."

"I was afraid you'd say that."

Metzger began to circle around some of the undead, effectively trapping the Prius between them and the few trucks Timmons spotted. Strangely, most of the vehicles here were tucked into the available parking spots, instead of awkward, random angles. Because the zombies remained spread out along the main road through town, Metzger would need to deal with them. Behind them, the mountains provided a beautiful backdrop that made Lake Placid such a gorgeous destination, particularly during the fall and winter months.

"See if you can get either of the trucks started, and I'll deal with the dead."

"Over there," Timmons said, pointing to a reasonably new Ford pickup.

In his mind, Metzger doubted it would start because it was the single vehicle parked awkwardly along the street, as though abandoned after it ran out of gas. Even so, he drove over to it, parking so the pilot could exit the car safely and attempt to start the truck. He watched momentarily as Timmons tried a passenger door, finding it locked. Timmons darted around the truck, trying the driver's side door, which wouldn't give either. He quickly jumped into the Prius, trying to catch his breath quickly before Metzger drove him to the next truck.

"That one," Timmons said, nodding in the direction of an older blue Chevy with a long bed.

Metzger sped over to the truck, knowing this time he needed to defend his friend. Once he parked beside the truck, Timmons jumped out and Metzger emerged from the driver's side of the Prius, already releasing his sword from its sheath for action. In his mind, he imagined he was in the worst movie trailer ever, armed with a sword in front of a hybrid car.

A comedic movie perhaps, he thought.

He began dismantling the line of the undead, slicing a few through their skulls before ducking down to sever a few legs, causing them to collapse and pile atop one another.

A few of them headed for Timmons, so Metzger quickly darted around the car, pulling one by the collar as it was about to grab the captain along one arm. He threw it to the ground, quickly stabbing it with the point of the sword in the skull. He sliced through another one that rounded the truck, eyeing the pilot ravenously.

"Any luck?" Metzger asked.

"It's unlocked," Timmons answered before scrambling inside to search for keys from the passenger side.

Although Timmons didn't shut the door behind him, Metzger gently pushed it closed, protecting the military man so he wouldn't personally be distracted while dealing with the undead. When no living people were around, he felt free to swing the sword more freely, severing heads while using a mix of power and precision. If the living were around, he sometimes hesitated, wanting to ensure he didn't hurt one of his allies in the process of protecting them.

A moment later, he heard Timmons attempt to start the truck, and though it sounded like it might turn over, it ultimately sputtered and did not. Timmons exited through the driver's side door, taking Metzger's side as he drew his knife.

"Put that away," Metzger said. "You might hurt someone."

"I'm going to help you with these things."

"I've got it handled."

"Oh, so I should leave all thirty-four of them to you?"

"You didn't really count them," Metzger said skeptically, slicing through the skull of a former tourist with a puffy jacket and some kind of winter hat on, as though she were about to get a lift on the slopes.

She barely made a hiss before the blade cut through her skull along the top of the ears from left to right.

"That's an approximation," Timmons said. "This thing will start if we can find some gas, which beats wearing ourselves out fighting the infected."

"Quit sounding so military," Metzger insisted. "Call them zombies, dead, undead, or dead heads. Anything but infected."

Timmons rolled his eyes.

"So sorry."

Metzger was about to head back to the Prius when a gunshot rang out, striking the tailgate of the truck Timmons had just checked.

"Get cover!" Timmons yelled as they both ducked behind the truck.

Timmons started to peer around the front of the truck when another shot rang out, striking the sidewalk beside him.

"Shit!" he yelled. "We need to get real cover!"

Metzger wasn't certain how good a shot the sniper was when it came to moving targets, but he hated the idea of sitting still. He also wanted to lead any bullets away from the Prius and the truck, knowing they might be his only modes of transportation out of town.

A mere ten feet separated the two men from a few brick buildings along the street. Metzger hoped at least one of the nearby doors might be unlocked, or they were about to meet an unlucky fate if the shooter had murder on his or her mind.

"The buildings," Metzger said, pointing to the doors he'd just spotted.

Timmons nodded.

"Ready?"

"Go!" Metzger said as they darted toward the abandoned business, and a shot rang out from somewhere across the town.

Eighteen

Two doors in adjoining businesses provided an opportunity to escape the projectiles that fired in their direction. Timmons made certain Metzger tried the door on the right, because the shells were fired from their left. One shell scuffed the sidewalk to their left, as though a warning shot, and another struck the wall closer to Metzger as he tried the door, finding it unlocked.

Both he and Timmons discovered safe havens in their buildings, but despite having walls that literally touched, the two men couldn't communicate through the doubled thickness of the bricks. Metzger considered heading directly next door and meeting up with his friend, but he didn't particularly want to be shot at again, in case the first volley of gunfire was the shooter's warm-up round.

Instead, he stood perfectly still momentarily, listening for sounds from Timmons, or the undead, before making his way through the ground level of the building. He found desks and filing cabinets galore, realizing he'd stepped into a former insurance office with absolutely nothing of use to him. Paperwork, clocks, and an old coffee maker filled out the remainder of the office, along with computers sitting atop the desks, collecting dust.

He weaved through the desks and dividers that gave employees some peace back in the day, until he found a storage closet, and through that, a rear exit that remained secured from the inside with a rather large manual deadbolt. He doubted any fire inspectors approved of such a crude security system, but apparently it worked.

After pulling the deadbolt aside, with a bit of effort, Metzger opened the door, finding an alley behind him where the captain was already bent over, staring at the ground.

"There's a zombie in there, if you'd like to take care of it," Timmons offered, thumbing towards the closed door behind him.

"What happened to your vow of keeping me safe at all times?" Metzger retorted with a grin.

"Well, I tried dealing with it, but my blade got stuck in the side of its skull and it snapped at me."

Now Metzger felt concerned.

"It didn't bite you, did it?"

"No," Timmons replied, holding up both arms as proof that his coat remained unscathed.

"Good."

"And for the record, I've stated that I would be fine going out with my boots on, but I didn't mean these."

He looked down at the duck boots, which likely paled in manliness to the cowboy boots he wore during warmer weather.

"You poor thing," Metzger said with a sarcastic edge. "I've seen you shoot, and you're definitely no Doc Holliday."

Metzger opened the door, finding a male zombie standing perfectly still in the center of an open ground floor. It wore blue jeans and some kind of flannel shirt, as though the elements weren't favorable when the apocalypse struck central New York. Only when it heard the door open did it turn his way, and a knife protruded from the skull where Timmons skimmed the edge of the bone structure, getting the blade lodged in bone, skin, and hair. It appeared as though the entire level was undergoing some renovation, or perhaps waiting for someone to lease it when people still had jobs and businesses to run.

Metzger used an old snake charming trick, putting his empty hand up, in front of the undead minion, and stabbing it with his own knife once it shifted its gaze. It began to fall to the floor, and he managed to retract both knives from the skull, wiping them off along the flannel shirt before heading out back.

"Here," he said, returning the Navy man's knife to him.

"Thanks," Timmons said flatly. "What are we going to do about our shooter?"

Metzger considered the possibilities momentarily. They could put their hands up, go to the Prius, and leave town peacefully, but that might simply make them stationary targets. Considering he possessed a notion about where the shots came from, Metzger thought about circling around, behind the buildings, and forcing a confrontation in whatever building the sniper used. He wondered if the shooter wanted the Prius, in which case he or she required the key fob from Metzger's pocket, and he wasn't about to surrender his only means out of town willingly.

"Of course we can't just walk into town and get a truck," Timmons lamented. "There's always some goofy bastard who has to make life hard for us."

"Did you consider maybe we're trespassing in their new home?"

"It's a town, Daniel. Do they really need to lay claim to the entire fucking town?"

Metzger shrugged, because he supposed they didn't. He felt as though the shots were warnings, rather than someone deliberately trying to murder them without provocation.

"They shouldn't get to us as long as we stay behind this row of buildings," Metzger reasoned aloud.

"I seem to recall a rather large gap between these buildings and where the shots originated," Timmons countered. "Unless you have a zipline or a jetpack, I'm not sure how we cross that area without getting gunned down."

"We don't. Unless we have a distraction."

Timmons looked at him with that concerned stare he sometimes provided when he didn't like Metzger's risky plans.

"Without getting shot, I want you to show yourself at the front door of this building so they focus on you."

"And what will you be doing?" Timmons asked skeptically.

"I'll be running to the end of this building, then across that open void, trying to locate them while they're spotting or shooting at you."

"It doesn't take much for them to turn that rifle in your direction."

"I know, but I'm faster, and I'll make sure to duck for cover when I can."

"That's not very reassuring when you're the one with the car keys."

Metzger reached into his pocket and pulled out the key fob, plopping it directly into Timmons' open palm.

"Please don't bail on me."

"You know I'd never," Timmons said with the most serious expression Metzger had ever seen from the man, which matched his tone.

"Okay," Metzger said, prepared to turn around and make a mad dash to the end of the row of buildings. "Give me two minutes and pop your head out."

"That's it?" Timmons questioned. "This is the extent of your plan?"

"Yup." Metzger turned and started jogging down the alley. "Two minutes!" he yelled to Timmons without turning around, picturing the man shaking his head.

Metzger darted to the end of the row as quickly as possible, picking up speed as he ran. Fortunate no zombies occupied the alley, he reached the last building, peeking around the side, and looking upward as a rifle fired from the window in the direction of the Prius and the truck. He spotted the muzzle flash and ran directly to the building without thinking, darting behind vehicles and the undead when possible. To a shooter, Metzger would stand out against sluggish undead and stalled vehicles as a backdrop. He didn't have time to deal with the dead, which immediately turned to follow him. Metzger quickly found himself seconds away from reaching the safety of the next row of buildings where the shooter remained hidden.

Hearing another shot, Metzger quickly looked up, seeing the barrel aimed in the direction of the Prius. Hoping Timmons remained unharmed, he continued to the back of the buildings without hesitation, trying to accurately pick the rear entrance to the building where the shooter remained. Finding it difficult after only a few cursory glances at the window in question, Metzger felt thankful the buildings were painted various colors so they didn't form one continuous bland color in front. Even better, the rear exteriors were painted to mirror the front, so he quickly found a light, olive-green color and stopped short of the back door.

Waiting just a few seconds to catch his breath, Metzger tried the knob, finding it locked. He debated a few seconds whether to kick it in, or head all the way around to the front and risk being spotted. Ultimately, he decided to save precious seconds, drawing his right foot back until another shot rang out. He targeted the area beside the doorknob, letting his leg thrust forward as though the rifle were a starter pistol. The door gave way, and he reached for the .357 at this side, trying to remain somewhat quiet as he headed inside.

Like most of the area buildings, this one stood three stories tall, and Metzger quickly found the rear staircase, hearing a thump upstairs. He scaled the stairs just short of a sprint, realizing there wasn't any way to do so quietly because the vacant building echoed virtually every noise. The sounds of scuffling feet reached his ears, and he knew the shooter was about to flee, or come directly at him.

As Metzger rounded the staircase to the top floor, he was about to check the first door to the left when someone holding a rifle came face-to-face with him at the door itself. He wasn't sure if he was more surprised that the rifle wasn't aimed at him, or the person carrying it appeared to be under ten years of age. By the time he suspected a trap, the door opened behind him, and another person emerged, sticking a gun barrel to his head. A side glance indicated a teenage girl held the gun to him, and the boy holding the rifle before him served as a decoy.

He remembered movies where kids were forced into horrific militaristic situations, wondering if this dynamic resembled those plots.

"We just wanted you to leave," the girl said, reaching for the revolver in his right hand.

Metzger's survival instincts told him that he could easily step back quickly and use momentum to throw her back into the open room, but he wasn't about to assault kids as a former school teacher.

"I'll need that back before I leave," he said, surrendering the weapon.

"It's doubtful you'll be leaving," the girl replied.

Both kids appeared unclean, as though they hadn't found a functioning shower or bathtub in months. Their faces were speckled with dirt and grime, and an odor followed them wherever they went that indicated hygiene wasn't a priority.

"My friends aren't going to let you keep me, and if you kill me, that'll make things worse."

"Just let him go," the boy argued.

"Why? So he can bring trouble like the last group?"

"I just came here for a truck," Metzger said, attempting to remain neutral. "I can even return it when I'm done."

He couldn't read their thoughts from their expressions, but Metzger guessed the two youngsters had been through far more than anyone their ages should have.

"Where are your parents?" he asked. "Where is anyone?"

"We're the only ones left," the boy answered.

"Don't tell him anything," the teen girl said, admonishing him.

Metzger stepped back, studying both of them momentarily. They didn't strike him as killers, but he wondered why they were in the town. If they possessed skills with guns or knives, they would have left a trail of unanimated bodies in the streets, and Metzger didn't recall seeing any of those.

He didn't necessarily see a resemblance between them to indicate a blood relation. While the boy had raggedy brown hair that screamed for a haircut, he didn't appear malnourished. With her black hair cut short, the girl appeared a bit thin, as though she sacrificed food and other necessities to keep the boy healthy.

"You two are just passing through," Metzger decided, speaking the words. "Just like me."

"And what if we are?" the girl asked, putting forth a brave face.

"Then there wasn't a need to shoot at me. Not everyone is an enemy."

"I shot," the boy admitted. "I was trying to shoot one of the zombies."

Metzger smirked.

"You missed."

"And I took over," the girl said, "because I knew you'd think we were shooting at you, and we didn't want you heading this way."

By now the three heard the sound of footsteps ascending the stairway below.

"Dan?" Timmons called from somewhere between the first and second levels. "You there?"

"Don't answer," the girl threatened, holding her gun on him.

"I have to," Metzger informed her, reasonably confident he wouldn't be shot in cold-blood. "He won't give up."

Metzger leaned over the railing.

"Top floor," he called.

Timmons joined them momentarily, a bit surprised to find his friend being held at gunpoint.

"What have we here?"

"We were just sorting a few things out," Metzger replied.

Timmons didn't aim his sidearm at the kids, but he didn't holster it, either. Metzger wanted to diffuse the situation before the captain felt compelled to protect him by any means necessary.

"Please give that back," Metzger said to the girl, nodding toward the revolver. "It belonged to my father, or I'd let you have it."

"I can't trust you," the girl said, reluctant to provide him with a weapon. "Our group trusted people before, and now there are less of us."

"Are you two the only ones left around here?" Timmons questioned, obviously probing for information. "It's not safe with the wildlife in this area."

"We're not the only ones."

Metzger turned to Timmons, asking him to remain quiet with nothing more than the exasperated expression on his face. He felt the girl wasn't telling them the whole truth, and the two kids didn't have additional people with them, or nearby.

"Just give the guy back his weapon," the boy said. "He's not going to hurt us."

"And how do you know?" the girl asked. "People lie."

"I'm Dan," Metzger introduced himself. "And this is Scott. He's a pilot in the Navy."

Now the girl looked at them very skeptically.

"How does a pilot wind up out here?"

"I wonder that myself, sometimes," Timmons replied.

"That's not much of an answer," the girl said.

Metzger stepped in once again.

"Look, we're getting supplies for our group. We just came here for a truck. You're welcome to come with us, or just let us get what we came for and we'll be on our way."

Growing impatient, or concerned for Metzger, Timmons began to push into his friend's backside. Metzger felt the metal of the gun against his back, despite the military man keeping the barrel aimed safely away from both of them.

Metzger blocked his path, putting himself directly in front of girl's firearm.

"Seriously, Scott?" he said aside to the captain, though the kids could certainly hear every word he spoke.

"We're burning daylight," Timmons grumbled. "We don't have time for this."

Without any further prompting, the girl handed Metzger his .357, which he accepted and holstered, nodding his thanks. He addressed the teenage girl directly.

"Are you two seriously going to be okay?"

"We have people," she answered. "We've lost some, but we get by."

Metzger still wasn't certain he believed the kids were part of a larger group.

"That truck needs gas," he said. "Have you come across any?"

"There's a gas station down the road," the boy said.

Metzger knew a gas station wasn't much help to him without power.

"There's no way to pump the gas," the girl added, "but there are four or five cars in the lot that looked like they were getting repaired."

"I appreciate it," Metzger said. "Good luck out there."

He dared not push the issue of the kids joining them. If they had a group, it seemed doubtful they required much assistance. His own group, which included his nephew, might very well run out of supplies before the end of winter, so he couldn't bring in more mouths to feed in good conscience. If he continued to push the idea of them coming with him, he suspected he might add to their mistrust, and Metzger suspected he might see them again in the future. Only so many towns and resources existed within the Adirondacks.

Metzger and Timmons left the kids behind a bit awkwardly, and Metzger could tell the boy wanted some adults in his life, or at least better people than he'd seen. He looked a bit longingly at the two departing men as though he wished they'd ask him to come along. Metzger didn't feel it was his place to ask, and he needed to put his family first. Harold and Phyllis took in extra people without complaint, but he didn't want to pressure his hosts into bringing in strangers.

"You're a little too trusting sometimes," Timmons said once they made their way into the alley where they couldn't be shot in the back from a high vantage point.

"They weren't a threat, Scott. I could see that from the beginning."

"It only takes one irrational second for one of them to put a slug in you."

"I don't want you harming kids to protect me. Ever."

Metzger felt sorry for them. He honestly didn't know if they had anyone else in their lives, and he didn't even know their names. Kids who shielded themselves from adults so fiercely harbored resentment, possibly from betrayal or abuse in their past. The apocalypse was no place to accept people at face value immediately, but something scarred them, particularly the girl, to keep them so independent.

"I see the gas station," Timmons said, looking down the street where a number of undead remained to impede their efforts.

Metzger didn't feel entirely safe, because he trusted the kids not to shoot him from behind, but he wasn't sure if more members of their group hid in the town. He kept glancing behind him, but saw no gun barrels or any sign of the kids monitoring them.

"You can't trust anyone out here," Timmons admonished him when they reached the gas station.

Each of them looked for a gas can, or means to check the fuel levels of the vehicles parked in the lot.

"You can't go aiming guns at every kid you encounter," Metzger said. "You're a father, aren't you?"

He jumped into a car, finding the keys in the ignition and no gas in the tank when he turned the ignition just far enough to check.

"I wasn't much of one," Timmons admitted with a hint of guilt, and perhaps a little sorrow at the thought of never seeing his son again.

"You're in the military," Metzger said. "It comes with the territory that you're not home a lot."

"It wasn't that," Timmons said as he located a gas can inside the shop and stepped outside to spy a few undead drawing near.

"I've got them."

Metzger had been practicing with handheld weapons the past month, so he twirled the sword a few times to see if he could do so under pressure. He spun the weapon so he was holding it backwards, which allowed him to swing his fist forward and let the blade cut through the first zombie's skull on the backside of his swing. It fell to the ground, and he kicked the second zombie, knocking it to the ground before he thrust the tip of the sword through its left eye, careful not to strike the tip against the concrete below.

"You're just showing off," Timmons scoffed, trying his second vehicle, and having success as it actually turned over.

Unfortunately, the vehicle was a compact car that didn't help them any more than the Prius.

"I'll get the car," Metzger said, always keeping a garden hose, minus the metal ends, in the back to syphon gas from vehicles when necessary.

He fetched the Prius, returning to find Timmons gaining access to the older vehicle's gas inlet. Unscrewing the cap, Timmons set it atop the car, monitoring his surroundings as more undead lingered in the area. The previously sunny, virtually cloudless sky gave way to clouds that continued to darken and block the sun. Metzger feared he might have guessed incorrectly about the weather, and the warm front was about to give way to more snow.

"We need to hurry this up," Timmons said, his breath showing in the cool air.

"Did you even try that?" Metzger asked of a truck parked off to the side of the parking lot.

It appeared intact, despite not being driven for some time.

"I haven't," Timmons admitted. "I got focused on the car."

Metzger walked over to the truck, quickly searched it, and found a set of keys tucked in the visor on the passenger's side. An older two-tone Silverado, the truck managed to start with a few tries, and Metzger felt surprised to see nearly half a tank of gas registering on the gauge. He hoped it didn't have some kind of transmission problem that might keep it from navigating the hilly roads to the resort.

"Well, I'll be," Timmons said. "I'd have bet fifty bucks it wouldn't start."

"Saves us some time and effort," Metzger sighed. "I'll drive this if you want to drive the Prius."

Timmons gave him a sour look.

"I'd rather you give me an enema with your sword," Timmons replied, motioning with a few fingers for Metzger to exit the truck.

"Don't say I didn't offer."

Metzger began gathering the hose and gas can for future use, putting them in the back of the Prius. He managed to remember the route back to the old store, but his mind kept wandering to the two youngsters, curious if they were part of some child cult, barely surviving, or if adults used them to carry out dirty work.

Unlike Timmons, he didn't consider everyone a threat, and he knew from experience he needed to be thorough when evaluating strangers. Metzger didn't want to be so hardened against newcomers that he didn't provide them an opportunity to prove themselves. While he wasn't looking for more roommates, allies in the apocalypse might make for safer travels and an exchange of information.

Even so, he occasionally glanced behind him to ensure that Timmons stayed close, and they weren't being followed. Metzger didn't want to be responsible for luring any groups with nefarious intentions back to the resort. He felt incredibly fortunate to live in such a place, with so many amenities he enjoyed on a daily basis. Granted, everyone who lived there chipped in and worked around the grounds, or fetched necessary items, but none of them complained. Even Nathan did what he could to help, though Metzger's nephew often appeared lonely without playmates or pets around. Farm animals made for subpar substitutes, and Metzger wished he could find a cat or dog to bring his nephew one day.

When he and Timmons arrived at the store, Metzger parked to the side so Timmons could back the truck close to the store's main entrance. Both stood a moment, listening for any signs of vehicles or people following them. Hearing nothing, they set to work, carrying cases of packaged foods out to the truck.

"What did you mean that you weren't a good dad?" Metzger inquired during the third trip the pair made together, each carrying a box.

"You're going to think I'm the shittiest person on the planet," Timmons answered before setting his box in the truck bed and shoving it back.

"You've already proven that you aren't."

"I told you my son lived in Las Vegas," Timmons stated as they walked inside. "What I didn't tell you was that he was living with my ex-wife who worked out there as a manager at one of the hotels."

"How old was your son?"

"He would've been about sixteen when the world collapsed."

Each grabbed another box of dried goods, navigating their way through the store once more.

"You said you and your son weren't on speaking terms," Metzger recalled aloud.

"That's a delicate way of putting it," Timmons replied. "And doesn't make me sound like quite the asshole I am."

Metzger began to question how Timmons, a level-headed pilot, very much accustomed to high-pressure situations, could be such a terrible parent. He felt certain the man exaggerated the extent of whatever poor decisions he made as a father. He waited for more elaboration as each of them set another box in the bed of the truck.

"Cooper, my son, was born autistic," Timmons said with a bit of a sigh. "I spent all of my life waiting to be a dad, and I just wasn't ready for what came with raising an autistic kid."

"It's not easy," Metzger said, knowing the difficulties from personal experience as a teacher.

He didn't personally teach disabled kids, but he saw them, and some of the issues their assigned teachers experienced during student meltdowns.

Timmons waited until they stepped inside to continue his story.

"At first, Sarah and I weren't sure of the extent," he admitted. "And, in the scheme of things, Cooper wasn't bad off. He had some ticks and some issues that set him off, and he occasionally wore the headset to keep the external stimuli from bothering him."

"But?"

"Things just got progressively worse, because I wasn't home very often. The kid needed stability, and I was flying missions, or stuck at the base, on-call half the time. Here I was, halfway to my pension in the Navy, so I couldn't just quit."

Timmons walked into the back room with Metzger close behind. Each grabbed another box, and Metzger led the way out.

"Things fell apart around Cooper's sixth birthday," Timmons admitted. "My own son never really bonded with me, because I wasn't home much. It hurt, but I guess my career was taking center stage. Sarah and I fought all the time about what to do for his education, and how she wanted me to take specialized classes for parenting an autistic kid. I just didn't have the time, and we were moving in different directions."

Each of them placed their cases in the truck bed, taking a second to observe their surroundings to ensure no one took notice of their stash.

"She got a job offer in Vegas, as an assistant manager, knowing she could move up the ladder, so we decided to call it quits."

"Just like that?"

"It hadn't been good for a few years," Timmons admitted. "I was always there financially for my son, but there wasn't really a relationship between us. Until the end, I helped pay for specialty schools, and I checked in when I could. Hell, at first, I used to send cards, and tried the video chat thing, but sometimes it was literally like talking to a wall. Cooper would stare off into space, and about two minutes into the conversation, he sometimes up and walked away. I guess it got easier over time to do the minimum and throw myself into my work."

"That doesn't make you a monster," Metzger said. "You're human."

"I only spoke to Sarah once after this all started," Timmons stated, his eyes glazed a bit as he stared at the glass of one of the dusty cooler doors. "It didn't sound like things were going very well out there, and she wasn't sure what to do with Cooper."

He turned to Metzger, his eyes misting a bit as he recalled the day in question.

"What do you say to that?"

Metzger couldn't provide an answer.

"I could've gone AWOL and stolen a plane to pick them up, but I knew right away there wasn't a place for someone like my son in this world. I couldn't even make time for him before, so what could I have done differently? Instead, I just followed orders like always, and told myself that made it alright."

Sniffling, Timmons breathed in hard from his nose, trying to mask the pain he felt from thinking about his decisions. Metzger felt certain the man had never spoken in such complete detail about his son and his failed marriage to another living soul.

"Sometimes I imagine their last hours on Earth, and it haunts me," he admitted. "I was kicked back inside a secured perimeter getting three square meals a day, and my ex probably died protecting my only child. I put on a brave face in front of the other pilots, but inside I was dying a little each day."

"Is that why you were willing to leave the base?"

"Partly," Timmons replied, wiping back what little moisture made it to the sides of his eyes. "Being trapped with your thoughts isn't always a good thing, you know."

"I'm very aware."

"I started showing you the aircraft in Norfolk to pass the time. Maybe I thought I could mentor you, kind of like a dad, in the beginning." Timmons paused, searching for the words. "But the truth is you're already a far better man than me. You probably think I'm protecting you because of the whole cure the world messiah thing, but it's more than that, Dan. I've said it before, and maybe you don't see it yet, but you're going to be a leader in this new world. I just plan on making certain nothing happens to you before you reach your full potential."

Metzger couldn't muster a reply, because he still wondered if Timmons told him such things with an angle in mind. He appreciated the captain coming clean, and he trusted the man, but Metzger didn't picture himself as a leader of men.

Not like Timmons, and certainly not like his brother.

Before their conversation could continue, a female zombie emerged from the nearby woods, spying the two men and heading directly at them. Snow, which fell lazily from the sky during their return drive to the old store, now picked up in both steadiness and thickness.

"I'll go get another box," Timmons said, openly looking for a reason to excuse himself and let Metzger deal with the minor threat.

When the captain ducked out of sight, Metzger realized he hadn't taken his sword from the car as he went to reach over his shoulder for it. Not feeling panicked against only one member of the undead, he gave a gentle kick to her stomach, driving her back a few feet while he picked up a nearby rock about twice the size of a softball. Deciding to try an experiment, he hurled the rock at her forehead, but it grazed the side of her skull instead.

"Guess I need to work on my aim," he muttered, kicking her back once again, buying time to pick up the rock for a second attempt.

His next throw hit the zombie squarely in the forehead, knocking her back before she reluctantly collapsed to the ground, as though the impact from the rock required a moment to register and kill the brain. Walking over, he kicked the zombie's arm, but it didn't move an inch. Hearing Timmons step outside behind him, Metzger turned around to see the Navy man load another box into the truck.

"Fetching the sword was too much effort?"

"Thought I'd try something," Metzger confessed. "How many more trips?"

"Three or four."

Metzger followed Timmons inside.

"You really don't think I'm a monster?" Timmons asked.

"No. Have you taken the time to picture what would've happened if you landed a plane out there? You would've been swamped, or worse."

Timmons nodded, seeing his point.

"It's because of you that I have a chance to find my brother," Metzger said. "Again."

"The least I could do."

"Really, it's not. You gave up a lot to fly us out here, and I know you're not entirely comfortable being around the dead. I doubt any of us really are. And I appreciate you being honest with me about your past."

"You don't think any less of me?"

"I think I understand where your head was at," Metzger replied, picking up one of the last boxes inside the storage room. "You weren't a deadbeat dad, because you provided support, and you made efforts to be in Cooper's life."

"Yeah, but a father should be there through thick and thin," Timmons said, beginning to slide into a cesspool of negativity again.

"You're here now," Metzger reasoned. "You've got my back, and I appreciate that more than you know. And what you've told me stays between us."

Timmons nodded.

"Thanks," the captain said, providing a thin smirk. "We'd better get this stuff loaded before the snow traps us here."

Metzger led the way through the store.

"Keep up, Pops," he said, trying to alleviate the tension Timmons brought upon himself by reliving his past.

"Okay," the pilot said, hesitating before adding a word he spoke with a hint of a chuckle. "Son."

Nineteen

"Is this our life now?" Luke asked Gracine in the center of a wooded grove. "We just hide from the government like hermits?"

Gracine carried an axe and a small gas can, while Luke toted a chainsaw. Behind them, Samantha skipped around several trees, simply being a kid.

"We're a far cry from hermits," Gracine said. "We got lucky and found a community."

Gracine found their current lodgings, and the community part of it came as a fortunate surprise.

After a month of being settled in, they brought their particular skills to those of the people already occupying the other houses. All of the houses were built with fireplaces, which made them desirable in the apocalypse, though some required conversion from natural gas to wood as their fuel source.

Fortunately, Virginia seldom reached cold temperatures that threatened the group significantly. Although they didn't have electricity, the collective showed Gracine and the others their plans to locate solar panels and create their own energy. A man who lived across the street from them worked as an engineer for years, possessing a solid understanding of how electrical grids worked. He felt confident he could create a system to power all twelve houses if they could locate the proper materials.

Today, however, the group simply required firewood to keep their houses warm with three full months of winter still ahead.

"We could've done a lot worse, you know," Gracine informed Luke. "We found people with little ones, which gives Samantha some playmates."

"She has been happier," Luke admitted. "It just feels like we've shifted gears completely."

"How so?"

"When we were with Dan, everything was about helping the military and finding the man responsible for all of this. Now we're just settling in, and no one's really talked about it."

"What's to talk about?"

"Is this just another stop?" Luke questioned. "Is this temporary lodging? Colby hasn't really said much."

"He hides his feelings, but he's been through a lot. I think he's ready to play it safe for a while."

Both of them stopped when they found a downed tree that simply needed to be cut into manageable pieces.

"That's already dry," Luke said, nodding toward the tree. "We could burn that right away."

"That's what we want."

Samantha continued to skip around several of the trees, and Gracine looked around to ensure no unwanted visitors took notice of her.

"Samantha, honey," Gracine called to the girl.

"Yeah?" Samantha answered, running over to her.

"Would you be a dear and ask Mr. and Mrs. Brown to bring the truck back here?"

Gracine nodded to Luke to ensure he thought it was okay for the girl to run a few hundred yards back to the pickup truck where their neighbors awaited word that a suitable tree was located.

"I can go with her," Gracine offered.

"That's alright," Luke said before turning his attention to Samantha. "I need you to be a big girl and head straight back to the truck, understand?"

Samantha nodded.

"Tell Mr. and Mrs. Brown to bring the truck down here to us. And if you see any of the monster people?"

"I run away and get help."

"You come to me, or you run to the Browns if you see the monster people."

Samantha nodded and ran in the direction of the truck.

"I hate doing that," Luke said once she was out of earshot.

"She needs to learn responsibility," Gracine said. "We didn't see any danger on the way down here, and it's a straight shot."

"Watch her as long as you can," Luke said, waiting a few seconds before priming and starting the chainsaw.

He and Gracine both knew the sound of a running chainsaw would draw the undead to their location, and they wanted Samantha to have a good head start, even if the truck was only a few hundred yards away.

Monitoring Samantha all day, every day simply couldn't be done, because like any kid she wanted to explore and have fun. Gracine taught her safety measures whenever possible, and Luke instructed her on firearms with the knowledge he gained from his partner at the start of the apocalypse.

Gracine didn't lose sight of the girl until she walked into a thicket of trees, and Samantha didn't deviate from her path. A few minutes went by, and Luke was already cutting the tree into smaller sections by this point. She considered leaving him to check on Samantha, but he'd never hear a zombie coming, and letting Samantha spread her wings didn't work effectively if they constantly checked on her.

She breathed a sigh of relief when the maroon Ford pickup truck headed in her direction. She saw Samantha wedged between Samuel and Karen Brown in the truck's bench seat, looking proud of herself for following through with her errand. Although Karen clearly ruled the roost in their marriage, Samuel drove the pickup truck, backing it closer to where Luke continued cutting the wood. Gracine knew the noise was going to attract the undead, and the group had already formed a plan for a few of them to chop wood while the others monitored the area for flesh-eating assailants.

"Any trouble?" Karen asked when she stepped from the truck, shouting loudly enough to be heard over the chainsaw.

A rugged woman who grew up on a farm, she knew how to shoot, work with heavy machinery, and maintain anything from a garden to a field with plant life. Her dirty-blonde hair was tied back in a ponytail today, and she wore a red and black checkered flannel shirt with stained blue jeans. She treated the people in her neighborhood better than she did her own husband, but Samuel didn't say much, as though he simply rolled with the punches. Perhaps she simply emasculated him in public and they had make-up sex in private.

"We're good so far," Gracine reported. "Can you and Samuel keep watch while I start splitting some logs?"

"Sure," Karen answered.

She looked to her husband, who nodded that he understood.

Self-sufficient in his own right, Samuel Brown maintained a repair shop where he carried out vehicle repairs on the farm he and his wife owned when he found time. In his spare time, he did woodwork in his shop, and because two of his fingers were missing their tips, close to the first knuckles, Karen said he wasn't very good with saws. Because they left the Maplewood community for work at their old residences, some neighbors said they had dual residency as a joke.

Slender, and nearly six feet in height, Samuel wore eyeglasses and somehow managed to keep a five o'clock shadow at all times, which looked like a beard in infancy. In his early forties, like Karen, his wavy light brown hair had yet to show any gray, and his hazel eyes typically appeared caramel in color. From what Gracine saw during their few trips into the open world, he handled himself well, with firearms and blades alike.

She thought she overheard him say he spent some time in the military, the Army perhaps, for a handful of years.

Luke cut the dead tree into pieces typically around a foot in length, allowing Gracine to prop them atop the ground and use an axe to split them. She and Luke managed to chop nearly half the tree into useable firewood before the Browns offered to swap places with them. Luke had cut up virtually all of the tree, so Samuel took to splitting the wood, and Karen began loading it into the truck with some help from Samantha, who carried smaller pieces.

A few minutes passed before the undead began staggering around nearby trees, eyeing their next potential meal in the form of four adults and a child. Luke dealt with a few by using his blade, penetrating their skulls to put them down permanently. Gracine did much the same, but a few zombies turned into a few dozen, and the group openly grew concerned. Karen and Samuel stopped their chores to draw their weapons, but the undead emerged from every direction.

"We need to go," Gracine said. "The wood will be here."

Samuel looked to his wife, who didn't usually express much concern, but she showed displeasure regarding the situation around them.

"Agreed. Let's take what we've got."

Karen assumed driving duties, while Samantha and Gracine occupied the front with her. Luke and Samuel found enough room in the truck bed to ride behind the wood, and six or seven zombies began groping at them just before Karen put the truck into drive and navigated around the trees. A short time later, she located the white Ford Escape they brought as a backup vehicle, handing her husband the keys so he could drive back to the neighborhood with Luke.

Soon enough, they reached the front gate, and Gracine jumped out to open it. She waited for both vehicles to pass through the opening before closing the gate and securing it with a latch one of the residents crafted specifically for the non-electrified double gate. Within a few minutes most everyone stepped outside to greet them, and Gracine exited the truck when she spotted Sutton standing in front of their new residence.

"What happened?" he asked, taking notice of the light load in the truck bed.

"We had more cut, but the dead heard the noise from the chainsaw. A few dozen surrounded us before we could deal with them."

"I should've come," Sutton muttered.

"We couldn't deal with them by hand," Gracine said. "And you and all of your guns would only attract more of them."

"I have lots of ammunition," Sutton assured her. "We could clear them all in a day if we lured them to us."

"We have nothing but time on our hands," Gracine said, reaching up to glide her fingers gently along his cheek. "We'll get the wood tomorrow."

Moving past him, Gracine stood a moment to look at their current residence, finding it difficult to believe they landed in such a good situation.

A two-story house with the lower half encased in stones of various, decorative earth tones, it felt like a palace to Gracine, who lived in apartments much of her life. Along the second story, natural wood siding was painted a neutral beige that worked well with the stones. Like every house in the neighborhood, the windows remained intact with energy-saving measures, and the shingled roof appeared virtually brand-new.

More than three-thousand square feet provided plenty of space for their group to stay, though they remained on a probationary term within the neighborhood. A partially finished basement provided them with even more space, and tolerable temperatures throughout the year if they chose to gather or sleep down there.

Conditions of permanent residence, which included the house, meant them not causing trouble, and doing their part to deal with the undead, and fetch supplies as needed. What Gracine learned in a short time, however, was how some people inside the gated community seemed far more adapted for the current world than others. She liked the Browns, and they often volunteered to risk their lives outside the gates because a few older members weren't suited for battling the undead or stacking firewood.

Sutton provided the supplies from the box truck as tribute to enter the community and be given a chance at permanent residence, but admitted he felt stripped of some independence. He drew the line at surrendering most of his weapons, but Buster's presence won over the adults and children alike inside the gates. Domestic pets weren't easily found once the undead outnumbered the living, though one of the children kept a predominantly orange calico cat named Pumpkin inside her home. Fortunately, Pumpkin remained indoors, because Sutton wasn't certain how Buster would react to seeing another animal outside.

"What have you been working on?" Gracine asked Sutton as she walked up to the house, leaving Luke and Samantha to go across the street so Samantha could play with the neighbor kids.

"Organizing our weapons so they're spread throughout the house. I wish we could find a candle store to raid so we had more lighting at night."

"Or a battery store so our flashlights didn't die all the time."

Gracine walked up the stone steps near the street that led to an inlaid path of bricks, creating a path to the front steps of the house.

"Where's Sean?" she inquired.

"He went out with another group to look for supplies. They took an RV because they might have to spend the night near one of the towns."

Virginia contained many small towns which might hold supplies, or danger, and it made more sense for a group to check several in a day, rather than head out each day and waste precious fuel.

"I'm surprised you let him go."

"It's worse if I make him stay," Sutton said. "Besides, he's an adult. I can't shelter him forever, even if I did just get him back."

"Did he take Buster?" Gracine asked, looking around for the canine.

"Nah. Buster's been sniffing around the fences. It's been good for him to see new people. He soaks up the attention."

Both were about to head inside their designated abode when Samuel Brown called to them.

"Hey! Can you guys help unload some of this firewood?"

"Where do you need it?" Gracine asked.

"We're going to take this load down to the McAllister family," Samuel replied. "If we can get a truckload or two a day, hopefully we can get enough for everyone to make it through winter."

From experience, Gracine knew Virginia winters didn't typically bring much snow, or even freezing temperatures much of the time. Where she stood, the air felt as though it might be just above fifty degrees on a December day. Walking down the steps, she joined Samuel at the truck, noticing Karen wasn't around.

"Where's the wife?" Sutton asked, never one to concern himself with pretenses.

"I'm sure she had something to work on at the house."

"So how did you two meet?" Gracine asked once they jumped in the truck with Samuel.

"We met after I left the Army," he answered, assuming the driver's seat. "Her family owned a few large farms and they knew my family because my father and grandfather worked on their tractors."

"Aren't you a mechanic?" Sutton asked.

"I learned it from them," Samuel replied. "Also picked up woodworking from my grandfather before he passed."

Samuel wiggled his fingers for both passengers to see.

"Lost one fingertip before my military days, and one afterwards."

"Did you ever consider giving it up?" Sutton asked with a raised eyebrow.

Samuel chuckled.

"Those injuries happened with my grandfather's old equipment. They didn't have much in the way of safety features."

"So, you and Karen met some warm summer night at her family farm?" Gracine asked, trying to draw the picture in her mind.

"Something like that. I'd gone over to help my dad work on a tractor, but he didn't really need my help, so I passed the time talking with Karen."

"Love at first sight?" Gracine asked, causing Sutton to roll his eyes.

"Not exactly," Samuel answered. "We got along, and saw each other once in a while, but it was her who came to me and asked me on our first date."

Sutton cleared his throat, and Gracine nudged him with her elbow, causing him to grunt.

"What did her parents think of you?" Sutton asked while rubbing his sore ribs.

"They loved me and my family, but I don't think they liked the idea of me dating Karen."

By now the truck had reached the correct house, and Gracine thought about Robert and Nancy McAllister, growing fonder of them as time passed.

"Like you weren't good enough?" Gracine asked Samuel once they all exited the truck.

"I didn't come from money," Samuel said. "I think they wanted her to marry a banker, or someone influential."

"No offense," Sutton said, "but it sounds to me like you've always been the hired help."

Samuel shrugged, grabbing a chunk of wood from the truck bed.

"Think what you want."

Letting Samuel walk ahead of them, Gracine waited to address Sutton.

"Rude," she said pointedly.

"He's whipped."

"He's a good husband."

"Of course you would say that," Sutton said, plucking a few chunks of wood from the truck. "You always want us to be agreeable."

"You who?"

"Women," Sutton answered, looking at her as though she asked just to pick on him.

Gracine knew, but she wanted to hear him say the word.

"My first wife thought she could change me," Sutton said, carrying the blocks of wood alongside Gracine. "She gave up after five years and served me with papers."

"Hard to believe, you being so charming and whatnot."

After a few more trips, Buster caught up with them and Gracine scratched his head as they returned to the truck. Samuel placed the wood behind the house, beside a dwindling pile of wood, and Gracine considered it fortunate they found a tree already downed and dried out for them to use immediately.

Just beyond the wrought iron gate surrounding the houses, numerous trees hid the community from the rest of the world. Such trees remained safe because they protected the residents, and because they were mostly the types of trees with needles and sap, which made them less desirable for burning. Despite the cover, and the shade they provided, Buster sensed something because he stopped walking beside Gracine, stiffened, and began growling as he pointed his nose at one particular side of the fencing.

Occasionally the undead paid the community a visit, usually in small numbers, and the group dealt with them through the iron bars with bladed weapons. A few times a week they collected the bodies and burned them a few miles down the road, keeping the neighborhood free of odors and any animals that might attempt to devour the carcasses.

"Looks like we got some customers," Sutton said, reaching for the knife at his side.

While the community felt like paradise compared to their previous destinations, the undead arrived often enough to bring them back to reality.

Reaching for her own knife, Gracine followed Sutton and Buster to deal with the few visible threats as they reached the gate. The dead stretched their arms inside, attempting to grasp prey.

"Here we go again," she muttered, prepared to earn her keep.

Twenty

Mid-January

Bryce only knew the date because he occasionally turned on the GPS tracking device to check his location, and it provided date and time like a cell phone.

Finally east of Buffalo, he and Molly found themselves slowed by winter weather in the second week of January. Food and fuel became increasingly difficult to find, especially on days where a foot or two of snow impeded their travel. They found shelter and warmth whenever possible, a necessary evil to avoid frostbite from the lake effect winds. Often, their visibility was cut to less than twenty feet, particularly on highways and interstates where no buildings blocked the harsh winds.

Grabbing a new vehicle, or syphoning fuel proved far more difficult when cars were caked with ice and layers of snow. Occasionally, they located one inside a garage, but currently they were nearing a rest stop in the middle of a snowstorm. A foot of snow already covered the ground, and the duo was forced to walk after their last truck ran out of diesel fuel. Although it wouldn't be heated, the small building would provide some shelter from the cold, and they might find something to eat or drink.

Carrying packs that the duo became exceptionally adept at loading with only essentials, Bryce and Molly seldom toted food, because what little they located, they ate soon after. A few lucky finds provided them with lightweight bedding and clothes typically used by recreational hikers before the apocalypse. Bryce had long since ditched the last of his military clothing, and he kept the tiny tracking device inside an RFID covering meant to block signals from credit cards. Because he understood the technology to be similar, he hoped the sleeve would keep the device from being read by tracking devices. He hadn't located any other clues or people associated with Nadeau, but the tracker might come in handy if his luck changed.

He considered testing it with the tracking device, but he didn't want to risk the military thinking they had located the previous target, and therefore, their missing lieutenant commander.

"I don't know when we'll see another building," Bryce virtually yelled over the snow and gusting winds to his travel partner. "Want to stop and wait it out?"

Molly required only a few seconds to look around at their bleak situation. Every vehicle required great effort to access, much less start, and visibility hampered their efforts anyway. Until they distanced themselves from the Great Lakes, the weather would be their greatest nemesis.

Before the fiercest snow struck, both picked up goggles and facemasks during their travels, which limited their exposure to the weather. If they had chosen to grab skis and poles, they might have fit in at a ski resort back in the day, but no sporting goods stores were visible from the roads they walked.

"We aren't going to get far like this," Molly reasoned. "Let's get some shelter."

Bryce preferred finding houses or cabins with fireplaces, but the timing seldom worked in his favor when it came to spotting a safe haven for the evening. Starting so far from New York also led him into winter weather before he could draw close to the Adirondacks. He felt like they covered a handful of miles per day with vehicles being difficult to procure. Numerous factors worked against him once colder weather settled in, and no lucky breaks came their way in the form of ready-to-go vehicles, or clear highways.

Fortunately, Bryce found a driving force within him, because his brother reached out to him after Colby Sutton provided a much-needed link between the two. He provided Metzger with Bryce's sat phone number, and Metzger reached out to his brother, assuring him they were safe at the resort. Willing to battle the worst of the elements to see his wife and son, Bryce still reached human limits, so he felt relieved to see the rest stop come into view through the whiteout conditions.

When they reached the building, Bryce found it slightly larger than he expected. Most of the rest stops acted as welcome centers with tourism brochures, and some possessed gas stations and eateries in the old world. This particular building appeared somewhere in between, with restrooms, a welcome center desk, an expanded gift shop with mostly barren shelves, and even shower stalls for truckers to rent.

"Luxurious," Molly commented sarcastically when the door closed behind them, leaving the snow and freezing winds just outside the thick window panes.

Napkins, newspapers, and brochures lined the floor like some kind of cost-effective carpeting, and Bryce could hear the wind howling outside. Both of them knocked on the nearest walls, hoping they didn't hear any other noises from within, because the building wasn't lit very well from the gloomy day behind the windows.

No enemies emerged, and Bryce could see to the end of the gift shop, finding its shelves picked clean from travelers who came before him.

"We need to clear it," Molly said, though both felt exhausted and chilled from the treacherous weather outside.

"Agreed."

Each of them drew the small flashlights they carried in the small pouches of their packs.

During their time in extremely cold weather, Bryce had learned that the undead didn't fare well in the elements. When they encountered them outdoors, Bryce and Molly discovered they moved sluggishly, and if they remained still long enough, they froze in place, making them incredibly easy to kill. When blasted with wind and snow, the undead often couldn't move, unless they'd remained continuously mobile, and they could barely emit any of their feral noises.

Bryce checked the shower stalls and behind the welcome center desk while Molly covered the restroom areas. Finding more mess, and nothing of use, Bryce met her at the entrance once he finished.

"I guess shelter is all we get," Molly said, forcing a grin.

"My kingdom for a garage with a warm car, a full tank of gas, and a full gas can," Bryce said despondently.

Leaving the highway in search of houses, or cars with fuel, consumed time Bryce didn't believe he could afford. Sometimes the weather worked in his favor, and sometimes it completely shut down a day of progress.

"What are we going to do?" Molly asked, her breath still visible despite them being indoors.

Without any heat, building interiors were only preferable because they cut off the biting wind.

"I don't think the weather is letting up anytime soon," Bryce said, stepping forward to look out the front door where strong winds and snow swirled everywhere. "We could make camp here."

Setting up a camp typically meant using their lightweight, thermal sleeping bags in the warmest area possible. Heat from a vehicle, or finding a kerosene heater felt like too much to ask for, and Bryce felt somewhat depressed that he wasn't reunited with his family.

"Let's wait it out a spell," Molly said.

Both of them took what items they required from their packs, including their firearms. Bryce currently carried a Smith & Wesson .40 caliber pistol because he possessed a small box of ammunition for it. He also carried a shotgun, typically strapped over his shoulder, while Molly opted for an AR-15 she found along the way. Her sidearm of choice was a nine-millimeter because ammunition remained abundant, comparatively, and it didn't weigh her down.

Each of them laid out their sleeping bags and settled inside, keeping their gear on because they didn't plan on sleeping. Instead, they covered their lower extremities with the bags and leaned against a wall in one of the smaller rooms. Bryce hoped what little body heat they generated might remain contained in the space, but their clothes and the sleeping bags were enough to keep them alive.

"I'm sorry," Bryce said once they settled beside one another, pulling their sleeping bags up to their necks.

"For what?"

"For getting you into this."

"I chose to come along," Molly assured him.

"You saved me," Bryce said with a grin. "You were willing to keep me from being a brainless carnivore when I died, and when that didn't happen, you stayed to make sure I reached my brother."

Molly chuckled.

"I really don't have anywhere else to be."

"Well, lucky for you we're in peak vacation season here in New York."

Both shared a laugh momentarily.

"I wish you had someone to find," Bryce said a moment later.

"This world, and the people who take advantage of it, made certain I had nothing left. If you're feeling survivor's guilt, don't. You and your brother are good people, and I look forward to meeting the rest of your clan."

Bryce grimaced.

"I wish we were days away, but it feels like weeks at the rate we're traveling."

"The weather will clear again," Molly said assuredly.

"Are you sure you lived in New York prior to this winter?"

"Yes," Molly said, laughing. "Born and raised. It's not all snow *all* the time, even in the winter."

"Maybe I was gone too long," Bryce thought aloud. "We don't really have snow on the open seas. At least not in the places I traveled."

Bryce wished they could start a fire, but the building didn't have the means to direct smoke outside, and an indoor fire presented numerous safety hazards. Locating houses with fireplaces, particularly in New York, didn't present much of a challenge, but the conditions kept them from leaving the highway. Although zombies didn't present much of a danger, the elements could easily get them lost since they didn't appear to be near any settlements.

Leaning his head back, Bryce heard the howling wind outside, and it sounded soothing because he didn't miss machinery and crowds most of the time. When he earned leave from the military, he always felt a little out of place in the civilian world. People bellyached about the problems in their lives, never knowing the worldly threats around them, and how their military shielded them on a daily basis. Most of those people were likely dead, and Bryce felt out of place again, because he didn't have a home, and his family felt so far away, despite being only half the state's distance.

"What are you thinking about?" Molly asked, beginning to relax, despite the frigid temperatures surrounding them.

"The future."

"We all do."

"I know, but if we keep going down the same paths, we'll never rebuild the world."

"You made it sound like they were restoring your base, and the town."

"They were, but having power doesn't feed thousands of mouths. I hope they have the foresight to plant crops, and save animals before everything is gone. They're listening to leadership that isn't suffering our fate. Those fat cats are sealed belowground, eating like kings, without the threat of zombies or assholes."

Molly stared straight ahead, which didn't provide much of a view except a wall stained with blood.

"You sound disillusioned for a career Navy man."

"Before, I had something to believe in. The people I worked with are smart, capable, but they're still listening to the same policies and people that got us into this mess. If we focused on getting the right people in the right places, we could get refineries going, bring servers online, and rebuild society from the coasts inward."

"Sounds like you have a plan."

"Not really," Bryce said, wondering if his words were wishful thinking. "I'm just worried that the longer we let this continue, the harder it'll be to restore order."

"What about Nadeau?"

"What about him?"

"Everyone seems to think he's out there, and if he is, what's to say he doesn't strike again?"

Bryce nodded in agreement. His own people put forth a meager effort when it came to locating the man, yet they were more than happy to try and retrieve him once they discovered the value running through his veins.

"If he has another wave of terror for us, I'm afraid there isn't much we can do about it," he said. "At least we have our major bases secured."

"Even with his planning, I wonder what kind of life he lives," Molly said thoughtfully. "Only so many places are safe from the dead."

"From what I understand, the man was kind of a genius. Maybe he's in a bunker, or some tower halfway to the sky, looking down at us peons."

Bryce felt somewhat chilled and sluggish. He wanted nothing more than to curl up in the bag and rest for a few hours.

"I'm going to get some shuteye," he told Molly. "Rest would do us some good before we head out in the cold again."

"Sleep tight," she replied, pulling her rifle close, evidently not ready for sleep quite yet.

***

Bryce wasn't certain how much time had passed when he heard a rhythmic tapping from the front of the building. At first his mind incorporated the noise into whatever dream his imagination had conjured, but by the third tap he opened his eyes, blinking furiously because he felt as though he hadn't slept sufficiently.

Already to her feet, Molly appeared determined to examine whatever noise disturbed their rest, and Bryce reached for his sidearm after unzipping the sleeping bag and kicking his feet from under its warmth.

"I've got it," Molly said, looking back to him. "Probably some dead brain stuck against the door."

"I'm coming," Bryce said, getting to his feet and following a few feet behind, despite her protest.

Crossing a central room, the duo made their way to the front where snow lined the windows, like some storefront display covered white frost from a can. Neither could see anything beyond the glass, and the noise had stopped, but neither would return to a peaceful slumber until they determined the sound's origin.

"It probably moved on," Bryce reasoned aloud.

"Probably," Molly said, though she pushed the front door open just the same.

Putting an arm up to shield her face from the slashing wind, Molly took a step outside, looking to the ground for clues.

"I see footprints," she said with a wary edge to her voice, as though something other than the undead might have visited them.

Bryce began to step forward, as she stepped back, beginning to let the door close without turning her back to it. Before the door could close, he heard a shotgun blast that sent Molly flying back from the doorway, landing hard on her back inside the building. Bryce immediately spied blood and ran to her side, seeing her stomach and lower chest were pelted with buckshot as blood made its way through the split flesh and her jacket.

"No!" he said repeatedly, drawing his sidearm and looking to the door, which did not open right away.

Caught between potentially defending himself and evaluating her, he frantically searched for the worst of the wounds, though Molly's eyes were already staring upward with the initial stages of shock.

Her lips quivered and moved, though no sound came out to indicate she was cognizant of her surroundings or what had transpired.

Bryce instinctively looked up, finding a man at the doorway holding a shotgun, appearing bewildered. He could barely see the clean-cut appearance of the man who wore a winter hat with the hood of his jacket pulled up over the top. Taking aim, Bryce briefly considered pulling the trigger without giving the action much thought, but the man lowered his shotgun to the ground, his eyes echoing a sentiment of sorrow.

"I'm so sorry!" he stammered. "I saw movement and I thought she was one of them!"

He appeared dressed for winter, and Bryce noticed he wore clothes very suited for the environment, just like the kind he and Molly found along their journey.

"Help me check her over," Bryce ordered, returning his attention to Molly and her injuries, hoping she could be saved.

Returning his attention to Molly, he couldn't feel any bumps along the surface of her flesh where his fingers checked in the bloodied areas, meaning the pellets went deeper than he'd hoped.

Before he made his next decision regarding Molly's care, Bryce felt his right side slammed from the impact of the shooter attacking him. Laid out on the floor beside Molly, he no longer possessed a firearm because he put it down when he attempted to assess her wounds. Immediately aware that the man who shot Molly, and now attacked him, meant them both harm, Bryce swung, connecting with the man's face. Although this stunned his attacker momentarily, Bryce couldn't get to his feet because the man kept hold of his legs and worked his way upward, determined to subdue the Navy man.

At first, Bryce reached for his sidearm, quickly deciding he couldn't reach it from his position. Unfortunately, the move provided the man with ample time to mount Bryce's torso and lay into him with several fists to the face, only some of which Bryce blocked.

"You're coming back with me," the man stated firmly. "You've been running like a coward all this time when you could've saved thousands by cooperating."

Bryce immediately knew why this man was here, and what he wanted. The words, however, sparked an ember inside of him that grew to a fury so intense that he used a sudden adrenaline rush to throw the man off to one side. Wasting no time, Bryce tackled him and returned the favor, striking the man several times in the jaw.

"You just shot an innocent woman," he said with venom in his tone. "That makes you a piece of shit!"

Attempting to defend himself, the man poked Bryce in one eye with his thumb, giving him a brief opportunity to free himself from under the Navy man.

"You're a traitor and a coward," the man said, equally angered. "She was aiding and abetting, so she got what was coming to her."

Both men stood, breathing hard with their breath visible in the frigid air, holding their fists at their sides.

"My people left me for dead," Bryce spat. "Then they have the nerve to send you mercenaries to drag me back when I'm suddenly useful."

"I don't need to hear your lies," the man said, and Bryce wasn't certain what branch the man served in, but he didn't care at this point. "They said you had to be breathing when I brought you back. That means I can beat you until you're a vegetable for all I care."

"Bring it on," Bryce said, motioning for the man to charge him.

Accepting the invitation, the man ran forward, tackling him through the front door like a football player, landing them both in the snow outside, with the door propped open by their bodies. A zombie, barely functional in the cold, took notice of their skirmish, and sluggishly made its way toward them.

"I was lucky to find you," the man said, wrapping his hands around Bryce's throat, much like the Marine who confronted Bryce in Indiana. "We knew where you were headed. We always knew."

Sounding incredibly assured, as though the military created some kind of background check, complete with psychological mockup, the man likely knew where Bryce was heading. Access to his personnel files only revealed so much, but they probably spoke to anyone who ever worked with him, including Mark Dascher, the man who captained his last ship.

If they knew details about the resort, that placed Bryce's entire family in danger, and he didn't want them used as leverage. He also didn't want Molly dying, so he wedged both of his hands between his attacker's grip and thrust them outward, breaking the hold. Bryce shot a fist directly upward, catching the man beneath the jaw, likely causing him to bite his tongue. Instinctively, the man reached for the shotgun he discarded during his ruse, stating he'd mistakenly shot Molly. Now he intended to strike Bryce with the butt of the weapon, but Bryce grasped his forearms, wrestling the man for the firearm before it left him incapable of defending himself.

With the shotgun turned sideways, the man began to press the weapon downward, towards Bryce's throat as the zombie rounded a vehicle parked near the building. Mere feet away from the battle, the zombie staggered through the harsh wind as Bryce fought to keep the shotgun from pressing down on his windpipe. Only a few inches away from feeling the cold metal against his skin, he pressed upward, knowing gravity wasn't on his side.

"You shouldn't believe everything they tell you," Bryce strained to say as he pushed upward, giving the shotgun one forceful heave, launching his adversary off to one side.

Infuriated, the man immediately went on the attack, and Bryce aimed the shotgun's barrel at the man, pulling the trigger to find the gun hadn't been re-loaded, based on the clicking sound it produced. His actions stopped the man in his tracks momentarily, as though he expected to be torn apart by pellets. When the man's eyes narrowed, focusing on Bryce before he took one step forward, a gunshot of a different kind rang through the small enclosure.

Struck in the side, where blood dribbled from the fresh wound, the attacker appeared stunned as he wiped his fingers against the injury, coating his fingers in blood. He leaned against the wall momentarily and stumbled forward, allowing Bryce to grab his belt with one hand and pull him forward where the zombie managed to grasp him with icy fingers. Pulling the man to the ground, the zombie sank its yellowed teeth into his neck and the man's screams pierced Bryce's ears until Bryce stood, returning to the slightly warmer shelter to check on Molly.

Still holding the AR-15 that dealt the ultimately mortal wound to Bryce's attacker, her eyes were fading, and her breathing labored.

"I'm so sorry," Bryce said, cupping her head with his hand. "Thank you."

She tried to speak, but words still weren't coming as her eyes focused on him for only a second or two before gazing upward to the ceiling. Blood saturated the entire front of her jacket, and Bryce knew nothing could be done to save her. Even in a modern world with ambulances and doctors, he questioned if Molly's wounds would be fatal.

He doubted anyone could survive a similar gunshot at close range.

Feeling a tear reach his right eye, Bryce dreaded continuing the journey alone. He chastised himself for being so selfish as a friend lay dying in his arms, but he couldn't do a thing to ease her pain.

"Don't let me," Molly managed to say as her eyes trained on him for a few seconds.

She didn't finish the sentence, but Bryce knew exactly what she meant. During their time together, they promised they wouldn't take any chances of the other joining the undead legions, even if no evidence of a bite or scratch presented itself.

"I won't," he promised. "I'm so sorry."

"Not your fault," she stammered before coughing up a bit of blood, which spilled onto her chest, blending with the already saturated cloth.

Her fingers gently touched his palm, and he clasped her hand, knowing her life measured in seconds.

"Find them," she said, coughing once more, violently this time, before her head fell back and her eyes remained open, staring beyond Bryce's left shoulder.

Unable to move for several seconds, Bryce remained on his knees, vigilantly at her side, feeling guilty if he left her too soon. No human eyes viewed his actions, yet he felt that Molly deserved better than dying on a cold floor, being left in a rest stop without a proper burial. Bryce couldn't help his parents, being thousands of miles away in foreign waters, but he felt obligated to protect Molly, or at least share the responsibility of keeping them both safe.

Instead, the target on his back got her killed.

Finally letting go of her hand, Bryce cupped his face in his hands, fighting back tears he needed to cry. He felt ashamed, though she wasn't a ward in his care like so many green sailors on his ship in the Navy. Fierce and capable until the very end, she saved him several times over, and Bryce knew why his brother respected the woman so much. Even so, Bryce questioned if he could keep his own family safe when the military kept sending personnel to track him down.

He waited a few minutes until his nerves began to settle. When the wind died down momentarily, he heard no wails from outside, and he couldn't even hear the zombie feasting on the man who attacked him a few minutes earlier. Bryce no longer wanted to stay inside, fearing the awful memories made here more than the cold and wind outside. He began gathering his belongings, along with the AR-15, stuffing everything useful into his pack for travel.

With his nerves collected, he knelt beside Molly, brushed his fingers over her eyes to close them, and drew the knife from his side. Without looking directly at his work, he slid the blade into the back of her skull, along the softer lower portion. Assured he reached the brain so she couldn't possibly reanimate, Bryce stood, sniffling back some mucus in his nose. He wiped the knife along her pants, cleaning the blood before setting it aside. Taking her head in both of his hands, he gently kissed her on the forehead, thankful she tagged along instead of striking out on her own.

Already bundled up for the cold, he shoved the door open, finding the zombie still focused on devouring the victim gifted to him. Bryce forcefully jabbed the zombie in the skull, putting it down before dropping to his knees to ensure the man sent for him didn't return for a second life as well.

Bryce searched the man's pockets, finding an Army identification, which he pocketed, along with the man's dog tags. Finding a few semitransparent shotgun shells in the man's pockets, Bryce determined they were the beanbag variety that police used to subdue unruly suspects. Obviously, they were meant for him, and for some reason the soldier didn't reload the shotgun.

He didn't know why the man felt compelled to shoot Molly, unless he wanted to make certain nothing interfered with him claiming Bryce as a prize. He considered the move a complete waste, because two people wound up dead. Bryce didn't want to be a liability, nor did he want the military to use him as an experiment for a vaccine. He didn't know what these military kids being sent for him were told, but he knew he needed to retrieve his family before anyone else located them.

Looking around, he saw the two bodies beside him already covered in a light blanket of snow. Visibility hadn't improved, but he felt determined to head east and retrieve his family. He wasn't certain what his next move was after that, but he didn't plan on going anywhere near military bases. If the military truly knew where his family was staying, he couldn't endanger them, or his in-laws, but he needed to find somewhere safe for their group to wait out the winter.

Beginning to walk along the interstate, Bryce hadn't gotten far when he felt certain he heard the sound of a running vehicle. Cautiously, he tracked the noise, weaving through stalled vehicles and ducking down to avoid detection. He finally spotted a Humvee in the distance, mostly clear of snow, sitting in the middle of the road. Bryce waited a few minutes before daring to approach it, thinking the dead soldier might have an accomplice, but Bryce finally discovered the vehicle was empty, and left running by the man as though he had decided to check out the rest area and discovered Molly and Bryce by accident.

Bryce opened the door, giving one last look around before examining the seats inside, finding them empty. He then slid inside, glad to be out of the cold, though he discovered the heater only provided warm air at best, because they were built with stock heating units. Sitting back, he got comfortable in the seat, trying to keep his thoughts from returning to the attack. He needed to focus, but his mind kept shifting to the loss of a close friend, and he began to understand the pain his brother endured during his travels.

"Let's hope you have some fuel," Bryce muttered before daring to steal a glance at the dashboard.

Twenty-One

Three Days Later

"That's a hell of a lot of snow," Timmons said, looking out the window of the main building at the resort.

Even in the late morning, the sky appeared dark and dreary without any sign of letting up on precipitation.

"I've seen worse," Metzger said, taking his side as pasty flakes landed on the glass and melted just as quickly.

"You can't go out in this," Timmons insisted.

"I don't have much choice," Metzger said. "We're running out of supplies, and our last few runs didn't exactly go as planned."

Some of the locations on the marked map Harold provided him were already picked clean, and in one case, the undead surrounded the area. Metzger knew how to deal with a fair number of zombies, but he couldn't handle a hundred at a time without a game plan. The property in question was an elementary school more than twenty miles from their location in Lake George, which housed some tourist attractions and a theme park Metzger recalled attending before his teenage years.

"You didn't need to do that Christmas run the way you did," Timmons said, referring to a particular trip Metzger took to find some holiday cheer for everyone at the resort.

"It worked, didn't it? Besides, I wasn't about to let my nephew go without anything for Christmas."

"That boy will be missing a lot more than presents in the future."

"We all needed a little cheering up, Scott. Nathan misses his dad."

Metzger missed his brother as well, and grew concerned with each passing day, particularly since Bryce knew where to find them.

He made a trip into one of the nearby small towns, finding small gifts for everyone at the resort around the Christmas holiday. Isabella's parents put up decorations and a nine-foot tree with colorful lights in the main building. Metzger even located wrapping paper and tape at a thrift shop he looted during one of the trips, finding a few food items and supplies as well.

To say Nathan's eyes lit up when he opened up the toys his uncle found for him would certainly be an overstatement, but the boy's thoughts were on the holiday for a day, and not the fact that he hadn't seen his father in months.

Metzger heard the dryer running in the nearby laundry room, which felt like a regular occurrence, sometimes lulling him into a false sense of normality.

"I don't like the idea of you making this trip alone," Timmons told him with a serious, concerned expression.

"It'll be quick and easy."

"None of these trips have been quick and easy."

"We just need a few things to tide us over until the weather breaks. The dead won't be an issue with the freezing weather."

"I'm not worried about the dead. Those kids we saw in the fall have a camp somewhere. They've been raiding the same places as us, and it's only a matter of time before we find them or their friends."

Staring at the accumulation of nearly six inches, Metzger worried slightly about getting stuck, but his previous trips helped him locate some vehicles capable of maneuvering through the snow.

"Those kids aren't a threat, even after the way you treated them."

"How exactly did I treat them?" Timmons asked with a raised eyebrow.

"Like they were murderous criminals."

"That sounds like a stretch."

Metzger shook his head.

"Let's just say kid gloves are *not* in your arsenal, Scott."

"Kids, adults, the infected, whatever, you shouldn't be going out there alone."

Metzger stared out the window a few seconds longer, considering the entire front of the building was comprised of glass and a few structural elements. He wondered how the building remained reasonably warm with so much glass, which certainly wasn't a good insulator.

"I dare say I won't be traveling today," Metzger decided aloud. "It's coming down a little too thick out there."

Jillian entered through the main door, located on the parking lot side of the building, spying the two men talking in the foyer. She immediately walked over and planted a kiss on Metzger's lips, which he enjoyed, taking a few seconds to savor the taste of whatever mouthwash she chose to use that morning. Enjoyable tastes and smells often eluded survivors of the apocalypse, so they savored them whenever possible.

"I think I liked it better when you two were keeping things secret," Timmons said, fighting to roll his eyes at them.

"Methinks flyboy is jealous," Jillian said with a grin when her lips parted from Metzger's.

Jillian walked behind the check-in counter where a refrigerator was located in a small room, taking a bottled water from the appliance.

"You two have a lot to learn about relationships," Timmons commented when she returned.

Instead of taking the bait and simply asking for an elaboration, Jillian chose a different path.

"Did you have one of those nicknames pilots always have in the movies?"

"They're called call signs," Timmons answered somewhat testily.

"Did they call you Salty Dog, or Silver Bolt maybe?"

Timmons scowled at the line of questioning, because he disliked ribbing about his age. He didn't consider himself that old, because he felt incredibly fit, but the median age changed drastically when the world fell to the dead.

"You're going to think it's funny when you need this pilot to fly you somewhere and he doesn't comply."

Metzger didn't particularly need his girlfriend and mentor bickering in front of him, but the winter caused everyone to go stir crazy inside the limited space the resort offered.

"Come on now, Jillian," he said, taking her hand. "Leave Gray Goose alone."

Timmons shook his head.

"Keep it up, you two. You really should respect your-"

"Elders?" Metzger finished for the pilot.

"You two are going to get there someday," Timmons said, pointing his finger back and forth between Metzger and Jillian. "I just hope your kids give you shit about being old each and every day."

His mention of children caused Metzger and Jillian to look at one another with odd expressions, because neither had ever mentioned their desires for the future. The apocalypse tended to leave them with dreams and plans that didn't extend past a week or two.

"You're going to have kids," Timmons assured them. "The world is going to run out of rubbers someday, and when you have little ones running around, guess who isn't going to babysit?"

"Come on," Jillian said, continuing to tease Timmons. "They're going to want to spend time with Grandpa Scott."

"Not funny," Timmons replied seriously.

Jillian noticed something out the mammoth front glass, walking toward the surface with undivided attention.

"Is that a person out there?" she questioned almost to herself.

All three of them rushed to the glass, like dogs thinking their owner was home, to find a young woman struggling up the hill that led to the parking lot. She stumbled and fell about fifty feet from them, and all three sensed her urgency as they backed away from the glass.

"I'll get Phyllis and Harold," Timmons said, prepared to head to the cabins as Jillian and Metzger went out the main door to assist the woman.

Dashing down the snowy drive to her side, they helped her to her feet, noticing immediately her face was pink from the cold, and several cuts and bruises covered her face and her hands.

"Come on," Jillian urged her as she and Metzger each took an arm to support the woman as they walked to the main building.

Once inside, they sat her down at one of the chairs inside the old lounge, letting her catch her breath and get warm.

"Are you injured?" Metzger inquired.

"Nothing too bad," the young woman answered.

Wearing some basic winter gear that appeared mostly dark gray or black, the woman wore a winter hat that barely covered half her ears, and gloves appearing tattered and torn from her trek through the woods.

"How did you get here?" Jillian asked.

Harold and Phyllis walked into the room, with Timmons directly behind them.

"Amber?" Phyllis inquired, drawing surprised stares from everyone except Harold.

Phyllis weaved her way around everyone else to kneel beside the exhausted woman. She reached up, feeling her way around Amber's forehead, face, and neck, checking for injuries or other issues.

"She used to work here," Harold explained to everyone else in the room, keeping his voice just above a whisper.

"What happened to you, dear?" Phyllis asked of their new arrival. "We figured you and your brother made it home once the apocalypse hit."

"We did," Amber said, sounding completely spent. "It's such a long story."

"It's okay, dear. Get warm, and we'll fix you something to eat. You must be starved."

Metzger motioned for Harold to speak to him away from the others.

"Where is she from?"

"Their parents lived an hour from Pittsburgh," Harold answered. "When things went bad, she and her brother said they were heading home to check on their folks."

"How do you know them, exactly?"

"They worked here for an internship last spring."

Although he didn't say anything, Metzger suspected Amber and her brother knew about the amenities at the resort, and how a person might live off the land, yet enjoy a small sense of luxury. A single person traveling from Pennsylvania to the Adirondacks felt out of place to him. Aside from the military base, he had yet to personally find a residence that resembled pre-apocalyptic conditions.

"You're thinking something," Harold commented with just a trace of a smirk on his lips.

"We really need to hear her story over a hot meal, Harold."

Timmons pulled Metzger aside next, the concern written on his face.

"This doesn't add up," the pilot said.

"I know. I want to hear what she has to say, then I might take a drive down the mountain."

"You just canceled your supply trip. Heading downhill for a different purpose doesn't make it safer. Or easier."

Timmons paced the floor a moment, just out of sight from everyone else.

"Personally, I wouldn't travel this far *hoping* this place was still standing and functional," he said, referring to Amber's journey.

Metzger tended to agree. After dealing with numerous threats, he suspected Amber might have friends lurking nearby if she was lying. He didn't want to suspect the worst of someone Phyllis and Harold knew personally, so he kept his notions to himself.

"Keep quiet until we hear her out," he said to Timmons. "We can't alienate our hosts."

Isabella and Nathan walked in through the rear entrance, and Metzger noticed the confusion on Isabella's face.

"We have a guest," he told her as she peered into the former lounge area.

"Who the hell hikes up here?" Isabella questioned.

"That's what we thought," Timmons said before biting his bottom lip in thought.

"What?" Metzger asked, curious what the captain was contemplating.

"We can't possibly secure this whole place against multiple people."

"You boys are getting a little ahead of yourselves," Isabella said. "I'd like to hear what she has to say before we go boarding up windows and doors."

Metzger looked to his nephew, who appeared rather excited at the prospect of another person joining their group. Nathan grew bored without other children around, and so little to do at the resort. Metzger refused to take his nephew with him on supply runs, though he often managed to find books, games, and other activities for Nathan in the towns. Nathan kept trying to get a closer look at their new guest, but Isabella held him back protectively.

Jillian left Amber's side, joining Metzger and the others in the adjacent room.

"What do you think?" Metzger inquired.

"I'm not sure," Jillian replied. "But I think we should get to cooking a warm meal."

"Any particular reason?"

"The sooner we all sit down, the sooner we get answers," Jillian said before heading for the kitchen to see what ingredients and supplies they possessed to create a decent lunch.

"I think I love her," Metzger told Timmons once she walked away.

"If you're not sure, you're probably thinking with your dick," Timmons responded.

"I meant it facetiously."

Timmons gave a knowing grin.

"Sure you did, son. Sure you did."

***

While Jillian prepared a lunch for the group, because she wanted the group present when Amber told her tale, Phyllis made the young woman a cup of hot chocolate to keep her warm.

Jillian cooked some Salisbury steaks with au gratin potatoes from a box, setting a table inside the main building for everyone. When they sat down as a collective, Metzger studied Amber, who had removed her wet winter clothing, exchanging the garments for dry sweat pants and a sweater that Phyllis managed to locate for her.

Metzger guessed Amber's age to be around twenty, which possibly explained Jillian's dislike for her. Despite Jillian's age, she had experienced a lifetime of tragedy and betrayal during the apocalypse. She also knew to remain suspicious of new arrivals until they proved themselves worthy of being part of their group.

Amber possessed strawberry blonde hair with a handful of reddish freckles dotting her face. Her hair looked like an unfinished bird nest, with hair fibers sticking out in every direction despite her efforts to tame it. She continued to shiver for nearly half an hour straight after coming inside, but Metzger didn't see any serious injuries on her, or lingering effects from the cold once Amber warmed her bones inside the resort building.

Everyone held off eating, wanting to avoid being rude as they waited for her to take a bite. She finally ate some of the steak, and then another bite, and then another. After the third bite, she licked her lips self-consciously as though she felt guilty for eating.

"What's the matter, dear?" Phyllis asked her, and Metzger couldn't tell if the older woman was genuinely concerned, or feigning until the group learned the truth.

Phyllis wasn't easily swayed, but her history with Amber might prove a weak spot.

"It's everything," Amber answered slowly, her eyes growing misty.

"Where is Ronnie?" Phyllis pressed cautiously. "Is he coming?"

"No," Amber said, looking down solemnly at her plate. "He didn't make it."

"I'm so sorry, dear," Phyllis said. "Finish your lunch and you can tell us what happened."

At this point everyone else began to eat, partly because they didn't want to make their guest feel as though they were staring at her, but also because the meal was a welcome change from eggs and random canned goods.

When they finished, Amber appeared weary, but everyone gathered in the lobby where they had moved seating enough for all of them during the past month. Harold washed dishes, and everyone from the group gathered to hear how Amber made her way back to the resort.

"When everything went bad, Ronnie and I were separated. I was living at home with our parents in Pennsylvania, but he was in Kentucky interviewing for a job."

"She and Ronnie are twins," Phyllis explained for the benefit of everyone in the room.

Metzger knew twins shared a bond likely stronger than the one he shared with his older brother.

"It took us a few months to reach a destination we picked when we last talked on the phone," Amber stated almost absently. "I got there first, and waited almost two weeks. I'd almost given up hope when Ronnie made it."

"What about your parents?" Timmons asked, barely masking his skepticism.

"I left them at home," Amber said. "They were going to make a stand there with some neighbors."

"They didn't want to go with you to find their son?"

"I didn't go alone," Amber said. "My boyfriend and a neighbor went with me. We had some food, and some weapons."

Metzger listened intently, but in his mind, he considered the possibility she wasn't alone at the moment. He wanted to take a trip down the mountain to see if he could locate any signs of additional strangers. One look outside indicated the snow wasn't going to let up anytime soon, which served to cover both footprints and tire tracks everywhere.

"My parents had other family to take care of," Amber said, directing her gaze directly at Timmons. "My brother and I had a plan, and maybe my parents didn't know I was leaving when I did, or they might have tried to stop me."

"So, you met your brother, and then what?" Phyllis inquired, her voice remaining calm.

"We lost our neighbor before reaching Pennsylvania," Amber said. "We had to stay the night in a trailer park and we couldn't see very well. The dead made their way into the manager's office where we were sleeping and attacked him."

She spoke the words numbly, staring at the wall, and not the people anxiously awaiting answers.

"We got back to town and ended up searching for days for our parents," she continued. "They weren't where they had talked about going, and after I left, maybe they changed their plans."

"Did they go looking for you?" Jillian asked, possibly seeing similarities to her own situation.

"I left a note so they wouldn't worry that I'd died, or run away," Amber said, wiping aside a tear. "They stayed close to home, probably because I had others with me, but they didn't make it. The dead were everywhere in the town, and they were locked in a church with at least twenty other people. By the time we got there, everyone inside was dead, and most of them were chewed up."

"That must've been terrible," Phyllis said sympathetically.

"My boyfriend went to check on his family," Amber continued. "We waited a few days, because they lived only a few towns over, but he didn't come back. I should've gone with him, but he insisted on going alone. He said he didn't know what he'd find over there."

"Did you eventually go?" Metzger inquired, keeping his tone neutral.

"We did," Amber answered, looking directly at him. "My brother and I looked through the town, hiding as best we could for another two days. I never found Adam, or his family, so I hope they took off, or found somewhere safe to lay low."

"But why come here?" Jillian asked of their guest. "This is a long way from home, and there was no guarantee the resort would be standing."

"We knew the risks," Amber replied. "It's only one state away, and we weren't sure if anyone would think to stay here or not. We knew it had what we needed to survive, and figured the dead wouldn't hike up a mountain to get us."

"Where is your brother, dear?" Phyllis asked, though her expression indicated she expected to hear tragic news.

Metzger wasn't certain if Phyllis bought the story without question, or used one of her management techniques, attempting to catch Amber in a lie. His own opinion wasn't completely formed, though he didn't like the idea of anyone else arriving at the resort unexpectedly.

"I lost him just east of Rochester," Amber answered, looking directly to the floor.

Metzger studied her movements, trying to see if she shed crocodile tears, or excessively mourned her lost brother for show. She shed a single tear, and looked to Phyllis seconds later, showing resolve despite all of the losses in her life.

"The snow slowed the dead, so they were barely a threat outside, but we needed shelter," Amber continued. "We found a show cabin near one of the exits and wanted to spend the night, but there were other people already there."

She hesitated.

"They shot Ronnie," she said. "I think he died instantly, but they aimed at me so I ran out the door. I just ran and ran, and they kept shooting. I don't know how I got away."

"Me either," Timmons grumbled so only Metzger heard his words.

Metzger ushered him away from the others, to one of the rear rooms in the main building.

"I can put this to bed pretty quickly," he said.

"How's that?"

"One little trip down the mountain will let us know if she had anyone else with her."

"You see that white stuff coming down outside, son?" Timmons questioned. "Tire tracks and footprints will be long gone before you could ever determine if anyone else was there. Besides, there's more than one way up here."

"The other ways involve a lot of effort."

"We're talking about young adults, here. If they're willing to hike from Pennsylvania to this place, a little mountain ain't gonna stop them."

Metzger felt frustrated, because he hated not knowing about threats. After some near misses early in the apocalypse, he didn't take people at face value any longer.

"You should stay here and protect your family," Timmons said earnestly.

"How long do we keep this up?" Metzger questioned. "We can't keep vigil day and night, hoping no one else shows up. This place might be compromised for us."

"We can't throw in the towel."

"We're not doing any such thing," Metzger said adamantly. "Until I know my brother is safe, and here, we'll do whatever it takes to keep this place."

In the background, Amber continued to provide details of her story to Phyllis and the others.

"She's starting to give more specifics about her journey here," he said. "Maybe she *is* telling the truth."

"She's had almost six months to manufacture that story," Timmons said, not budging. "Whatever happened, this place is her endgame."

Metzger stared at the snow continuing to fall heavily outside, knowing he couldn't travel safely down the mountain without a large vehicle. Everyone was snowbound until the snow ceased, or the temperature climbed enough to melt the white substance once again.

"We keep an eye on her," Metzger decided aloud. "Until we can figure out if her story is true, we watch her like hawks and we don't let her near Nathan."

Turning his attention to the room where the conversation continued, Metzger felt uneasy, knowing any shreds of truth to be discovered would soon be revealed. Until then, he required proof to fully trust Amber, because he realized Timmons spoke from experience, and the man had good reason not to take people at their word.

Taking one last look outside, Metzger decided he would travel when the weather broke to learn what he could about Amber's travels.

And any secrets she left behind.

Twenty-Two

The Next Morning

Brad Weir arrived in the town of Conway, South Carolina in a timely manner with Mullins, but the search for his family didn't go well. One of the members of his church chose the town of Conway because he had family there, and because the town was located on the waterfront, and not far from Myrtle Beach. The colorful, picturesque images in his mind were replaced by the sepia reality of the apocalypse where zombies roamed the streets and dust covered everything.

For over a month, the two former cops remained in the town, and the surrounding area, looking for signs of Weir's family. They fished the waters for food after locating some poles, tools, and bait. Much of their problem lied in larger groups prowling the area, and Weir quickly realized why his family and the others might have moved on to a safer location. He wasn't certain all of the groups were dangerous, but he dared not approach them, simply hoping for a favorable outcome.

Each day they tried a different location, often outside of town, typically locating abandoned vehicles, the undead, and every so often, other survivors. Traveling light, the duo carried sidearms and a few rifles. Clothes, they learned along the way, could be found inside any house they deemed safe to search, and they often times kept only a spare shirt and some extra underwear with them.

On this day, he located a small bus outside of a grade school that gave him promise. Clothes flapped along a makeshift clothesline outside of the school, and voices could be heard from within. Now shortly after dawn, several birds chirped, and insects hummed, living comfortably in the warmer climate of South Carolina. He and Mullins had parked their latest vehicle, an old S-10 pickup truck, several blocks away and approached the facility on foot. Trying to avoid looking like intruders or terrorists, they kept their hands away from their sidearms, approaching the school cautiously. Weir fought to keep his emotions in check, listening to the voices from within, hoping one of them might belong to his wife.

"South Conway Elementary School," Mullins read the lettering along the front entrance's awning.

A reasonably modern facility, the school was a place the two men visited previously, but they found no activity on those occasions. Hearing conversational voices, Weir felt drawn to the school because the bus out front looked similar to the bus the group left with from New York. He wondered if the group chose a similar bus to the one they abandoned because they wanted to stick it out for his benefit.

Both men gave up shaving a few months back, sporting beards that contained more gray hair than either recalled seeing the last time they grew them out. Both had done some undercover work, earlier in their careers, and the years had changed their appearances, expedited by the conditions brought about with the apocalypse.

"You okay?" Mullins asked when Weir stood frozen a moment, staring at the school, feeling too apprehensive to approach it.

He experienced heartbreak repeatedly when he and his friend located small groups that turned out to be families or banded survivors that he didn't recognize. Often, they scouted the areas first, seeing the people from a distance so they didn't risk getting shot or captured.

"I can't take much more of this, Mike," Weir confessed. "I'm sure this makes me an asshole for saying it, but I envy you because you had your answers pretty quick."

"It makes you human, brother," Mullins said. "I hate seeing you in this much pain, not knowing where they went."

Voices of children reached the ears of the two men, possibly from the school playground behind the school, and Weir felt as though the apocalypse didn't exist for a few fleeting seconds.

Without giving it thought, he stepped forward, wanting to see the people who lived devoid of concerns in a world ruled by the undead.

"Brad," Mullins cautioned.

"Stay back if you want, Mike," Weir said. "I've got to see this."

Weir approached the front entrance, finding the double doors propped open by rocks, as though people were in the middle of moving items inside, and didn't want them closing. Aside from the bus, no other vehicles appeared as though they were parked at the school in recent days or weeks. The scene appeared more like parents preparing for a fund-raiser bake sale instead of moving their belongings into the latest shelter.

Stopping just short of the entrance, Weir felt numb with shock when he saw a familiar woman rounding the corner, down the hall, heading his way for a return trip to the bus. Both of them stood momentarily, unable to move or speak, even as Weir felt a wave of emotion wash over him as he locked eyes with Jolene, his wife.

Both of them remained frozen, and a few seconds felt like an eternity to Weir, until his two sons rounded the corner, turning to spot him. He darted forward, dropping to his knees and pulling them both into a large hug, kissing each of their foreheads. He fought back tears, trying to remain strong for his boys, because there wasn't room for softness in the apocalypse.

"You made it," Jolene said quietly when he stood to embrace her.

"I just kept trying," he said, pulling away briefly to take them all in, finding them all in good health. "When we found the bus, I was so worried."

"It broke down," Jolene said. "We traveled in separate cars until we found another one."

Over the next few minutes, hardly any of them spoke as they simply enjoyed the moment, feeling a range of emotions after completing a nearly impossible task in the apocalypse by finding one another. It didn't take long, however, for Weir to regain his survival instincts that allowed him to travel from state to state safely.

"Why were the doors propped open?" he asked his wife.

"A few of the guys are checking the school from front to back," Jolene answered. "We were more fearful of what they might find in here than outside."

"It isn't always as peaceful as it is this morning."

Mullins finally approached them after respectfully giving them some family time. The boys appeared a bit apprehensive of the former cop, but Weir quickly spoke up.

"You remember my friend Mike, right?" he asked them. "He's the reason I made it all the way down here to find you."

Jolene gave Mullins a quick hug to thank him, and the boys joined in as well. His oldest, Colton, was just turning twelve, and the younger boy, Layton, was two years younger than his brother. Many days passed where Weir found himself regretting letting them go ahead without him. He trusted the people his family traveled with, but he didn't feel as though he accomplished as much good in the Buffalo area as he'd hoped to.

"Thank you," Jolene said to Mullins, who simply nodded graciously with a grin.

Weir had detected a bit of unease with his travel companion after they left the Navy base in Virginia, though Mullins never elaborated on what thoughts ran through his mind.

"You're welcome," Mullins said to Jolene before looking down to the boys. "Your dad saved my bacon a few times out there, you know."

"Did you have to kill the monsters?" Layton inquired.

"Oh, yeah," Mullins answered. "We had to kill some monsters."

"We'll have time for scary stories later," Weir said. "Let's get this place cleared so we can settle in."

***

By late afternoon everyone had gotten acclimated to one another, and Weir learned that only one person on the bus trip was fatally wounded because she chose to venture too far into a wooded area to relieve herself. A small band of zombies heard her movement and bit her several times, slowing the group's travel when they were forced to tend to her wounds. She held out almost two days before succumbing to the infection, and the group dealt with her body accordingly.

Weir spent a little bit of his day catching up with everyone else from the bus, thanking them for keeping his family safe during their travels. Traveling in small groups, they cleared the school within one hour, finding no other settlers inside. Many useful supplies were gone, though a few items remained, along with adequate space for everyone to have their own space inside the large building.

Sitting in the playground area with a fire started in a pit the group constructed, they cooked some cans of beef stew from a small, virtually hidden pantry someone discovered inside the maintenance room. Like the walls of a castle, the school itself surrounded the playground, providing a safe habitat for the children and adults alike. Weir spent the afternoon shoring up several doors to ensure any curious travelers or marauders didn't simply enter the school without someone hearing them.

"What's wrong?" Weir asked Mullins, who sat beside him in classroom chairs everyone brought outside to the bonfire where they cooked the stew.

At his feet, the boys barely moved, having stayed by his side all morning and afternoon.

"What do you mean?" Mullins retorted with a confused look.

"You've been quiet all day," Weir noted. "Hell, you've been quiet since we left the Navy base. What gives?"

Mullins drew a pensive breath, looking skyward at the stars above the school. Weir considered the location ideal, with water around them for drinking and fishing, while the density of the dead appeared lower than other areas the duo visited during their travels. Even so, he suspected Mullins felt differently.

"I can't stay," Mullins answered after a few seconds.

"What do you mean you can't stay?" Weir asked incredulously. "This place is a paradise compared to some of the areas we've seen."

"It's not about settling down for me," Mullins answered. "When we were at the base, I felt like part of something bigger. I want to help track the guy responsible for all of this."

"That's a pipe dream, Mike."

"Dan didn't think so," Mullins said. "He tried to do his part, even though he didn't have a dog in the fight."

"We all have a stake in this, Mike," Weir said. "That guy is still out there, and there's nothing saying there isn't another phase to his plan."

Jolene cleared her throat, drawing the attention of both former cops.

"Can you two take it elsewhere before you scare the boys?" she requested.

"Stay put, boys," Weir said as he and Mullins rose from their chairs to speak somewhere else.

Mullins led the way inside the school, which provided them with barely enough light to see one another as dusk quickly approached. Standing in the hallway, Mullins leaned against a nearby wall while Weir paced the floor.

"We just got here," he said. "You can't just up and leave. Or at least you shouldn't."

"I'm happy for you," Mullins said. "You found your family, and your paradise."

"Then share it with me, brother."

"I've got to do more than simply exist."

"What does *that* mean?"

"It means I want to help with the search for this guy. You saw the clues plain as day with me when we came across those survivors. They were heading towards sanctuary with that Nadeau guy. This isn't over, Brad."

"I can't repay the favor," Weir said, feeling exasperated, saddened, and trapped. "I can't go with you."

"I know," Mullins said, providing a comforting grin.

"I'm begging you to reconsider. If something happens to you, I'd never live with myself."

"If something happens to me, you'll never know."

"And that's what scares me, Mike. Please don't do this to me."

Mullins straightened from the wall, taking a few steps into the hallway.

"I'm not asking anything of you," he said. "This is something I have to do with what time I have left."

"What do you mean by that?"

"We talked about this," Mullins said. "You know I had pancreatic cancer, right?"

"Of course."

"There's nowhere left for me to go for checkups, Brad. Eventually, it's going to return, and there won't be any stopping it."

"You don't know that," Weir said, ready to say just about anything to get his friend to stay.

"I'm no psychic," Mullins admitted, "but I know my luck is eventually going to run out."

"Then live your life. Don't go on some suicide mission just because you think the military is acting too slowly on the Nadeau search."

Mullins took a deep breath and exhaled audibly.

"I want to do some good while I still have time. You did me a huge favor when you helped me track down my family. I repaid in kind. We're even, Brad."

Mullins took a few seconds before speaking again.

"I'm heading back to Virginia to see if I can help in the search, help Dan, help anyone I can along the way."

"There has to be another way."

"There isn't," Mullins said, his mind very much made up from the resolve scrawled in his expression.

Both stood silently a moment, neither able to muster their next words for the person they each spent the past six months traveling with through all kinds of mortal danger.

"I've known for a while," Weir admitted.

"Known what?"

"You were yearning for something else. I felt like I was holding you back, because you wouldn't have left Virginia if you weren't helping me."

"We're even," Mullins insisted. "Seriously."

An awkward silence filled the air before Mullins spoke again.

"If not for you, I might not have made it out of Buffalo. I might've been devoured by the undead, or put a gun to my head after a while. Every single thing I lived for died in that city, and if I didn't have a living person around me, God only knows how things would have gone."

"I guess I'm not talking you out of this," Weir said, depressed about losing the only steady companion in his life since the start of the apocalypse.

"You'll know where to find me," Mullins assured him. "If they can light up that town next to the base, maybe they can restore the world before it gets too fucked up."

Weir gave a heavy sigh.

"When are you leaving?"

"Tomorrow morning."

Wier shook his head, still incapable of believing what his friend told him.

"I'm exhausted," he admitted. "You can't be doing much better. Give it a day or two."

"I'll be fine. Without having to stop so often, I can make good time back to Virginia."

Weir thought of the numerous times they took short detours to look for his family, or search for supplies. Traveling alone made that aspect of the journey easier, but it also left a single person vulnerable to packs of the undead.

"We can get you food and supplies to get you started," Weir offered. "A car."

"I appreciate that," Mullins said. "We can talk in the morning, Brad. For now, let's go spend some time with your family before I leave."

Weir smirked, hoping the overnight might prove enough time to change his friend's mind about heading north alone.

He doubted it, but he didn't plan on giving up.

Twenty-Three

Two Days Later

Bryce Metzger felt relieved when he finally reached the edge of the Adirondacks, knowing only hours remained before he was reunited with his family. He wanted to call his brother and possibly ask for a ride to the resort, but the charger he used to charge his satellite phone broke, and the phone finally lost the last of its power.

Still reeling over the loss of Molly, Bryce drove the military vehicle less than halfway to the resort, managing to syphon fuel to it once from a diesel truck. With such terrible mileage, he only drove another hour or so, weaving around traffic, before the fuel gauge reached empty once again. Unfortunately, an hour didn't net many actual miles because he spent so much time on and off the interstate, dodging stalled vehicles and small herds of the infected.

He managed to spot a very vocal group of younger survivors at one point. He ducked for cover before any of them could spot him. Bryce didn't have time to make friends or get entangled in any skirmishes with unfamiliar groups. His brother had luck on his side when meeting people most of the time, but Bryce didn't take chances with civilians. He couldn't even trust people in uniform at this point, because someone at Naval Station Norfolk wanted him there in a bad way, and thankfully he understood his value to them.

Unfortunately, he no longer provided them with undying loyalty, because he felt they hadn't returned the favor.

His final travel issue came in the form of weather, because the snow hadn't ceased in days. At long last it broke in the overnight, and a warm front appeared to sweep through his home state. Like other survivors, Bryce began to feel changes in the weather, allowing him to anticipate the climate in the coming hours. A rise in the temperature might turn the snow into slush, but unplowed roads still created an issue for him when it came to ascending the road to the resort.

Not incredibly familiar with the area, Bryce knew he needed to reach elevation to spot the resort. Cursing himself for breaking the charger by slamming it in a car door during a hurried attempt to hide from the undead, he simply made his life more difficult. Finding that particular charger wasn't impossible, but it also wasn't easy the past few days with car doors frozen shut and the frigid weather nipping at every exposed body part. Sheer willpower kept Bryce moving, because he found the need to swap vehicles a few times after the Humvee ran out of diesel.

He currently drove a 1989 Ford pickup truck that didn't have four-wheel-drive, meaning it wouldn't be taking him up any steep hills.

"Who lives in New York and doesn't have four-wheel-drive?" he muttered when the driving began to get tougher.

Not in a good position to be stranded, Bryce either needed to find another vehicle, or don appropriate gear for hiking in the Adirondacks until he found some sign of the resort.

He parked in the middle of the road, because no one was traveling any roads near the mountains as daylight diminished. Soon, the purple hue of the winter sky would silhouette the towering peaks, leaving him little time to make a decision or find shelter for the night. Bryce had no intention of hiking through the mountains after dark, knowing they covered several thousand square miles in total. Pulling out his area map, he narrowed down the area from memory, familiar with the tourist towns near the resort. If he could draw a bit closer to them, and assess the highest points from the area, he might locate his family by the next day.

"Lake Placid," Bryce said the name of one of the towns aloud.

Recalling its history, he suspected he might find a place to stay, if nothing else, because winter athletes often trained near the old Olympic grounds. He didn't bank on finding supplies, since other people likely flocked to the area during warmer weather. Bryce began saving only food and essential warming supplies when the temperatures remained frigid most of the time. Finding a house, lodge, or hotel with a fireplace wasn't always difficult, but he still needed to ensure he possessed the means to start a fire.

He managed to plot a course to the town, wanting to arrive before dark, but knowing better because travel throughout the mountains wasn't an easy task in normal conditions. Looking up from the map, he saw the sky begin to darken and change color, indicating he didn't have much time to reach his destination before dusk.

***

When Bryce reached the edge of town, nearly three hours later, he parked the truck and studied the town momentarily. Shutting off the lights, he was still able to see much of the town because the moon made a rare winter appearance, illuminating the buildings. He didn't see any lights, which wasn't uncommon, but he saw no signs of human life, including any outdoor fires, or glowing windows along any of the buildings. Strangely, a number of vehicles were parked in all kinds of positions along the main drag, as though abandoned for other vehicles.

He considered the possibility that their owners didn't survive the trek to Lake Placid, because at least a dozen undead were visible, showing signs of thawing from the frigid temperatures that finally began to rise.

Feeling uneasy for some reason, Bryce decided to drive down the main drag without his headlights on, glancing at each building he passed for signs of life. The undead were immediately drawn to the noise of the truck, beginning to follow him, which made any attempt to stay in town incredibly dangerous.

Eventually, Bryce drove down some side streets, ahead of the undead, looking for houses with chimneys. Although gas heat was a possibility in virtually any house, he suspected people around the mountains stuck with wood-burning fireplaces. Except for the zombies, much of the town appeared undisturbed, as though the apocalypse left it intact for newcomers. He recalled his parents taking him on several family vacations as a kid, sometimes to theme parks, and sometimes to places like the Adirondacks with family activities like museums and interactive historical experiences.

One look at the gas tank indicated the truck wouldn't get him much farther, and Bryce had to forego heat to keep the windows defrosted. For some reason, heat wafted from the vents, as though the blower system was dead or dying. Growing colder by the second without any daylight, Bryce searched desperately for any house that appeared to have a chimney. Most of the dead were left in the snowy streets behind him, and he wasn't going to be noticed on a side street in the small town.

Finding a two-story house, he pulled over, stopped the truck, and grabbed his gear for a dash to the front door of the house. He gave a quick, cursory rap on the front door, hearing nothing for the next few seconds. He tried the doorknob, finding it unlocked, so he let himself inside.

He stood silently in the mudroom momentarily, listening for any movement within the house. Hearing none, he moved forward, finding the house illuminated from the moon outside, though he stepped slowly to avoid attracting unwanted attention. Barely warmer than the outdoors, the house's interior showed Bryce his breath whenever he exhaled. As his eyes adjusted to the darkness, he placed his right hand atop the sidearm holstered safely along his hip.

Within a few minutes he covered the entire house, finding no living or dead person inside. Breaking out a flashlight, he took a more careful look through the residence for anything useful, coming across a few snack-sized bags of chips. He rummaged through the kitchen drawers, finding several electronic devices like a Kindle and a tablet possibly used for schoolwork. He suspected that someone who liked technology lived in the house, because a laptop computer was sitting atop one of the kitchen table chairs.

Beneath the devices in the drawer, Bryce discovered a universal charging cord. On one end, he found a USB port, and it split into four various inserts for devices. Already possessing a USB car adapter, he quickly grew excited about the prospect of calling his brother and arranging an easy ride to the resort.

Bryce couldn't recall if the old truck had a suitable cigarette lighter port, but a few other vehicular options weren't far from the house. He took a few minutes to look out the front windows, seeing only a few undead staggering through the snow nearby. No other vehicle or signs of life appeared along the street in either direction.

Taking the cord and the phone, he walked to the truck, finding it didn't have a functional port for the adapter. He trudged through the snow to the next house over, seeing two cars parked awkwardly in the yard instead of the short driveway. Both were unlocked, but the first had a dead battery, so he tried the second, finding it capable of charging the satellite phone once he plugged in the various, necessary adapters. The phone produced a chime to indicate it began charging, and a red light appeared on the charger portion plugged into the car's port. Bryce hid the phone beneath the seat, keeping it hidden, and turned the charger so the light faced the floor. He also covered the charger with a discarded sock he found in the car, draping the sock over the glowing red dot on the cord.

Because the keys were in the ignition, he took them, locking the car as he walked away. Crossing through the snow in the road, rather than the yard, Bryce found two members of the undead community had made their way through the elements, now close enough to threaten him. Even so, he outmaneuvered them, making his way to the front of the house where a third zombie emerged from the shadowy side of the building. Able to attack him before he could dodge to one side, or enter the house, the zombie took Bryce down as it lurched at him. He landed hard in the snow, immediately feeling the cold substance run down his back as the zombie snapped at him with its teeth, trying to take a bite out of his face.

Only his forearm against its neck kept it from fulfilling its wish, and the other two undead now found ample time to catch up and head directly at him.

Using his left hand, Bryce clasped the zombie by the throat, shoving it far enough back that he was able to use his right hand to draw his sidearm. He didn't want to use the gun, but he couldn't reach the knife on his left side as easily, and the other two zombies were closing in fast, meaning he needed to dispose of them quickly.

Instinct caused him to wince, attempting to shelter his ears from the impending gunfire, but when he fired the first shot through the attacking zombie's skull his ears immediately rang from the noise. He threw the dead weight aside, since the undead typically didn't weigh as much as the living, rolling to his knees and taking aim at the other zombies. Bryce waited until they drew close enough to ensure his aim hit the mark, putting holes in each of their skulls respectively before they collapsed atop the slushy snow.

His ears continued to ring as he frantically looked around, feeling certain someone heard the gunfire. No lights flipped on, and no cars veered around the block on either side of him, but Bryce felt more paranoid about the living than the dead in that moment.

Bryce possessed little of value to other survivors, but people tended to gravitate towards one another just the same. He threw some snow over the undead bodies, knowing little could be done to hide his footsteps. If anyone came looking for him, he wouldn't be able to fend off more than two people without suffering a gunshot or knife wound. Perhaps he felt paranoid because he drew so close to seeing his family again, but he dashed for the front door and locked himself inside, trying to collect his nervous breath.

"Calm down," he said to himself. "No one is going to come poking around because of some shooting."

Even so, he hid the car keys within a lazy chair's innards where the upholstery wrapped around to the underside of the chair and a staple had come loose, creating a small pocket. If someone located him, they might want him to hand over everything he possessed, and that sat phone, along with the car charging it, held more value to him than anything.

He also made certain not to use any flashlight, which made navigating the house a more difficult process. Although he located a fireplace, and virtually everything necessary to start a fire, Bryce couldn't risk calling additional attention to his location. Being out of the wind and elements felt better, and he dressed for the winter as always, so he didn't fear freezing to death.

A few times he checked the windows before chastising himself for moving curtains aside. He needed to wait long enough for the phone to reach a sufficient charge before heading to the car next door. Each minute ticked by, feeling more like an hour to Bryce as he fought to keep busy by searching the house again and getting some items together to start a fire if he ever felt safe enough to light the kindling he discovered beside the fireplace.

Nearly ten minutes passed, and Bryce harbored thoughts of checking outside to see if the satellite phone possessed enough power for a call to his brother. He suspected it did, but he didn't want to make himself an easy target if anyone had decided to search the area for a shooter. Even worse, the noise surely reached the ears of the undead, drawing them to the area as the moonlight guided them.

Still fully dressed, Bryce waited another few minutes until a noise reached his ears from the front yard. Unable to continue any activities without knowing the property remained secure, he took a peek out the front window to put his mind at ease. Instead, he found additional undead gathering on the property, which might as well have been a beacon to let survivors know his location.

"Fuck," he muttered, drawing the knife from his left side, prepared to deal with them quietly and hide the bodies in the snow, or behind some of the vehicles.

Zipping up his jacket, he drew the knife and stepped outside, poised to stab the undead closest to him when he received a powerful fist to his jaw, dropping him to the snow. His consciousness faded in and out as he saw footsteps from regular people around him that didn't drag and flop sideways like those of the undead.

"Finish those things off," he heard a male voice say.

"Don't kill him," a young woman's voice warned the man who struck Bryce and currently stood over him.

"I won't," the man replied testily.

Bryce tried to get to his feet, or perhaps his knees because everything around him continued to spin, but the man held him down, standing on his wrist that held the knife while he stripped Bryce of his sidearm.

"Don't move," he said as he patted Bryce down from head to toe, still standing on the wrist. "Let go of the knife or we'll have to shoot you."

Bryce obeyed, releasing the knife, because these people didn't seem to want him dead, and he hoped they proved to be reasonable. He struggled to regain his bearings, shaking his head as he began to realize the man who struck him was a towering figure, young and powerful, possessing the ability to hurt him far more than a fist to the face. Assessing his build proved difficult because all three of the younger people around him wore thick winter jackets.

Pinned to the ground, Bryce heard the distinct sounds of knives plunging into the skulls of the undead as they emitted final throaty noises before falling to the ground. Half a dozen or so kills took place before the trio turned their attention to him. The powerful man yanked Bryce to a seated position in the snow, and the Navy man wasn't sure what the intention of the young people around him might be. All of them appeared to be in their early twenties, the third of them being a young man of average height and build with dark hair.

Bryce didn't struggle as his taller assailant dragged him to the front of the house, placing his back against it so they could address him.

"We don't plan on killing you, but we can't have you interfering with our activities," the woman said.

Assuming her side, the shorter of the two men appeared protective as though they might have been a couple.

"I'm just trying to survive," Bryce said, trying to sound more scared than he truly felt. "I wanted to spend the night here before I moved on."

"What are you doing here?" the smaller man asked. "In this particular area."

"My parents brought me here as a kid," Bryce answered with a partial truth. "I knew there were tourist towns here, along with sources of water. It's a good place to get away from swarms of the dead."

"How do we do this?" the larger man asked the other two, concerning Bryce immensely.

He wondered if they put him at ease so he wouldn't struggle, planning to ultimately kill him anyway. His cooperation remained based on the fact they hadn't immediately killed him, and appeared to be against doing so.

Mostly.

"Disable the vehicles," the shorter man said. "All of them. Then we need to disable him."

He nodded in Bryce's direction when he spoke the words, causing Bryce to struggle once again, which proved to be useless against the power of the towering man.

"We aren't killing him," the young woman insisted.

"No," the taller man answered. "But he may wish he was dead when we get done."

Bryce wasn't physically harmed, but they bound his wrists around a pillar inside the house while they removed items from the residence. He saw them carrying clothing and several blankets outside before rummaging through the backpack he carried, taking most of the items for themselves. Saying little between one another, as though they were worker ants communicating via other means, the young group cleared the house quickly. They removed specific objects, possibly filling their needs, before the shorter man walked inside from the cold, approaching Bryce.

"We're done," he said, drawing a firearm from behind his back, taking aim at Bryce's chest. "I'm going to cut the rope, and you're going to strip down to your underwear."

Bryce said nothing, feeling certain the stranger was pranking him as he simply stared incredulously.

"I'll freeze," he stated when the man didn't crack so much as a smirk.

"We can't have you following us."

"I won't," Bryce said emphatically.

Bryce heard a strange noise outside, and a glance through the window indicated the trio had set the truck he last drove on fire, which included most of the items removed from the house.

"Okay," Bryce agreed, allowing the man to slice the rope with a pocketknife.

He undid his jacket first, tossing it to the floor, followed by his shirt and the pants he'd found that worked perfectly within winter weather. An entire ensemble built from months of travel and clearing dangerous houses was about to be wiped out, or used by kids who assaulted him with their secretive motives.

"This seems excessive," Bryce commented after being ordered to remove his shirt and pants next.

"We need to make sure you can't go anywhere for a while. We know you're not going to get far without any clothes, and the fire outside is going to have you surrounded by the dead before long."

"I don't even know you people," Bryce said. "How could I have foiled your plan?"

"You ask a lot of questions," the younger man said, growing impatient as Bryce removed his pants, immediately feeling the sting of the cold, despite being inside. "You should concern yourself with starting a fire in here and staying warm until daybreak."

Already shivering, Bryce looked at his pile of clothes on the floor, doubting he could replicate a set as good to combat the cold. The man picked them up, still holding the gun as his friends reached the door.

"You can keep your underwear," he said, "since there's a lady present."

"Thanks," Bryce replied sarcastically.

"Good luck," the man said before all three of them exited the house, closing the door behind them.

Bryce saw the glow of the fiery truck through the front window, immediately darting to the bedrooms to look for some sort of coverings. He quickly discovered the group left only women's clothing in the closets, taking every single winter garment outside, regardless of gender assignment. Fortunately, they left several blankets behind, so Bryce covered every inch of his skin possible before returning to the living room area to make an attempt at starting a fire.

He heard the groans and growls of the undead outside within minutes, and one look outside the window revealed their numbers heading directly at the truck.

"Damn it," he grumbled, knowing they would eventually form a wall capable of keeping him from reaching the car next door.

In the darkness, temperatures dropped significantly, and he knew they dipped well below freezing. Mere minutes remained for him to retrieve the phone from the car, or risk being downed and devoured like a gazelle in the Serengeti by ravenous lions. With some of the components already in place to light a fire, he debated his options only a few seconds before overturning the chair and reaching for the keys to the car next door. Frigid from the lack of heat and gloves, his hand fumbled momentarily before locating the set of keys that went to the car, clutching them for dear life.

His gun and knife were taken, leaving him no defense against the growing horde. Options were few as the youngsters had, in fact, disabled him without taking his life.

Drawing a deep breath, he dropped the blankets to keep them dry for his hopeful return. Bryce walked to the door, and threw it open, dashing outside toward the car next door. He saw no signs of his three younger assailants, doubting they found reason to stick around after stripping him of his clothes, weapons, and dignity. Some of the undead immediately turned their focus to him, away from the burning truck, and a few more staggering nearby headed directly for Bryce.

He used the electronic key to unlock the door before reaching the car, hearing the click of the locks. Tugging open the passenger side door in desperation, he felt damage to a fingernail on his right hand as though he might have torn part of it off. Ignoring the minor pain, he dropped to the ground, despite the cold snow clutching at his legs, reaching for the phone without climbing inside. Seeking refuge from the car meant likely getting trapped inside without weapons, and Bryce needed warmth that the car couldn't provide if it lacked fuel or the ability to start.

Managing to grab both the phone and the charging components, he stood, finding a zombie dangerously close to him. He kicked at it with his bare foot, sending it flailing to the ground as it tried to maintain its balance. Able to escape the closing circle of predators around him, Bryce dashed directly for the door. By now the fire from the truck was simply a few flickering flames and a thin plume of black smoke, giving the undead little else to occupy their attention. He crossed the threshold with freezing feet, shut the door behind him, and began shivering uncontrollably.

He wanted to make a call immediately, but his teeth chattered and he kept hunching over, trying to get warm. Throwing the blankets over his body, he dropped to the floor, cocooning himself inside, which helped after a few minutes. Bryce knew he needed to start a fire to have any realistic shot at getting warm, but doing so meant exposing his naked flesh to the freezing elements inside the house. He put off doing so for another minute before finally getting the fireplace set with wood and kindling, using the box of matches to start the fire, hoping the chimney wasn't somehow clogged. Burning the house down didn't help his situation, though it would get him warm that much quicker.

Patiently stoking the fire to life, Bryce began to slowly thaw from the trek outside. He couldn't believe the trio took every useful piece of clothing from the house, but that, coupled with them flattening the tires of virtually every nearby vehicle, ensured their plan succeeded.

Bryce would not be following them anytime soon.

Once his body reached a suitable temperature and he stopped shivering and convulsing, Bryce dared open the phone, finding it halfway charged. He'd kept it close to him, or in the blankets the entire time to keep it warm. Sitting mere feet from the fireplace, Bryce embraced the warmth, looked at the phone once more, and decided to call for a rescue from his predicament.

Twenty-Four

On most nights, when darkness swept across the Adirondacks, Metzger headed to bed unless he found a reason to stay up and work on something. Tonight, being a reading and project night for him prompted Jillian to use her own cabin for a change. Both felt worn out after a day of helping Harold split firewood outside, so they decided to avoid any sexual temptations.

Already in bed, covered with two blankets, Metzger knew the flames dancing in the fireplace would last most of the overnight. Occasionally, he needed to throw a small log in the fireplace if he awoke in the early morning hours, but his body was accustomed to the cold, allowing him to sleep through the night most of the time.

Snuggled in bed, he began to drift off when he heard the sound of a ringtone, writing it off to a dream at first. When the noise didn't stop, Metzger jumped out of bed and grabbed the phone, which sat nearby atop a nightstand. Without bothering to look at the number, he flipped it open and answered.

"Hello?"

"Dan, it's Bryce. I need your help."

"What? Where are you?"

"In Lake Placid."

"Oh my God," Metzger muttered. "Why didn't you call sooner?"

"I thought I could make the drive up there and surprise you guys, but I ran into some trouble."

"What happened?" Metzger asked as he walked toward a random pile of clothes in one corner of the room.

"The vehicle I had wouldn't make it up the hills to the resort, so I stopped for the night," Bryce answered. "Some kids jumped me and took everything I had. Said they couldn't have me messing up some plan of theirs."

"Kids?" Metzger questioned, thinking back to the incident he and Timmons had in the same town.

"Young adults is more accurate."

Metzger knew it couldn't be the same kids he encountered, though perhaps their companions weren't as friendly.

"Are you okay?" Metzger asked, holding the phone against his shoulder while dressing himself the best he could.

"I'm okay. The one guy hit me once, and they tied me up, but I'm free now."

"How do I find you?"

"Look for the crispy truck where a hundred zombies are standing."

"Great," Metzger muttered, removing the phone from his ear long enough to slide a shirt over his head and shoulders.

"Oh, and please bring me some clothes if you can."

"Why?" Metzger questioned, finding such a request rather odd.

"These kids disabled all of the vehicles around here, and took my clothes so I couldn't stay outside for very long. They really didn't want me following them."

"Okay," Metzger replied, thankful Bryce escaped with his life and his health.

"This phone's battery is dying," Bryce said. "Be careful coming here. I don't know where these kids went, or what they were planning."

"I will. See you soon."

Metzger flipped the phone shut, donning more clothes, including winter gear before stuffing the phone inside a jacket pocket that zipped shut. Knowing what lay ahead, he grabbed the short sword he commonly used, along with a few sidearms since it sounded like Bryce was weaponless. He also plucked a shotgun from the corner of the room, already questioning which vehicle he wanted to take. He decided to take a Prius because he didn't have *any* vehicles guaranteed to ascend snowy hills, and a hybrid would at least deliver him to Lake Placid.

Another advantage to the Prius was the fact that it didn't roar to life like a few of the trucks he and Timmons drove to the resort during their treks to towns and campsites. With everyone already tucked away in their cabins, Metzger didn't want to wake them, or have them question where he was going at such an hour. Until he returned with Bryce, there wasn't much point in getting everyone excited and hopeful. A shift in the weather, or the lack of a vehicle capable of traveling uphill might keep them away for a day or more.

Lake Placid wasn't a simple drive down the road, and Metzger always tended to plan for the worst.

Even so, he decided to head over to his friend's cabin, knocking lightly on the door. Timmons answered the door a moment later, wearing white long johns from head to toe.

"If you're looking for sex, you have the wrong cabin," the pilot said groggily.

"You were already asleep?"

Timmons simply gave him a grouchy stare in reply. For someone who considered himself a rebel among military men, the captain typically kept his face smooth, except for his mustache, which caused Metzger to question his renegade nature. Tonight, however, Timmons' face revealed untouched stubble, indicating he hadn't shaved at all during the day.

"Get in here," the man finally said.

Metzger stepped inside, finding his friend shared the same ideas about keeping warm with a ripe fire going in the fireplace.

"What's going on, kid?"

"I have to head down to Lake Placid."

"Now?"

"Now. My brother is there."

Timmons gave him a perplexed stare.

"He called on the sat phone and said he had some trouble with some strangers."

"I'll get dressed," Timmons offered, heading toward some clothes draped over a chair.

"No," Metzger said. "I need you to stay here and keep watch over everyone. I could be down there until at least tomorrow if the weather gets bad."

"You need backup."

"I *need* someone to watch over my nephew. Amber has been fitting in, so far, but if anyone comes for her, or strangers show up, this place needs to be defended."

"Fine," Timmons agreed. "Isabella will be happy to hear her husband is back."

"You can't tell her," Metzger said.

"Why not?" Timmons countered, openly surprised.

"Look, I don't want them freaked out. Just tell them I went on a supply run early in the morning when they wake up."

"Dan, you've got *me* worried. What aren't you telling me?"

Metzger paused, drawing a deep breath.

"I'm not entirely sure what I'm getting into, but I'll handle it. Please, just keep this place secure until I get back."

"Sure," Timmons conceded. "Just make sure you get back here in one piece."

"I plan on it."

Metzger went on supply runs whenever possible, but he never left for more than half a day. With the weather in question, and unknown strangers in the mix, he wasn't sure how long extracting his brother from Lake Placid might take.

He lingered momentarily, as though he and Timmons both knew something felt different, dangerous perhaps, regarding what should have been a simple run to the valley below. Metzger finally gave a nod and ducked out the door, returning to his own cabin just long enough to grab some spare clothes for his brother. He stuffed them into a spare duffel bag he located during one of their searches, finding the key fob for the gray Prius.

Fortunately, the car remained parked in the primary parking lot, away from the cabins, allowing him to escape without detection because the car ran silently when the electric motors powered it. Getting up to speed caused the engine to kick in when driving, but he planned on being far enough away by then that no one would hear. Metzger crossed the parking lot, finding the snow crunchy on top, and slushy underneath. He kicked the white chunks off his feet before stepping into the vehicle.

From the parking lot, only the two closest cabins were visible, and he pictured Timmons looking out the window, like a concerned parent, wishing him a safe trip.

Metzger appreciated the man's protective nature, but he didn't know that he shared the captain's outlook on his future. Like everyone else, Metzger simply wanted to survive, not be a leader of the masses. He planned on picking up the person he considered a perfect candidate for a leadership position, though he wondered how his brother ended up stripped of every belonging except for a sat phone. Pushing the ignition button, Metzger didn't hear a sound from the car as the dashboard lights illuminated the interior. He left the radio on, often scanning for channels when he traveled, only to hear static across the spectrum. The chances of hearing anything on the radio felt like a longshot, mostly because the Adirondacks had very few listening options in the first place.

Driving carefully in the snow, Metzger reached what he considered the valley in about twenty minutes, finding an odd sight when he turned to the right. By now he knew the area reasonably well, and planned on reaching Lake Placid without the use of a map, but a red, four-door car sat halfway on the road, and partly tipped into a ditch. Metzger drew to a stop, examining the vehicle momentarily, trying to decipher how long it might have rested there, and what happened to its occupants.

Opening the door, he stepped from the Prius, walking over to the car. He looked for tracks, but the recently melted snow created a glistening white path along the roads and the woods alike. For the most part, the undead population around the mountains remained low at all times, so he doubted the travelers were attacked. Even so, he questioned where the people who last occupied the car might have gone.

He felt compassion for anyone having to trek in the Adirondack elements, but he selfishly hoped they didn't head up the mountain toward the resort. Taking one last look at the car, he stepped into the Prius and continued on his way to find Bryce.

About a mile down the road, he found a member of the undead staggering in the center of the snow-covered path. He stopped the car, grabbing his sword as he stepped out, prepared to see if the deceased person might be related to the red car. As he shut the Prius door, the dead woman turned to confront him, and Metzger could tell she recently passed away. He didn't see trauma along her body, but she didn't have winter gear on, meaning she might have run out of fuel and died shortly thereafter. Her skin, barely paler than a living person's during the winter months, let him know she hadn't expired by more than a week.

Perhaps the cold prevented her from wandering very far, because freezing temperatures froze muscles and joints inside the dead, keeping them from actively walking.

Metzger hated the idea of someone freezing to death so close to safety, but he couldn't be everywhere at once, finding people to save. He drew closer to the woman, and as she growled at him, slowly raising a frigid arm to grab at his coat collar, Metzger stuck the sharp end of the sword into her forehead, followed by the brain, bringing the ordeal to a close.

He dragged the body to the ditch beside the road, ensuring no one struck it with a vehicle. His act was partly out of respect for the dead, and also to protect future travelers. Returning to the Prius, he gave a lengthy stare at the woman's body, praying he would never have to put down someone he cared about.

***

Nearly an hour later, he approached the Lake Placid area, finding the town rather tranquil, at least along the main drag. He prowled the streets, searching for evidence of his brother, or a large gathering of the undead, and after about ten minutes, he located a charred truck and a few dozen zombies lingering in the area.

"Oh, Bryce, what have to gotten yourself into?" he questioned aloud as he parked a safe distance from the undead horde.

Stepping from the car, he grabbed his sword and went to work immediately, taking a combination of precision and baseball swings at the skulls of his adversaries, cutting them all in half. In the cold, they appeared slow to advance, giving him an opportunity to catch his breath after dealing with the first dozen. He considered the easier method of using a gun on the remainder of the dead, but he didn't know how long he and Bryce needed before heading back to the resort.

Huffing a moment, Metzger leaned against the Prius, smelling burnt flesh from where the undead drew too close to the truck while it was on fire. Some of them possessed obvious burn marks, a few sporting clothes burned onto portions of their body where they were completely engulfed by flames. Metzger couldn't fathom how the undead felt nothing, yet they could see, smell, and hear just fine, if not better than the living. It stood to reason that some of their senses were dulled in death, leaving the others to be enhanced.

Being perpetually surrounded by snow and frigid weather kept Metzger from being in top condition like he was when he constantly battled zombies and occasionally ran from them. He took notice of smoke rising from the chimney of the house in front of him. Bryce likely didn't come out to assist him because it sounded like he didn't possess any usable clothing. A distraction might have been nice, Metzger thought, but he began to catch his second wind and raised the sword to deal with the last of the undead stumbling in his direction.

A few fell on their faces, tripping in the snow, giving him a free pass to stab them in their skulls and end their misery. The rest, he disabled by slicing through their skulls, and even stabbing a few of them in their mouths when they drew close and hissed at him.

With six or seven undead still coming at him, Metzger realized several more in the distance had picked up on the noise and started heading his way. Giving a sigh, he cleanly severed one more head and darted to the house before completely draining his stamina. He rapped twice on the door, and opened it, finding his brother inside, shivering beside the fireplace.

"I'm glad to see you," Bryce commented between chattering teeth.

Metzger pulled his brother into a tight hug, making certain he didn't knock the blanket loose from Bryce's shoulders. He held the hug a few seconds longer than normal, because he remembered a time when he thought he'd never see his older brother again.

"Likewise," he replied, "but you're going to have to tiptoe through the snow, because I left your bag of clothes in the car."

"What kept you?" Bryce kidded, knowing the obstacles his brother battled to reach him.

"Well, you didn't exaggerate about the party you threw out front," Metzger replied. "The bad news is there's still a handful left for us to avoid or kill."

"I can dig up a steak knife," Bryce offered.

"I'll be fine. Just follow my lead and we'll be inside a nice, warm car in less than a minute."

Metzger noticed half a dozen more entering the yard, and his heart sank because he didn't want to put his brother at risk.

"Let's play this smart," he told Bryce, who looked out the front window beside him. "I can use the car and lead them away."

"What if the assholes who left me stranded and naked are still around?"

"Something tells me they aren't. I didn't see anything unusual when I was driving around looking for this place."

Metzger stole another glance outside, finding the undead begin to approach the house, seeing the flicker of the dying fire through the open curtains.

"Does this place have a back door?" he asked.

"It's all covered up with boxes and weight-lifting equipment. They didn't want anyone getting inside."

Metzger groaned, wishing good luck would follow him more often.

"Look, give me ten minutes and I'll lead them away. I'll come back for you, you'll get dressed, and we'll surprise everyone at the resort. One big, happy ending."

Bryce answered with a doubtful expression.

"I'll be *right* back," Metzger promised.

"Fine," Bryce conceded.

Holding his sword in his right hand, Metzger pushed his way out the front door, knocking the three zombies pressed against it to the ground. Another made an attempt to bite at his neck and shoulder area, but Metzger shoved it back and cleanly lopped off the top of its skull the way a skilled gardener trims a shrub. With a clear path to the Prius, Metzger headed toward the car with several zombies stalking him. He managed to start the vehicle and drive away, debating whether or not to honk the horn.

While the noise would provide incentive for the undead to follow him, it might alert survivors to his presence, and he didn't need additional hurdles to clear before getting his brother up the mountain. He also didn't want to risk Bryce thinking he was honking for him to come outside into a dangerous situation. Metzger played it safe and drove slowly with the undead following him like marchers in a parade that didn't keep their balance in the snow very well.

Only the sound of the defroster kept him company as he slowly drove into the downtown area of Lake Placid. Metzger cautiously looked around for signs of trouble, namely survivors, finding no artificial lighting, vehicles, or people walking along the slick sidewalks.

Although he didn't spot any of those signs, he did notice numerous flat tires accompanying every vehicle he passed. These people, whoever they were, didn't want Bryce following them. Metzger couldn't help but wonder if they were aligned with the kids he and Timmons encountered, but these new survivors appeared very tactical, organized, and surprisingly compassionate because they could have killed Bryce.

Thoughts of making another turn and trying to leave the dead behind crossed his mind, but a red light appeared on the dashboard, immediately concerning Metzger. As impossible as it seemed, at least in his mind, the Prius informed him it was running low on fuel.

"Shit," he muttered, knowing he needed to syphon gas from another vehicle.

Between the swarm of undead still following him, the dark of night, and the dropping temperatures, he decided the return trip to the resort needed to wait until morning. Stopping the car, he stepped out, sword in hand, and dealt with a few of his pursuers to thin their numbers. By attacking them, he also drew the attention of any stragglers.

Already worn down, Metzger didn't feel like dealing with more of them, so he returned to the car and started down the block. Ensured they followed him along his most recent right turn, Metzger turned right again and headed back to the house. Because the car made so little noise, he hoped most of them lost track of him and simply wandered the streets of Lake Placid aimlessly.

He pulled up to the house, finding no undead in the immediate area, a few minutes later. Grabbing his weapons and the duffel bag with clothes, he stepped from the Prius and approached the house. Bryce anxiously opened the door, obviously ready to head to the resort, still cocooned within the blanket.

"Hold your horses," Metzger said, handing his brother the bag.

"What's wrong?"

"The car is on empty."

"Then we get some gas from one of these other vehicles."

"Or we stay the night and syphon gas when we can see and we don't freeze our dicks off."

Bryce immediately expressed his displeasure about the circumstances.

"I can get dressed and we can get gas right now."

"The dead aren't far away, Bryce. Any noise brings them right back here. We take the night, we rest up here, where it's warm, and we deal with our issues in the morning."

"And what if those people come back and torch the car? Then we're stranded."

"You said it yourself that they had someplace to be. Seems doubtful they're going to linger in Lake Placid."

"We're immune to the dead."

"That doesn't mean I want to get bitten," Metzger countered. "And we aren't immune to the cold, or bullets. We shelter in place and we hit the road at first light."

Bryce still appeared unhappy, but he dropped the blanket, beginning to dress himself with the selections from the bag.

"I get it," Metzger said. "I want to get back, too, but playing it safe guarantees that you get back to Izzy and Nate, and I get back to Jillian."

Bryce smiled.

"You found her?"

Metzger realized he and his brother had a number of things to catch up on when time permitted.

"They were coming to get me when your wife broke me out of the base."

"Unfortunately, I don't think the military is done searching for either of us."

"It's just a matter of time before they come sniffing around here," Metzger reasoned aloud.

Bryce appeared deeply concerned.

"If they talk to the people I worked with, they'll get answers," he said, drawing a bit closer to the fire, despite being fully dressed and having a blanket. "They'll also have some of my personal information from the databases once they have their system fully functional again."

"I don't want to spend the rest of my life running, or looking over my shoulder," Metzger said.

"Me either. Believe me, we'll get this settled one way or another."

"I hope you have a plan."

Bryce gave a reassuring smile.

"Little brother, I always have more than one plan."

Twenty-Five

Timmons didn't sleep particularly well in the overnight, knowing Metzger traveled down the mountain to get his brother. Heading to any of the nearby towns wouldn't have been easy during the cold months prior to the apocalypse, but untreated snow and ice left the roads treacherous. He felt a bit of relief that he hadn't spoken to anyone else at the resort yet. Daylight was often slow to reach the resort through the trees, and cloud cover ensured that the impending illumination remained almost an hour away.

Getting dressed, he decided to make some coffee in the main building, and prep some breakfast items before the others joined him. Their routine tended to have them in bed at dark, and up around dawn, with so little to do. Everyone made certain to keep all lighting turned off in the main building, and Timmons often worked by flashlight or candlelight before the sun peeked over the trees. With so much glass in the building, any kind of natural illumination helped him navigate his way through the building's interior.

Already wearing warm gear, including duck boots, Timmons threw on a winter coat and opened his cabin door to find something unsettling in the distance.

Like a beacon in the night, the main building appeared to have every single light turned on, probably causing it to be seen for miles. Only Timmons knew Metzger left, potentially bringing his brother back with him, and he resisted the urge to turn on any lights to lead his friend back to the resort.

He also couldn't picture his friend returning, and performing such a careless act, even if everyone else awoke to greet him there.

Shutting his door, the pilot grabbed a Smith & Wesson stainless steel 10 millimeter semi-automatic that he sometimes carried. Finding such an odd size in ammunition wasn't usually difficult, because most survivors tended to ignore it when it didn't fit their firearms. He opened the door once again, stepping outside into the brisk air.

His cabin was behind several others along the two rows, but the main building easily caught his attention. He wondered how no one else noticed, unless their window coverings shielded the light from entering their cabins. Just enough starlight appeared to light his way, allowing him to look at the ground for footprints, and ahead for any strange vehicles or people. Timmons wanted to believe someone made an honest mistake, but after months of living at the resort, everyone there knew better, including the youngest member of the group.

When he approached the entrance everyone tended to use, he found the area cleared of snow and slush, indicating someone had done some morning shoveling. Feeling more confused than before, he assumed one of his fellow residents shoveled the area near the door as a courtesy, forgetting to turn off the lights afterwards. Timmons opened the door, holding his firearm in a ready position as he slowly crossed the threshold. A realization suddenly reached his mind that someone might have shoveled the area to cover up footprints.

He hoped to find someone making breakfast after absentmindedly turning on every single light inside the building, but as he entered, two strong hands clasped his hands, virtually crushing them over the firearm he held.

Timmons yelped in pain, barely seeing the figure looming over him before the gun was stripped from his hands and he was literally picked up and thrown across the room. Landing hard, his back struck several bar chairs and a sofa, which brought him to an abrupt stop. He felt a sharp pain in his right wrist, causing him to wonder if he broke a bone while being manhandled, or tossed like a lawn dart. One of the chairs fell over him, and as he swept it clear with one arm, Timmons found four younger people approaching him from across the room, already armed with various guns.

One of them was Amber, the girl Harold and Phyllis took in and trusted based on her brief stay the previous year. Timmons hadn't noticed anything particularly odd about her behavior the past few days, but he now understood she played a part and infiltrated their small group so she could bring in her real friends.

"This really isn't necessary," Timmons said, trying to get up from the floor, only to receive a hard shove from the large man who assaulted him.

"Stay down, old man," he warned.

"I didn't have much choice," Amber said, kneeling down a few feet from him. "I didn't know if anyone would be here after all this time. I needed backup."

"You didn't need to lie and sneak around," Timmons said.

"People are more accepting when there's only one survivor," Amber said evenly. "They don't ask as many questions."

"It's a matter of supply and demand," the shorter of the two men said, taking a step forward.

"And who the fuck are you?"

"This is Ronnie, my brother," Amber answered.

"Enough with the introductions," the taller man said. "Let's shoot the old-timer and take this place."

Now Timmons felt a shot of adrenaline at the thought of being ruthlessly murdered in a place he temporarily called home. Before he decided to act, however, cooler heads prevailed.

"We aren't killing anyone," the other young woman said. "That was never part of the plan."

"You want to let them walk out of here so they can come back and take the place back? We'd be looking over our shoulders forever."

Timmons got himself to a seated position on the floor without attracting attention. He felt as though reason might prevail, so he decided not to attack any of the young adults.

"Amber's been here two days and she knows you can't keep this place up and running yourselves," he said.

"You did an internship here, babe," the tall man said. "You got this."

"Adam, he's right. It's changed."

"Then we keep the old folks around until they teach you what to do."

"I can't believe you're talking about murdering innocent people, Adam," Amber said emphatically. "This isn't *you*."

"Wake up, Amber. We can't afford to feed extra mouths. You've been out there."

"Everyone deserves a chance to make it," Ronnie said, siding with his sister. "If we're going to slaughter people, we're no better than the dead."

"We've made it here by working together," Timmons said, deciding to speak up while the odds were in his favor.

"Shut up, old man," Adam demanded, taking a threatening step in his direction.

"You shoot me, and everyone comes in here with guns a blazing," Timmons warned.

"Maybe I'll just strangle you with my bare hands," Adam retorted. "Or gut you like a fish."

"That's enough!" Amber shouted with a constrained volume. "We never talked about murdering people, or forcing them to work for us."

"What did you think was going to happen?" her boyfriend retorted. "There's a reason we didn't knock on the front door."

"We didn't think anyone would be here," Ronnie said.

"You wanted a way in, and I got that for you," Amber said to her boyfriend. "An introduction."

"Some introduction," Timmons muttered, holding his injured wrist as he felt the onset of swelling.

"Shut up," they both told him simultaneously.

"This isn't going to work," Ronnie said to his sister. "I don't want to hurt anyone, but the Padgetts aren't going to welcome us after you lied to them."

Timmons suspected the four young adults had time to catch up and discuss recent events before he entered the main building. He wasn't sure if the other woman was Ronnie's girlfriend, or simply an acquaintance they brought to their new forever home.

"Look," he said, daring to speak again. "I'm a pilot. I can get you kids wherever you want to go if you leave these folks alone. Florida, Texas, somewhere nice and warm where you don't have to worry about all this snow."

"Where people have guns, and the zombies don't freeze to make them easy targets," Amber countered.

"And how the fuck do you expect to get us out of here?" Adam asked. "We had to hike up half of the mountain just to get here."

"Getting down is much easier," Timmons assured him. "And we left a plane just west of here."

"West of here?" Amber said with a furrowed eyebrow. "Buffalo isn't exactly one town away."

Now caught in an omission of the truth, Timmons lost any footing he might have gained with his abductors.

"Phyllis can be quite talkative once you get her started," Amber said, tilting her head sideways in a sassy fashion.

As though on que, Phyllis and Harold walked through the door, immediately rushed by the young adults and held at gunpoint. Fortunately, they weren't handled as roughly as Timmons had been, but they vocalized a need for answers. Very little was said to them, as they were placed near the pilot, and Adam stated a desire to get everyone else in the main building before moving forward.

"What the hell is going on?" Harold asked of Timmons.

"Your former intern seems to have betrayed you."

"That little bitch," Phyllis uttered disgustedly, just above a whisper.

After a few minutes, Amber went out the main entrance to check on her boyfriend, and in short order, the pair returned with Isabella, Nathan, and Jillian. Only Timmons knew about Metzger leaving in the middle of the night, and he intended to keep it that way in case his friend arrived in time to deal with the situation. Thus far, none of them were bound, being held at gunpoint only, so a distraction might provide them an opportunity to surprise the young adults by rushing them.

Timmons heard them make mention of the fact that Metzger wasn't in his cabin, or anywhere else on the grounds, dismissing it as him going on a supply run with one of the cars gone.

Everyone around him looked confused and scared, and for his part, Timmons wasn't sure of what action to take. His attempts at being conversational and trying to bring about a resolution like Metzger would have tried, failed utterly. It seemed as though three of their captors remained steadfastly against murder, but Adam appeared to have some sort of control over them. Perhaps sheer intimidation because of his size kept them in line, or maybe he spearheaded the entire plan to take over the resort once Amber and Ronnie told him about the self-sufficient nature of the property.

"We can't run this place without them," Amber insisted to her boyfriend, trying to keep her voice low enough that she couldn't be heard.

Timmons knew well enough that virtually every sound inside the building could be heard when there weren't appliances running in the background. Remaining calm, he studied his surroundings, ignoring some of the conversation as he looked for the means to escape the situation or overtake the young adults. Other than bulky furniture, few weaponry options presented themselves. If he were determined to be selfish, he could make a run for the building's other door, ducking into the woods and escaping if his captors weren't good shots.

He already knew he wasn't going to run, which would force him to continue using his weaker skill set of negotiating. Turning the other three against the taller, stronger man wasn't going to be easy, but Timmons knew only fear kept them under his thumb. No matter the size of a man, a bullet proved a great equalizer, and he needed to convince only one of them of that fact.

"We have everything we need," Adam insisted, touching his girlfriend's face gently, trying to manipulate his way into converting her mindset.

"You do?" Phyllis chimed in. "You know where to go for supply runs?"

Her question was met with silence and mildly surprised stares.

"You know how to raise chickens, keep plants alive all year round, and replace a solar panel when it goes bad?"

More silence.

"We run this place as a team," Harold added. "You youngsters wouldn't last a month without something important breaking down."

"You seem to forget we worked here," Ronnie said, his voice not as confident as the stoic front he put forth.

"So that's it?" Harold questioned. "Because we built this place up, and you think you know how to run it, you're going to systematically murder us and bury us out back?"

Ronnie didn't answer, and the look crossing his face indicated he didn't want to harm anyone.

"This wasn't your idea, was it, son?" Harold asked the younger man, using language Timmons often used with Metzger, possibly to drive his point home.

"There are other camps in the area," Isabella stated, trying to reason with the four young adults. "All of them have fireplaces, nearby water, and some supplies. You could make a go of it there, and even trade supplies with us. I have a son here."

"A son who enjoys hot showers," Adam said with a hint of envy and anger. "Why shouldn't *we* get to live the good life?"

Timmons felt his face flush with anger, and he foolishly blurted his words without forethought.

"Because we were invited, and you're an entitled piece of shit trying to steal something that doesn't belong to you."

Holding a pistol in one hand, Adam stormed over to the pilot, clutching Timmons by the throat with his free hand, hoisting him off the ground as Timmons felt the large fingers begin to cut off the oxygen he desperately needed to survive.

"Old man, it's time for you to go."

Timmons felt the fingers squeeze inward and he involuntarily made a gurgling croak that came from asphyxiation.

"Leave him alone!" Isabella shouted, and some of the others chimed in, but Timmons felt no easing from the powerful fingers wrapped around his throat.

He felt light-headed, and Timmons saw sparkling orbs of light as the room began to dim.

"Let the old man go," a voice from across the room ordered, and all heads turned to find Metzger and his brother standing near the entry that led to the rear entrance.

Timmons felt the hand completely release him, and he dropped to the ground in a heap, quickly gulping a few deep breaths.

"Bryce!" Isabella shouted, prompting her husband to hold up a hand, letting her know to stay put until the life and death business concluded.

"Dad!" Nathan exclaimed as his mother held him back.

Both Metzger brothers held firearms on the newcomers to the resort, keeping them at bay.

All of them except Amber appeared to recognize Bryce, possibly wishing they killed him outright instead of trusting that the elements would keep him in check. They didn't immediately put down their firearms, so Metzger took the next step in controlling the situation.

"Drop your weapons or we open fire and risk fucking this place up for all of us. It's the only reason I didn't come in shooting."

"How can we trust you won't shoot us?" the other girl asked.

"If I wanted you dead, I would've come in shooting. I'm giving you one last chance."

Amber's boyfriend wasn't having it.

"We can kill all of them and take this place," he said.

"We never agreed to killing anyone," Amber argued, putting down her weapon as her brother and the other woman followed suit. "This was your plan, and a bad one at that."

"It sounds like only one of you is the problem," Metzger said. "I can't kick the four of you out of here and expect you to stay away, which poses a dilemma."

"How much did you hear?" Phyllis asked Metzger.

"Enough," he responded. "It's time we settle this without damaging this place."

He continued to keep his weapon aimed at the taller man, who remained dangerously close to the hostages.

"How do you propose that?" Ronnie asked, keeping his hands raised just above his waist, indicating he didn't plan on making any sudden moves.

"Me and the big fella over there are going to have it out to see who stays here. No one dies needlessly, and we settle this like men."

"I like that idea," Adam said with a scowl.

Instead of immediately complying, however, the taller man remained near the hostages in case Metzger provided a ruse instead of a solution. Of the four intruders, only he continued to hold a firearm, which he didn't appear ready to put down.

Timmons got to his feet, inching a bit closer to Metzger as everyone appeared to be in compliance with his idea. The pilot felt certain everyone in the room wanted Metzger to kick this bully's ass, but he wasn't convinced his friend possessed the ability to follow through.

"You can't do this," Timmons said, keeping his voice low, fearing for the safety of his flying protégé.

"I can, and I will," Metzger replied.

"What I mean, is you can't possibly beat him."

Metzger looked at him directly with the most serious look he'd ever provided the pilot.

"Manchester."

Twenty-Six

"No, *not* Manchester," Timmons insisted, taking hold of Metzger's right arm for emphasis. "You can't do this."

"I'll be fine," Metzger promised, appearing reassured to the Navy captain.

He continued to hold both his sidearm, and the short sword, moving toward the other three young adults who trespassed at the resort.

"He's playing for blood," Timmons said just above a whisper, extremely worried about his friend. "I don't want to see you end up dead."

"I've got this, Scott," Metzger assured him with a grin. "What matters is we get him away from everyone else. I don't think the others are much of a threat."

"Just shoot the motherfucker, Dan."

"No. He needs to learn a lesson, and the others need to see the consequences of their actions."

"Why do you always have to do things the hard way?"

"I've known him almost thirty-four years, and I've yet to find out," Bryce chimed in.

Because someone finally spoke it, the group knew Adam's last name to be Hewitt. He continued to argue with his group members, who appeared to be turning on him completely, asking why he would accept a challenge when they were clearly outnumbered and the three of them surrendered their weapons.

He didn't really have an answer for them, but Timmons recognized the classic signs of a bully in the man with a sociopathic streak.

Metzger removed his jacket, even though he had stated a desire to carry out the fight outside.

"Talk him out of this," Timmons said, turning his attention to Bryce.

"Nope."

Timmons remained silent a moment as Metzger went forward with his plan, speaking before anyone else could interrupt.

"Outside," he said, addressing Hewitt. "No weapons. The winner is the last one conscious."

"You'll be more than unconscious," Hewitt promised.

"I'm sure you'll try, but this isn't going to end well for you."

Timmons drew close to Bryce before speaking into the man's ear.

"Is he just doing this for show?"

"No," Bryce answered. "He means it."

"Why aren't you stepping in? You're his big brother."

Bryce shot him a quizzical stare.

"If he gets pummeled, it's on your watch," Timmons added.

"He won't get pummeled."

"Fighting *that* isn't like fighting the dead."

"I'm aware," Bryce said. "Just like you, I was on the receiving end of those big paws."

Bryce turned to acknowledge his wife and son as they ran up to him, knowing they were no longer in danger. He broke away from Timmons to embrace them and tell them comforting words. Timmons knew their anguish, and decided not to pester Bryce during the family reunion. He wasn't sure how he would react if he learned that his son and ex-wife were alive, but he seriously doubted that possibility in his own life.

Because of that, and seeing that Bryce might remain preoccupied for at least a few minutes, the pilot made the decision that he wasn't going to let any serious harm come to the man he considered the son he always wanted.

Timmons watched as Metzger and Hewitt walked to the main door after Hewitt handed his last firearm to Amber, who quickly set it down in compliance with the rules Metzger set. She didn't want to be harmed by the people she betrayed, because no one knew which way the impending skirmish would end. Bryce seemed confident, which unnerved Timmons even more, because the lieutenant commander wasn't sharing his insider knowledge.

Harold, Phyllis, and Isabella had already collected the other firearms, ensuring that they definitely controlled the situation. Like Timmons, they appeared equally perplexed about Metzger's reasons for wanting to battle a larger, stronger foe. Timmons wouldn't have personally advocated for shooting all four of them, but he didn't have a better solution. In his line of work, he occasionally dropped a bomb on a designated target without having to witness the aftermath. Perhaps Metzger framed a plan within his mind, heading toward a feasible conclusion, or he simply wanted to dish out some punishment on Adam Hewitt.

Already dressed for the weather, everyone stepped outside, barely able to see their breath in the cold because the warm front returned for the break of dawn. Even the clouds began to break, and the sun's rays crept closer to the mountain, causing Timmons to wonder if he would be spying blood in the snowy carpet of the parking lot that much easier.

Before following the others outside, he grabbed the firearm he'd been carrying recently, stuffing it behind him with a purpose. He wasn't going to stand by and watch Metzger get maimed or killed by Hewitt, though he did plan on winning the Manchester bet before he interfered. He expected the slap he would place on Metzger after winning would be the least of the man's injuries, yet he wondered how Bryce remained so calm about the whole affair.

"How are you okay with this?" he asked the lieutenant commander, who had taken his side with Isabella and Nathan beside him.

"Because I know my brother and what he's capable of when provoked."

"That's not much of an answer."

"Stand back and watch, Captain Timmons," Bryce said. "You're about to see a clinic."

***

Metzger shook his arms, getting them loose when he stepped outside, sizing up his opponent and testing his footing along the snowy parking lot. He found it slick beneath the mix of soft and slushy snow, knowing it might be difficult to evade punches. Taking his sword and his sidearm, Metzger set them off to the side where it wouldn't be easy for anyone to grab them on a whim, himself included.

He understood his friend's concern for his well-being, but there were a few things he never told Timmons about his past. Metzger didn't pick fights, but in this case, he needed to assess Hewitt before deciding how to move forward with the four trespassers. It seemed the others got mixed up with an assertive person who took advantage of information Amber likely provided about the resort. Having food, water, electricity, and especially heat, sounded like a dream come true, and he wouldn't blame anyone for taking a stab at such a life.

Bryce helped clarify a few things for him, and the brothers decided to drive the Prius back, despite its lack of fuel, knowing they could use the electric motors if they drove slowly, without having the engine kick in and consume fuel. Metzger decided to try this route with virtually every other vehicle in the area burned or disabled, trying desperately to recall any abandoned cars or trucks on the way back to the resort that might provide some gas.

Although they failed to find any fuel, they arrived at the resort shortly after the four young adults.

"Why did you come here?" Metzger asked Hewitt as the two squared up along the snowy parking lot.

"Why do you ask so many questions?"

"You could've gone anywhere else," Metzger said, ignoring the comment. "You're just being a lazy fuck."

"What would you know about that?"

"I taught school once, and I saw kids from broken homes who turned out just like their parents. You're one of those kids who would've lived off the system in the normal world. Now you're mooching off people who paved the way, including the people who brought you here."

"You don't know a thing about it," Hewitt said as he closed the distance between the two men, raising his fists.

Metzger didn't stand perfectly still, but he didn't assume an aggressive stance, or step forward, either.

"I know you're a bully, and a piece of shit," Metzger said, trying to get a rise out of the man. From the change in expression on Hewitt's face, from mean to angered, he felt he succeeded. "You think you were built for the apocalypse, and whatever you want is yours, but that isn't the case."

"Well, fuck you!" Hewitt yelled before launching a right fist at Metzger, which the former teacher easily ducked.

Now he knew Hewitt to be right-hand dominant, and a hothead. Hewitt swung with his left hand, which Metzger also anticipated and moved his head back to avoid contact. He wasn't ready to engage the man quite yet, wanting to give Hewitt every opportunity to show that a shred of humanity, or normal human behavior, resided within him.

He suspected his friends and family surrounding him wondered why he didn't simply put a bullet in the man's head when he possessed ample opportunity. Metzger believed in giving people second chances, and taking a human life didn't come easy to him. Hewitt didn't appear willing to change, and letting the man go free likely wasn't a realistic option. Regardless, Metzger wanted to teach the young man a lesson and punish him a bit before his fate was decided.

Metzger also knew his brother and Timmons wouldn't let anything terrible happen to him if Hewitt somehow got the upper hand.

Based on the expression on Hewitt's face, and the various growls and grunts the man produced during his next two swings of the fist, Metzger knew his adversary was growing more agitated. Easily dodging the first punch, Metzger narrowly ducked from the second, knowing anything that connected with his face or neck might put him down. He heard gasps from his friends and family, but also Amber and her brother, as though they were genuinely concerned Hewitt might land a solid blow.

"You can do better than that," he commented, trying to antagonize Hewitt into wearing himself down with more attacks.

"Fight me," Hewitt spat in return. "Quit ducking me like a pussy."

"Not so easy without a gun, is it?" Metzger asked, infuriating his adversary so the man charged him and threw a wild punch.

Metzger evaded the blow, delivering a side kick to Hewitt's ribs before the man could react. He caught a glance of Bryce saying something to Timmons, and he suspected his brother might be informing the pilot that Metzger briefly attended some martial arts classes as a child. Sports got in the way of classes later, but he continued to practice the techniques he learned as he matured.

Delivering the kick nearly cost Metzger his balance, and in a game of evasion, he could ill afford to slip and fall to the ground. By no means a weak man, Metzger still needed to avoid taking damage from his larger opponent. Each day was a matter of life and death against the undead, and Metzger didn't want to be nursing injuries that slowed his movements. Despite what Hewitt believed, he wasn't dodging him to avoid contact altogether, but simply to wear him down and watch for a mistake. After all, Hewitt could slip along the snowy parking lot just as easily.

"You're not going to let me live anyways," Hewitt said, drawing close enough that only Metzger heard him. "So I might as well snap your neck for the satisfaction."

"Not everyone thinks in absolutes," Metzger replied. "It's not always a kill or be killed world."

"Don't try and talk your way out of this," Hewitt growled before throwing another punch at Metzger's face.

Metzger blocked the blow by deflecting it to one side with an open palm.

"I'm not," he answered, rattling off two quick punches to Hewitt's sternum, sending the larger man staggering in reverse.

Now on the attack, Metzger caught him in the jaw with a fist while his other fist aimed at the man's ribs, connecting for more damage. Hewitt grunted, but recovered quickly enough to grab Metzger by the throat, much as he had Timmons. Metzger anticipated such a move, however, and used both of his forearms in an upward motion, breaking the hold. He dropped to the ground, but Hewitt immediately threw a straight punch that caught Metzger beside the nose, staggering him to the brink of unconsciousness for a few seconds.

He recovered just before Hewitt would have connected with a haymaker, ducking out of the way before taking a few defensive steps back. Shaking his head, Metzger regained his senses within a few seconds and waited until Hewitt lurched forward once more before landing a kick squarely in the man's groin, flooring him instantly. Deciding he didn't want to take any more chances with the elements playing against him, Metzger mounted his adversary on the torso and threw several punches that bloodied the man's nose. He kept the man's arms pinned so there wasn't much resistance, and despite Hewitt attempting to buck him, Metzger acted as a human paper weight. Twice, Hewitt's head slammed back against the snowy blacktop of the parking lot, putting him in a helpless predicament.

Metzger had thoughts of putting the man out, but a throaty growl distracted him from the nearby woods as several zombies staggered forward, freed from a frozen state by the warm front, and likely lured by the illuminated main building.

Standing from his bloodied adversary, Metzger walked over to grab the short sword, spying three zombies with their vacant eyes locked on him because he stood the closest to the woods. A glance at Hewitt indicated the man was dazed, and unlikely to rise from snow-covered parking lot now dotted with blood. Drawing the sword from its sheath, Metzger dissected the heads of the first two zombies rather quickly, letting their decapitated bodies fall to the hard surface. As he began marching toward the last undead threat, however, he heard panicked yells from behind him.

"Adam, no!" he heard Amber scream.

Someone else warned of a knife at the top of his lungs, so Metzger jabbed the last zombie squarely in the forehead with the tip of the sword, killing the brain, before immediately turning with the sword as audible footsteps grew dangerously close to him.

Believing his sword could deal with any threat closing in on him, Metzger spun around, seeing a few blood droplets fly from his blade. He controlled the weapon with both hands allowing the blade to carry out its work, much like he would against the undead. Instead of cutting cleaning through a skull, however, it just barely grazed the abdomen of Hewitt, creating a thin red line where it drew blood. Considering the sword had just disposed of three zombies, coagulated blood dripped from portions of the saturated blade. The sharpened tip did its job, cutting through the man's clothing with precision sharpness, reaching just enough flesh to do some damage.

Both Metzger and Hewitt stared at one another momentarily in shock, because both knew what a bite or infected cut meant. Metzger mentally prepared his defenses in case Hewitt attacked him, but the man simply took a few steps back, opting to study the wound with bewilderment. His right hand still held the knife that he intended to use on Metzger, having likely hidden it somewhere in his jacket, or along the back of his pants. Hewitt refused to be bested, which probably prompted him to keep a weapon hidden during the fight, but even he couldn't defeat the infection.

He turned, looking to Amber, who simply stared at his injury, unable to muster words of sympathy, or contempt. Metzger couldn't read her emotions, though he suspected she no longer sided with him in the least, because he took advantage of her knowledge, forcing his own desires ahead of the small group. Metzger decided they could deal with the other three young adults later, but first he needed to ensure Hewitt posed no further threat to the group. To this point, the man hadn't said a word, clearly shocked by the fact that he wouldn't survive the next few days.

Before Metzger could deal with the man, Hewitt darted down the hill, into the cold, where trees swallowed him.

"That was odd," Timmons said when he approached Metzger.

"He didn't exactly have many options, Scott. That cut was a death sentence."

"That's not on you," Timmons said assuredly. "That fucker had a knife and he wasn't planning on giving you a papercut."

Metzger wondered if Hewitt would freeze to death before the infection set in and slowly took his life. With luck, the man might locate a gun and end his misery quickly, but Hewitt seemed like the type to cause misery and chaos as long as his body permitted.

Jillian walked over and gave him a long hug, pulling him close.

"Don't do anything like that again," she whispered. "You scared me to death."

"No promises," he replied softly.

Taking her by the hand, he walked over to the three young adults, who appeared apprehensive, frightened, and uncertain at the same time.

"I'm very disappointed in you both," Phyllis told the twins. "You *dated* that man?"

Her question was aimed directly at Amber.

"He wasn't like that before, I swear."

"The apocalypse changed a lot of people," Metzger reasoned.

"What are you going to do to us?" Donnie questioned.

"We should turn you loose and let the dead have you," Harold said.

"Or take their clothes and see how they like running through the woods," Bryce countered, obviously still raw over his earlier treatment.

Within a few seconds, all eyes fell to Metzger, and he wasn't certain why everyone valued his opinion so much.

"They stay with us," he decided aloud, since evidently the choice was his to make.

All three youngsters appeared ecstatic and a bit surprised at their good fortune.

"You three are going to earn your keep," Metzger said sternly. "I'm giving you the benefit of the doubt, because Harold and Phyllis spoke fondly of you in their stories about running the resort. Don't step out of line, because we've got a good thing going here, and I *will* do what it takes to defend my family."

All three nodded sheepishly.

Within a few minutes, Harold and Phyllis began making arrangements for living quarters once everyone stepped inside the main building. While Jillian appeared to have some sympathy for the three lost souls, because she fought for survival much the same, Timmons stepped over to prod Metzger for some answers.

"You sure this is wise?"

"They're young and impressionable, Scott. We need to at least give them a chance, and we could use some experienced hands around here."

"More mouths to feed," Timmons lamented. "I'm not sure this is how you protect your family, Dan."

"It's a trial basis. They're going to prove themselves so they can stay here with Harold and Phyllis when the rest of us move on."

Timmons looked at him with mild bewilderment.

"This isn't our forever home?"

"No. We're going to have to return to the base at some point, or at least I am."

"And why the fuck would you do that?"

Metzger framed his answer carefully.

"If Nadeau is out there, and alive, who's to say there isn't a second wave coming? Or what if something didn't explode the first time around and the air is filled with this virus again?"

"It's not your responsibility to save the world, Dan."

"How can you possibly say that, when there are so few of us left?"

"Humans reproduce, son. It's what we do. Maybe it's time for you to start worrying about yourself a little more."

"No. We're going back to Virginia when the winter weather breaks."

Timmons sighed through his nostrils.

"There's no talking you out of this, is there?"

"No. I'm not dragging you or Bryce into this. It's something I'll deal with on my own."

"I'm not letting you go back there alone. They might throw me in the brig, but there's no way you're stepping foot on that base by yourself."

Metzger appreciated the sentiment, suddenly wishing he hadn't revealed his future plans. He didn't want his brother or Timmons to suffer because of choices he made on his own. He doubted a reasonable serum was created from his blood in the time he spent on the base, so he wanted to provide more samples for the military, even if doing so meant sacrificing his own freedom.

"We're staying long enough to make sure these kids work out before any of us leave."

"And your girlfriend is okay with all of this?"

"I haven't told her yet," Metzger replied.

Timmons chuckled.

"I want to be a fly on the wall for *that* conversation."

"This is bigger than any one person," Metzger stated. "Maybe they've found others who are immune, but if they haven't, I may be the only person with blood they can use."

"Again, not your problem, kid."

"I'm not running from it, Scott. Tracking Nadeau is nothing but dead-ends, so it's time to prepare for the worst."

"Sounds like you're not optimistic about the future."

"I'm just making sure there *is* a future. Now let's quit talking about it, and get some work done around here."

Metzger hesitated before following Timmons back to the others.

"What's wrong?" the Navy man asked with a furrowed brow when he turned around.

"I forgot something."

"What?"

Metzger provided a sudden, yet moderate slap to the man's right cheek, prompting a knowing smile from Timmons following the act. Everyone else looked over with mild surprise, as though they might be witnesses to a scuffle, quickly realizing the two men weren't having an altercation, but rather a moment of horseplay.

"I had that coming," Timmons admitted.

"Just remember that before you go teaching me your military traditions," Metzger said with a grin.

Twenty-Seven

Mid-February

Sutton adapted to life in a community better than he expected to, but aspects of cohabitating with other people continued to elude him. Some of the neighbors got together for game nights, dinner, or the occasional church service on Sundays. Telling time and the day of the month wasn't incredibly important to Sutton, but some people continued to cling to the old traditions as though their lives might suddenly be returned to normal someday.

On this particularly cold morning, he took Father Paul with him to hunt some wild game just before daybreak. Without hunting seasons to keep them in check, and sense enough to keep away from the undead much of the time, deer and other wild animals found fewer predators to thin their numbers. Sutton planned on taking advantage of their higher numbers, their false sense of security, and the fact that he had lured them close to the community with salt licks and other tasty treats.

"This doesn't seem very sporting," Father Paul said as he and Sutton assumed a prone position atop a hill overlooking some of the food laid out for the deer.

Just enough morning light emerged for them to see their surroundings.

"It beats starving."

Without conservation laws, Sutton was free to use whatever methods he chose to hunt animals, which became one of his staple contributions in Maplewood. Typically, he brought a spotter with him, not so much to locate deer, but to watch his back against the undead. He usually asked his son, or Gracine, but

Gracine had started spending time with a man inside the community, and Sean was busy helping with other chores on this morning, so the priest volunteered.

Dressed in a winter gear that concealed his collar, Father Paul appeared as though he couldn't get warm on the chilly morning. Sutton agreed that the light wind possessed the means to chill a person to the bone, but he covered his body from head to toe, leaving only his cheeks exposed to the elements before heading out. Perhaps the priest wasn't accustomed to the winter weather, or underestimated the temperature, because his teeth occasionally chattered.

Sutton sighted in the POF Renegade rifle he brought along, complete with long-range scope and bipod for stability atop the hill. Without the scope, the rifle would prove quite adept in a gunfight, and might be overkill for hunting, but Sutton wasn't freezing his ass off for sport. He wanted dinner for himself and more than two dozen people who craved something other than canned goods, rations, and boxed sides.

Father Paul rolled over to his back, watching behind them for any lurking undead, though very few stragglers made their way to the community unless something happened to attract them. A bullet fired from the POF Renegade would certainly gain their attention, though it might take hours for them to amble to the spot the two men occupied.

"You going to be okay?" Sutton inquired, staring through the scope at a doe near the far edge of the feeding area.

She appeared apprehensive about entering the worn patch of ground, possibly because she didn't have any companionship with her for safety.

"I'll be fine," Father Paul responded. "The Lord provides for us as needed."

Sutton felt safe in their location, both from the undead and being spotted or smelled by deer. Below, the feeding area was a few hundred yards away, and he could make an accurate shot with the rifle. So long as the duo didn't make any loud noises, the wind would cover their movements and low-volume chatter.

"What does your good book tell you about the dead roaming the Earth?"

"I'm pretty certain that chapter was omitted from the copy I use."

"Then what does your gut tell you?"

"It tells me our interpretation of the Rapture may be off a bit."

"Isn't that where all the good people in the world go to the afterlife, and the wicked are left here?"

"Something like that," Father Paul answered Sutton's question with less detail than Sutton wanted.

"There are a lot of good people left in this world, Father."

"I'm aware of that, Colby. Perhaps His work isn't finished yet."

"Maybe He didn't have a hand in it, and people are just shitty."

Father Paul looked at him thoughtfully.

"The Lord typically takes a hands-off approach and allows us to make our own mistakes."

"And the balance is usually restored," Sutton commented, "but I'm not sure how we do that with ninety-nine percent of the population now dead."

"Maybe the balance isn't always about people," Father Paul suggested. "We may not have factories and computers, but are we not provided for with supplies, water, and the food we're hunting right now?"

"You like answering questions with questions, don't you?"

"Isn't life just a series of questions?"

Father Paul provided a smirk with his latest reply.

Sutton hadn't spent much time around the priest, partly because he didn't want to get into questions about the afterlife. Losing his youngest son changed him, mainly because searching for his boys kept him going. Now, he went through life like the zombies he occasionally battled, simply existing to eat, sleep, and repeat life the following day.

He found purpose in hunting to keep the others fed with much-needed protein, but any number of residents could hunt. Sutton just happened to be the best shot.

"I feel like we're just biding our time, Father," Sutton said.

"How so?"

"We keep doing these things, staying alive, but the world isn't going to return to what we knew."

"It sounds like you're ready to quit."

"I'm not saying that. I still have a son to watch over."

Father Paul waited a moment before speaking again. Looking through the scope, Sutton spied another curious deer, this one a young buck, nearing the feeding area. Perhaps they detected the scent of humans on some of the food, or something else kept them from sampling the buffet.

"I'm sorry about your youngest," the priest finally said. "Gracine told us what happened at your last stop during dinner one night."

Likely one of the dinners Sutton skipped, because he didn't typically feel like socializing.

"Father, I need to ask you something."

Sutton felt weird calling a man close to him in age "Father" at any time, but it was how Catholics operated, so he wanted to be proper about addressing the man.

"What is it?"

"Do you believe in something after all of this? I mean *really* believe."

"Absolutely. Becoming a priest isn't some trade school class we take for a semester or two. It's a lifelong devotion, and there were a number of times that I questioned if it was my calling, but I *never* found myself doubting a higher power."

Spying a member of the undead heading their way, Father Paul stayed low to the ground, virtually crab-walking away from the hilltop's crest before standing to deal with the intruder. Sutton remained focused on the two deer below, which hadn't taken notice of the priest moving away, or using his weapon of choice to puncture the zombie's skull. Even as the spiked end of the weapon entered the zombie's cranium, it gave a final, defiant growl that went unnoticed by the mammals below.

"Now, where was I?" Father Paul asked when he returned to Sutton, lying on his back to keep watch for more threats. "Oh, my calling. I can only assume you're asking on behalf of your deceased son?"

"His name was Jacob."

"I'm sorry, Colby," the priest said with genuine empathy. "I can only imagine what you went through, losing him like that."

"No offense, but I'm not sure you can relate, Father."

"Don't be so sure," Father Paul answered without removing his eyes from the area he watched meticulously. "I may not have children, but I've been to dozens of wakes and funerals where I didn't have answers for parents who lost their children to suicide, or careless accidents, or even child predators. I know there's evil in this world, Colby, because God gives us free will. I also know there's something else eating at you. Gracine said something happened with the other half of your group, but she didn't say what."

"She's good at spreading gossip."

"She cares about you."

"Is that why she's been spending so much time with Reggie?"

Sutton wasn't happy about Gracine seeing the man, perhaps because he felt a bit jealous, but he also understood that he wasn't good company recently. Reggie Mitchell was a former Army sergeant who became a cop in the regular world after his discharge. Sutton considered the man a bit bland for Gracine, but she appeared to enjoy being around him.

"You've been emotionally detached," Father Paul answered. "She has strong feelings for you, but you haven't been reciprocating them."

"How would you know that?"

"I may not have a wife or kids in my profession, but I have eyes."

A noise reached Sutton's ears from behind his position.

"Excuse me a moment," Father Paul said, inching his way away from the hilltop.

Sutton looked through the scope, finding one of the deer beginning to eat as a third, younger fawn dared to approach what Sutton came to call the kill box. He didn't consider his methods the least bit fair for the deer, or any other creatures that happened into the area, but Sutton needed to provide for more than just a handful of people.

Behind him, he heard a thwack as Father Paul likely used his makeshift crucifix sword to down their latest intruder. A moment later, the priest returned, setting the weapon beside him as he reclined against the crest of the hill once more.

"You were saying about Gracine?"

"Oh, so now you care?" Father Paul asked coyly.

"I've always cared. I just didn't realize she thought about me like that."

"She's never said anything, but I feel very certain the woman has feelings for you. But we're getting off-topic. What happened with the other half of your group?"

Sutton groaned.

"Does anything I say have lawyer-client privilege? Well, the equivalent."

"Discretion comes with my vocation, Colby."

Sutton peered through the scope once more, finding a more mature, thicker buck making his way near the box. He visited the area nearly every day to put out apples not fit for human consumption, and salt licks the group had acquired before his arrival. Most of the apples were harvested in the fall and dried by one of the residents with the intention of using them as bait. The method didn't preserve the apples perfectly, but they remained fresh enough that deer didn't seem to mind.

"I just about have a shot," he informed the priest. "I might try for a second target if the doe gets close enough."

"In the meantime, feel free to start talking about what happened before you came here."

"You're awful pushy, Father."

"Comes with the territory. You can be a little feisty when God has your back."

Sutton smirked, though the butt of the rifle kept the priest from seeing. Strangely, the priest might have been his favorite hunting companion thus far, keeping him on his toes and providing interesting conversation.

"Someone from the other half of the group thinks I killed her father," Sutton finally said, realizing he hadn't really spoken about the event since it happened.

"What do *you* think?"

"I think it was a perfect storm of bad circumstances."

"Did you mean for any harm to come to her father?"

"No. I didn't even know her father was alive, much less living in the town where me and my new group were heading."

Sutton paused a moment, seeing no new activity below.

"I knew the new group was trouble, but I didn't know just how bad. I'd gotten separated from the others, and knew I needed to survive if I wanted to see them again. Well, it backfired, and they ended up getting into a skirmish with my former group. That's when Jillian's father was shot."

"It sounds like you're leaving out quite a few details."

"I killed three of the four men in my new group, saving everyone except Jillian's dad. That doesn't make up for what happened, but I never meant to bring trouble to them."

"Does killing other people bother you?" Father Paul inquired, possibly angling towards learning about Sutton's religious beliefs.

"I don't enjoy it, if that's what you mean. I've never killed anyone outside of self-defense."

"I've only known you a few months now, Colby, but you don't strike me as a danger to yourself or others. We've all made mistakes, particularly in these dark times when survival is far from guaranteed."

"So, even a man of God like you has made mistakes?" Sutton inquired.

"I'm far from infallible. During the early days of the apocalypse I made some critical errors when people were looking for help."

"You're not a survivalist, Father. How could they expect help from you?"

"Spiritual help. I didn't have answers for them."

"My shot isn't going to get any better than this, Father," Sutton said, seeing the buck in close proximity to a mature doe. "I might be able to nab a pair."

Father Paul made a sign of the cross across his head and torso, saying a silent prayer that Sutton's shots hit their marks.

Taking the first shot, Sutton hit the buck squarely in the chest, causing all four of the deer to jump and take a second or two to collect their bearings. The buck immediately staggered after taking a few steps, but Sutton was already focusing his attention on the large doe, knowing only a few crucial seconds remained for him to take the shot or go without extra meat. He lined up a shot in the back of her neck, taking the slight breeze into account before squeezing the trigger.

His shot struck home, and the deer immediately felt the pain, though she ran out of the kill box with blood trickling from the wound.

"We've got a runner," Sutton reported.

"We're going to have dead heads coming our way once they hear those shots."

Sutton and the priest made their way to the black Ford pickup they borrowed from the ample supply at Maplewood. Once they were inside, Sutton began driving around the hill to a spot where they could access the kill box without taking an extreme angle down the hill.

"When you said you hadn't been perfect, you didn't mean anything with kids, right?" Sutton asked his companion, half-kidding.

"I've taken a vow to be a man of peace," Father Paul began, "but that vow can be broken if you're going to be insulting."

"Just wanted to make sure."

"A few bad apples give us a bad name," Father Paul assured him. "I like to think most of those men have had their day or reckoning."

"That's not very Christian of you."

"Neither is violating children, my son."

Sutton reached the bottom of the hill, driving to the edge of the kill box where he and Father Paul were able to load the buck into the back of the truck with reasonable ease. Far tougher was locating the doe and loading her body into the truck bed before the dead located her and began devouring the corpse. As a rule, the dead didn't feed on something unless they took it down or spotted it falling, but Sutton didn't want to waste one second.

"Tracking isn't going to be easy in a truck," he commented when the two men returned to the vehicle's cab.

"It won't be bad unless she made it to the woods."

Sutton agreed, and the open field around the kill box continued anywhere from a quarter to half a mile, depending on the direction. Most of the grass and weeds were low to the ground and tan from the winter weather. Although snow seldom visited the area, freezing temperatures bullied the plants and wildlife as badly as any other climate.

As though sent from above, the sun emerged from mostly cloudy skies, helping Sutton search for blood along the ground. He spotted the occasional blood droplets, which increased in both occurrence and volume, letting him know they were getting closer. Unfortunately, the woods ahead threatened to conceal his kill, and a hearty dinner for the villagers, if they didn't locate the doe soon.

"I see trouble," Father Paul said, pointing ahead of them, slightly to the left, where three undead stragglers appeared to be heading for something.

"Shit," Sutton muttered. "Pardon my French, Father."

"Forgiven, Colby. Just get your ass over there before they do, because that's probably where your deer fell."

Sutton parked the truck as close as he could to the area before both men jumped out. Father Paul grabbed his weapon from the truck bed and immediately took to swinging at the closest of the zombies, striking it in the skull and making himself the primary target of the two remaining threats. He led them away from their original target, allowing Sutton to scour the ground for signs of blood or a fallen deer. After spying a small pool of blood, he quickly located the dead deer, which remained undisturbed by the attackers pursuing the priest.

He tried lifting the deer by himself, but it proved just heavy enough to give him pause. Not wanting to throw out his back, he decided to assist Father Paul so the man could return the favor and help him load their haul.

Father Paul swung his weapon into the head of one of the two remaining threats, knocking it to the ground, but as he went to pull the makeshift sword free, it remained lodged inside the skull. While he attempted to free the weapon, the other zombie managed to draw close enough to grasp at his arms. Unaccustomed to dealing with numerous threats, the priest panicked a bit and fell to the ground, allowing the zombie to fall on top of him, snapping its brownish teeth at his neck. He managed to fend it off with a forearm under its chin, but he couldn't shove it aside, so Sutton rushed over, using a knife to end the threat with a jab to the side of the zombie's skull.

"Thanks," the priest said, trying to catch his breath after the scare.

"You're welcome," Sutton replied, offering a hand to help the priest get to his feet. "Let's get this thing loaded and head back for a hearty dinner."

Between them, the pair loaded the doe into the truck bed, beside the buck, before heading down several miles of calm, cleared roads. Riding the high of a successful morning that would feed their fellow residents, the two men joked and chuckled until they neared the gated community. Sutton saw the issue first, and Father Paul went from a beaming smile to a solemn expression in a split-second.

Parked in the road leading up to Maplewood, three military transport vehicles showed no signs of personnel, which caused Sutton to wonder if soldiers invaded the community.

"Oh, shit," he muttered.

"Is this a problem?" Father Paul inquired, knowing about the group's issues with the military as told over several dinners.

"It could be."

Sutton had parked far enough away that they probably wouldn't be spotted unless they drove closer. The tan military vehicles, two Humvees and a larger troop transport, stuck out against the backdrop of the community.

"Take your sidearm, get out, and leave the hunting rifle in the back," Father Paul ordered more than suggested. "I'll tell them I was hunting alone and see what's going on."

Sutton didn't immediately comply, giving the preacher a mildly suspicious look. Trust still didn't come easy for him, because the living typically wanted to stay that way at any cost.

"We don't want the military around here any more than you do, my son," Father Paul assured him.

Giving a nod, Sutton opened the door, leaving it ajar as Father Paul walked around the front of the truck. He gave Sutton an encouraging tap on the shoulder before assuming the driver's seat. As Sutton watched him drive in the direction of the military vehicles, he said his own prayer that the military presence was coincidence, and not his past returning to haunt him.

Twenty-Eight

Shortly after dawn, Gracine emerged from bed to put a log on the fireplace inside the house she currently shared with Reginald Mitchell. Mitchell lived in the residence with a family of four who occupied the downstairs, while he lived upstairs. Due to the cold weather, everyone stayed in the living room during the overnight, beside the fireplace, which left anything intimate off the table for Gracine and Mitchell.

"You good?" Mitchell whispered to her when she returned to the oversized sleeping bag they shared in the overnight.

"I am," she replied quietly.

Her fingers intertwined with his and they grinned at one another.

Because Mitchell was black, Gracine sometimes wondered if the villagers believed they should naturally belong together. She didn't much care about what they thought, or about race for that matter. The apocalypse didn't discriminate, and neither did she when it came to choosing friends and allies.

Mitchell kept his hair cut short for practicality, and Gracine considered him handsome, with smooth features. Although he wasn't quite as independent or mechanically-inclined as Sutton, Mitchell proved himself worthy as a leader in the small community. Gracine tried holding out for Sutton to make some sort of romantic advance toward her, but he became more of a recluse, depressed over losing his son, and speaking less to her about his thoughts. Sutton didn't exactly wear his emotions on his sleeve, or talk about things that bothered him freely, and Gracine grew tired of waiting for a relationship that wasn't about to blossom.

She felt bad for Sutton, and technically, Gracine still shared a house with him, Luke, Samantha, and Sean, but she spent most of her time around Mitchell. Overall, their group was accepted with open arms into the community, and they all did their share to keep Maplewood running smoothly. Samantha attended classes with other children who lived inside the walls, and the group was extremely close to having a community with power, plumbing, and even propane gas for each residence. They had amassed books that taught them how to reconfigure each house for such things, and the McAllisters specifically brought people who formerly worked in trades into the fold.

"Maybe we should go to my place for breakfast," she whispered to Mitchell. "Everyone should be up."

Quietly getting up, the couple retreated to the room upstairs, got dressed, and managed to leave the house without disturbing their housemates. Outside, the weather felt cold and dry, as though it might spit snow that never fell.

"You giving any more thought to moving in with me?" Mitchell asked during the walk to the other house.

"I feel bad leaving the others."

"You mean you feel bad leaving Colby," Mitchell said sourly.

"I'm not with Colby," Gracine assured him, stopping to look him in the eyes. "Who am I staying with every night?"

Mitchell paused, acting sheepish a moment before answering.

"Me."

"That's right," Gracine said, touching his face gently before giving him a quick kiss.

Not much for public displays of affection, Gracine kept her time with Mitchell mostly under wraps because she didn't want to emotionally hurt Sutton. Part of her wanted him to know what he was missing, but she didn't want to be cruel. She spent the first month of their time at Maplewood trying to bring Sutton around to a normal state, putting off advances from Mitchell, but she eventually moved forward.

When they made it into the house, Gracine found a few items to cook for breakfast, including eggs from some of the chickens kept in a coop within the community. With so many people, and numerous outbuildings added to Maplewood, Gracine felt as though the place needed to expand. Members of the group had taken storage sheds from abandoned houses, built a greenhouse, and created a weapons depot from one of the garages. Many of the yards felt cluttered with necessary buildings, gear, and firewood, leaving very little recreational space.

With winter weather keeping residents indoors much of the time, their everyday lives weren't too bad, but once spring arrived, many residents would feel claustrophobic inside the gated walls.

She wished they had more essentials, and while power, water, and plumbing were close to being in place, the group struggled to find live animals. Even if they somehow located cows, pigs, and other farm animals, they didn't really have sufficient means to house them. The dead tended to wipe out any living thing that stood in their path, which made restoring the world to any sense of normalcy nearly impossible.

"It's good," Mitchell said as they finished eating at the kitchen table.

"It's tolerable."

When they arrived, the pair didn't find anyone in the living room area near the fire, meaning the others slept in their rooms, or stepped outside. No one really locked their doors, because sentries often kept watch in the overnight, and anyone trusted in the community kept weapons inside their assigned houses. At this point, Gracine, Sutton, and the others were trusted members of Maplewood.

"Sometimes I feel like you're slow-rolling this thing between us," Mitchell said, keeping his voice down in case others were within earshot.

"This community is a dozen houses," Gracine replied. "Everyone knows everything about everybody," she added, speaking the words slowly for emphasis. "We've only been here a few months, and I don't need people starting rumors."

"I'm not ready to put a ring on your finger if that's what you're worried about."

"That's the least of my worries right now, Reggie."

"You know I'm willing to wait for us to move forward."

"I think we're well past the prom night formalities," Gracine said, stroking his chin with several fingers.

"We are, but I'm sick of having you half the time."

"Patience, Reginald."

"You know I hate being called that."

Both of them looked up when the front door opened, revealing Samantha entering with a concerned expression.

"What's wrong, baby girl?" Gracine asked.

"The Army men are here!"

"What do you mean?"

"They brought three cars with them."

To an eight-year-old, any vehicle with four wheels could be referred to as a car, and Samantha's education was stunted the day her parents were torn apart by the undead and she went to live with Luke and his partner.

"Get Luke," Gracine told the girl, immediately shaking her head because she spoke incorrectly. "I mean your dad."

She tended to forget that Samantha now called Luke her father, and struggled to remember to call them by the titles they called one another.

"Meet us outside, honey," Gracine added, taking Mitchell by the hand before heading to the already open door.

Stepping outside, she found a number of people in the community already standing at the front gates, with more heading that way. She spied three tan vehicles just outside the gates, trying not to fear the worst, but concerned her past, or rather Sutton's, had followed them. Squeezing Mitchell's hand, Gracine put on a brave face and stepped forward to begin collecting facts.

"What is this about?" she heard Robert McAllister asking the military personnel through the front gate.

"We're on a routine patrol," a man in military fatigues answered. "I'm Major Dawkins with the Army."

"What can I do for you, Major?"

"We're searching for some persons of interest," Dawkins said, reaching into an inside pocket to produce two photographs.

"Oh, no," Gracine said under her breath, recognizing Metzger and his military brother as the two individuals in question.

She had pushed forward a little, through the growing crowd, in order to hear and see what transpired, but she didn't want to be recognized in case one of the few soldiers she initially encountered at the base were in this group.

"Can they recognize you?" Mitchell asked quietly.

"Doubtful."

She squeezed his hand a bit tighter.

"Robert will cover for your people," he said with more assurance than she felt.

"I can't say we've seen them," McAllister said. "Wish I could be of more help."

"Do your people get outside often? Could they have possibly seen these two men?"

"Major, if we leave these walls, it's to hunt, fish, or collect supplies. We don't go associating with strangers, and we certainly don't have room to bring more people in."

Dawkins didn't appear satisfied with the answer, as though he knew something more than he stated to the mayor of Maplewood.

"Would you object to us taking a look around?"

"I would very much," McAllister replied. "It's early morning, and you just woke up most of our residents. And they are armed residents, I might add."

"Where are you lads from?" Nancy McAllister inquired.

"The base at Norfolk."

"You've driven a long way to search for these men, haven't you?"

"We're just one of several teams, ma'am. It's important we find these individuals for the sake of national security."

"National security?" McAllister chuckled. "This village is the only sovereign state we recognize at the moment. You haven't blessed us with your presence the past six months, so I question how much of a nation we have left."

"More than you think, sir," Dawkins stated. "We're working to restore society, but even for us, things are spread a bit thin."

Gracine kept attempting to avoid eye contact with the military personnel on the other side of the gate.

"Quit deflecting," Mitchell said quietly. "You're going to look guilty."

"I need to hear what they're saying."

"They aren't going to recognize you based on what you told me," Mitchell assured her.

Gracine doubted anyone could pick her out of a lineup based on the brief encounter the group had with a few guards the day they brought Metzger to the military installation.

Even so, she felt the military came to this particular community for a reason.

Before more discussion took place, a pickup truck approached the gate, and Gracine feared Sutton might do something irrational to get them in hot water, or raise suspicion amongst the armed soldiers. When she spotted only one person inside the truck, and the person who stepped out was Father Paul, she grew even more concerned.

"Where the hell are you, Colby?" she muttered, hoping he wasn't about to create trouble when the situation appeared to be ending.

***

"What's going on here?" Father Paul asked the man in charge once he parked the truck and stepped out.

Appearing reasonably young, but capable, the major immediately spied the collar beneath the winter gear the priest sported.

"Father?" the man questioned, more about the priest's affiliation with the village than Father Paul's chosen vocation.

"I live here, my son."

Dawkins introduced himself, briefly stating his business at the community.

"I can assure you we haven't seen either of those men," Father Paul stated.

Wearing a concerned expression, Dawkins motioned with his head for the priest to talk to him away from the others.

"Can I confide something in you, Father?"

"It's kind of my thing, Major."

Dawkins smirked.

"I am Catholic, Father, but I need to ask you something to make certain I get the truth."

"Of course."

"We've been searching much of the state for these two men, or anyone they're affiliated with, and one of the men who helped them owned a box truck. One of our drones spotted a box truck in your gated community."

Father Paul scoffed.

"Major, box trucks aren't uncommon. But if you must know, one of our members found it and brought it here with some supplies."

"Very well, then."

Dawkins hesitated a moment.

"Is there something else, my son?" Father Paul asked.

"It's been well over six months since I went to church, Father. Do you hold services here?"

"I do, but they're less formal, and unfortunately, not very well-attended."

"Would I be welcome to attend mass if I were to ever make it this way again?"

"Everyone is welcome, my son."

Father Paul wasn't entirely sure if the man continued to be a devoted Catholic, or his military nature wanted to get inside the community for a closer look. In truth, Maplewood had nothing to hide from the military. Neither Metzger brother was hidden inside the gates, and neither had stepped foot inside the community, though most of the residents now knew about the men through stories told to pass the time.

"We hope to expand the walls and build a church," Father Paul said, trying to be conversational so the soldier didn't think of him as rude, or someone with secrets. "At some point, we want to travel to Lynchburg to get some items from my old church."

"Sometimes, they hold services on the base," Dawkins said, "but they're not exactly Catholic. Plus, the military keeps us pretty busy, so it's hard to make time."

Already near the pickup truck, the major sauntered over to the truck bed, spotting the two deer inside.

"You lift those yourself, Father?"

"Not if I want to keep my back in working order. I had some help, and he's still out there hunting, while I deliver these for our designated butcher to start cleaning."

Dawkins stared in the direction the priest drove from, and Father Paul hoped Sutton managed to keep himself well-hidden.

"Food is about to be our biggest struggle on the base," the major noted. "We have supplies stored in bulk, spread out across the country, but we have thousands to feed. I hope you'll say a prayer for our families, Father."

"I will, my son."

Father Paul turned toward the truck, trying to divert the man's attention away from the hunting area where Sutton might still be hiding.

"You've traveled quite a way to find these two men, Major. They must have done something dreadful if the military wants them so badly."

"It's classified, but it's also not as cut and dried as you might think."

Father Paul nodded his understanding.

"I wish you luck, my son."

Dawkins shook his hand before signaling for the military men behind him to pack up and head to their next destination. Once the three vehicles began leaving the area, Father Paul jumped into the truck and drove it through the front gate as the Maplewood residents opened it for him.

"Where's Colby?" Gracine asked him immediately when he parked and stepped from the vehicle.

"He stayed back at my request. I told him I'd handle the situation."

"What did you tell them?"

"What they needed to hear, my dear. They said they spotted a box truck inside these walls with a drone and decided to check it out. I told them one of our members brought us supplies in it."

"You lied?" Mitchell asked from beside Gracine.

"Not so much a lie as a spin on the truth, Reginald."

"I'm gonna sleep with one eye open around you, Father Paul," Mitchell kidded, drawing a chuckle from the priest as Sutton made his way to the front gate.

"What was all that about?" he inquired.

"They saw your box truck with their drone," Gracine answered.

"Fuck," Sutton muttered, forgetting the priest stood beside him. "I mean darn."

"They were asking about Dan and Bryce," Gracine said as McAllister approached their discussion.

"That can't be good," Sutton said.

"Is there anything you weren't telling us about your friends?" McAllister asked. "The military wouldn't be sending out search parties if those brothers weren't important to them."

"They're important, because they're immune to whatever infects the rest of us," Gracine said, reiterating previous dinner discussions. "That's it. The military wants to make a vaccine from their blood and hold them prisoner."

"Your friends could relieve the rest of us from a lot of stress if a vaccine was created," McAllister thought aloud.

"You're assuming the military would share it with outlanders like us," Sutton noted. "In my experience, they aren't the giving types."

McAllister wandered away from them, appearing to be deep in thought. Gracine began questioning their status and security within the community, but she also held more loyalty to Metzger than anyone she'd met in Maplewood. While Metzger put his family above their original group, he made no secret about his intentions, and he did his best to get them shelter within the military base once they got him there.

"You should call and warn them," Gracine said quietly enough that only Sutton heard her words.

"I can't. For all we know, the military could be monitoring sat phone traffic. I have a feeling they're the reason we still have operational phones at all."

"They can't just trace calls, or listen in, can they?" she asked, realizing Mitchell had overheard everything both of them said.

He simply shrugged because he didn't have an answer, while Sutton remained stoic.

"They just drove half a state away to fly a drone and spot my old box truck," Sutton said. "I'd say they're pretty serious about finding Dan and his brother."

"They have to know they aren't in Virginia."

"I'm saying they're as in the dark as we are about Dan's location, or they wouldn't have come here."

"Or maybe they came here because we're their last hope of finding him," Gracine figured aloud.

"Now you sound like me," Sutton commented.

"Yeah, you do," Mitchell said sourly, hating when Gracine was on the same page with her former traveling companion.

Mitchell walked away, putting his displeasure on display for Gracine, while Father Paul approached Sutton and Gracine.

"I would keep dinner conversation about something other than your friends," he suggested.

"Why is that?" Sutton questioned.

"The military could come back," the priest noted, "and loose lips, well, you know."

Sutton and Gracine looked at one another with concerned expressions, hoping Maplewood didn't have anyone who might sell them out to the military, especially after they earned their keep within the walls.

"Hey," Father Paul said, rapping Sutton on the arm. "We need to get these deer cleaned, or dinner isn't going to happen."

Sutton nodded, following the priest to the truck, leaving Gracine to hope Metzger and his family remained safely away from the military and their plans.

Twenty-Nine

Early March

After more than a month at the resort, the three youngsters proved their worth by helping clean, cook, and scavenge a few areas they remembered from their travels. Seldom did the weather cooperate, often dumping snow on the Adirondacks, accompanied by frigid temperatures and gusty winds. On days like this particular afternoon, however, the weather showed it might break after a southern wind brought some warmth to the area.

"We're losing daylight," Timmons said as he and Metzger gathered a few belongings into a newer Ford pickup they found at a house where the residents no longer needed it.

Inside the house, the men found ample supplies to last the group for weeks, but they also found that the older couple who occupied the cabin decided apocalypse life wasn't for them, and hung themselves from one of the cabin's thick structural beams inside. Metzger cut them down, simply to end their existence forever, as they had long since turned and become part of the undead legion.

Metzger always found tokens of the living in the vehicles and belongings he looted from stores and residences. He liked to think that part of them lived on with him in his adventures, but his mind often wandered to images of them in their second life, where they wanted nothing more than to devour him.

"Sure you don't want an extra set of hands?" Bryce volunteered, holding a hot mug of coffee in the kitchen area, wearing fuzzy slippers and pajama bottoms with a long-sleeve, white flannel shirt.

Despite having the tools to shave after his return to semi-civilization, Bryce kept the beard he grew during his travels to New York.

"You're not exactly dressed for action," Metzger commented.

"That's easily fixed."

"We've got this," Timmons assured his fellow Navy officer. "It's still too cold for fishing, so we're hoping to find some food stashes."

Timmons hadn't shown Bryce the level of respect he gave Metzger, and it wasn't clear whether he respected the younger brother more, or he kept things more formal since he and Bryce were technically military personnel. For his part, Bryce didn't exactly try bonding with Timmons at all, leaving Metzger in an awkward situation because he didn't want to show favoritism to either man. Navigating through the subtle nuances of adult behavior felt trying sometimes, causing him to wish he could return to being a teacher surrounded by children.

Metzger scooped up a small pack of supplies from a nearby table in case they didn't return by nightfall.

"Besides, we've got Hannah coming with us this time."

Hannah Miller was the young woman who accompanied the twins to the resort along with Hewitt, and she was certainly the least culpable in the ill-conceived plan to overthrow Harold and Phyllis for control of the property. Metzger would say she was along the for ride, just trying to survive, like every-one else, in such dire times.

From what the youngsters said, Hannah was Amber's high school friend who lived in the same town as the twins. She attended a different college, but their paths crossed in their hometown shortly after the apocalypse began. Blessed with a pretty face and light brown hair that stopped just short of her shoulders, she put her education to use by helping upgrade the greenhouse and brainstorm some ideas about additional food resources, along with supplemental energy ideas that might rely on nature instead of fossil fuels.

Both of the twins had participated in short supply runs, and Hannah made it known that she wanted to contribute more to the group. Metzger noticed the young adults went above and beyond to atone for their mistake of siding with Hewitt. Making amends wasn't easy because the siblings were additional mouths to feed, who initially entered the resort with seemingly hostile inten-tions. None of the adults could say they fully trusted the three quite yet, and

Isabella in particular didn't allow Nathan anywhere near them unless her parents or Bryce happened to be nearby.

"About ready, kid?" Timmons asked Hannah when she entered the building through the rear entrance, carrying a small pack around her right shoulder.

"I'm good whenever," she answered casually, setting the pack on one of the chairs.

Jillian walked in, ready to see Metzger before he departed, as she often did.

He'd taken notice that Hannah paid him more attention than anyone else at the resort, and he felt certain his girlfriend wasn't the least bit thrilled. Timmons enjoyed giving him a hard time, saying Jillian and Hannah were practically the same age, which wasn't untrue. To Metzger, Jillian felt lightyears ahead of the young adults in maturity because of everything she endured, both in losing her family and living on the road among the undead for so long.

"You be careful," Jillian said, wrapping her arms around Metzger, giving him a kiss that lasted longer than usual, possibly for Hannah's benefit.

"I will," he said when their lips parted. "We may be gone all night, so don't wait up."

"I may sleep in here tonight," Jillian said, referring to the main building. "Wouldn't want any more surprises cropping up."

Metzger didn't reply, because he knew her words were meant as a jab at Hannah and the twins for bringing Hewitt directly to their residence.

Feeling a bit uncomfortable, he turned to Timmons.

"We ready?"

"We are," the pilot said with a knowing smirk.

Without additional fanfare, the trio loaded the last of their supplies into the truck, and Timmons assumed the driver's seat while Metzger rode shotgun. Hannah shared the equally comfortable rear seats of the crew cab with a few of the bags. None of them initially fastened their seatbelts, throwing conventional safety to the wind, but the truck's warning alarm wouldn't shut off until they buckled up.

"Technology," Timmons grumbled as he started the truck down the hill towards their first destination.

"Says the guy who flies multi-million-dollar aircraft," Metzger commented.

Looking back, Metzger spotted Hannah with her nose in a book, oblivious to their conversation.

"What are you reading?" he inquired.

"It's a book on how to install solar panels," she answered without looking up.

"Not exactly riveting," Timmons commented.

"I agree," Hannah said, "but we're eventually going to have to replace the resort's panels if we want to maintain hot showers, and last I checked, none of us are licensed electricians."

"Point taken," Timmons said. "Carry on."

Almost halfway down the hill, they encountered a zombie trying to stagger up the road, and Timmons started to swerve at it.

"Don't," Metzger said with more of a scolding tone than he intended. "It's not worth hurting the truck."

"You're no fun, but we *do* need the truck."

Timmons returned to his original lane, letting the zombie turn around as its attention now focused on the truck. Metzger looked in his mirror, seeing it stagger a few steps before hitting a slick spot, which sent it tumbling down the hill and into the woods where it disappeared.

"I wonder if Harold and Phyllis remember where the solar panels came from," Hannah said, as though she hadn't heard a word of their minor disagreement.

"Unlikely, if contractors did the work," Metzger said. "Why?"

"If we knew where they were produced, or stored, we could possibly make a road trip and grab some extras."

"How do you know there would be any left?" Timmons asked.

"Solar panels probably aren't at the top of anyone's survival list," Hannah retorted. "It takes a little knowhow to install them."

"We'll have to check with them when we get back," Metzger said. "Any other ideas?"

"We need renewable food. The greenhouse and the chickens are nice, but we need more."

"That's why we'll hunt and fish," Timmons said. "We aren't going to find cows and pigs unless we come across a farmer that's protected them all this time. And I ain't gonna be the one to negotiate with a loaded shotgun pointed at me."

Somewhat disappointed, Hannah went back to burying her nose in the book, and Metzger could tell Timmons didn't mean to shoot down her ideas and crush her spirit. He gave the older man a sideways glance, indicating the pilot needed to atone for his lapse in manners. In response, Timmons bobbled his head a moment, meaning he would make amends in his own time.

For the most part, the roads appeared tolerable, with just enough crunchy, melting snow to keep the truck from slipping on the layer of ice below.

"How much have you dealt with the dead?" Metzger asked Hannah when they neared Lake Placid, where Metzger wanted to check a few houses at the edge of town before they moved to some of Harold's other mapped locations.

"A little," she answered. "Adam did most of the work when we traveled. He seemed to like that kind of thing."

Not feeling surprised, Metzger decided he wouldn't place Hannah in any perilous situations until he knew she could contend with undead attackers.

When they reached the town limits, the group spotted numerous vehicles picked over, along with bodies strewn across the street. Metzger recognized his own handiwork a few times, and he directed Timmons to drive past the areas he had previously checked, finding some houses on the other side of town. As they passed the area, however, he noticed their doors kicked in, indicating someone had already raided them. He made a mental note of the vehicles on this end of town that might still run, or offer useful finds.

"There are houses dotting this whole area," Metzger noted aloud.

"I'm sure your kids have found all of them by now," Timmons said, looking along his side of the road for any prospective looting areas.

"What kids?" Hannah inquired.

"We ran into some teenagers during one of our trips here," Metzger answered. "They said they were in a group with some adults, but I wasn't sure I believed them."

"I *definitely* didn't," Timmons said grumpily.

"Big surprise," Hannah commented, drawing an inadvertent snort from Metzger as he chuckled.

Timmons ignored their fun at his expense, continuing to drive around the area until he found a row of houses that appeared undisturbed along a street slightly offset from the other roads.

"Either no one located this place, or people live here," he thought aloud.

"There's only four houses here," Metzger commented. "Maybe our local friends haven't bothered with them yet."

Timmons stopped the truck in front of the first house. All three of the travelers stepped from the truck, quietly closing their doors. Not a single member of the dead had appeared, roaming the streets, which left Metzger mildly concerned. If the undead weren't around in any capacity, he suspected someone, or multiple people, thinned their numbers. Anyone capable of dealing with undead efficiently wasn't a person Metzger wanted to cross, because he never knew how survivors felt about strangers.

"Got the keys?" Metzger asked his friend.

"Yeah," Timmons answered, dangling them as proof. "I'm never very trusting when we come to these places."

Metzger unhooked the sheathed knife from his belt, turning to hand it to Hannah.

"You're trusting me with this?" she asked, surprise in her eyes and her tone.

He placed the ensemble in her hands, giving her a nod.

"I don't expect you to lead the charge, but just in case anything comes at you."

Hannah appeared appreciative of his trust, and examined the knife as she swallowed hard, openly hoping to avoid using it.

Once everyone was in position around the front door of the first house, Timmons opened the door and swung it inward while Metzger held his sword in front of him. Knocking on the door heavily three times, Timmons backed away and the group waited for any sounds of the undead. Only the breeze entering the residence and echoing throughout reached their ears, so Metzger led the way inside, stepping cautiously through the living room until they reached the kitchen.

"See what you can find," he told Hannah. "Use trash bags or boxes if you find anything worth taking back to the resort."

She nodded affirmatively, beginning to search cabinets and the pantry area as Metzger and Timmons walked room to room throughout the one-story house, making certain no threats awaited them.

Timmons opened each door, if they weren't already open, and Metzger stood ready to deal with any threats. When they reached the second bedroom, obviously the room where the parents of the household slept, Timmons scoured the area visually, spotting something that interested him. He walked straight to the dresser where an alarm clock and a few other small items rested, each with a thin layer of dust coating them.

"Fuck yeah!" Timmons shouted with contained excitement.

"What is it?" Metzger asked, approaching his friend.

Timmons held up a green bottle of cologne with a small brown horse printed on the bottle. He sprayed it on Metzger's hand without waiting for permission, or further inquiry on the younger man's part. Metzger waited a few seconds before placing his hand close to his nose, once the initial potent odor wore off, finding the cologne to smell a bit musky, outdoorsy almost, and not potent like some of the French scents.

"It's nice," Metzger said with a small shrug.

"Nice?" Timmons asked incredulously, his eyes growing wide with surprise. "This is *my* scent, son. I can't tell you how much play I got wearing this and a nice pair of shitkickers on weekends."

"Well, I'm glad the two of you are reunited."

Shoving the bottle into a back pocket, Timmons helped Metzger clear the remainder of the house, and the duo found only a few small boxes of ammunition, and a .44 Magnum for their trouble. When they reached the kitchen, Hannah already had boxes and cans of food stuffed inside two trash bags. She left anything questionable inside the pantry, and set aside a few utensils the group needed at the resort.

"Nice job, kid," Timmons said before heading outside, a skip in his step that Metzger hadn't seen since they landed in New York.

"What's his deal?" Hannah asked.

"I guess you could call it a small victory. Let me help you with those."

Each of them toted a bag to the truck, tossing them into the truck bed. Timmons was already at the next door, ready to head inside.

"Wait for us," Metzger called, seeing daylight wane in the distance, knowing his friend wanted to explore all four residences quickly.

He questioned why no one had bothered to explore the four houses, because their street, and general location, wasn't that far removed from most of Lake Placid. Possibly a few hundred houses dotted the town, and surrounding roads, but six months was a long time for a variety of people to pick them over, including this street.

"Come on," Timmons urged, reaching for the doorknob as Metzger heard an odd thumping sound coming from ground level.

It wasn't simply a single thump, but rather powerful as though several people were throwing themselves against a door or wall.

He looked to the second house in the row, seeing metal bulkhead doors along the side of the house that led to a cellar beneath. Much to his horror, Metzger realized why no one wanted to deal with the row of houses, because at least one concealed a deadly secret within its walls. At the same moment Metzger learned the truth, the handles being secured by a single lock warped and snapped, allowing the bulkhead doors to burst open. Metzger also saw his friend begin to turn the knob on the front door, oblivious to the commotion along the side of the house.

"Scott! No!" Metzger screamed as the front door swung inward and a group of zombies emerged and lurched at the pilot ravenously, sending him to the ground.

Thirty

For a brief moment, Metzger watched his friend engulfed by at least five zombies, and he started forward to deal with the situation after getting over the initial panic of losing another person he cared about. By some small miracle, Timmons fell to the ground, and backed up like a crab until he was able to get his footing. He darted over to Metzger, who spied a number of undead emerging from the exterior cellar doors.

"Get ready," he told Hannah. "I'll get the ones I can, but a few might slip past me."

"Holy shit!" Timmons exclaimed as he took Metzger's side, reaching for his sidearm. "I didn't expect that!"

"I saw the danger too late," Metzger told his friend. "Don't shoot unless you have to. Maybe I can keep this quiet."

"Okay."

Metzger chose to stand his ground and let the undead filter his way, where he was able to slice the first few through the skull with ease. The numbers began to catch up with him soon, and he kicked a few aside before stabbing and slicing a few more, ending their existences. A glance at each of the doors showed more of the undead emerging from the front, and the cellar. Metzger wasn't sure he could handle so many without tiring, but he didn't want gunfire attracting more of their kind.

"Get in the truck," he ordered Timmons and Hannah.

"What about you?" Timmons asked without moving.

"I've got a plan. Get in the truck and start it. You can help distract them for me."

"Okay," Timmons said with a tone that indicated he hoped Metzger knew what he was doing.

Metzger had some doubts, but he wouldn't let his body tire to the point that he risked being overtaken.

He heard the truck doors open and shut behind him, because he kept his eyes on the ravenous zombies stumbling his way, some with mangled hands, and others with feet that didn't face forward. Timmons started the truck as asked, and Metzger dealt with a few more of the undead, opting to behead them at the neck to ensure his sword didn't get stuck within a skull. Unfortunately, the heads remained animated, gnashing their teeth and constantly searching for food they could no longer catch with their dull eyes that creepily followed anything that moved.

About a dozen undead drew dangerously close to him, and Metzger knew the risks of getting his blade stuck or broken, so he backed away, circling around the truck.

"Stay right here," he told Timmons, who responded with a nod.

As a collective, the undead appeared uncertain of how to maneuver while hunting Metzger around the truck. Most followed him directly while a few acted as though they lost track of him completely. He quickly rounded the truck and swung his sword at two consecutive zombies before they turned and spotted him. Their heads plopped against the ground, leaving bloody marks in the melting snow before rolling to a stop.

Now, every lifeless eye looked to him, and Metzger decided to jump up in the truck bed, rather than continue being pursued. He didn't want to risk slipping on a patch of ice, because much of the snow and ice remained, despite the warming trend. He managed to get a foot on the rear bumper and propel himself over the tailgate as gray, cold hands groped at him. Standing, Metzger allowed the undead to file around the truck bed and reach for him, desperately wanting a warm meal.

"Want me to take off?" Timmons inquired after rolling down his window slightly.

"No," Metzger said emphatically. "I've got this."

Taking the blade over one shoulder, Metzger carefully lined up his shot, bringing the sword down upon fingers, necks, and any other body part that crossed the blade's path. His efforts required a few more swings until one undead woman remained, grasping desperately at him. Taking a few seconds to study her, he wondered if she lived locally, or migrated to Lake Placid, hoping for a chance at life. Several bite marks along her neck indicated her life was cut short by unimaginable circumstances at some point in her journey.

Metzger swung the sword fluidly, severing her head at the ears as the top portion of the skull fell into the truck bed. Holding the weapon, he climbed to the ground, opened the tailgate, and brushed out all of the body parts that now littered the bed. Timmons and Hannah climbed out of the truck, both appearing impressed with his skills.

"You okay?" his friend asked.

"Will be once I catch my breath," Metzger answered, panting slightly from the excitement. "And you?"

"Not a scratch," Timmons said, lifting his arms as though he needed to prove it to himself once more. "Glad I put the bottle in the truck before I fell on my ass over there," he added, thumbing inside the truck where the green bottle of cologne rested in one of the cup holders.

"I'm so happy for the two of you," Metzger said with a bit of sarcasm.

"If that bottle had been on me, my ass would've smelled awesome and you two would've had a delightful ride home.

Both Metzger and Hannah rolled their eyes slightly, and Metzger couldn't imagine dealing with the full contents of the bottle being unleashed and trapped inside the truck's cab with them.

"Why would anyone trap the dead inside a house like that?" Hannah questioned.

"It can't be with good intentions," Metzger reasoned aloud. "Getting them in there would be dangerous as hell."

Timmons stepped forward, staring at the house.

"I say it's worth a look."

"Of course it is," Metzger added, looking over his shoulder and guessing they had about an hour of daylight left.

Using flashlights from the truck, Metzger and Timmons began clearing the house, leaving Hannah outside to watch for any undead or living threats. Timmons had moved the truck closer to the house, with the hope that they would hear any activity themselves. Metzger led the way to the cellar, locating a radio complete with CD player that could run on batteries. He suspected it lured the undead downstairs, but he didn't know if someone wanted an easy way to deal with them, or planned to weaponize the zombies.

Only one undead straggler remained inside one of the bedrooms, a man dressed like he was ready to hit the nearby golf course, with a chunk missing from his left forearm. His teal golf shirt, now soiled with numerous stains and bodily fluids, gave the impression he didn't know death was coming for him while he planned on leisurely activity. Only one of his two-tone shoes remained, the other lost in his struggle for life, or as a shuffling member of the undead.

"Poor sap never saw it coming," Timmons muttered as Metzger used the pointed tip of his blade to jab through the left eye socket, downing the man permanently.

"What about you?" Metzger asked his friend. "Did you see it coming?"

"I was a little preoccupied right before the bombs went off that day," Timmons admitted. "My military life was on the ropes, and I had a decision to make."

"Oh?"

Timmons walked into the kitchen, opening a few cupboards as Metzger did the same. Much of the floor throughout the house appeared slimy, as though bananas had been left to blacken and rot, leaving filth and black sludge trails throughout the building that smelled even worse than they appeared. From experience, Metzger compared the odor to a city dump where food items had been left to rot for days in the hot sun, except the house absorbed the scent over time, making the structure an equal partner in distributing foul odors.

"The Navy was ready to put me to pasture," Timmons said, grabbing a few cans from a cupboard, setting them on the countertop.

Metzger realized the two had discussed this previously, but the Navy man didn't go into much detail.

"Retirement?"

"Well, it's never really brought up in conversation, but pilots have a shelf life in the Navy's eyes. Fighter pilots more so than us transport guys, but there comes a time where you either promote, or look at your civilian options."

Metzger chuckled.

"What?" Timmons asked, a bit irritated.

"Sorry. I'm just trying to picture you in one of those airline pilot uniforms."

"Yeah, well I *wasn't*."

Timmons stepped sideways to a different cupboard, opening it to find only plates and bowls.

"If you're a captain, that's a big step if you promoted, right?"

"Rear admiral lower half, to be specific. I'd be on the water, or cooped up inside an office, which is not something I'm accustomed to."

"You'd be a boss."

"Also not something I'm really accustomed to. Technically, I supervised some pilots, of course, but it's more of a brotherhood than a pissing match. I was in a pinch, Daniel."

Metzger located some coffee and hot chocolate containers, checking each to make certain they were sealed before setting them aside for bagging. Each of them appeared unopened, and he didn't trust open containers, because some survivors were capable of leaving poisoned wells in the world of scavenging.

"And then the apocalypse came along and saved your career," he put his friend's situation into a one-sentence summary.

"Something like that," Timmons said, his voice trailing off.

He piddled momentarily, and Metzger could see a crack in the usually rugged façade of the pilot.

"What is it?" Metzger asked.

"It's just that I never had a contingency plan beyond flying planes for the Navy," Timmons answered, looking a bit despondent about the past. "Of course I thought about it, but they were ready to kick me out the door, or pin some stars on my uniform. I wasn't really ready for either."

"I think I know you well enough to say you would've felt like you didn't have a purpose."

Timmons nodded, sniffling a bit in a rare show of emotion.

"Even when the apocalypse struck, and they suddenly needed me, I still didn't feel right about it. It took a manpower shortage to make me valuable again. Maybe that's why I was happy when you came along, because it gave me something to do. And it pissed me off when they asked me to use our friendship to their advantage."

"I appreciate your loyalty, Scott. You could've easily screwed up my family reunion."

"You fought like hell to get to Bryce. Even though it didn't work out the way we figured, you two finally got what you wanted."

An awkward silence fell between them momentarily.

"That about it?" Metzger asked about the available supplies, seeing the pair had cleared the kitchen.

"I think so. Wasn't much in the other rooms, as though someone went through here before they locked up the infected."

Heading for the front door, Metzger had a question for his friend.

"What about you? How much longer are you going to be happy saddled with us?"

Timmons gave a crooked smirk.

"Haven't given it much thought. I don't have a home with the Navy now, so I'm going to play it by ear."

"You were more than just our ride here," Metzger said. "You're welcome to stick around as long as you want, if I haven't said that before, or you didn't think so already."

"I appreciate it," Timmons said as the two men walked through the front door, finding Hannah waiting patiently with the truck.

"Looks like a light haul," she commented without judgment.

"It was probably picked over before our friends were put inside," Metzger said. "Do we have time to try the last two? With a little more caution, perhaps?"

Timmons gave a slow nod that indicated he accepted the blame for putting all three of them in jeopardy when he opened the front door without expecting any traps.

"If I could find some matching deodorant, I'd be in heaven," the pilot commented.

Hannah shook her head, amused by Timmons and his simple pleasures.

"Your generation just buried their heads in their tablets and cell phones," he said in response. "Couldn't be bothered to mow lawns, shop in stores, or attend meetings in person."

"We survived the apocalypse," she said. "Must've been doing something right."

"You mean *you* survived. Ninety-nine percent of your generation didn't."

"Ninety-nine percent of everyone didn't survive," Metzger noted.

"My point exactly."

Despite their mild bickering, the three cleared the last two houses in short order, finding some food, a little ammunition, some toilet paper and trash bags, and most importantly, no undead.

As they placed the last of their bounty into the truck, and the purple hue of dusk glowed before them, Metzger saw his friend staring at the mammoth lodge in the distance, at the western edge of Lake Placid.

"Why haven't we checked that place before?" Timmons asked.

Looming in the distance, like some kind of movie backdrop, portions of Whiteface Lodge stood four stories tall, constructed mainly of heavy timber, and appearing luxurious, even in the face of the apocalypse. Topped with a green roof and large windows, the building possessed a haunted house feel, even from a distance. Several trees on the grounds nestled the mammoth building, providing an appearance of nature with modern amenities. Metzger couldn't imagine how cozy and inviting it might appear if only its lights still had power.

"You think someone isn't already calling that place home?" Metzger retorted.

"Surely, it would've been one of the first buildings picked over around here," Hannah added.

"We need a place to stay for the night," Timmons said. "Our truck has a lot more room left, and daylight will come early."

"There are a hundred houses around here with fireplaces," Metzger said, waving his arm at the rows of buildings just east of their location.

"He's not going to give in," Hannah told Metzger, because even she knew Timmons and his idiosyncrasies in the short time she lived at the resort.

"I'm aware," Metzger said. "Okay, Captain. Let's go check the place out."

"Don't call me that," Timmons said, fishing the keys from his pocket with a bit of excitement. "I'm driving."

On the way there, Metzger contemplated why Timmons wanted to visit this massive resort so badly. He felt as though his friend always liked bigger and better things in life, and military life certainly allowed the pilot to experience culture and architecture. Bryce sometimes talked about shore leave when ships reached ports both domestic and abroad, giving the sailors freedom to see the world. Perhaps Timmons occupied himself with taverns, and the company of mysterious women, prior to the world falling apart.

When they drew closer to the lodge, Metzger realized how isolated it was from the main portion of town. Sitting north of Highway 86, it possessed the entire side of the road, surrounded by woods, while a few other small inns, and stores, occupied the other side. Metzger felt uneasy in his stomach, as though the trio was about to experience something dangerous.

"No one could maintain this place by themselves," Timmons said, staring at the complex as they approached the main driveway.

"I never said *one* person would."

"Then who?" Hannah asked.

"I always suspected the kids we met before might live here."

"Who are these kids?" she asked, more for clarification than anything else.

"The ones who shot at us?" Timmons said more than asked.

"Why would they shoot at you?"

"They were actually trying to help us," Metzger answered. "I think."

Timmons slowed the truck as they pulled into the driveway, and he purposely kept the headlights off in case someone inside observed their approach.

"This is eerie," the older man admitted.

"That's putting it mildly," Hannah added.

Nearly a minute later, the truck came to a stop in the circle driveway in front of the building where guests likely checked in as recently as the previous August. No other vehicles were parked there, and Metzger saw no indications of the undead milling around the area. He felt gravely concerned, but curiosity ate at him about the building, because he once researched the place for a romantic vacation with his girlfriend, and Whiteface Lodge reached the top three on his short list.

"I think there's more than one building," Metzger said, trying to recall the online brochure he examined almost a year prior, before he and his girlfriend parted ways.

Each of them grabbed a flashlight as dusk took hold of the area, and Metzger felt certain someone claimed the property at some point because no undead lingered on the grounds. He led the way to the main entrance, which he found unlocked, so he opened one of the two doors, stepping inside to find the front desk to the right. Beyond it, backlit by moonlight through French doors and some windows, he saw a large dining area with a fireplace on each side. No fires currently warmed the room, and he could actually see his breath in the flashlight's beam as nighttime brought about colder temperatures.

A number of small, round tables occupied the room with one large, rectangular table that held seating for at least eight, occupying the center. The walls, handrails, floor, and even the ceiling were constructed of stained wood, reminiscent of pioneer days to Metzger. Even without lighting, the place looked magnificent, and virtually untouched because everything appeared to be made of wood, leaving little to loot or destroy.

"I've never seen so much wood in all my life," Hannah said quietly as the three fanned out around within the dining room.

Metzger noticed several offshoot hallways that likely led to various rooms, stairs, and elevators that no longer moved. He felt drawn to the picturesque French doors at the back of the dining area overlooking a recreational area. Between the darkness and the snow, he couldn't see details clearly, but he spotted a water fountain centerpiece surrounded by a circular walkway that stemmed from other concrete walking paths. The walkway had melted just enough compared to the lawn surrounding it that Metzger could tell where a person might walk. In fact, he believed as he squinted, that some of the snow was trodden in the lawn and the walking area. Footprints appeared to travel back and forth from the main building and another building across the recreational park.

Snow hadn't abandoned the Adirondack area for weeks, so he couldn't make an accurate guess when the tracks were created, but Metzger felt certain he saw tread details in a few of the closer prints when he shined his flashlight out the door. He was about to suggest they leave when the beam of light caught something closer to the fountain that he couldn't quite make out. At first, he thought perhaps someone stacked some firewood there, but the shapes appeared rounded in some areas. He wondered if a person cleared the dead and decided to leave them on the property. Burying them during the winter months couldn't be accomplished, because New York winters froze the ground solid for months, and burning them didn't exactly dispose of the bodies.

"Stay here," he said to Timmons and Hannah, finding he needed to unlock the French doors to access the back patio, and the walking paths beyond it. "I'll be right back."

Suspecting a trap, or possibly a gruesome scenario before him, Metzger marched through the snow slowly, keeping his flashlight turned off to avoid making himself a target. The two buildings on the property were now silhouetted by moonlight on a virtually cloudless evening, adding to the eerie feeling that he and his companions weren't alone on the grounds. He could barely see his breath as the purple skies turned black, with only a handful of stars to provide illumination.

Drawing close to the fountain, Metzger felt a sense of dread as he spied four rows of stacked bodies. They appeared to be piled upright and efficiently, almost the way someone might place firewood beside a house. As though left for decoration, or some sort of triumphant monument, the bodies symbolized something, and as he shined his light across several faces, he saw eyes wide open, pale like those of the undead. These people hadn't turned, however, and some of them appeared to have looks of horror or shock on their faces. Upon further examination, he noticed these same people had bullet holes in the backs of their skulls, or bloody stab wounds in their necks.

Bouncing the flashlight beam between the various bodies, he noticed several victims close to him in age, a few older, and quite a few young adults and teenagers in the piles. He wondered what happened to these people, because the undead weren't suspects based on the way these people were murdered. Metzger found no evidence of bite marks, or any other reason these people might have been infected and put down before nature ran its course.

His mind frantically ran through the possible scenarios that left these people in the bitter cold where even scavengers hadn't torn at the bodies yet. Metzger didn't detect a scent from the bodies, as though the freezing temperatures stunted the decay and odor that would normally attract far more sensitive noses than his to the area.

"Who would do this?" he wondered under his breath.

While effective at killing the living or the dead, the military wouldn't condone genocide so far as he knew. They would press people for information, or whatever else they wanted, but killing people in cold-blood wasn't in their nature.

Even worse, and more mysterious, a new group might have decided to claim the Adirondacks for themselves, killing everything in their path. A bit of observation and sufficient firepower went a long way in taking over virtually any area in a hurry. Despite imminent danger possibly everywhere around him, Metzger needed to take a few extra seconds to examine the horrific scene before him.

Swallowing hard, he moved to the third of the four stacks, noticing something familiar about one of the bodies about midway down. Although the bodies were placed with no particular theme or reasoning, Metzger spied the boy with the disheveled brown hair who shot at him during his first visit to the area. A face frozen in time, etched with terror, the child likely knew his end was near, and blood along his chest indicated he was shot. Likely trying to flee his inevitable fate, the child likely saw members of his group slaughtered. Metzger began to realize his instincts were correct, that these kids and their group lived in the lodge, but someone, somehow, ended their lives in mere months.

"We need to get out of here," he muttered, turning before sprinting as best he could toward the French doors.

In this instance, he hated being right, realizing he should have pressed Timmons harder about avoiding the lodge, particularly under the blanket of darkness.

Reaching the French doors in a matter of seconds, Metzger tried the handle the first time and the door wouldn't open. Thinking he'd been locked out, or set up from the beginning by some unseen group, he tried the door again, putting his shoulder into it. This time the door gave way, because it had been wedged against the frame from the cold, allowing Metzger to enter the dining room once more.

Stepping inside, Metzger's eyes were immediately drawn to Hannah being held captive by a large hand covering her mouth. Another hand holding a firearm gripped her, pulling her tight against his body with the gun dangerously close to her face. Hannah's muffled cries couldn't escape the hand, and although Metzger couldn't see the face of her assailant in the darkness, he knew by the size of the man it could only be one person.

He just couldn't fathom how this person before him survived the frigid winter and a wound that should have killed him to terrorize numerous innocent people.

"Hello, Adam," Metzger said, less prepared to deal with his most dangerous adversary to date than the first time around.

Thirty-One

More details reached Metzger's eyes as they adjusted to the darkness, including the fact that a prone Timmons was just a few feet away from Hewitt's left foot. It appeared a hatchet might be buried in the pilot's skull, because a slender piece of wood emerged from that area, but Metzger quickly realized a broken chair duped his interpretation of the scene.

Hewitt wore dark winter clothing, which caused him to blend in with the surroundings in such low lighting. All of his attire appeared different from the last time Metzger saw him, and the man likely pilfered from the stacks of victims outside.

"Don't worry," Hewitt sneered, glancing at an unconscious Timmons. "Pops is fine. For now."

"You don't have to do this," Metzger said.

"I don't?" Hewitt countered, openly surprised at the wording. "You *made* me into this. I barely survived, making my way to this town after you left me for dead. For weeks, I scrounged together what food I could, wondering how I survived that cheap shot wound you gave me."

Hannah continued to squirm, and any doubt Metzger possessed about her working with Hewitt passed, because the firearm in the man's right hand proved very convincing.

"You singlehandedly murdered this entire village?" Metzger asked, not masking his disdain.

"It wasn't hard," Hewitt remarked, giving an evil smile. "They left a few at a time to get supplies, and it occurred to me that those supplies would go a lot further for one person than twenty-two."

Metzger believed the number sounded correct, based on what he found in the courtyard.

"You're an absolute monster," Metzger muttered.

"What's that?" Hewitt asked, waving the gun slightly to taunt Metzger. "Maybe you should watch your tone."

Metzger hadn't given up the notion of reaching for his own firearm, and his eyes shifted to the available cover behind the tables. Hewitt hadn't given his plan much thought, trying to control a situation with three adversaries who were no longer caught off-guard. Metzger could almost assuredly survive the situation by diving for cover, or running out the doors behind him, but he wasn't about to leave Hannah and Timmons to die like the unfortunate souls in the courtyard.

"You going to add us to your pile out back?" he asked Hewitt.

"Maybe, but I've got some special plans for you first. You're going to watch this traitor die, along with the old man. I'm a lot better off than I would've been. But there's still the fact that you tried to kill me."

"You kind of had it coming," Metzger responded. "But before you hurt anyone, there's something you need to know."

"Nothing is going to change what I plan on doing."

"You say that, but the military could definitely use you."

"Use me?" Hewitt asked skeptically. "I don't have any interest in working for anyone, especially the people who let this happen."

"Not working," Metzger explained, his eyes still looking for cover and possible weapons other than his sword and sidearm. "They're looking for people immune to the infection. You'd be a commodity."

"What do you mean by that?" Hewitt asked, openly intrigued as he loosened his grip slightly on Hannah.

"A commodity is something valued," Metzger answered, uncertain if Hewitt meant the definition or the specifics when asking about the word.

"I know what it means. I'm asking what that would mean for *me*."

"It would mean living where there's electricity, having three square meals a day, and being protected by the military day and night."

Hewitt contemplated the words nearly all of three seconds before responding.

"You're lying."

"I'm not. My brother worked there, and he knows how desperately they're searching for anyone immune to the disease."

Metzger purposely left out his personal, harrowing ordeal with the military because he wanted Hewitt to feel special. Planting the seed of opportunity was only the first phase of his plan, because he needed the man to contemplate the offer before producing additional information.

"What good does someone like me do for the military?"

"They can create a vaccine from your blood."

Now Hewitt attempted to pull Hannah in tight once more, but she managed to wriggle her head free from his grip.

"Shoot him!" she shouted, pleading with Metzger.

"Don't try it," Hewitt warned, "or they both die right here and now."

"Your best option is to accept my offer and let us take you to the military," Metzger said steadfastly.

"I don't trust you. You're just waiting for a chance to shoot me."

Metzger couldn't reveal the reason why he *wasn't* lying. Taking Hewitt to the military scientists might very well keep them from trying to find him or his brother. It felt inevitable, somehow, that their former allies would eventually locate them and drag them back to Virginia, or some secret, undisclosed location.

"Believe me, the last thing I want to do is shoot you."

Metzger noticed a look of panic in Hannah's eyes when he spoke the words, and before he could do anything to prevent her next action, she got her mouth free once again and bit into Hewitt's left wrist, which held her captive. He screamed in pain, and went to retaliate against her by taking aim with his right arm as she ran away. Metzger quickly drew his own sidearm, firing before he took careful aim, merely clipping Hewitt in his right shoulder.

Hewitt chose his best option rather quickly, attempting to flee the dining room area as Timmons came to and reached for the small revolver he kept hidden in one of his winter boots.

"Don't!" Metzger yelled to his friend, but Timmons was already firing as Hewitt reached the edge of the dining room and headed down one of the branching hallways.

Metzger couldn't tell in the poorly lit conditions if his friend actually struck Hewitt or not.

"Do *not* shoot him if you can help it!" he instructed both Timmons and Hannah as he darted from the room, prepared to take down Hewitt however he needed to.

Hannah remained on the floor, trying to catch her breath from her ordeal while Timmons shook his head, still trying to loosen the mental cobwebs after somehow being rendered unconscious by Hewitt.

Metzger quickly discovered Hewitt wasn't difficult to follow because he left blood droplets on the floor wherever he went. So far as he knew, Hewitt didn't have the benefit of a flashlight, but he knew the building's layout. Exercising caution, Metzger wished he had backup, because he wasn't about to let his adversary escape cleanly. He felt responsible for unleashing the man on an unsuspecting group in Lake Placid that could have easily brought harm to Timmons, and him, during their initial visit.

Whenever he came to a corner or intersection, Metzger turned off his flashlight and studied the area before moving forward. He didn't want to be an easy target for Hewitt, but he needed to locate the man soon. If Hewitt escaped, and wasn't gravely injured, it would only be a matter of time before he repeated his cruelty to others in a different location.

Continuing to follow the trail of droplets, Metzger ended up heading up some stairs, wondering if Hewitt had chosen one of the numerous rooms to call his own suite at some point. Most, or all, of the rooms contained fireplaces, which provided warmth, and obviously the man helped himself to any goods the former residents collected. Deep down, Metzger felt rage about how the man singlehandedly murdered nearly two dozen individuals, feeling tremendous guilt for not finishing the job the first time. Despite his growing hatred for the man, Metzger kept his emotions in check, because keeping Hewitt alive meant solving a few of his own problems, while helping mankind in general.

At the top of the stairs where the second floor led to a handful of suites, Metzger found larger droplets of blood, as though Hewitt might have rested a few seconds at that very spot before continuing down the hallway. Metzger carefully stepped into the hallway, concerned that Hewitt might be lying in wait for him in one of the recessed doorways. His eyes bobbed between the blood trail and the hallway ahead, and Metzger stayed near the wall along his right side in case he needed to duck into cover as well.

He waited only a few seconds before moving forward, realizing the droplets stopped at one particular door, which likely accessed the room Hewitt chose as his personal quarters. Metzger stopped at the door, debating how to proceed, because he envisioned the man on the other side, taking cover, waiting to put two slugs in Metzger's chest. Standing safely to one side, Metzger tried the doorknob, which in this case was a pushdown thumb latch. The doors appeared to have modern, electronic key entry slots, but in the case of power outage, he wasn't sure if they would work without a generator or backup battery.

In this case, the door remained secured, and now Hewitt likely knew he was on the other side for certain. Although made of wood, the door wasn't especially thick, or heavy in appearance, so Metzger figured he might be able to bust through with a running start. Holding the pistol in his right hand, he walked to the other side of the hallway, sucked in a quick breath, and charged at the door, leading with his left shoulder. Striking it with a good amount of force, he heard the door crack slightly from within, but it remained solidly on its hinges.

He knew using his shoulder as a battering ram a few more times would likely result in injury, which he couldn't afford in a showdown with Hewitt. A thought crossed his mind that Hewitt might be weakening from blood loss, and simply nursing his wounds, or on the verge of passing out. Any number of scenarios ran through his mind, but Metzger wasn't about to waste time taking every precaution possible. He wasn't about to let the man elude him and bring harm to more innocent survivors, so he backed up and launched himself into the door once again, beginning to compromise the latch near the handle.

Despite his shoulder feeling a bit tender after the second attempt, Metzger reared back one last time and hurled his body against the door, sending it flying inward as he tumbled to the ground. He intended to stay low in order to avoid being shot, but lost his balance in the process of the door breaking into several chunks. Expecting gunfire immediately, he rolled to one side, and into a sofa without hearing anything.

Getting to his knees, Metzger frantically looked around the room, seeing no sign of Hewitt, though a fire flickered in the suite's fireplace. Wondering how they hadn't spotted a plume of smoke from outside the lodge, Metzger regained his footing, finding the double doors wide-open that led to an exterior deck.

"Oh, shit," he muttered, wondering if Hewitt had attempted to jump from the exterior balcony, or wanted Metzger to fall for some sort of trick.

Before running blindly toward the balcony, he checked the bathroom and closets to make certain Hewitt didn't plan to lure him outside just to toss him over the railing. Finding them empty, he carefully stepped onto the balcony area, which remained covered with snow, discovering several footprints and a rope ladder. An escape ladder, like those found in hardware stores for fleeing a burning home on an upper level, was hooked to the balcony, and before Metzger could look over the railing, he heard a pained yelp from below.

He immediately panicked that Timmons had somehow gotten himself injured by the maniac, so he rushed to the railing, looking down to find Hewitt lying on the ground. Because the ladder fell short of the ground, the man might have dropped down, or possibly slipped on the device. Now clutching his right ankle, Hewitt rocked back and forth in pain, groaning out loud as Timmons and Hannah exited the back of the resort to the courtyard where Hewitt's chosen room faced.

Metzger spotted Hewitt's gun beside him on the ground, and he immediately felt compelled to keep his friend and Hannah away from the man.

"Stay back!" he yelled, catching them both by surprise as they had to look around, before spotting him on the second story.

Freezing in their tracks, they appeared to ask Metzger for direction, and he motioned for them to return to the rear doors. Timmons held out his left arm, like a boom gate, keeping Hannah from taking another step forward, but

Metzger worried that his protective friend might try to resolve the situation himself. Indeed, the Navy captain appeared uncertain of which action might prove the best, and his eyes drifted in the direction of the piles of corpses nearby. He stared momentarily, taking a few deep breaths, and Metzger felt certain his friend would rush forward and risk a confrontation with the wounded Hewitt. In the end, he trusted Metzger enough to heed his request. Backing away with Hannah, both kept their eyes on Hewitt until they reached the doors and returned inside.

Hewitt continued to lament his likely broken ankle, not trying to rise from the ground, so Metzger left the room through the broken door and briskly went down the stairs, navigating his way to the dining area. There, he found a concerned Timmons who grabbed him by the arm as he attempted to pass through to the rear doors.

"You need to finish him," Timmons said sternly. "He's a danger to all of us."

"We *need* him, Scott."

"We need him like a hole in the head, Dan. There's no reason to keep him around."

"Please, just kill him," Hannah added, her face etched in fear after nearly being killed by her former ally.

"I don't want to keep him around," Metzger said, looking to both of them. "We need to take him to Norfolk."

"What?" Timmons asked, his expression indicating he thought Metzger had lost his mind.

"He has the same immunity as me," Metzger stated. "He survived that cut from my sword that was covered in zombie blood."

"That could be a fluke," Timmons argued.

"How?" Metzger countered. "When everyone else dies from it. This could be our one chance to get the military off our backs, because you know they're looking for us."

Timmons started to say something, but his open mouth froze momentarily, giving Metzger an opportunity to say what he needed to.

"Stay here," he said to both of his companions. "I'm going to deal with Hewitt."

Again, Timmons started to say something, but Metzger cut him off by holding up a finger and making a statement.

"That's final," he said sternly.

He started to walk away, but turned around sharply as something crossed his mind.

"Find me some rope, or handcuffs, or something. We're taking this fucker back with us. *Alive.*"

Metzger tried to read the captain's thoughts, but Timmons maintained a neutral expression. He turned to head outside once again, prepared to deal with Hewitt, knowing his plan might easily fail for a number of reasons. If it did, his situation wouldn't really change, but it certainly wouldn't improve. They sent specialized soldiers after Bryce, and Sutton had called to warn him that the military paid a visit to the area where he, Gracine, and the others were currently staying.

When he stepped out the back doors once again, Metzger spied Hewitt in the distance trying to stand on his bad ankle, and utterly failing. As the man tried to put weight on it, he collapsed, hitting the snowy concrete hard. Walking with a purpose, Metzger assumed Hewitt still possessed his pistol, because it wasn't lying on the ground. He needed to ensure he didn't get shot while he either subdued Hewitt, or reasoned with the man.

"Stop!" he shouted, as though a police officer pursuing a suspect.

Hewitt indeed froze in his tracks, and his right hand slowly reached for what Metzger assumed was his gun tucked somewhere in his jacket. Metzger continued closer, spying cover to his right in case he needed to avoid gunfire.

"Don't be stupid," he said. "You have a sniper rifle trained on you right now."

He wasn't positive the man bought the lie, but his hand stopped short of reaching into his jacket.

"Just kill me and be done with it," Hewitt said, though his words didn't sound like a man ready to die.

"I'm not going to kill you unless you make me."

"You tried once before."

"Believe me, if you didn't have immunity to the virus, I would've put a bullet in you a few minutes ago."

Hewitt appeared conflicted, but ultimately, he signaled he was going to slowly reach for the gun, which he tossed several feet away from him once he pulled it out. Knowing he was in the clear, Metzger let his anger get the best of him, rushing forward to stomp Hewitt in his injured ankle, causing the man to howl in pain. Not only had the man murdered almost two dozen people, but he threatened to kill Timmons without a shred of doubt or remorse. Metzger couldn't let such sociopathic behavior go unpunished.

Metzger tucked his own firearm behind him, taking a deep breath as he debated how to deal with Hewitt. Dropping down and mounting the man's chest, pinning his arms to the ground, Metzger lit into him with several punches to the face, repeatedly and rhythmically until he began to feel pain in his own knuckles. Even so, he continued to pummel Hewitt, knowing he needed to keep the man alive, but not in pristine condition.

"Whoa!" Timmons said, rushing up behind Metzger and pulling him off the man, allowing Metzger to see the blood and busted skin on Hewitt's face as the man groaned, rolling over on the frozen path.

Timmons released his solid grip on Metzger's arms, but kept a hand on his shoulder to make certain no further beatings occurred.

"This is kind of a role reversal," Timmons admitted.

"I can't kill him, but he can't go unpunished for what he did," Metzger muttered, looking at his reddened, sore knuckles.

"Yeah, I know," the pilot said slowly, glancing in the direction of the bodies.

Once he felt assured Metzger wasn't going to batter his adversary again, Timmons walked over to grab the discarded firearm.

"We can't be keeping him prisoner for too long," he said. "It's dangerous for everyone at the resort."

"I know. That's why we need to get him to Virginia as soon as the weather allows."

Timmons shook his head, though Metzger wasn't sure his action was based on the notion of heading south.

"What is it?"

"Hannah and I got blindsided by this creep and you've had the wherewithal to talk him down, subdue him, and realize his importance within seconds.

Hell, if it was me, I would've put a bullet between his eyes and never realized the wasted opportunity."

"That option is still on the table if he gives us any trouble, Scott. But delivering him to the military might get them off our backs."

"I hope you're not planning on walking up to their front gates, son."

"Hardly. I'll hammer out the details, but I've got a plan for that, too."

Hannah approached them from behind with several synthetic portions of rope.

"It's all I could find," she said, looking a bit guilty for being taken hostage, or her earlier alliance with Hewitt when she didn't know better.

"Neither of you need to feel bad about him surprising you. He's been here a while and knows the lay of the land. And he's obviously gotten some practice at killing the living."

Metzger looked to the bodies, and Hannah got her first real look at them, drawing closer momentarily until she realized exactly what happened to them. Putting both of her hands to her face, she withdrew, on the verge of sobbing because she realized how close she came to joining the victims that once occupied the lodge.

"No," she muttered, shaking her head before retreating to the main building in a dead run.

"I'll keep an eye on her," Timmons volunteered. "You going to be okay?"

Metzger nodded, understanding his friend was really asking if he could keep a level head.

As Timmons walked away, Metzger went about the business of flipping Hewitt over and tying both his hands and his feet for the time being. He didn't want the man to put up any kind of resistance until he formulated a solid plan to transport him back to the resort, keep him prisoner, and somehow get him back to Virginia. With the sat phones continuing to function, he had an idea how to make contact with the military brass, but he also considered the risk of giving away any information that might lead them to the Adirondacks, or his loved ones.

Metzger struggled with the risk versus reward, because he didn't want such a dangerous man around his family. He reached for the gun behind him, stopping just short of clasping it, because he knew killing Hewitt doomed any chances of the military ceasing their search for him and his brother. Looking to the piles of bodies, he wondered how many of them were blood relatives, or risked their lives for one another before their senseless murders.

His hand slowly wrapped around the gun's handle, but he stopped just short of lifting it from his belted pants. For several conflicted seconds, Metzger contemplated the appropriate move, watching Hewitt writhe in pain along the ground, somewhere between a cognizant and unconscious state. Looking skyward, he wanted to let out a yell to vent his frustration, but Metzger knew the dangers of doing so. Instead, he released his grip and decided he'd come this far, and he wasn't about to let Hewitt go to waste when his blood might help create a vaccine or a cure for the plague.

Timmons returned a few minutes later, his face registering a bit of surprise that Metzger hadn't changed his mind about keeping Hewitt alive.

"We're staying the night," Metzger decided aloud. "We'll use his room since he already has a fire going."

"There's enough supplies in there to last us for months," Timmons said, thumbing towards the lodge.

"They'd last a single person a lot longer than that."

"Don't beat yourself up. You couldn't have known."

"And now that I *do* know, I'm not letting it go to waste. I've got some pretty good ideas how to deliver him without any of us getting caught up in the military's web."

"That's good, because they'll be looking to pin something on me other than an admiral's star."

"Don't worry," Metzger said, placing a hand on his friend's shoulder. "With this, they won't have much cause to be pissed at us."

Timmons chuckled doubtfully.

"It's pretty obvious you don't know my former employers very well."

***

Nearly an hour later, the three found a spot in the lodge where they were able to use a small chain and some handcuffs to secure Hewitt to a metal railing behind a bar located in the dining area. Metzger did most of the work because

Hannah remained traumatized, and Timmons didn't feel especially well after being struck in the head.

Each room, it turned out, was like a hotel suite, complete with fireplace, furnishings, walk-in showers and hot tubs that didn't appeal to Metzger without electricity for hot water. Beds, some disheveled, and some appearing they were made that morning by housekeeping, appeared equally luxurious. Wood adorned virtually every wall, and every piece of furniture in the lodge, and Metzger understood why a group of just over twenty people chose to call Lake Placid their home.

"I thought I knew him," Hannah lamented, sitting on the floor close to the fire, which provided them warmth enough to comfortably sleep in the room.

"You couldn't have known," Metzger told her. "The apocalypse. It changes people."

All three of them sat near the fire, soaking in the warmth momentarily. Although they located candles and other supplies, in addition to the food, they chose to let the fire be the sole illumination within the suite.

"You sure he can't escape?" Timmons asked, barely glancing in the direction of the dining area one level below them.

"I'm not sure of anything," Metzger replied. "He never even stirred when I moved him. He's either a really good actor, or I busted him up worse than I thought."

"Those people," Hannah said, her voice trailing off momentarily. "How did he kill so many of them?"

"They're like anyone else, Hannah," Metzger answered. "They left this place to find supplies, and he probably picked them off a few at a time. We all know that sometimes people don't make it back, so by the time they had an idea what was going on, there weren't enough of them left to make a stand against him."

A monster among men, Hewitt could easily defeat most people with his bare hands, but given a gun or a knife, his lethal nature was amplified.

"If he wants to escape, he's going to have to earn it," Metzger said, knowing from testing the railing personally that it wasn't going to give without a fight.

"Why do you have to let him live in the first place?" Hannah questioned.

Her fear of Hewitt remained apparent after nearly dying at his hands.

"He has immunity to the disease," Metzger explained.

"I know," Hannah answered somewhat testily. "It's not worth the risk."

"Tell that to anyone bitten by the infected," Timmons butted in, slight irritation in his tone. "Dan has risked life and limb for his family and people he didn't even know. Yourself included. You saying you don't have faith in him?"

"I don't have faith in our chances of survival if Adam gets loose. A normal person doesn't stack bodies like firewood in their back yard."

"I've already taken steps to make certain he doesn't get out of that room without us knowing," Metzger assured her.

He planned on securing their room, and checking on Hewitt throughout the night to make certain the man didn't escape. To ensure Hewitt didn't escape without detection, Metzger used some baby monitors he found in a storage area to listen to the dining area. They ran on electricity or battery backup, so he was able to power them with some extra batteries, thankful for both finds.

Hannah took the bed, with insistence from Timmons and Metzger, while both men slept on the floor, practically cocooned in blankets with fresh pillows that never saw use after the crumbling of society. Reasonably accustomed to the warmth a fire provided, Metzger discovered it felt slightly better on this particular evening after such an exhausting day of travel and combat. Images of the bodies in the courtyard ran through his mind at first, but he soon drifted off, knowing such horrors were a regular occurrence in the new world.

Metzger experienced an odd dream in which he was home with his parents for a weekend, and Bryce was supposed to join them shortly because he was between tours. For some reason, Isabella and Nathan weren't coming, which Metzger considered odd, but in the recesses of his mind the entire dream felt awkward, and not because his parents were deceased. Whenever he dreamed about the days of having a normal life, he questioned why his mind ventured there. He supposed those better days comforted him, allowing him to escape his current living conditions.

What woke him from the odd dream was the jingling of chains through the baby monitor he set beside his makeshift bed on the floor. Somewhat groggy, he propped himself up on one elbow and looked at the monitor, finding the volume knob turned lower than he recalled setting it before lying down. A few feet away, Timmons continued his uninterrupted slumber, snoring lightly, so Metzger looked up to the bed, finding it empty. At first, he figured Hannah went up to use the restroom, but he heard the chains again through the baby monitor and perked up, looking to the suite's door, finding it slightly ajar. The bathroom door was also ajar, which he saw by firelight, knowing Hannah would have taken a candle inside and closed the door behind her, were she using the bathroom.

"Oh, fuck," he muttered, clamoring to his feet, startling his friend in the process as he grabbed his gun and his sword before exiting the room in a hurry.

Immediately regretting not putting on footwear, Metzger headed for the stairwell in sock feet, carrying his weapons. Dust atop the wooden floors kept him from sliding as he started and stopped several times in his hurry to get downstairs to the dining room. He navigated several stairwell landings by what little natural light made its way inside the lodge, finding the main level shortly.

From there, it wasn't far to the dining area, and as he reached the mammoth room, he stepped inside, hearing nothing at all. Cautiously taking a few more quiet steps over the cold floor, Metzger eyeballed the bar area, needing to step closer for a full view of the area. Natural light from the moon and stars made its way inside the French doors, and numerous windows, providing adequate lighting for him to make out some details.

When he neared the end of the bar, he found a pair of feet sticking out from behind the wooden structure that he knew didn't belong to Hewitt. Sucking in a nervous breath, Metzger held the firearm in his right hand and his sword in his left, prepared to shoot first and stab if necessary. He immediately assumed Hewitt somehow got Hannah in his clutches, or lured her downstairs, but decided not to call out until he saw how the scene before him unfolded. Trying to keep his breathing quiet, slow, and calm, he began to round the edge of the bar, unable to hear his own footsteps, which he considered a blessing.

All the while, his heart pounded in his chest because he wasn't mentally prepared for a third encounter with Hewitt, despite his senses being heightened beyond belief.

"She came down here to kill me," Hewitt's voice finally broke the silence, startling Metzger enough that his feet left the wood flooring.

Now knowing the voice came from behind the bar, Metzger stepped around, aiming the gun at Hewitt, who sat on the cold floor, still handcuffed to the chain looped around the bar railing by one hand. His voice sounded monotone and matter-of-fact when he spoke, as though entirely incapable of experiencing human emotions at this point.

"Here's the knife," Hewitt said, kicking a large knife towards Metzger that stopped a few inches short of his sock feet.

Metzger knelt down, pulling Hannah by the left foot from behind the bar so he could evaluate her. She didn't have any outward wounds, but she wasn't conscious, or responsive, during the few seconds required to remove her from immediate danger.

"I'm not sure if she's alive," Hewitt said indifferently, without inflection in his tone.

"Why would you do this?" Metzger said, trying to feel for a pulse and finding none.

Hannah's neck and his fingers both felt cold because they were exposed to the frigid temperatures of the lodge, just like Metzger's appendages. He was about to try again for a pulse, and potentially begin CPR, when Hewitt spoke.

"She came down here and tried to stab me with a knife," he said evenly. "I managed to grab her neck and squeeze."

Metzger saw red marks along Hannah's neck, even in the dim lighting, and he began to doubt his ability to breathe life into her. He bent down over her mouth and nose, trying to see if he felt any breath against his cheek, and he did indeed feel a little warmth against his skin, so he delayed starting CPR.

"I pretended she was your girlfriend as I squeezed the life out of her," Hewitt said, trying to get a rise from Metzger. "And I appreciate this thin-ass blanket you provided to keep me from dying in this wooden freezer."

Metzger refused to let Hewitt agitate him. Assured Hannah was safely away from the man, he slumped his back against the bar, safely away from the shackled Hewitt. Unsure if Hannah was taking her last breath, or simply unconscious, he decided to take a moment and see what happened. Even at the resort where his brother's in-laws possessed basic medical supplies, there wasn't equipment enough to help anyone with serious injuries or health issues.

"I really can't stand you," he said, addressing Hewitt without looking around the corner at the man.

"Oh, the feeling is mutual. Believe me."

Metzger placed a hand on Hannah's stomach, feeling the rise and fall from her chest, leaving him a bit more reassured she was simply unconscious.

"I know you can't kill me, for whatever reason," Hewitt said, his words piercing Metzger, because Metzger no longer wanted to hear the man.

If removing his vocal cords were an option, he might consider the procedure.

"I'm welcoming the military," Hewitt continued. "Free meals and safety behind secured fences sounds awfully good."

"Sure you can resist the urge to murder people for no reason?"

"I had my reasons," Hewitt retorted, still not raising his voice or speaking with any emotion. "Survival of the fittest, and you can see who's still breathing."

Metzger wasn't thrilled about Hewitt's sudden acceptance of his future, but the man cared about his own survival above all else.

"She's alive, you know," Metzger countered in their verbal game of chess, referring to Hannah, who showed more signs of life with a light moan and movement in her fingers.

"That's fine," Hewitt said, as casually as he might place a restaurant lunch order.

Hannah began to regain consciousness, and Metzger helped her to her feet once she blinked a few times, prepared to help her upstairs.

"I might get bored at the base," Hewitt added, as though needing to get in the last word. "Maybe I'll decide to come look you up someday."

"Doubtful," Metzger replied, feeling reasonably assured the military wouldn't let him leave their complex once they had a new guinea pig and tested his blood.

Metzger assisted Hannah to the stairway, glad she hadn't gotten killed for doing such a boneheaded thing as attacking Hewitt. He kept her arm around his neck to help steady her as she walked.

"What happened?" she asked groggily, coughing a bit.

"Apparently you attacked Adam with a knife and he choked you out?"

"Sounds about right," she said wearily, still trying to regain her senses.

"What were you thinking?"

"I didn't want to risk him living near us at the resort," Hannah answered. "You had the guns, so I grabbed the only thing I could find."

"I know you don't want to hear this, but I need him alive so I can take him to the military," Metzger said as he helped her up the first few steps. "They'll stop badgering me, and Adam won't be our concern."

As Metzger reached the first landing, heading upward, he heard the sound of clopping winter boots coming at him.

"Did I miss something?" Timmons asked with wide eyes, holding a pistol, when he encountered the pair on the landing.

Metzger and Hannah looked to one another, then to the pilot, giving audible sighs as they brushed past him to get some much-needed sleep.

Thirty-Two

Two Days Later

Gracine hadn't spent much time with certain members of her new community, and that list included Sister Rosa. During their interactions, the two were certainly amicable, but they came from very different backgrounds. Internally, Gracine ranked the Maplewood residents in the order in which she trusted them, and Rosa and Father Paul were certainly near the top.

Each Sunday, the pair held mass, and Father Paul made efforts to accommodate various denominations without making attendees feel as though they needed to convert to Catholicism. Rosa spoke very little to her community members, often letting her work ethic speak for her. She helped in any number of ways, preparing meals, providing school lessons for the children and young adults, and sometimes venturing outside the walls to help gather supplies for the residents.

Gracine occasionally helped with supply runs, but they tended to save her spot in the rotation for those times when a big rig required driving back to the community. During a few instances, particularly in the larger, more dangerous towns, they were able to locate a tractor-trailer filled with a variety of goods that didn't arrive to whatever store ordered the goods. She hated finding a zombified driver stuck inside the cab, but they were easy to deal with before taking the truck. Seeing them reminded Gracine of how her own life might have ended if she hadn't chosen to abandon her profession and get away from populated areas when she did.

"Where are we headed, exactly?" Gracine asked as she drove a small green Honda a few miles outside of Maplewood in the direction Rosa provided.

"To Lynchburg," Rosa answered. "It's where Father Paul and I lived, and worked. I may know a few more areas that weren't touched by looters."

"You don't just call him Paul when you're not around him?"

"It's disrespectful," Rosa said with an absolutely serious expression. "He is one of the few conduits we have with God left on this planet."

"I guess I don't know much about your religion," Gracine admitted. "Pretty much any religion for that matter."

"I noticed you haven't been to any services," Rosa noted without judgment in her tone.

Gracine continued driving, framing her answer to be less abrasive than the words swimming in her mind.

"Maybe I'm not much of a believer, considering how few of us are left."

"Perhaps God left you here for a reason. Are you not helping others?"

"I'm just trying to stay alive."

From the corner of her eye, she saw a knowing smirk from Rosa.

"If that were the case, you wouldn't be joining me on this run."

"Sister, are you questioning my honesty?" Gracine asked, using a tone that indicated she wasn't being a hard-ass.

"Are you avoiding a real conversation about religion?"

"I've noticed you and Father Paul are good about answering questions *with* questions. Colby says the same thing."

Rosa chuckled.

"Speaking of Colby, you two seem reasonably chummy for people who aren't dating."

"Dating?"

"You know what I mean."

Gracine gave a sigh, reminded of the one thing that bothered her most about the community. With only so many people, gossip spread like wildfire, and no one appeared capable of minding their own business, particularly regarding relationships.

"Colby is hot and cold all the time," she answered, speaking as neutrally as possible. "I'm not sure I can deal with that."

"You're not that much different," Rosa pointed out. "Most of the time you're very task-oriented and serious."

"Colby has a lot on his plate," Gracine countered. "The death of his son, and taking care of the other one."

"His son is an adult. And, while no one gets over the death of a child, most people move forward. You could help him with that."

Gracine swerved to avoid a zombie in the center of the road just ambling and looking skyward for some reason.

Along this particular stretch of highway, they found very few stalled cars as fields and trees surrounded them. Occasionally, they spotted a house off the road, but checking individual houses often offered greater risk than reward in rural areas.

"I'm with Reggie," Gracine said. "And it doesn't seem very Christian of you to suggest I betray his trust."

"There's no ring on that finger," Rosa noted, nodding toward Gracine's left hand.

Gracine groaned.

"I'm sure you and Father Paul could take care of that if things ever got that serious."

"We could certainly help."

Several seconds of silence passed.

"And what about you?" Gracine inquired.

"What about me?"

"With the end of the world upon us, are you forever committed to celibacy?"

"I wasn't committed in the first place."

Gracine gave her a quizzical stare.

"Girl?"

"I'm a sister, not a nun," Rosa answered.

"There's a difference?"

"*Yes*. Becoming a nun is something far more binding. My position allows me to back out and return to a normal life if I choose to."

Gracine arched an eyebrow before speaking her next words.

"We're half a year into the apocalypse and you're still rapping little kids on the knuckles with rulers?"

"Look, I didn't choose my vocation on a whim," Rosa explained, her accent a bit thicker than usual as she stressed her point. "I take this very seriously."

"Okay, okay," Gracine said, removing her hands from the wheel briefly in a defensive posture to indicate she wouldn't pursue the topic further.

A moment later, every ounce of civilization disappeared as fields surrounded them in every direction. One solitary tree stood defiantly in the center of a cornfield on their right where the corn had long since submitted to the elements, mostly hunched over like an elderly person using a walker. Most likely, the deer and birds helped expedite the battered appearance of the cornstalks by eating what exposed kernels they could find.

"Just one more question," Gracine pressed, drawing an audible sigh from her passenger. "Don't you Catholic folks worship Mary for some reason?"

"Mary?" Rosa asked for clarification.

"You know, the mother of Jesus."

Rosa started to answer, but a strange sight ahead in the road caught their attention, and Gracine pulled to the right shoulder, a safe distance away from the two people who appeared to be literally supporting one another. A man and a woman struggled to walk, and though both remained among the living, Gracine wasn't certain how much longer they could survive without intervention.

She turned to Rosa.

"What do you think?"

"They look legit," the sister answered. "There's literally nothing else out here, so they can't exactly surprise us."

Gracine looked around for anywhere a sniper might post up, peering at them through his sights, finding nothing except the tree, which didn't offer cover without its leaves. Not one house, barn, or outbuilding could be seen, and unless someone chose to lie within the fading corn, good cover wasn't readily available.

As they drew closer, the pair in the road wore haggard expressions, not looking for assistance, or backing away, as they trudged forward. The man's head appeared shaved, giving him a military or police appearance, with a thin, but fit frame as he wore blue jeans and an olive-green work shirt with long sleeves. By contrast, the woman kept her dark hair pulled back with a band, though she also wore blue jeans and a red jacket, possibly from a high-end store that sold jackets for urban people who wanted to appear rural. Like most clothing, it likely came to her through whatever journey brought her to the western portion of Virginia.

"How are we doing?" Gracine asked when she stepped from the car, her hand already placed atop the pistol holstered on her right side.

She saw both the man and the woman toted firearms at their sides, but neither made any move for the weapons. Their expressions displayed their exhaustion, and it took a few strides for them to come to a stop and acknowledge the two women before them.

"We've been better," the man answered. "Out for a drive on this lovely day?"

Gracine already liked that the man possessed a sense of humor, though she wasn't ready to drop her guard completely.

"We were about to check some areas for supplies," Gracine said, seeing little point in being deceptive or untruthful.

"We can save you the trouble," the woman answered, showing bruises and bloody marks upon closer inspection. "The towns we passed through were mostly picked over."

"Are you two okay?" Rosa inquired, opening the car's trunk to get them some bottles of water.

"We're trying to reach the military base," the woman answered, before glancing sideways at her companion. "Against his advice."

Gracine stiffened at the words, knowing her and her group worked hard to *avoid* the military and the base at all costs for several reasons.

"I'm not a fan myself," she said. "We had some poor customer service from them when our group reached their gates."

"Do you have family at the base?" Rosa asked, handing the pair two unopened water bottles.

Gracine took notice that the weary travelers eyeballed her religious garb.

"I have information to deliver," the woman answered, her expression immediately indicating she believed she said too much.

"We can help you," Rosa offered. "We can at least get you some supplies."

Gracine looked to her, remembering when the sister offered to help her group, only to be chastised by Father Paul for speaking out of turn.

"They need help," Rosa said in her own defense so only Gracine heard.

"We can make it on our own," the man said, openly not trusting strangers to assist with their task.

"At the rate you're crawling, it would take you a month to reach Norfolk," Gracine said, beginning to agree with Rosa.

Both of the travelers opened their water bottles and downed the water in virtually one swig. Neither appeared ready to speak about their mysterious agenda, which caused Gracine to wonder what could be so important and secretive at the same time.

"You say you need to reach the base," she said, addressing the woman directly. "They weren't exactly hospitable when my friends went there."

"I work for the government," the woman said, appearing slightly taken aback after speaking the words. "*Worked* for them. They'll listen to me. They'll have to."

Gracine looked to Rosa, who returned her concerned glance.

"You went to Naval Station Norfolk?" the man questioned, his eyes meeting Gracine's.

"We did, back in the fall."

"And?"

"They turned us away, mister. We escorted a friend there, and they let him inside, because his brother was a Navy officer, but they wanted nothing to do with the rest of us."

A perplexed expression crossed the man's face.

"I wonder why they would turn people away."

"They didn't have the room, and they were still working on setting up, and clearing the dead."

"It's their job to protect us," the man said, taking the situation a bit personally.

"They were overwhelmed," the government woman said. "I doubt they had much of a choice."

"We were told our politicians are living in bunkers, safely tucked away in secret locations," Gracine said. "That sounds like the same old shit to me."

"Can you trust them?" the man asked of the government woman. "Will they even believe you?"

"I have to try," she answered. "There's nowhere else to go."

Now the man shook his head negatively.

"What is it?" Rosa asked, noting that something left him unhappy about heading to the base.

"I had an acquaintance who was being held against his will at the base," he answered. "And this was after he assisted them, risking his own life. I'm not entirely sure the military can be trusted."

"It wasn't Dan Metzger, was it?" Gracine asked with surprise, uncertain how any other human being could meet the same criteria.

"It was," he answered, openly stunned.

"Just so we're clear, a guy who carries swords and decapitates zombies like nobody's business?" Gracine questioned further.

"Don't know that I saw too much of the beheading, but he was carrying a couple swords in some kind of backpack when I saw him in Buffalo."

"Sounds like we need to have a little talk," Gracine said, motioning for the weary duo to join them in their car. "Supplies can wait."

***

"Why exactly are we meeting outside of Maplewood?" Sutton asked from the passenger's seat of an SUV that he, Gracine, Rosa, and Father Paul borrowed from the community. "And who?"

Although Gracine provided an excuse that their other vehicle was running rough, and they were heading out for supplies, she intended to meet Mike Mullins and Brooke Palacio at an abandoned residence several miles down the road. After leaving the pair there, for safety reasons, Gracine went back to get the most trusted person in her life, and the priest, whom Rosa vouched for repeatedly.

"This is a bit peculiar," Father Paul said, addressing Rosa more than Gracine.

"We have people who need help," Rosa explained. "We weren't sure how the McAllisters would react to bringing them to the community, so we decided to bring them supplies."

"So, we're your muscle?" the priest asked with a furrowed eyebrow, indicating he probably wasn't the best choice.

"It's more than that," Gracine answered. "These people are heading to the Navy base."

Sutton groaned.

"I know, I know, Colby. I want you to talk them out of it."

"And why should I give a crap?" he inquired, minding his language with religious folks riding behind him.

"I have this feeling if they go to that base, no one will ever hear from them again."

Sutton shot her a wide-eyed, suspicious stare.

"You're starting to sound like me."

"The man has met Dan. And the woman has classified information."

"What kind of information?" Father Paul asked from behind Gracine.

"We think she may know where the man responsible for the apocalypse is hiding."

"She told you this?" Sutton asked with surprise in his tone.

"She implied it," Rosa answered. "Just before we left, she indicated she was following someone before the apocalypse struck who compromised national security."

"This sounds like a lot of speculation," Sutton said, shaking his head. "We should probably give these folks some food and water and send them on their way."

Gracine looked over to him before nodding at a house just ahead of their SUV on the right.

"Well, we're here, so you can talk to them yourself and see what you think."

Set off the highway, the two-story farm house sat surrounded by vast fields of crops that never saw harvest. A barn, untended for years, showed only flecks of red paint from its last paintjob some decades prior, beginning to fall in because the roof showed early signs of structural failure. Gracine knew the community used it for temporary storage of vehicles and other goods that couldn't be hauled away by hand.

Once the group parked, they slowly emerged from the vehicle because no one came out the front door to greet them. Gracine felt her heart begin to race at the thought of the duo having left the farmhouse and moved east toward the base. If her instincts proved correct, the information the woman possessed might be better told to their group instead of military personnel who proved they couldn't be trusted.

"Well, this is creepy," Father Paul commented after a few seconds of gusting winds providing the only noise around them.

A few seconds later, the door opened, and both Mullins and Brooke walked outside.

"I didn't know you were bringing others," Brooke spoke her disapproval.

"We aren't exactly threats," Father Paul said, pulling lightly on his collar to show his position within the church.

His actions did little to calm the situation.

"Let's just everyone take a breath," Mullins suggested before thumbing behind him. "There's lovely, smelly furniture inside where we can talk."

Everyone agreed to head inside, where they were safe from any interruptions or prying eyes.

"You weren't kidding," Rosa said of the furniture, indicating she hadn't stepped foot inside previously.

As though the property had been on the market when the apocalypse struck, the house possessed very little furniture inside. A few chairs, a couch, and a kitchen table with a complement of chairs appeared to be the only pieces located on the ground floor. A few spots along the floor appeared to be in disrepair, either with holes or stains, and Gracine wondered if the house was abandoned, being renovated, or about to be marketed for an as-is sale before the dead rose.

"I think I'll stand," Sutton said, leaning against an opening between the kitchen and living room.

"We brought you supplies," Gracine said after daring to sit down on a couch that possessed at least one mysterious stain. "I'm worried about you going to the base after how they treated our friend."

"What did they do to your friend, exactly?" Brooke questioned.

"He was kind enough to be their guide in two missions," Sutton answered, "as a civilian, mind you. And when they discovered another use for him, they kept him imprisoned at the base."

"That doesn't make much sense," Brooke replied, far from sold on their pitch.

"He's immune to the sickness, so they wanted his blood to create a vaccine," Rosa added, drawing penetrating stares from Sutton and Gracine. "Well, why beat around the bush? We're trying to earn their trust, aren't we?"

"The military lives just a little better than we do," Sutton confessed. "But they answer to politicians who remain hidden in their bunkers to this day."

"Then there is still democracy," Brooke said assuredly.

"If you can call it that," Sutton scoffed.

"Taking away someone's civil liberties, including their freedom, isn't something this country should do," Father Paul added. "From what I know, their friend did nothing wrong, yet they stole his freedom because he served a purpose. We're worried that you could tell them what you know and be deemed a threat."

"Why would I be a threat? I may know exactly where the person responsible for the apocalypse is hiding."

Brooke's expression first indicated she believed she spoke too freely, but she shrugged, as though accepting that strangers knowing the truth didn't matter in the scheme of things.

Mullins looked to each of the people in the room.

"It's true. She's been carrying this burden since the beginning."

"Why did it take you so long to get here?" Rosa asked.

"It wasn't a linear journey, to say the least," Brooke answered. "I only met Mike recently, and he had the same goal in mind."

"I also know what they did to Dan," Mullins admitted. "The last time I saw him, they were keeping close watch over him."

"It wasn't just that," Sutton said, visibly upset. "I'm no fan of the government, much less the military, but they treated his brother like shit, too."

"How so?" Brooke asked, growing invested in their story.

"They sent both of them on a mission with some Marines, and his brother was left for dead," Sutton answered.

"He was bitten," Gracine added.

"So, he was already dead," Brooke reasoned aloud.

"No," Sutton said, shaking his head slightly. "Bryce is immune, too, and the bastards knew it."

Brooke put her fingers up to her temples.

"This is all a bit difficult to process."

"Both brothers bent over backwards, trying to help the government find this Nadeau person," Gracine said. "And for their troubles, they got stabbed in the back."

"They know about Nadeau?" Brooke asked skeptically.

"Yeah," Sutton answered. "It's no big secret. The secret is where the prick is hiding."

"How long have they known?" Brooke inquired, a stunned look crossing her face.

Sutton shrugged.

"They had to have known within the first few months."

"It took me months just to peel back the layers and get my first true lead," Brooke said. "With their manpower, and the equipment they possess, they could have located Nadeau by now."

"You have no doubt about that?" Father Paul asked with empathy.

Appearing exasperated, Brooke looked to each of them, likely feeling as though she undertook a dangerous journey for nothing.

"All this time, I've been killing the dead, avoiding most living people, and doing unspeakable things to the people Nadeau recruited," she said almost numbly.

"How did you even get involved in all of this?" Rosa questioned.

"I worked for the CIA," Brooke finally admitted. "The funny thing is, the government didn't trust Nadeau, and they knew he was up to something before he put those bombs in place."

"And yet capitalism won out," Sutton said sourly.

"You can't arrest someone for what they *might* do," Brooke said as a matter of fact. "I was simply one spoke in the wheel, monitoring the activities of one of his most trusted associates. No one knew the extent of his plans, or his reach." She paused a few seconds, reflecting on the circumstances. "Until it was too late."

A few seconds passed, and the only noise anyone heard was one of the house's shutters smacking against the siding because its latch no longer worked correctly.

"You said you had tracked Nadeau's hiding place," Gracine said calmly, and gently, but she knew they all wanted the information Brooke Palacio had kept to herself thus far.

"Months of painstaking work have left me with two possible destinations," she said. "Both of them were too far for me to travel and check by myself. Turning my findings over to the military sounded like the best option, because they could quickly and easily verify, or dismiss, my findings."

"Two locations, huh?" Sutton asked no one in particular. "What if we could offer our services and help you find out for certain before you talked to the military?"

"Driving me thousands of miles doesn't exactly save me time," Brooke replied.

"Who said anything about driving?"

Everyone except Gracine looked at him skeptically, and in her mind, she believed she knew what Sutton was proposing.

"Let's compare notes, because we can get you a pilot and your answers," Sutton offered.

"It wouldn't be as simple as doing a flyby to see if Nadeau is home."

"He's responsible for the woes in all of our lives from the sound of it," Father Paul said. "I'm not sure he should wait until the afterlife for justice."

Brooke looked to Mullins for some reassurance.

"If they're friends of Dan Metzger, they can be trusted," he said. "I feel certain of that."

"Alright," Brooke said. "Let me start from the beginning, and we'll see if we can make this work."

With that, she went into complete detail, spending over an hour giving specifics about discoveries, encounters, and several near misses, keeping her audience riveted the entire way.

Thirty-Three

The Next Day

Commander Mark Dascher rose from bed half an hour before daybreak, dressing in fatigues without waking his wife and children in the large apartment the military provided for him. Officers with higher ranks were blessed with better living conditions and some amenities by the new combined military force. Except for generals and admirals, officers were allowed to dress in fatigues, rather than traditional uniforms. For most meetings, particularly with superior officers, they were expected to wear clean uniforms and polished shoes.

Norfolk, Virginia remained safe from the dead, because soldiers and sailors went through, building by building, clearing the area of the infected during the warmer months. While they still washed up from the ocean, almost daily, the bodies were dealt with and disposed of in a proper fashion. Dascher didn't personally deal with the efforts, because his obligation remained with his ship, *USS Ross*, which remained docked beside the Navy base.

Living in a four-story apartment building with his family, Dascher shared the third floor with three other families. While he enjoyed one of the better buildings in Norfolk, he knew the men and women under his command certainly weren't homeless. Virtually every square inch of the city that wasn't dedicated to greenhouses, storage, or raising livestock, was converted to living space. A number of personnel slept on the base, or in the ships, because military assets couldn't be left unguarded, even in the apocalypse.

Dascher affectionately referred to living in town as "off-campus" because the city was adjacent to the base, but not directly part of the military in any sense. Leadership wanted civilians off the base completely to create a division of work and labor, as civilians were expected to hunt, fish, organize, and police the residential areas for the undead, or skirmishes among the living. Much like the old world, citizens had jobs, though now they were paid in food and housing.

Stepping outside from the apartment building, Dascher looked around, seeing the city lit up as people stirred, getting ready for their workdays. He enjoyed the sense of normality the military provided for their people and their extended family. Dascher felt bad for people roughing it in the newfound wilderness, battling the dead without benefit of heat, readily available food, or hot water. He walked to the corner, waited only a few minutes, and spied the golf cart that went around the city, picking up officers to transport them inside the base.

Enlisted personnel traveled by bus or trolley during designated times because shifts were staggered for them. Security wasn't as streamlined as it had been when computers and databases were fully functional, but slipping into the base wouldn't prove easy for nefarious individuals. Dascher stepped from the golf cart, flashed his ID badge to the guards at the shack who were already very familiar with him, and walked through the gate where another golf cart with an Army corporal at the wheel took him to his ship.

Virtually everyone received a promotion when they reached Norfolk, or the San Diego base, keeping morale stable. No one wanted to remain a private forever in the Army, or a seaman recruit in the Navy. When the commander boarded his ship, he was saluted a few different times by enlisted men, before requesting status updates from officers. Finding no changes in his ship or personnel, he walked to his quarters, prepared to grab a few items before meeting with the executive officer who replaced Bryce Metzger.

When Bryce was left behind in New York, Dascher was never given much information, or clarity, about his former executive officer's status. Provided with discretion to choose a new XO, Dascher wasn't certain if the military considered Bryce deceased, MIA, or a deserter. Rumors circulated, as they always did around the base, that Bryce likely survived the attack because his brother possessed immunity to the infection. The scientists on the base apparently concluded that the brothers shared the same markers in their blood that kept them from contracting the terminal condition.

Before the apocalypse struck, Dascher began formulating plans for retirement, and what opportunities awaited him in civilian life. About a year short of locking in his military pension, the commander knew survival for him and his family was about the only thing the government could promise now. Some days, he questioned how much longer they could keep their word, because food grew short. Each day, more and more groups of civilians and soldiers alike went out searching for resources, because rations began to run low. Gardens didn't grow overnight, and sustainable animals were mostly wiped out by the infected.

Unfortunately, some of the people who left the base never returned. No reasons were ever given, and no search parties sent outside the walls, which deepened the mystery for those who remained. They never knew if the dead got to their people, or worse, other survivors, and often memorials were held by family and friends in small groups. Graveside services didn't happen because there was never a body, unless the next wave of adventurous souls happened to locate them in their travels.

Grabbing a pen, his pad of paper, and a new book to read at the apartment from his selection beside his bunk, Dascher walked into his personal bathroom. He dabbed a bit of cologne on his face, finding the bottle near empty, which explained why he only used it on days he felt optimistic about the day going well. His intuition proved correct about half the time, which meant the commander endured his share of bad days on the job.

About to exit his room, Dascher heard the phone in his breast pocket begin to ring.

Many of the crucial officers possessed satellite phones because the military needed to be able to reach them at a moment's notice. Even before the apocalypse, Dascher was issued a sat phone as a last resort in case ship communications failed. The military grew to love redundancies if nothing else, but the commander couldn't recall the phone ringing one time since his ship docked at Naval Station Norfolk.

"Commander Dascher," he answered, hearing a slight croak in his voice that kept him from sounding as official as he wanted.

Dascher blamed a head cold for keeping him stuffed up the past few days.

"Commander, this is your former XO," a voice from the past said, causing Dascher to stiffen, because Bryce Metzger was the *last* person he expected to hear over the line.

"Oh my God! How are you?" Dascher inquired, returning to his room so no one meandering the halls of the ship heard his conversation.

"Alive."

"Glad to hear it. They had their doubts around here."

"The Marines made certain to nab my brother and leave me behind. That's a story for another time."

"Are you doing alright? Is there something you need?"

"Don't be fishing for information, Mark. You're better than that."

"I wasn't," Dascher said truthfully. "I swear. They would like nothing more than to put you and your brother under a microscope."

"I know. I need you to get me an audience with General McCall, Mark."

"General McCall?" Dascher repeated, swallowing a bit as he gave a light groan. "You're assuming he'll see me."

"You aren't that far down the ladder, Mark. He'll see you, especially when you tell him it's me who wants to speak with him."

"Okay," Dascher agreed, hoping to catch the general and his staff in favorable moods.

"You have half an hour to get this phone to him before I call back."

"Half an-" Dascher started to object as the call went dead. "Fuck."

***

General James McCall sat behind his desk, ready to start his morning, concerned about any number of things in the back of his mind.

He and an admiral in San Diego acted as the only direct links to the President and the scores of politicians protected in various bunkers and shelters across the nation. Although he understood the frustration of his own people, and the surviving civilians, they didn't understand the consequences of disobeying direct orders.

A delicate balance kept the government functioning at a scaled down level, and orders from government officials kept the military from searching for Nadeau. McCall assumed some form of truce was reached, though he didn't trust the Canadian one bit. He had personally reviewed the files taken from the man's offices, and he felt frightened for the future of the human species. McCall didn't scare easily, but he grasped the grand plan Nadeau envisioned, and he felt reasonably certain the human race had only seen the first phase of the mogul's entire scheme.

Although McCall delegated some of the daily tasks and problem-solving to colonels, admirals, and a few scientific civilians, he worried about the days ahead. Preserving American life in any sense of the word required groups going beyond Norfolk, and likely Virginia, to find animals, seeds, and other long-term sources of food. For the most part, the civilians were willing to pitch in and risk going beyond the city limits of Norfolk, but their military spouses didn't want them to. Unfortunately, the military was already stretched thin carrying out duties required of them, even in the apocalypse. In addition to maintaining their ships and vehicles, they now provided security, went on missions to find food and supplies, and dealt with the dead that constantly seemed to reach the base via ocean currents.

McCall bore the brunt of government officials, and the survivors on his base for much different reasons, but he shouldered the responsibility and kept from public view to remain as neutral as possible. His allegiance remained to the government that employed him, but the residents within in the city and the base far outnumbered the politicians.

Housed inside a spacious office customized for him to work alone, or hold small meetings within the conference area, the general felt the ire of angry eyes on him when he did step into view of the local civilians. To them, he was likely as bad as the politicians who lived safely in bunkers, unable to feed his people or vaccinate them against a deadly threat.

McCall cared about the people serving under him, and their families, but virtually everything that could be done *was* being done.

About to start reading through the stack of papers on the left side of his desk, McCall heard a quick knock on his door before a Marine colonel assigned to his staff stepped inside. Formalities had long since been dismissed, because the men interacted with one another dozens of times each day.

"Sir?"

"What is it, Curt?"

"Commander Dascher is here, asking for a minute of your time."

McCall remembered the name, but he couldn't immediately place the Navy man's current assignment.

Colonel Curt Ramsey possessed a light-skinned face that came with having red hair, and safely tucked away from the sun. He read the general's perplexed expression, as only he could.

"He commands the *USS Ross*, sir."

"The ship Metzger was assigned to?"

"Yes, sir."

McCall grumbled under his breath, thinking he caught Ramsey suppressing a smirk.

"Not funny, Colonel."

"No, sir."

"Tell him I have about two minutes."

"Yes, sir."

Knocking and entering less than a minute later, Dascher stepped inside, holding his hat while standing at attention, which the general quickly dismissed. He wore the Navy's winter khaki uniform, appearing starched and pressed, along with his hat, which meant he likely changed before coming to see the general.

"At ease, Commander."

"Sir."

Dascher appeared a bit uncomfortable, sweating just a bit despite the winter weather.

"What can I do for you, son?"

"Lieutenant Commander Metzger just made contact with me, sir."

"I'm assuming he provided you with a time and place to rendezvous with our forces, or you wouldn't be here."

"No, sir. He's calling back, and asked to speak with you directly."

McCall placed his hands on the desk momentarily, staring at them while contemplating what the lieutenant commander wanted from him.

"He asked, eh?" McCall inquired.

"Well, more like demanded," Dascher said with a bit of hesitation.

"Put the phone on my desk, Commander," McCall ordered.

Dascher complied, and began to step back as though expecting to be dismissed.

"You're staying, Commander," McCall said, dashing the Navy man's hopes of avoiding an uncomfortable situation.

"Yes, sir," Dascher said, remaining in a standing position in front of the desk.

"Sit, Commander."

"Yes, sir."

Unable to disguise his level of discomfort, the commander sat in one of the two provided chairs, visibly restraining his body from fidgeting.

"Does he trust you?" McCall asked the commander.

"I like to think so."

"We need to convince him to return home."

Dascher appeared skeptical.

"Speak freely, Commander."

"He's been gone almost six months, our people left him for dead, and he's with his family, sir. I'm not sure I have proper motivation for him to return."

McCall looked at the commander shrewdly.

"Who said we left your man for dead, Commander?"

"The Marines did, sir."

McCall couldn't directly control everyone on the base, and the Marines tended to talk about the parts of their missions that weren't classified.

"We can protect his family here," he emphasized for Dascher's sake. "We have walls, food, and clean water."

"With all due respect, sir, you kept his brother prisoner. There might be some trust issues."

"Semantics, Commander. We need both of them back here."

McCall could tell Dascher wanted to inquire about specifics, but he wasn't cleared for such details. No one else had proven to be a match for vaccine testing at either of the major bases, meaning the Metzger brothers were the only viable hope against further chemical attacks from Nadeau or his followers. Dascher still hadn't managed to sit still for more than a few seconds since taking a seat.

"Jesus, son, quit fidgeting," McCall said, noticing the commander stealing glances at the phone every few seconds.

"Sorry, sir."

A few minutes later, the phone rang, and McCall nodded for the commander to answer it. Dascher did so, putting it on speaker mode so the general could hear the conversation.

"Bryce?" Dascher asked as he set the phone on the desk once again, scooting his chair a bit closer to hear better.

"This is Dan Metzger," the voice said. "Is this General McCall?"

Before Dascher could say a word, McCall ushered with one hand for the commander to give him some privacy, and Dascher wasted no time standing and hastily exiting the room. He felt a bit surprised that the younger brother was calling instead, which forced him to change his tactics on the fly.

"This is McCall," the general said. "You've been an absolute thorn in my side, kid."

"That was never my intention, sir," Metzger said. "I remained loyal, even after what your people did to me and my brother."

"Mistakes were made," McCall said, adding empathy to his tone, but actually believing the mistake was providing Metzger with any freedom at all.

"Do you mean mistakes like sending soldiers after my brother?"

McCall groaned inwardly.

"One of the men I sent is still missing. Know anything about that?"

"Let's just say both sides have suffered casualties," Metzger replied. "None of which were at my brother's hand."

"So, I can accept your brother's word through you as gospel?"

"There aren't any living witnesses, if that's what you're asking."

"My position isn't an easy one," McCall said. "I have thousands of people surrounding me who don't happen to have the luxury of immunity to the infection. You're a smart, resourceful young man, Daniel. If you were me, and this danger was lurking out there, what would you do?"

Metzger didn't answer immediately.

"That's what I thought," McCall added.

A few seconds of silence passed between them, and McCall sensed Metzger wanted to be of help, but several issues complicated the relationship between him and the government.

"I'm calling because I may have solved a few of your problems," the younger man said over the line.

"Is that so?" McCall asked skeptically.

"First, I've located someone with the same immunity as me and my brother, and I'll be making arrangements to deliver him to you soon. The man has murdered at least twenty-two people I know of, and he's not to be trusted."

"I'm sure we can find appropriate accommodations for him. How do you know he's immune? Did you get your degree in biological sciences?"

"I cut him with a blade that had the blood of the infected on it last fall, and he survived the winter."

"That would solve one of my issues," McCall admitted.

Around the base, Metzger had become somewhat of a folk hero, because the Marines spoke of his prowess when dealing with the undead on their missions. Word continued to spread of how he left the base to go find his brother and save him in their home state. Naturally, stories were blown out of proportion, and Metzger sounded more like a mercenary ninja with a heart instead of a normal man capable of dealing with a reasonable number of undead.

"Nice as that may be, I could use you and your brother back here."

"That's not happening," Metzger said. "At least not yet."

"Got a full calendar, do you?"

"I've located a government operative who can lead us to Nadeau."

McCall sat pensively a moment, torn between admitting what he knew and keeping the oath he took to the government and the military.

Ultimately, he decided to maintain his silence and reveal no classified information to a civilian.

"I really wish you wouldn't pursue Nadeau, son."

"Because you've done such a bang-up job of bringing him to justice?"

"He's dangerous," McCall said, growing irritated at the young man who complicated his life long before this particular phone call.

"I'm aware. If it makes you feel better, I won't go in there with guns blazing."

"I'd feel better if you left this to the professionals. I'd also feel better if you and your brother returned, and brought a certain pilot with you."

"You've already stated as much," Metzger responded. "I think we're about done here."

"You could tell me where Nadeau is hiding, and we could strike a deal," McCall offered, trying to garner any information possible from the younger man.

"My government official has it narrowed down to two locations," Metzger offered. "Maybe you'll understand why I'm not very trusting or forthcoming when I tell you both of these spots are bunkers once used by our government. General, I'm not sure who to trust these days, and until I get some answers, you *won't* see me again."

"Who is your government official? Unless he can prove it, he can't be trusted."

"She. And she's proven her worth. I'm going to find Nadeau for you, then my brother and I will return to the base. Not until then, General."

"I'm guessing there's no talking you out of this crazy plan?"

"No," Metzger answered. "And once I'm finished, my brother and I will return to the base, but I have conditions."

"Okay," McCall said, trying to avoid lacing his voice with any particular tone, though he grew irritated with this civilian who dared give him commands.

"My friends are allowed to stay at the base this time around."

"Is that all?"

"No. No one in my party receives any kind of punishment, and none of us are incarcerated, especially me and Bryce."

"Sounds like you don't want your buddy to pay for abandoning his military duties."

"That's not a yes or a no," Metzger pushed.

"Fine. No one gets locked up, and your people can stay on the base, or in the town."

"I know things are tight, but we'll all chip in, General. And if you're lying to me, I will have contingencies in place to make certain things don't work out in your favor."

"You realize we have lots of personnel, and guns, right?" McCall said, deciding to flex his muscle just a bit.

"You're not the only one, General. I'll see you soon."

With those final words, the line went dead, leaving a slightly perplexed McCall to wonder what the future held for him, his base, and mankind, if Metzger stirred the hornet's nest by tracking down Nadeau.

End Volume 3.